WONDER WOMAN™
WARBRINGER

— DC ICONS —

Wonder Woman: Warbringer
by Leigh Bardugo

Batman: Nightwalker
by Marie Lu

— COMING SOON —

Catwoman
by Sarah J. Maas

Superman
by Matt de la Peña

WONDER WOMAN

WARBRINGER

– DC ICONS –

LEIGH BARDUGO

Random House New York

Wonder Woman created by William Moulton Marston

This is a work of fiction. Names, characters, places, and incidents either are the product of the author's imagination or are used fictitiously. Any resemblance to actual persons, living or dead, events, or locales is entirely coincidental.

Jacket art by Jacey

All rights reserved. Published in the United States by Random House Children's Books, a division of Penguin Random House LLC, New York.

Random House and the colophon are registered trademarks of Penguin Random House LLC.

Visit us on the Web! randomhouseteens.com

Educators and librarians, for a variety of teaching tools, visit us at RHTeachersLibrarians.com

Library of Congress Cataloging-in-Publication Data
Names: Bardugo, Leigh, author.
Title: Wonder Woman : Warbringer / Leigh Bardugo.
Other titles: Warbringer
Description: First edition. | New York : Random House, [2017] |
Series: [DC Icons]
Identifiers: LCCN 2016044698 | ISBN 978-0-399-54973-1 (hardback) |
ISBN 978-0-399-54975-5 (ebook) | ISBN 978-0-399-54974-8 (lib. bdg.) |
ISBN 978-1-5247-7098-3 (intl.)
Subjects: LCSH: Wonder Woman (Fictitious character)—Juvenile fiction.
Classification: LCC PZ7.B25024 Won 2017 | DDC [Fic]—dc23

Printed in the United States of America
10 9 8 7 6 5 4 3 2 1
First Edition

To Joanna Volpe—
sister in battle

"Draw nigh, come through the press to grips with me, so shall ye learn what might wells up in breasts of Amazons. With my blood is mingled war!"

—Quintus Smyrnaeus, *The Fall of Troy*

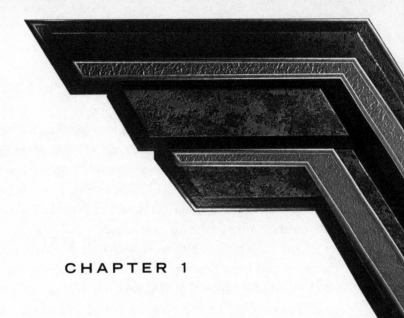

CHAPTER 1

You do not enter a race to lose.

Diana bounced lightly on her toes at the starting line, her calves taut as bowstrings, her mother's words reverberating in her ears. A noisy crowd had gathered for the wrestling matches and javelin throws that would mark the start of the Nemeseian Games, but the real event was the footrace, and now the stands were buzzing with word that the queen's daughter had entered the competition.

When Hippolyta had seen Diana amid the runners clustered on the arena sands, she'd displayed no surprise. As was tradition, she'd descended from her viewing platform to wish the athletes luck in their endeavors, sharing a joke here, offering a kind word of encouragement there. She had nodded briefly to Diana, showing her no special favor, but she'd whispered, so low that only her daughter could hear, "You do not enter a race to lose."

Amazons lined the path that led out of the arena, already stamping their feet and chanting for the games to begin.

On Diana's right, Rani flashed her a radiant smile. "Good luck today." She was always kind, always gracious, and, of course, always victorious.

To Diana's left, Thyra snorted and shook her head. "She's going to need it."

Diana ignored her. She'd been looking forward to this race for weeks—a trek across the island to retrieve one of the red flags hung beneath the great dome in Bana-Mighdall. In a flat-out sprint, she didn't have a chance. She still hadn't come into the fullness of her Amazon strength. *You will in time*, her mother had promised. But her mother promised a lot of things.

This race was different. It required strategy, and Diana was ready. She'd been training in secret, running sprints with Maeve, and plotting a route that had rougher terrain but was definitely a straighter shot to the western tip of the island. She'd even— well, she hadn't exactly *spied*. . . . She'd gathered intelligence on the other Amazons in the race. She was still the smallest, and of course the youngest, but she'd shot up in the last year, and she was nearly as tall as Thyra now.

I don't need luck, she told herself. *I have a plan*. She glanced down the row of Amazons gathered at the starting line like troops readying for war and amended, *But a little luck wouldn't hurt, either*. She wanted that laurel crown. It was better than any royal circlet or tiara—an honor that couldn't be given, that had to be earned.

She found Maeve's red hair and freckled face in the crowd and grinned, trying to project confidence. Maeve returned the smile and gestured with both hands as if she were tamping down the air. She mouthed the words, "Steady on."

Diana rolled her eyes but nodded and tried to slow her breathing. She had a bad habit of coming out too fast and wasting her speed too early.

Now she cleared her mind and forced herself to concentrate on the course as Tekmessa walked the line, surveying the runners, jewels glinting in her thick corona of curls, silver bands flashing on her brown arms. She was Hippolyta's closest advisor, second in rank only to the queen, and she carried herself as if her belted indigo shift were battle armor.

"Take it easy, Pyxis," Tek murmured to Diana as she passed. "Wouldn't want to see you crack." Diana heard Thyra snort again, but she refused to flinch at the nickname. *You won't be smirking when I'm on the victors' podium*, she promised.

Tek raised her hands for silence and bowed to Hippolyta, who sat between two other members of the Amazon Council in the royal loge—a high platform shaded by a silken overhang dyed in the vibrant red and blue of the queen's colors. Diana knew that was where her mother wanted her right now, seated beside her, waiting for the start of the games instead of competing. None of that would matter when she won.

Hippolyta dipped her chin the barest amount, elegant in her white tunic and riding trousers, a simple circlet resting against her forehead. She looked relaxed, at her ease, as if she might decide to leap down and join the competition at any time, but still every inch the queen.

Tek addressed the athletes gathered on the arena sands. "In whose honor do you compete?"

"For the glory of the Amazons," they replied in unison. "For the glory of our queen." Diana felt her heart beat harder. She'd never said the words before, not as a competitor.

"To whom do we give praise each day?" Tek trumpeted.

"Hera," they chorused. "Athena, Demeter, Hestia, Aphrodite, Artemis." The goddesses who had created Themyscira and gifted it to Hippolyta as a place of refuge.

Tek paused, and along the line, Diana heard the whispers of other names: Oya, Durga, Freyja, Mary, Yael. Names once cried out in death, the last prayers of female warriors fallen in battle, the words that had brought them to this island and given them new life as Amazons. Beside Diana, Rani murmured the names of the demon-fighting Matri, the seven mothers, and pressed the rectangular amulet she always wore to her lips.

Tek raised a blood-red flag identical to those that would be waiting for the runners in Bana-Mighdall.

"May the island guide you to just victory!" she shouted.

She dropped the red silk. The crowd roared. The runners surged toward the eastern arch. Like that, the race had begun.

Diana and Maeve had anticipated a bottleneck, but Diana still felt a pang of frustration as runners clogged the stone throat of the tunnel, a tangle of white tunics and muscled limbs, footsteps echoing off the stone, all of them trying to get clear of the arena at once. Then they were on the road, sprinting across the island, each runner choosing her own course.

You do not enter a race to lose.

Diana set her pace to the rhythm of those words, bare feet slapping the packed earth of the road that would lead her through the tangle of the Cybelian Woods to the island's northern coast.

Ordinarily, a miles-long trek through this forest would be a slow one, hampered by fallen trees and tangles of vines so thick they had to be hacked through with a blade you didn't mind dulling. But Diana had plotted her way well. An hour after she entered the woods, she burst from the trees onto the deserted coast road. The wind lifted her hair, and salt spray lashed her face. She breathed deep, checked the position of the sun. She was going to win—not just place but win.

She'd mapped out the course the week before with Maeve, and they'd run it twice in secret, in the gray-light hours of early morning, when their sisters were first rising from their beds, when the kitchen fires were still being kindled, and the only curious eyes they'd had to worry about belonged to anyone up early to hunt game or cast nets for the day's catch. But hunters kept to the woods and meadows farther south, and no one fished off this part of the coast; there was no good place to launch a boat, just the steep steel-colored cliffs plunging straight down to the sea, and a tiny, unwelcoming cove that could only be reached by a path so narrow you had to shuffle down sideways, back pressed to the rock.

The northern shore was gray, grim, and inhospitable, and Diana knew every inch of its secret landscape, its crags and caves, its tide pools teeming with limpets and anemones. It was a good place to be alone. *The island seeks to please*, her mother had told her. It was why Themyscira was forested by redwoods in some places and rubber trees in others; why you could spend an afternoon roaming the grasslands on a scoop-neck pony and the evening atop a camel, scaling a moonlit dragonback of sand dunes. They were all pieces of the lives the Amazons had led before they came to the island, little landscapes of the heart.

Diana sometimes wondered if Themyscira had called the northern coast into being just for her so that she could challenge herself climbing on the sheer drop of its cliffs, so that she could have a place to herself when the weight of being Hippolyta's daughter got to be too much.

You do not enter a race to lose.

Her mother had not been issuing a general warning. Diana's losses meant something different, and they both knew it—and not only because she was a princess.

Diana could almost feel Tek's knowing gaze on her, hear the mocking in her voice. *Take it easy, Pyxis.* That was the nickname Tek had given her. Pyxis. A little clay pot made to store jewels or a tincture of carmine for pinking the lips. The name was harmless, meant to tease, always said in love—or so Tek claimed. But it stung every time: a reminder that Diana was not like the other Amazons, and never would be. Her sisters were battle-proven warriors, steel forged from suffering and honed to greatness as they passed from life to immortality. All of them had earned their place on Themyscira. All but Diana, born of the island's soil and Hippolyta's longing for a child, fashioned from clay by her mother's hands—hollow and breakable. *Take it easy, Pyxis. Wouldn't want to see you crack.*

Diana steadied her breathing, kept her pace even. *Not today, Tek. This day the laurel belongs to me.*

She spared the briefest glance at the horizon, letting the sea breeze cool the sweat on her brow. Through the mists, she glimpsed the white shape of a ship. It had come close enough to the boundary that Diana could make out its sails. The craft was small—a schooner maybe? She had trouble remembering nautical details. Mainmast, mizzenmast, a thousand names for sails, and knots for rigging. It was one thing to be out on a boat, learning from Teuta, who had sailed with Illyrian pirates, but quite another to be stuck in the library at the Epheseum, staring glazed-eyed at diagrams of a brigantine or a caravel.

Sometimes Diana and Maeve made a game of trying to spot ships or planes, and once they'd even seen the fat blot of a cruise ship on the horizon. But most mortals knew to steer clear of their particular corner of the Aegean, where compasses spun and instruments suddenly refused to obey.

Today it looked like a storm was picking up past the mists of the boundary, and Diana was sorry she couldn't stop to watch it. The rains that came to Themyscira were tediously gentle and predictable, nothing like the threatening rumble of thunder, the shimmer of a far-off lightning strike.

"Do you ever miss storms?" Diana had asked one afternoon as she and Maeve lazed on the palace's sun-soaked rooftop terrace, listening to the distant roar and clatter of a tempest. Maeve had died in the Crossbarry Ambush, the last words on her lips a prayer to Saint Brigid of Kildare. She was new to the island by Amazon standards, and came from Cork, where storms were common.

"No," Maeve had said in her lilting voice. "I miss a good cup of tea, dancing, boys—definitely not rain."

"We dance," Diana protested.

Maeve had just laughed. "You dance differently when you know you won't live forever." Then she'd stretched, freckles like dense clouds of pollen on her white skin. "I think I was a cat in another life, because all I want is to lie around sleeping in the world's biggest sunbeam."

Steady on. Diana resisted the urge to speed forward. It was hard to remember to keep something in reserve with the early-morning sun on her shoulders and the wind at her back. She felt strong. But it was easy to feel strong when she was on her own.

A *boom* sounded over the waves, a hard metallic clap like a door slamming shut. Diana's steps faltered. On the blue horizon, a billowing column of smoke rose, flames licking at its base. The schooner was on fire, its prow blown to splinters and one of its masts smashed, the sail dragging over the rails.

Diana found herself slowing but forced her stride back on pace. There was nothing she could do for the schooner. Planes crashed. Ships were wrecked upon the rocks. That was the nature of the mortal world. It was a place where disaster could happen and often did. Human life was a tide of misery, one that never reached the island's shores. Diana focused her eyes on the path. Far, far ahead she could see sunlight gleaming gold off the great dome at Bana-Mighdall. First the red flag, then the laurel crown. That was the plan.

From somewhere on the wind, she heard a cry.

A gull, she told herself. *A girl*, some other voice within her insisted. *Impossible*. A human shout couldn't carry over such a great distance, could it?

It didn't matter. There was nothing she could do.

And yet her eyes strayed back to the horizon. *I just want to get a better view*, she told herself. *I have plenty of time. I'm ahead.*

There was no good reason to leave the ruts of the old cart track, no logic to veering out over the rocky point, but she did it anyway.

The waters near the shore were calm, clear, vibrant turquoise. The ocean beyond was something else—wild, deep-well blue, a sea gone almost black. The island might seek to please her and her sisters, but the world beyond the boundary didn't concern itself with the happiness or safety of its inhabitants.

Even from a distance, she could tell the schooner was sinking. But she saw no lifeboats, no distress flares, only pieces of the broken craft carried along by rolling waves. It was done. Diana rubbed her hands briskly over her arms, dispelling a sudden chill, and started making her way back to the cart track. That was the way of human life. She and Maeve had dived out by the boundary many times, swum the wrecks of airplanes and clipper ships and sleek motorboats. The salt water changed the wood, hardened it so it did not rot. Mortals were not the same. They were food for deep-sea fishes, for sharks—and for time that ate at them slowly, inevitably, whether they were on water or on land.

Diana checked the sun's position again. She could be at Bana-Mighdall in forty minutes, maybe less. She told her legs to move. She'd only lost a few moments. She could make up the time. Instead, she looked over her shoulder.

There were stories in all the old books about women who made the mistake of looking back. On the way out of burning cities. On the way out of hell. But Diana still turned her eyes to that ship sinking in the great waves, tilting like a bird's broken wing.

She measured the length of the cliff top. There were jagged rocks at the base. If she didn't leap with enough momentum, the impact would be ugly. Still, the fall wouldn't kill her. *That's true of a real Amazon*, she thought. *Is it true for you?* Well, she *hoped* the fall wouldn't kill her. Of course, if the fall didn't, her mother would.

Diana looked once more at the wreck and pushed off, running full out, arms pumping, stride long, picking up speed, closing the distance to the cliff's edge. *Stop stop stop*, her mind clamored. *This is madness.* Even if there were survivors, she could do nothing for them. To try to save them was to court exile, and there would be no exception to the rule—not even for a princess. *Stop.* She wasn't sure why she didn't obey. She wanted to believe it was because a hero's heart beat in her chest and demanded she answer that frightened call. But even as she launched herself off the cliff and into the empty sky, she knew part of what drew her on was the challenge of that great gray sea that did not care if she loved it.

Her body cut a smooth arc through the air, arms pointing like a compass needle, directing her course. She plummeted toward the water and broke the surface in a clean plunge, ears full of sudden silence, muscles tensed for the brutal impact of the rocks. None came. She shot upward, drew in a breath, and swam straight for the boundary, arms slicing through the warm water.

There was always a little thrill when she neared the boundary, when the temperature of the water began to change, the cold touching her fingertips first, then settling over her scalp and shoulders. Diana and Maeve liked to swim out from the southern beaches, daring themselves to go farther, farther. Once they'd glimpsed a ship passing in the mist, sailors standing at the stern. One of the men had lifted an arm, pointing in their direction. They'd plunged to safety, gesturing wildly to each other beneath the waves, laughing so hard that by the time they reached shore, they were both choking on salt water. *We could be sirens*, Maeve had shrieked as they'd flopped onto the warm sand, except neither of them could carry a tune. They'd spent the rest of the afternoon singing violently off-key Irish drinking songs and laughing themselves silly until Tek had found them. Then they'd shut up quick. Breaking the boundary was a minor infraction. Being seen by mortals anywhere near the island was cause for serious disciplinary action. And what Diana was doing now?

Stop. But she couldn't. Not when that high human cry still rang in her ears.

Diana felt the cold water beyond the boundary engulf her fully. The sea had her now, and it was not friendly. The current seized her legs, dragging her down, a massive, rolling force, the barest shrug of a god. *You have to fight it*, she realized, demanding that her muscles correct her course. She'd never had to work against the ocean.

She bobbed for a moment on the surface, trying to get her bearings as the waves crested around her. The water was full of debris, shards of wood, broken fiberglass, orange life jackets that the crew must not have had time to don. It was nearly impossible to see through the falling rain and the mists that shrouded the island.

What am I doing out here? she asked herself. *Ships come and go. Human lives are lost.* She dove again, peered through the rushing gray waters, but saw no one.

Diana surfaced, her own stupidity carving a growing ache in

her gut. She'd sacrificed the race. This was supposed to be the moment her sisters saw her truly, the chance to make her mother proud. Instead, she'd thrown away her lead, and for what? There was nothing here but destruction.

Out of the corner of her eye, she saw a flash of white, a big chunk of what might have been the ship's hull. It rose on a wave, vanished, rose again, and as it did, Diana glimpsed a slender brown arm holding tight to the side, fingers spread, knuckles bent. Then it was gone.

Another wave rose, a great gray mountain. Diana dove beneath it, kicking hard, then surfaced, searching, bits of lumber and fiberglass everywhere, impossible to sort one piece of flotsam from another.

There it was again—an arm, two arms, a body, bowed head and hunched shoulders, lemon-colored shirt, a tangle of dark hair. A girl—she lifted her head, gasped for breath, dark eyes wild with fear. A wave crashed over her in a spray of white water. The chunk of hull surfaced. The girl was gone.

Down again. Diana aimed for the place she'd seen the girl go under. She glimpsed a flash of yellow and lunged for it, seizing the fabric and using it to reel her in. A ghost's face loomed out at her from the cloudy water—golden hair, blue gaze wide and lifeless. She'd never seen a corpse up close before. She'd never seen a boy up close before. She recoiled, hand releasing his shirt, but even as she watched him disappear, she marked the differences—hard jaw, broad brow, just like the pictures in books.

She resurfaced, but she'd lost all sense of direction now—the waves, the wreck, the bare shadow of the island in the mists. If she drifted out much farther, she might not be able to find her way back.

Diana could not stop seeing the image of that slender arm, the ferocity in those fingers, clinging hard to life. *Once more*, she told herself. She dove, the chill of the water fastening tight around her bones now, burrowing deeper.

One moment the world was gray current and cloudy sea, and

the next the girl was there in her lemon-colored shirt, facedown, arms and legs outstretched like a star. Her eyes were closed.

Diana grabbed her around the waist and launched them toward the surface. For a terrifying second, she could not find the shape of the island, and then the mists parted. She kicked forward, wrapping the girl awkwardly against her chest with one arm, fingers questing for a pulse with the other. *There*—beneath the jaw, thready, indistinct, but there. Though the girl wasn't breathing, her heart still beat.

Diana hesitated. She could see the outlines of Filos and Ecthros, the rocks that marked the rough beginnings of the boundary. The rules were clear. You could not stop the mortal tide of life and death, and the island must never be touched by it. There were no exceptions. No human could be brought to Themyscira, even if it meant saving a life. Breaking that rule meant only one thing: exile.

Exile. The word was a stone, unwanted ballast, the weight unbearable. It was one thing to breach the boundary, but what she did next might untether her from the island, her sisters, her mother forever. The world seemed too large, the sea too deep. *Let go.* It was that simple. Let this girl slip from her grasp and it would be as if Diana had never leapt from those cliffs. She would be light again, free of this burden.

Diana thought of the girl's hand, the ferocious grip of her knuckles, the steel-blade determination in her eyes before the wave took her under. She felt the ragged rhythm of the girl's pulse, a distant drum, the sound of an army marching—one that had fought well but could not fight on much longer.

She swam for shore.

As she passed through the boundary with the girl clutched to her, the mists dissolved and the rain abated. Warmth flooded her body. The calm water felt oddly lifeless after the thrashing of the sea, but Diana wasn't about to complain.

When her feet touched the sandy bottom, she shoved up, shifting her grip to carry the girl from the shallows. She was eerily light, almost insubstantial. It was like holding a sparrow's body between her cupped hands. No wonder the sea had made such easy sport of this creature and her crewmates; she felt temporary, an artist's cast of a body rendered in plaster.

Diana laid her gently on the sand and checked her pulse again. No heartbeat now. She knew she needed to get the girl's heart going, get the water out of her lungs, but her memory on just how to do that was a bit hazy. Diana had studied the basics of reviving a drowning victim, but she hadn't ever had to put it into practice outside the classroom. It was also possible she hadn't paid close attention at the time. How likely was it that an Amazon was going to drown, especially in the calm waters off Themyscira? And now her daydreaming might cost this girl her life.

Do something, she told herself, trying to think past her panic. *Why did you drag her out of the water if you're only going to sit staring at her like a frightened rabbit?*

Diana placed two fingers on the girl's sternum, then tracked lower to what she hoped was the right spot. She locked her hands together and pressed. The girl's bones bent beneath her palms. Hurriedly, Diana drew back. What was this girl made of, anyway? Balsa wood? She felt about as solid as the little models of world monuments Diana had been forced to build for class. Gently, she pressed down again, then again. She shut the girl's nose with her fingers, closed her mouth over cooling mortal lips, and breathed.

The gust drove into the girl's chest, and Diana saw it rise, but this time the extra force seemed to be a good thing. Suddenly, the girl was coughing, her body convulsing as she spat up salt water. Diana sat back on her knees and released a short laugh. She'd done it. The girl was alive.

The reality of what she'd just dared struck her. All the hounds of Hades: *She'd done it. The girl was alive.*

And trying to sit up.

"Here," Diana said, bracing the girl's back with her arm. She couldn't simply kneel there, watching her flop around on the sand like a fish, and it wasn't as if she could put her back in the ocean. Could she? No. Mortals were clearly too good at drowning.

The girl clutched her chest, taking huge, sputtering gulps of air. "The others," she gasped. Her eyes were so wide Diana could see white ringing her irises all the way around. She was trembling, but Diana wasn't sure if it was because she was cold or going into shock. "We have to help them—"

Diana shook her head. If there had been any other signs of life in the wreck, she hadn't seen them. Besides, time passed more quickly in the mortal world. Even if she swam back out, the storm would have long since had its way with any bodies or debris.

"They're gone," said Diana, then wished she'd chosen her words more carefully. The girl's mouth opened, closed. Her body was shaking so hard Diana thought it might break apart. That couldn't actually happen, could it?

Diana scanned the cliffs above the beach. Someone might have seen her swim out. She felt confident no other runner had chosen this course, but anyone could have seen the explosion and come to investigate.

"I need to get you off the beach. Can you walk?" The girl nodded, but her teeth were chattering, and she made no move to stand. Diana's eyes scoured the cliffs again. "Seriously, I need you to get up."

"I'm trying."

She didn't look like she was trying. Diana searched her memory for everything she'd been told about mortals, the soft stuff— eating habits, body temperature, cultural norms. Unfortunately, her mother and her tutors were more focused on what Diana referred to as the Dire Warnings: War. Torture. Genocide. Pollution. Bad Grammar.

The girl shivering before her on the sand didn't seem to qualify for inclusion in the Dire Warnings category. She looked about the same age as Diana, brown-skinned, her hair a tangle of long, tiny braids covered in sand. She was clearly too weak to hurt anyone but herself. Even so, she could be plenty dangerous to Diana. Exile dangerous. Banished-forever dangerous. Better not to think about that. Instead, she thought back to her classes with Teuta. *Make a plan. Battles are often lost because people don't know which war they're fighting.* All right. The girl couldn't walk any great distance in her condition. Maybe that was a good thing, given that Diana had nowhere to take her.

She rested what she hoped was a comforting hand on the girl's shoulder. "Listen, I know you're feeling weak, but we should try to get off the beach."

"Why?"

Diana hesitated, then opted for an answer that was technically true if not wholly accurate. "High tide."

It seemed to do the trick, because the girl nodded. Diana stood and offered her a hand.

"I'm fine," the girl said, shoving to her knees and then pushing up to her feet.

"You're stubborn," Diana said with some measure of respect. The girl had almost drowned and seemed to be about as solid as driftwood and down, but she wasn't eager to accept help—and she definitely wasn't going to like what Diana suggested next. "I need you to climb on my back."

A crease appeared between the girl's brows. "Why?"

"Because I don't think you can make it up the cliffs."

"Is there a path?"

"No," said Diana. That was definitely a lie. Instead of arguing, Diana turned her back. A minute later, she felt a pair of arms around her neck. The girl hopped on, and Diana reached back to take hold of her thighs and hitch her into position. "Hold on tight."

The girl's arms clamped around her windpipe. "Not that tight!" Diana choked out.

"Sorry!" She loosened her hold.

Diana took off at a jog.

The girl groaned. "Slow down. I think I'm going to vomit."

"Vomit?" Diana scanned her knowledge of mortal bodily functions and immediately smoothed her gait. "Do *not* do that."

"Just don't drop me."

"You weigh about as much as a heavy pair of boots." Diana

picked her way through the big boulders wedged against the base of the cliff. "I need my arms to climb, so you're going to have to hold on with your legs, too."

"Climb?"

"The cliff."

"You're taking me *up the side of the cliff*? Are you out of your mind?"

"Just hold on and try not to strangle me." Diana dug her fingers into the rock and started putting distance between them and the ground before the girl could think too much more about it.

She moved quickly. This was familiar territory. Diana had scaled these cliffs countless times since she'd started visiting the north shore, and when she was twelve, she'd discovered the cave where they were headed. There were other caves, lower on the cliff face, but they filled when the tide came in. Besides, they were too easy to crawl out of if someone got curious.

The girl groaned again.

"Almost there," Diana said encouragingly.

"I'm not opening my eyes."

"Probably for the best. Just don't . . . you know."

"Puke all over you?"

"Yes," said Diana. "That." Amazons didn't get sick, but vomiting appeared in any number of novels and featured in a particularly vivid description from her anatomy book. Blessedly, there were no illustrations.

At last, Diana hauled them up into the divot in the rock that marked the cave's entrance. The girl rolled off and heaved a long breath. The cave was tall, narrow, and surprisingly deep, as if someone had taken a cleaver to the center of the cliff. Its gleaming black rock sides were perpetually damp with sea spray. When she was younger, Diana had liked to pretend that if she kept walking, the cave would lead straight through the cliff and open onto some other land entirely. It didn't. It was just a cave, and remained a cave no matter how hard she wished.

Diana waited for her eyes to adjust, then shuffled farther

inside. The old horse blanket was still there—wrapped in oilcloth and mostly dry, if a bit musty—as well as her tin box of supplies.

She wrapped the blanket around the girl's shoulders.

"We aren't going to the top?" asked the girl.

"Not yet." Diana had to get back to the arena. The race must be close to over by now, and she didn't want people wondering where she'd gotten to. "Are you hungry?"

The girl shook her head. "We need to call the police, search and rescue."

"That isn't possible."

"I don't know what happened," the girl said, starting to shake again. "Jasmine and Ray were arguing with Dr. Ellis and then—"

"There was an explosion. I saw it from shore."

"It's my fault," the girl said as tears spilled over her cheeks. "They're dead and it's my fault."

"Don't," Diana said gently, feeling a surge of panic. "It was the storm." She laid her hand on the girl's shoulder. "What's your name?"

"Alia," the girl said, burying her head in her arms.

"Alia, I need to go, but—"

"No!" Alia said sharply. "Don't leave me here."

"I have to. I . . . need to get help." What Diana needed was to get back to Ephesus and figure out how to get this girl off the island before anyone found out about her.

Alia grabbed hold of her arm, and again Diana remembered the way she'd clung to that piece of hull. "Please," Alia said. "Hurry. Maybe they can send a helicopter. There could be survivors."

"I'll be back as soon as I can," Diana promised. She slid the tin box toward the girl. "There are dried peaches and pili seeds and a little fresh water inside. Don't drink it all at once."

Alia's eyelids stuttered. "All at once? How long will you be gone?"

"Maybe a few hours. I'll be back as fast as I can. Just stay warm and rest." Diana rose. "And don't leave the cave."

Alia looked up at her. Her eyes were deep brown and heavily

lashed, her gaze fearful but steady. For the first time since Diana had pulled her from the water, Alia seemed to be truly seeing her. "Where are we?" she asked. "What is this place?"

Diana wasn't quite sure how to answer, so all she said was "This is my home."

She hooked her hands back into the rock and ducked out of the cave before Alia could ask anything else.

CHAPTER 2

Should I have tied her up? Diana wondered as she scaled the cliff, the noon sun warming her shoulders after the chill of the cave. *No.* She didn't have any rope, and tying up a girl who had almost died didn't seem like the right thing to do. But she'd need to have answers ready when she returned. Alia had been shaken by the wreck, but she was coming back to herself, and she clearly wasn't a fool. She wouldn't be content to stay in the cave for long.

Diana lengthened her stride. There was no point in going to Bana-Mighdall to retrieve the flag. She would return to the arena and make some kind of excuse, but she couldn't think beyond that. The farther she got from the cliffs, the more foolish her decision seemed. A cold, prickling fear had coiled just beneath her ribs. The island had its own rules, its own prohibitions, and there were reasons for all of them. No weapons were carried except for training and exhibition. The few off-island missions permitted were those sanctioned by the Amazon Council and the Oracle—and then only to preserve the isolation of Themyscira.

She needed to get Alia back to the mortal world as soon as

possible. Days would pass among the humans while Alia waited in her cave. Rescue ships might be sent for her lost boat. If Diana moved quickly enough, maybe she could get Alia out there on another craft so that she could rendezvous with them. Even if the girl tried to tell the authorities about Themyscira and by some chance they believed her, Alia would never be able to find her way back to the island.

The deep bellow of a horn sounded from the Epheseum, and Diana's heart gave a sick thud. The race was over. Someone had claimed the laurel crown she'd been so sure she would wear today. *I saved a life*, she reminded herself, but the thought was hardly comforting. If anyone found out about Alia, Diana would be sent from her home forever. Of all the island's rules, the prohibition against outsiders was the most sacred. Only Amazons who had won the right to a life on Themyscira belonged here. They died gloriously in battle, proving their courage and heart, and if, in their last moments, they cried out to a goddess, they might be offered a new life, one of peace and honor among sisters. *Athena, Chandraghanta, Pele, Banba.* Goddesses from all over the world, warriors of every nation. Each Amazon had earned her place on the island. All but Diana, of course.

That prickling coil tightened in her gut. Maybe rescuing Alia hadn't been a misstep, but something fixed in Diana's fate. If she had never really belonged on the island, maybe exile was inevitable.

She hurried her steps as the towers of the Epheseum came into view, but her feet felt weighted with dread. How exactly was she going to face her mother after this?

Too soon, the dirt of the road became thick slabs of Istrian stone, white and weathered beneath her bare feet. As she entered the city, she felt as if she could see people staring down at her from their balconies and open gardens, their curious eyes dogging her path to the arena. It was one of the most beautiful buildings in the city, a crown of glowing white stone perched atop slender arches, each emblazoned with the name of a different champion.

Diana passed beneath the arch dedicated to Penthesilea. She could hear cheering and feet stamping, and when she emerged into the sunlit arena, the sight that greeted her was worse than she'd expected. She hadn't just lost. She was the last to return. The victors were on the podium, and the presentation of the laurels had already begun. Naturally, Rani had placed first. She'd been a distance runner in her life as a mortal and as an Amazon. The worst part was how much Diana liked her. She was relentlessly humble and kind and had even offered to help Diana train. Diana wondered if it got tiring being splendid all the time. Maybe heroes were just like that.

As she made her way toward the dais, she forced herself to smile. Though the sun had helped to dry her, she was keenly aware of the rumpled mess of her tunic, the seawater knots in her hair. Perhaps if she acted like the race hadn't mattered, it wouldn't. But she'd only taken a few steps when Tek emerged from the crowd and slung an arm around her neck.

Diana stiffened and then hated herself for it because she knew Tek could tell.

"Aw, little Pyxis," Tek crooned, "you get bogged down in the mud?"

A soft hiss rose from the people standing nearby. They all understood the insult. Little Pyxis, made of clay.

Diana grinned. "Miss me, Tek? There's got to be someone else around here for you to judge."

A few chuckles bubbled up from the crowd. *Keep walking,* Diana told herself. *Keep your head held high.* The problem was that Tek was a born general. She sensed weakness and knew exactly where to find the cracks. *You've got to give as good as you get,* Maeve had warned Diana, *or Tek won't back down. She's cautious around Hippolyta, but eventually you're the one who's going to sit that throne.*

Not if Tek has her way, Diana thought.

"Don't be cross, Pyxis," said Tek. "There's always next time. And the time after that."

As Diana moved through the spectators, she heard Tek's allies chiming in.

"Maybe they'll move the finish line for the next race," said Otrera.

"Why not?" Thyra replied. "There are different rules when you're royalty."

That was a direct slight to her mother, but Diana grinned as if nothing in the world could bother her. "Amazing how some people never tire of the same song, isn't it?" she said as she strolled toward the steps that led to the royal loge. "You only learn one dance, I guess you have to keep doing it."

Some of the onlookers nodded approvingly. They wanted a princess who didn't flinch at the easy barbs, who stood her ground, who could spar with words instead of fists. After all, what real harm had Tek caused? Sometimes Diana wished Tek would challenge her outright. She'd lose, but she'd rather take a beating than constantly pretend the taunts and jabs didn't bother her. It was tiring knowing that every time she faltered, someone would be there to notice.

But that wasn't the worst of it. At least Tek was honest about what she thought. The hardest thing was knowing that, though many of the people smiling at her right now might be kind to her, might even show her loyalty because she was her mother's daughter and they loved their queen, they would never believe Diana worthy—not to walk among them, certainly not to wear a crown. And they were right. Diana was the only Amazon who had been born an Amazon.

If Tek found out about Alia, if she discovered what Diana had done, she'd have everything she ever wanted: Diana banished from the island, the clay girl lost to the World of Man—and Tek would never have to challenge Hippolyta outright.

Well, she's not going to find out, Diana promised herself. *There has to be a way to get Alia off the island.* Diana just needed to secure a boat, get Alia on it, and find some human to hand her off to on the other side of the boundary.

Or she could tell the truth. Face ridicule, a trial if she was lucky, instant exile if she wasn't. The dictates of the goddesses who had formed Themyscira were not to be taken lightly, and no offerings to Hera or prayers to Athena would change what she'd done. Would Diana's mother speak on her behalf? Offer excuses for her daughter's failings? Or just follow the punishment demanded by law? Diana wasn't sure which would be worse.

Forget it. She would get a boat somehow.

She scaled the steps to the queen's loge, keenly aware that all attention had shifted from the victors' podium to her. Light filtered through the silken overhang, casting the shaded platform in red and blue, jasmine tumbling from its railings in sweet-smelling clouds. There were no seasons on Themyscira, but Hippolyta had the vines and plants changed with every equinox and solstice. *We must mark time,* she'd told Diana. *We must work to maintain our connection to the mortal world. We are not gods. We must always remember we were born mortal.*

Not all of us, Diana had thought but hadn't said at the time. Sometimes it was as if Hippolyta had forgotten Diana's origins. Or maybe she just wanted to. *There are different rules when you're royalty.*

Diana had no doubt that her mother had seen her as soon as she entered the arena, but now Hippolyta turned as if glimpsing her for the first time and smiled in welcome.

She opened her arms and embraced Diana briefly. It was the proper thing to do. Diana had lost. If her mother showed too much warmth, it would be perceived as foolish or inappropriate. If she treated Diana too coldly, it might be seen as a rejection and could have far-reaching repercussions. The embrace was as it should be and nothing more, balanced on the sword's edge of politics. So why did it still prick her heart?

Diana knew her role. She remained at her mother's side as they placed the crowns of laurel on the victors' heads, and smiled and congratulated the morning's competitors. But the cold coil of worry in her belly seemed to have sprouted tentacles, and with every passing moment they squeezed tighter. She told herself not to fidget, to stop checking the position of the sun in the sky. She felt sure her mother could tell something was wrong. Diana could only hope Hippolyta would blame her behavior on the shame of losing the race.

The games would continue through the afternoon, followed by a new play at the amphitheater in the evening. Diana hoped to be back at the cave long before then, but there was no escaping the first feast. Long tables had been set in the gardens beside the arena, laden with warm bread, heaps of poached cuttlefish, grilled strips of venison, and pitchers of wine and mare's milk.

Diana forced herself to take some rice and fish, and pushed a piece of fresh honeycomb around her plate. It was usually her favorite, but her gut was too full of worry. She caught Maeve's questioning glance from the end of the table, but she had to remain with her mother. Besides, what exactly was she going to tell Maeve? *I definitely would have won but I was busy transgressing against divine law.*

"In Pontus we would have had lamb grilled on the spit," Tek said, pushing at the venison on her plate. "Proper meat, not this gamey stuff."

No animals were raised for slaughter on the island. If meat was wanted, then it had to be hunted. It was not a rule created by the goddesses or a condition demanded by the island, but Hippolyta's law. She valued all life. Tek valued her stomach.

Hippolyta just laughed. "If you can't find meat worth eating, drink more wine."

Tek raised her glass and they clinked cups, then bent their heads together giggling like girls. Diana had never seen anyone make Hippolyta laugh the way Tek did. They'd fought side by side in the mortal world, ruled together, argued together, and together they'd chosen to turn from the World of Man. They were *prota adelfis*, the first of the Amazons on Themyscira, sisters in all but blood. Tek didn't hate Hippolyta—Diana was fairly sure she *couldn't* hate her—only what she'd done when she'd created

Diana. Hippolyta had made a life from nothing. She'd brought a girl into being on Themyscira. She'd made an Amazon when only the gods could do such a thing.

Once, when Diana was just a child, she'd woken in her palace bedroom to hear them arguing. She'd slid from her bed, the marble cold beneath her feet, and padded down the hall to the Iolanth Court.

This was the heart of their home, a wide terrace of graceful columns that overlooked the gardens below and the city beyond. The palace was full of objects that hinted at the world her mother had known before the island—a golden cup, a shallow black kylix painted with dancing women, a saddle made of tufted felt—pieces of a puzzle Diana had never been able to fit together into a whole story. But the Iolanth Court held no mysteries. It ran the length of the western side of the palace, open on three sides so that it was always flooded with sunlight and the sound of fountains burbling in the gardens below. Sweet, waxy plumeria twined around its columns, and its balustrade was marked by potted orange trees that drew the gossipy buzz of bees and hummingbirds.

Diana and her mother took most of their meals there at a long table that was always cluttered with Diana's schoolbooks, half-full glasses of water or wine, a dish of figs, or a spill of freshly cut flowers. It was where Hippolyta welcomed new Amazons to Themyscira after they had been purified, her voice low and gracious as she explained the rules of the island.

But with Tek, Hippolyta ceased to be the dignified, benevolent queen. She was not the mother that Diana knew, either; she was someone else, someone a little wild and careless, someone who slouched in her chair and snorted when she laughed.

Hippolyta was not laughing that night. She was pacing back and forth on the terrace, the silks of her saffron-colored robe billowing behind her like a banner of war.

"She is a *child*, Tek. There is nothing dangerous about her."

"She is a danger to our very way of life," Tek said. She was seated on a bench at the long table in her riding clothes, elbows resting on the table, legs stretched out before her. "You know the law. No outsiders."

"She isn't an outsider. She's a little girl. She was made of this island's very earth, fashioned by my own hands. She's never even been *outside*."

"There are rules, Hippolyta. We are immortal. We're not meant to conceive, and the island was intended for those of us who have known the perils of the World of Man, who know what it is to fight against the endless tide of mortal violence, who choose to turn away from it. You had no right to make that decision for Diana."

"She will be raised in a world without conflict. She'll walk a land in which blood has never been spilled."

"Then how will she know to value it? The gods did not intend this. They made their laws for a reason, and you have subverted them."

"The gods blessed her! They endowed her with living breath, made my blood to flow in her veins, bestowed their gifts upon her." She sat down beside Tek. "Be reasonable. Do you think it was my power that gave her life? You know none of us have magic like that."

Tek took Hippolyta's hands in hers. Seated like that, hands clasped, they looked like they were making a pact, like they were colluding over some wonderful plan.

"Hippolyta," Tek said gently, "when do the gods give such a gift without exacting a price? There is always a danger, always a cost, even if we haven't seen it yet."

"And what would you have me do?"

"I don't know." Tek rose and rested her hands on the balustrade, looking out at the dark stretch of city and sea. Diana remembered being surprised by how many lanterns were still lit in the houses below, as if this were the appointed hour in which adults argued. "You've put us in an impossible position. There will be a reckoning for this, Hippolyta, and all for the sake of something to call your own."

"She belongs to *us*, Tek. All of us." Hippolyta laid a hand on Tek's arm and for a moment, Diana thought they might make peace, but then Tek shrugged her off.

"*You* made the choice. Tell yourself what you need to, Highness, but we'll all pay the price."

Now Diana watched Tek and her mother talking as if that argument and all the others that had followed didn't matter, as if Tek's regular torment of Diana was a fond game. Hippolyta had always waved away Tek's behavior, her coldness, claiming that it would fade as the years passed and no disaster befell Themyscira. Instead, it had gotten worse. Diana was almost seventeen, and the only thing that seemed to have changed was that she presented a bigger target.

Diana's eyes flicked to the sundial at the center of the feasting grounds. Alia had been alone in the cave for nearly three hours. Diana didn't have time to fret over Tek. She needed to figure out how she was going to get her hands on a boat.

As if she could read Diana's mind, Tek said, "Somewhere you need to be, Princess?" Her eyes were slightly narrowed, her gaze speculative. Tek saw too much. It was probably what made her such a great leader.

"I can't think of anywhere," Diana said pleasantly. "If I didn't know better, I'd think you wanted me to leave."

"Now, what would give you that idea?"

"Enough of that," Hippolyta said with a flick of her hand, as if she could simply wipe away discord. And sure enough, the musicians began to play and the feast table filled with song and laughter.

Diana moved the food around on her plate and did her best to be merry as the sun arced westward. She couldn't be the first to leave and risk looking like she was sulking after her loss. At last, Rani rose from the table and stretched. "Who wants to run to the beach?" she asked. She held the red silk flag aloft and shouted, "Catch me if you can!"

Chairs were shoved backward as the Amazons rose, whooping and cheering, to follow Rani down to the shore before the next round of games began. Diana took the chance to slip away to the alcove where Maeve was waiting. She wore a crushed-velvet tunic in pale celadon that barely counted as a dress and that she had paired with nothing but sandals and a circlet of leaf-bright green beads braided into her red hair.

"I think you may be missing your trousers," Diana said as Maeve looped an arm through hers, and they headed toward the palace.

"Two things I love best about this place—the lack of rain, and the lack of propriety. Sweet Mother of All Good Things, I thought that meal would never end."

"I know. I was seated across from Tek."

"Was she terrible?"

"No more than usual. I think she was on good behavior because of my mother and Rani."

"It *is* hard to be petty around Rani. She always makes you feel your time would be better spent improving yourself."

"Or emblazoning her profile on a coin." They passed beneath a colonnade thick with curling grape vines. "Maeve," Diana said as casually as she could, "do you know if the Council has mentioned a mission on the horizon anytime soon?"

"Don't start that again."

"It was just a question."

"Even if by some chance they did, you know your mother would never let you go."

"She can't keep me here forever."

"Actually, she can. She's the queen, remember?" Diana scowled, but Maeve continued on. "She's going to use any excuse to keep you here, and you gave her a good one today. What happened? What went wrong?"

Diana hesitated. She didn't want to lie to Maeve. She didn't want to lie to anyone. Still, if she shared this secret, Maeve would be forced to either reveal Diana's crime or keep Diana's confidence and risk exile herself.

"There were rocks blocking the northern road," said Diana. "Some kind of landslide."

Maeve frowned. "A landslide? Do you think anyone followed you? Knew your route?"

"You're not actually suggesting sabotage. Tek wouldn't—"

"Wouldn't she?"

No, Diana thought but didn't say. *Tek doesn't think she has to sabotage me. She thinks I can fail all on my own.* And Diana had proven her right.

"Hey," Maeve said, giving Diana's shoulders a squeeze. "There will be other races, and—"

Maeve seized Diana's arm. Her eyes rolled back and she swayed on her feet.

"Maeve!" Diana gasped. Maeve crumpled to her knees. Diana curled an arm around her waist, supporting her. Her friend's skin felt wrong. It was too hot to the touch. "What's the matter? What is it?"

"I don't know," Maeve panted, then bent double, releasing a low howl of pain. Diana felt it a second later, the echo of Maeve's anguish. All Amazons were connected by blood, even Diana through her mother. When one felt pain, they all shared it.

Women were already running toward them, Tek at the lead.

"What happened?" Tek asked, helping Diana raise Maeve to her feet.

"Nothing," said Diana, her panic spiking. "We were just talking and she—"

"Hell's hounds," swore Tek. "She's burning up with fever."

"An infection?" asked Thyra.

Diana shook her head. "She has no wounds."

"Could it be something she ate?" Otrera suggested.

Tek scoffed. "At the feast? Don't be absurd. Maeve, were you foraging today? Did you eat anything in the woods? Mushrooms? Berries?"

Maeve shook her head. Her body convulsed on a thready sob.

"Let's get her to bed and try to cool her body down," said Tek. "Fetch water, ice from the kitchens. Thyra, go get Yijun. She has experience as a field medic. We'll take Maeve to the palace dormitory."

"Maeve lives in the Caminus now," said Diana. New Amazons spent their first few years in the dormitory connected to the palace before they chose which part of the city they wanted to live in. Diana had visited Maeve's new lodgings just the other day.

"If this is a contagion, I want it isolated. The dormitory is empty and easy to quarantine."

"A contagion?" said Otrera in horror.

"Go," commanded Tek.

Thyra ran toward town to find the medic, and Diana bolted down to the palace kitchens to fetch a pitcher of ice. When she found Maeve and Tek in the dormitory, Maeve was huddled beneath a thin sheet, quivering. Diana set the pitcher beside the bed and stared helplessly at her friend.

"What is this?"

"It's a fever," Tek said grimly. "She's sick."

This couldn't be happening. It wasn't possible. "Amazons don't get sick."

"Well, she is," snapped Tek.

Thyra raced into the room, her golden hair flying. "The medic is coming, but two more alarms were raised in town."

"Fevers? Were they at the feast?"

"I don't know, but—"

Suddenly, the whole room seemed to shift. The walls shook, and the floor heaved like a beast waking from a deep sleep. The pitcher of ice tipped and shattered on the tiles. Thyra slammed into the wall, and Diana had to grab the doorjamb to keep from falling.

The shaking stopped as quickly as it had started. The only signs that anything had happened were the broken pitcher and the lanterns that continued to sway on their hooks.

"Freyja's braids!" said Thyra. "What was that?"

Tek's expression was bleak. "An earthquake."

"Here?" said Thyra disbelievingly.

"I need to find the queen," said Tek. "Wait for the medic." She strode from the room, boots crunching over shards of pitcher and ice.

Diana unfolded a blanket and tucked it around Maeve. She brushed the red hair back from her friend's face. Maeve's skin was too white beneath her freckles, and her eyes moved restlessly beneath her pale lids. *Contagion. Quarantine. Earthquake.* These words did not belong on Themyscira. *What if they'd come with Alia?* What if Diana had brought this language of affliction to her people?

No mortal was to set foot on Themyscira. The law was clear. In Amazon history, only two women had dared to violate it. Kahina had brought a mortal child back from a mission, desperate to save her from death on the battlefield. She'd begged to be allowed to raise the girl on the island, but in the end they'd both been exiled to the World of Man. The second was Nessa, who had tried to secret her mortal lover aboard a ship when she returned to Themyscira.

As a child, Diana had asked to hear Nessa's story again and again, wriggling in her bed, anticipating the horrible ending, the image of Nessa standing on the shore, stripped of her armor, as the earth shook and the winds howled, so angered was the island, so angered were the gods. Diana always remembered the final words of the story as told by the poet Evandre:

> *One by one, her sisters turned their backs as they must, and though they wept, their salt tears were as nothing to the sea. So Nessa passed from mercy into the mists, and to the lands beyond, where men breathe war as air, and life is as the wing-beat of a moth, barely seen, barely understood before it is gone. What can we say of her suffering, except that it was brief?*

Diana had shuddered at the shrug in those words. She had watched the moths that gathered around the lanterns of her mother's terrace and tried to fasten her gaze on the blur of their wings.

There and gone. That fast. But now it was Evandre's other words that she recalled with a terrible feeling of recognition: *The earth shook and the winds howled, so angered was the island, so angered were the gods.* When Diana had rescued Alia, she'd believed the risk she was taking was for herself alone, not for her sisters, not for Maeve.

Diana squeezed Maeve's hand. "I'll be back," she whispered.

She hurried out the door and ran across the columned court that connected the dormitory to the palace.

"Tek!" she called, jogging to catch up with her.

As Tek turned, another tremor struck. Diana careened into a column, her shoulder striking the stone painfully. Tek barely checked her stride.

"Go back to your friend," she said as Diana trailed her up the palace stairs to the queen's quarters.

"Tek, what's causing this?"

"I don't know. Something is out of balance."

Tek strode into the upper rooms of the royal quarters without hesitation. Hippolyta was at the long table, consulting with one of her runners, a fleet-footed girl named Sabaa.

Hippolyta looked up as they entered. "I know, Tek," she said. "I sent for a runner as soon as the first earthquake hit." She folded the message she'd penned, then sealed it with red wax, marking it with her ring. "Get to Bana-Mighdall as fast as you can, but be cautious. Something is wrong on the island."

The runner vanished down the stairs.

"There have been at least three reports of illness," said Tek.

"Are you sure that's what it is?" Hippolyta asked.

"I saw one of the victims myself."

"Maeve," Diana added.

"It may be striking the younger Amazons first," said Hippolyta.

"Not all of them," muttered Tek, casting a sidelong look at Diana.

But Hippolyta's gaze was focused on the western sea. She sighed and said, "We'll have to consult the Oracle."

Diana's stomach clenched. The Oracle. There would be no hiding then.

Tek nodded, a look of resignation on her face. Visiting the Oracle was no small decision. It required a sacrifice, and if the Oracle found an Amazon's tribute wanting, she could inflict any number of punishments.

"I'll light the signal fires to gather the Council," Tek said, and was gone without another word.

It was all happening too quickly. Diana followed Hippolyta into her chambers. "Mother—"

"If they ride hard, the Council should be here within the hour," said Hippolyta. Some members of the Council lived at the Epheseum or Bana-Mighdall, but others preferred the more isolated parts of the island and would have to be summoned by the fires.

Hippolyta shucked off the comfortable riding clothes and silver circlet she'd worn at the arena, and emerged from her dressing room a moment later in silks the deep purple of late plums, her right shoulder covered by a golden spaulder and scales of gleaming mail. The armor was purely ornamental, the type of thing worn for affairs of state. Or emergency Council meetings.

"Help me bind my hair?" Hippolyta said. She seated herself before the large looking glass and selected a golden circlet studded with heavy chunks of raw amethyst from a velvet-lined case.

It seemed bizarre to Diana to stand there plaiting her mother's ebony hair into braids when the world around them might be falling apart, but a queen never appeared as anything less than a queen to her people.

Diana summoned her courage. She needed to tell her mother about Alia. She couldn't let her go into a Council meeting without that knowledge. *Maybe it isn't Alia. It could be a disturbance in the World of Man. Something. Anything.* But Diana did not really believe that. When the Council consulted the Oracle, Alia would be discovered and Diana would be exiled. Her mother would look weak, indulgent. Not everyone loved Hippolyta as Tek did, and not everyone believed that a queen should rule the Amazons at all.

"Mother, today, during the race—"

Hippolyta met Diana's eyes in the mirror and clasped her hand. "We'll talk about it later. But there is no shame in the loss."

That wasn't remotely true, but Diana said, "It's not that."

Hippolyta set two more amethysts in her ears. "Diana, you cannot afford more losses like that. I didn't think you would win—"

"You didn't?" Diana hated the hurt that spread through her, the surprise she couldn't keep from her voice.

"Of course not. You're still young. You are not yet as strong as the others or as experienced. I hoped you might place or at least—"

"Or at least not humiliate you?"

Hippolyta lifted a brow. "It takes more than the loss of a little race to bring low a queen, Diana. But you were not ready, and it will mean you must work even harder to prove yourself in the future."

Her mother's assessment of her chances was the same as her measured embrace on the platform, just as practical, just as painful.

"I *was* ready," Diana said stubbornly.

Hippolyta's look was so gentle, so loving, and so full of pity that Diana wanted to scream. "The results speak for themselves. Your time will come."

But it wouldn't. Not if she was never given the opportunity. Not if even her mother didn't think she could win a damned footrace. And Alia. *Alia.*

"Mother," Diana tried again.

But Hippolyta was sweeping out of her chambers. Lamplight sparked off the gold in her armor. The earth shook, but somehow her steps did not falter, as if her very stride declared, "I am a queen and an Amazon; you are wise to tremble."

In the mirror's glass, Diana saw herself reflected—a dark-haired girl in disheveled clothes, her blue eyes troubled, teeth worrying her lower lip like some hand-wringing actor in a tragedy. She squared her shoulders, set her jaw. Diana might not be queen, but the Council members weren't the only ones who could petition the Oracle. *I am a princess of Themyscira,* she told the girl in the mirror. *I'll find my own answers.*

CHAPTER 3

Diana hurried to her room to change clothes and fill a traveling pack with a blanket, rope, lantern and flint, and the rolled bindings she used for her hands when sparring—they would do for bandages in a pinch. Four hours had passed since Diana had left Alia in the cave. The girl must be terrified. *Hera's crown, what if she tries to climb down?* Diana winced at the thought. Alia had all the substance of a bag of kindling. If she tried to get out of the cave, she'd only end up hurting herself. But there was no time to return to the cliffs. If Diana was going to fix this, she needed to speak to the Oracle before the Council did.

She opened a green enamel box that she kept by her bed, then hesitated. She had never been to see the Oracle, but Diana knew she was dangerous. She could see deep into an Amazon's heart and far into the future. In the smoke from her ritual fire, she tracked thousands of lives over thousands of years, watching the way the currents moved and what could be done to alter their courses. Access to her predictions always came with a steep cost. The most essential thing was to approach with an offering that would please her, something personal, essential to the supplicant.

The green enamel box held Diana's most cherished objects. She shoved the whole thing into her pack and ran down the stairs. She'd been pocketing food throughout the feast, but she stopped at the kitchen for a skin full of hot mulled wine. Though the kitchens were always a tangle of clatter and chaos, today the staff worked with grim determination and strange smells rose in billows of steam from the cook pots.

"Willow bark," said one of the cooks as Diana peeked beneath a lid. "We're extracting salicylic acid to help bring the fevers down." She handed over the goatskin. "You tell Maeve we hope she feels better soon."

All Diana said was "Thank you." She didn't want to add to her list of lies for the day.

The city streets were full of bustle and clamor as people ran back and forth with food, medicine, and supplies to shore up buildings damaged by the quakes. Diana pulled up her hood. She knew she should be at the center of it all, helping, but if her suspicions about Alia were right, then the only solution was to get her off the island as quickly as she could.

A glance at the harbor told her that stealing a boat would be close to impossible. The wind had risen to a full gale, and the sky had gone the color of slate. The docks were crawling with Amazons trying to secure the fleet before the storm descended in full force.

Diana took the eastern road out of the city, the most direct path to the Oracle's temple. It was bordered by groves of olive trees, and once she'd entered their shelter, she broke into a run, setting the fastest pace she dared.

Soon she left the olives behind, traversing vineyards and tidy rows of peach trees clustered with fruit, then passed into the low hills that bordered the marsh at the center of the island.

The closer Diana drew to the marsh, the more her unease grew. The marsh lay in the shadow of Mount Ptolema and was the only place on the island that existed in a state of near-permanent shade. She had never ventured inside. There were stories of Amazons entering its depths to visit the Oracle and emerging weeping or completely mad. When Clarissa had sought an audience at the temple, she'd returned to the city gibbering and shaking, the blood vessels in both of her eyes broken, her nails bitten down to ragged stumps. She'd never spoken of what she'd seen, but to this day, Clarissa—a hardened soldier who liked to ride into battle armed with nothing but an axe and her courage—still slept with a lit lantern beside her bed.

Diana shivered as she entered the shadows of the marsh trees, draped in veils of moss like funeral-goers, the gnarled masses of their exposed roots reflecting sinister shapes in the murky waters. She could hear no sounds of the approaching storm, no familiar birdsong, not even the wind. The marsh had its own black music: the lap and splash of the water as something with a ridged back broke its surface and vanished with the flick of a long tail, the scuttle of insects, whispers that rose and fell without reason. Diana heard her name spoken, a chill breath at her ear. But when she turned, heart pounding, no one was there. She glimpsed something with long, hairy legs skittering over a nearby branch and quickened her steps.

Diana kept heading what she hoped was due east, farther into the marsh as the gloom deepened. She was sure now that something was following her, maybe several things. She could hear the rustle of their creeping legs above her. To her left, she could see the glint of what might be shiny black eyes between drooping swags of gray lace moss.

There is nothing to be afraid of here, she told herself, and she could almost hear the swamp's low, gurgling laugh.

With a shudder, she pushed through a curtain of vines bound together by milky clusters of cobwebs and stopped. She had imagined the Oracle's temple would be like the domed buildings in her history books, but now she was confronted with a dense thicket of tree roots, a woven barricade of branches that stretched as high and wide as a fortress wall. It was hard to tell if it had been constructed or if it had simply grown up out of the swamp. At its center was an opening, a gaping mouth of darkness deeper and blacker than any starless sky. From it emanated a low, discordant hum, the hungry murmur of a hive, a hornet's nest ready to crack open.

Diana gathered her courage, adjusted her pack, and stepped onto a path of wet black stones that led to the entry, leaping from one to the next across water the dull gray of a clouded mirror, her sandals slipping over their glossy backs.

The air near the entrance felt strangely thick. It lay heavy against her skin, damp and unpleasantly warm, wet as an animal's lolling tongue. She lit the lantern hanging from her pack, took a shallow breath, and stepped inside.

Instantly, the lamp went out. Diana heard whispering behind her and turned to see the roots knotting closed over the mouth of the tunnel. She lunged for the entrance, but it was too late. She was alone in the dark.

Her heart set a jackrabbit pace in her chest. Over the vibrating insect hum, she could hear the vines and roots shifting around her, and she was suddenly sure they would simply close in, trapping her in the tangled wall forever.

She forced herself to shuffle forward, hands held out before her. Her mother wouldn't be afraid of a few branches. Tek would probably give those roots one withering look and they'd literally wither.

The hum grew louder and more human, a sighing, keening sound that rose and fell like a child's weeping. *I'm not afraid. I am an Amazon and have nothing to fear from this island.* But this place felt older than the island. It felt older than everything.

Gradually, she realized the tunnel was sloping upward and that she could see the dim shapes of her hands, the woven-root texture of the walls. Somewhere up ahead, there was light.

The tunnel gave way to a round room, its ceiling open to the sky. It had been late afternoon when Diana set out, but the sky she was looking at now was black and full of stars. She panicked, wondering if she'd somehow lost time in the tunnel, and then she realized that the constellations above her were all wrong. Whatever sky she was seeing, it was not her own.

The bramble walls held torches alight with silver flames that gave no heat, and a moat of clear water ringed the room's perimeter. At its center, on a perfectly flat circle of stone, a cloaked woman sat beside a bronze brazier hanging from a tripod by a delicate chain. In it, a proper fire burned vibrant orange, sending a plume of smoke into the star-strewn sky.

The woman rose and her hood fell back, revealing coppery hair, freckled skin.

"Maeve!" Diana cried.

The Oracle's face shifted. She was a wide-eyed child, then a wizened crone, then Hippolyta with amethysts in her ears. She was a monster with black fangs and eyes like opals, then a glowing beauty, her straight nose and full mouth framed by a golden helm. She stepped forward; the shadows shifted. She was Tek now, but Tek as touched by age, dark skin lined, gray at her temples. Diana wanted nothing more than to turn and run. She stayed where she was.

"Daughter of Earth," said the Oracle. "Make your offering."

Diana willed herself not to flinch. *Daughter of Earth. Born of clay.* Had the Oracle meant those words as an insult? It didn't matter. Diana had come here with a purpose.

She set down her pack and reached inside for the green enamel box. Her hand hovered over a jade comb Maeve had given her on her last birthday; a carnelian leopard, the little talisman she'd carried for years in her pocket, its back bowed in the spot where she'd rubbed her thumb against it for luck; and a tapestry of the planets as they had appeared at the hour of her birth. It was lumpy and full of mistakes. She and her mother had made it together, and greedy for Hippolyta's time, Diana had pulled rows of threads out every night, hoping they could just keep working on the project forever. She felt along the box's lining, fingers closing over the object she sought.

She looked at the moat. There was no obvious way across, but Diana was not going to ask for instruction. She'd heard enough people speak of the Oracle to know that—if her sacrifice was accepted—she would be permitted three questions and no more.

She stepped into the water. She could see her foot pass through it, see her skin, paler beneath the surface, but she felt nothing. Maybe the river was mere illusion. She crossed to the stone island. When she set foot on the smooth rock, the hum of voices dimmed as if she had entered the eye of a storm.

Diana stretched out her hand, willing it to steadiness—she did not want to tremble before the Oracle—and uncurled her fingers, revealing the iron arrowhead. It was long enough to cover most of her palm, honed to a cruel point, its tip and crevices stained in a red so dark it looked black in the torches' icy light.

The Oracle's laugh was as dry as the crackle of the fire. "You bring me a gift you despise?"

Diana recoiled in shock, hand closing protectively over the arrowhead and drawing it close to her heart. "That's not true."

"I speak *only* truth. Perhaps you are not ready to hear it." Diana glanced back at her pack, wondering if she should attempt some other offering. But the Oracle said, "No, Daughter of Earth. I do not want your jewels or childish trinkets. I will take the arrow that killed your mother. Though you despise a thing, you may value it still, and the blood of a queen is no small gift."

Reluctantly, Diana extended her hand once more. The Oracle plucked the bloodied arrowhead from her palm. Her face shifted. She was Hippolyta again, but this time her black hair was unpinned and unbraided, curling around her shoulders, and she wore a white tunic embroidered in gold. She was as Diana remembered her the day Hippolyta had found her daughter crying in the stables after Diana had overheard two of the Amazons talking before their daily ride. *They said I'm a monster,* she'd told her mother. *They said I'm made of mud.* Hippolyta had dried her tears with the sleeve of her tunic, and that night she'd given Diana the arrowhead.

Now the Oracle spoke with Hippolyta's voice, the same words

she'd said sitting in the lamplight beside Diana's bed. *"There is no joy in having been born mortal. You need never know the sorrow of what it is to be human. Among all of us, only you will never know the pain of death."*

The words had meant little to Diana at the time, but she'd never forgotten them, and she'd never been able to explain why she treasured the arrowhead so much. Her mother had intended it as a warning, as a reminder to value the life she'd been given. But to Diana, it had been the thing that tied her to a larger world, even if it was through something as gruesome as her mother's blood.

The Oracle wore the face of an aged Tek once more. She tossed the arrowhead into the brazier, and a shower of orange-hued sparks shot upward.

"You bring me gifts of death today," said the Oracle. "Just as you have brought death to our shores."

Diana's head snapped up. "You know about Alia?"

"Is that your first question?"

"No!" Diana said hurriedly. She was going to have to be smarter.

"The land shakes. The stalk that never wilts grows weary."

"All because of me," Diana said miserably. "All because of Alia."

"And those that came before her. Speak your questions, Daughter of Earth."

Some tiny part of Diana had hoped she might be mistaken, that Alia's rescue and the disasters on Themyscira had been mere coincidence. Now she could not hide from the truth of what she'd done and the trouble it had wrought. If she was going to make things right, she would have to word her questions carefully.

"How do I save Themyscira?"

"Do nothing." The Oracle waved her hand, and the smoke above the brazier arced over the moat. Through it, Diana saw a figure looking back at her from the water. It was Alia. Diana realized she was seeing into the cave on the cliff side. Alia huddled beneath the blanket, shaking, eyes closed, forehead sheened with sweat.

"But she wasn't injured—" Diana protested.

"The island is poisoning her just as she is poisoning the island.

But Themyscira is older and stronger. The girl will die, and with her will pass the taint of the mortal world. Most of your sisters will survive and return to health. The city can be rebuilt. The island can be purified once more."

Most would survive? *Will Maeve live?* The words burned on Diana's tongue, begging to be spoken. "I don't understand," she said, careful not to ask a question. "I'm not sick, and Alia was fine when I left her."

"You are of the island, born uncorrupted, *athanatos*, deathless. You will not sicken as your sisters do, and your proximity may prolong the girl's life, may even soothe her, but it cannot heal her. She will die, and the island will live. All will be as it should."

"No," Diana said, surprised at the anger in her voice. "How do I save Alia's life?" Her second question, gone.

"You must not."

"That isn't an answer."

"Then call her by the name given to her ancestors, *haptandra*, the hand of war. Look into the smoke and know the truth of what she is."

Again the smoke billowed up from the brazier and spread over the water, but this time when Diana looked, it felt as if she'd been engulfed in flame. She stood at the center of a battleground, surrounded by fallen soldiers, their bodies strewn over a ruined landscape, limbs like driftwood on a black-ash shore. She flinched as a massive armored vehicle roared by, a war machine of the type she'd seen in books, crushing bodies beneath its treads. She could hear a rattling sound in the distance, explosions that came in rapid bursts.

As her eyes focused on the horror around her, a helpless moan escaped her lips. There, only a few feet away, lay Maeve, her heart pierced by a sword, pinned to the ground like a pale insect. The bodies that surrounded Diana were Amazons. Her eye caught on a splash of dark hair: her mother, battle armor smashed and broken, her body discarded like so much refuse.

She heard a war cry and turned, reaching for a weapon she

did not have. She saw Tek, her body glazed in sweat, her eyes battle-bright, facing down some kind of monster, the kind from stories, half-man, half-jackal. The jackal's jaws closed over Tek's throat, shook her like a doll, tossed her aside. Tek fell, blood gushing from her torn jugular. Her eyes focused on Diana, blazing with accusation.

"Daughter of Earth."

Diana gasped, struggling for breath. The image cleared, and she was looking at her own face in the water, her cheeks wet with tears.

"You're getting salt in my scrying pool," said the Oracle.

Diana wiped the tears from her face. "That can't be. I saw monsters. I saw my sisters—"

"Alia is no ordinary girl. She is polluted by death."

"As all mortals are," Diana argued. What was different about Alia? The island had rejected her as it would any human presence. If Diana could just get her away from Themyscira, everything would return to normal.

"It is not *her* death she carries but the death of the world. Do you think chance brought her boat so close to our shores? Alia is a Warbringer, born of the same line as Helen, who was herself sired by Nemesis."

"Helen? Not Helen of—"

"Ten years the Trojan War raged. No god was spared. No hero. No Amazon. So it will be if Alia is allowed to live. She is *haptandra*. Where she goes, there will be strife. With each breath, she draws us closer to Armageddon."

"But it was Helen's beauty that caused the war."

The Oracle cut a dismissive hand through the air and the torches flickered. "Who tells those stories? Tales of vengeful goddesses who wager in human lives for vanity's sake? Of course men believe a woman's power must lie in the fineness of her features, the shapeliness of her limbs. You know better, Daughter of Earth. Helen's blood carried in it war, and in her seventeenth year, those powers reached their peak. So it was with every Warbringer. So it will be with Alia. You have seen it in the waters."

"A line of Warbringers." Diana turned the words over. Was it possible? How could a mortal—even a mortal whose ancestry could be traced to Nemesis, goddess of retribution—cause so much misery?

The Oracle was watching her closely. "Heed me, Daughter of Earth. When a Warbringer is born, destruction is inevitable. One has been the catalyst for every great conflict in the World of Man. With the coming of the new moon, Alia's powers will reach their apex, and war will come." She paused. "Unless she dies before then."

"The explosion wasn't an accident," Diana said as understanding came. "Someone wanted Alia dead."

"Many someones will do all they can to make sure that the world does not enter an age of bloodshed. But you need do nothing. Simply wait, and the girl will die, as she was meant to in the shipwreck. It is the best way."

Diana's eyes narrowed. She'd read the stories. She knew how oracles spoke. "The best way," she considered. The Oracle's mouth turned down at the corners as if she truly could read Diana's thoughts. For the first time, Diana asked herself why the Oracle had chosen to appear with Tek's face. To frighten her? To intimidate her? "The best way, but not the *only* way."

The Oracle's eyes flashed silver fire, as if they blazed with the same light as the torches on the walls. "Ask your final question and be gone from this place." Diana opened her mouth, but the Oracle raised a graceful hand. "Think carefully. I am not always so obliging in the gifts I accept. You worry over the fate of one girl when the future of the world hangs in the balance. Worry instead for your own future. Wouldn't you like to know if Tekmessa is right about you? If you will bring glory or despair to the Amazons? Eventually, your mother will grow weary of rule. Wouldn't you like to know if you will ever truly be a queen or if you are doomed to spend your life in half shadow? I can show you all of it, Daughter of Earth."

Diana hesitated. She thought of Tek's words, of her mother's denials. The Oracle might tell her she was an abomination, secretly reviled by the gods, destined to bring only misery to her people. But what if the Oracle told her she carried the gods' blessing, that she could be a boon to her sisters instead of a curse? It would absolve her mother, cease the endless speculation about Diana. Tek would never be able to say a word against either of them again.

But would it make Diana any more of an Amazon? *I could ask how to obtain their approval. I could ask how to win glory in battle.* She thought of Alia's hand gripping the hull, Alia's pulse beating beneath her questing fingers. A girl restored to life by Diana's own breath.

Save my people and Alia dies. Save Alia and I'll watch my sisters slaughtered. Really, it made the question simple.

"How do I save everyone?"

Fury suffused the Oracle's features. Her image flickered—a serpent, Tek, a skull, a black-gummed wolf. Her eyes were gemstones, snakes writhed upon her head and poured from her mouth. "Stubborn as all girls are stubborn," she snarled. "Reckless as all girls are reckless."

The words were out before Diana thought better of them. "And were you never a reckless, stubborn girl?" A pointless question, but it didn't matter now. Diana had asked the important question first, and the Oracle's anger made her believe it had been the right one.

The anguished hum rose around them, an aching lament layered with wild sorrow, and in it Diana heard the echoes of her sisters' cries on that terrible battlefield.

When the Oracle spoke, she was no longer Tek, but wore a different face, one that seemed hewn from light itself: "The Warbringer must reach the spring at Therapne before the sun sets on the first day of Hekatombaion. Where Helen rests, the

Warbringer may be purified, purged of the taint of death that has stained her line from its beginning. There may her power be leashed and never passed to another."

Therapne. Greece. It would mean leaving the island. Impossible. And yet . . .

"The line of Warbringers would be broken?"

The Oracle said nothing, but she made no denials. If Alia died on Themyscira, a new Warbringer would be born—maybe in a month, maybe in a hundred years, but it would happen. If they could reach the spring in time, if Diana brought Alia there under her protection, that would all change.

"I see you, Daughter of Earth. I see your dreams of glory. But what *you* do not see is the danger. Factions in the World of Man hunt the Warbringer. Some seek to end her life that they may ensure peace; some seek to protect her life that they may bring about an age of conflict. In less than two weeks, Hekatombaion begins. You cannot hope to reach the spring in time. You are one girl."

Diana clenched her fists, thinking of the bloodied arrowhead the Oracle had accepted as sacrifice. Her mother's blood. The same blood that flowed in Diana's veins. "I am an Amazon."

"Are you? You are not a hero. You are not battle tested. This quest is far beyond your skills and strength. Do not doom the world for the sake of your pride."

"That isn't fair," Diana said. "I'm trying to do what's right." Even as she said the words, Diana knew they weren't entirely true. She did want glory. She did want the chance to prove herself, not just with a footrace or a wrestling match, but with a hero's quest, something no one could deny. She wanted to argue with the Oracle, but what was the point in debating an all-seeing ancient?

"Go home," said the Oracle. "Go back to the Epheseum. Comfort your sweet friend. Let her know her suffering will soon be at an end. When the Council comes, I will tell them nothing. No one ever need know what you have done. Your crime will remain a secret, and you need not fear exile. The island will return to what it was, the world will be safe, and you may live in peace with your sisters. But should you take the girl from the island . . ."

The hum rose to a howl, a thousand howls, screams rising from the charred earth, the clash of swords, the lamentations of the dying, her sisters' misery amplified a thousand times. The sound of a future Diana could prevent by simply doing nothing.

"*Go,*" commanded the Oracle.

Diana turned and ran, back into the tunnel, into the dark, unable to escape that terrible howl. She ran without caution, scraped her shoulder against the bramble wall, tripped as the tunnel slanted downward, stumbled to her knees. Then she was back up, running again, that horrible chorus of anguish building to a shriek that vibrated through her bones and hammered at her skull.

The roots parted before her, and she tumbled out of the temple and into the brackish water of the marsh. She dragged herself upright, breathless, and lurched toward the banks. Through the gloom of the marsh, she fled, trying to put as much distance as she could between herself and the temple.

Only after Diana burst from the darkness of the trees and crested the first set of low hills did she allow herself to stop. She could smell the sweet, green scent of honey myrtle, feel the fresh spatter of rain on her skin. But even here she did not feel safe.

I am an Amazon.

In the whispers of the leaves, she heard the Oracle sneering, *Are you?*

She could not risk it. She could not risk her sisters' lives for the sake of a girl she barely knew. She'd been foolish to dive into the sea this morning, but she could make the right choice now.

The earth rumbled beneath Diana's feet. Lightning split the sky. She hitched her pack more securely on her shoulders and headed for the cave. Alia was dying. If Diana could not save her, at least she could make sure she did not die alone.

CHAPTER 4

The giant was back. Alia thought that maybe after the wreck, in her panicked, adrenaline-fueled state, she'd exaggerated the details of her rescuer. But, no, the girl was back in the cave, and she was just as Alia remembered her—six feet tall and gorgeous, built like someone who could sell weird fitness equipment on late-night television. The Ab Blaster. The Biceps Monger.

Maybe I'm delirious. She knew she had a fever and chills, but she couldn't make sense of her symptoms. The headache and the nausea could be the result of a concussion. No doubt she'd been banged around pretty badly when the *Thetis* went down. But she didn't want to think about that—the shock of the explosion, Ray screaming, the gray weight of the water as it dragged her down. Every time her mind brushed up against it, her thoughts stuttered to a stop. Better to focus on the cave, the blanket tucked around her, the terrible pounding in her head. If it was just a bad concussion, then her job was to stay awake until help came—and she'd done it. Here was help. In the form of a girl who looked like a supermodel who moonlighted as a cage fighter. Or vice versa. But where was the rescue team? The helicopter? The EMTs to flash a light in Alia's eyes and tell her everything was going to be all right?

"Just you?" she croaked, unnerved by how weak her voice sounded.

The girl sat down beside her. "Have you eaten anything?"

"Not hungry."

"At least some water?" Alia didn't have the strength. Dimly, she was aware of something being pressed to her lips. "Drink," the girl commanded.

Alia managed a few sips. "Is help coming?"

The girl hesitated. "I'm afraid not."

Alia opened her eyes fully. She'd succeeded in keeping her panic in check so far, but she could feel it trying to claw free. "Is it the earthquakes?" At the first tremor, Alia had dragged herself to the cave opening, terrified the rock above her would give way and she'd be crushed. But one glance at the drop to the sea had sent her scrambling backward. She'd huddled in her blanket, fighting her rising fear. *One thing at a time*, she'd told herself. *I'm on an island—maybe there's volcanic activity. Just wait for help to come.* She'd done her part. She'd kept conscious, managed not to expend her energy on crying or screaming. So where was her rescue?

The girl's expression was troubled, her gaze trained on her sandaled feet. Alia realized she'd changed clothes. Back on the beach she'd worn some type of white tunic, but now she was in brown leather trousers and what looked like a cross between a tank top and a sports bra. "This island is very isolated," she said. "It's . . . Contacting help wasn't possible."

"Then the rest of the crew . . . ?"

"I'm sorry. I wish I could have saved them all."

Her words didn't quite make sense to Alia. Nothing did. She closed her eyes, the ache of tears filling her throat. Her best friend, Nim, liked to joke that Alia was a jinx because trouble seemed to follow her everywhere. Fights erupted at parties. Couples started arguing over nothing. Then there was that time a free concert in

Central Park had somehow turned into a riot. It didn't seem so funny now.

Thinking about Nim, about home, about the safety of her own bed, made the tears spill over.

"Were they your close companions?" the girl asked quietly.

"I barely knew them," Alia admitted. "I need a doctor. There's something wrong. I think I hit my head during the wreck. There may be internal bleeding." Though even as she spoke, she realized that since the girl had appeared, the pain in her head had receded. Maybe she'd been more dehydrated than she realized.

"There was an explosion on your craft," said the girl. "Before it sank."

Alia leaned her head back against the cave wall. "I remember."

"On the beach, you said it was your fault."

Those words felt like a fist pressed against her heart. "I did? I must not have been thinking clearly."

"Do you think . . . Is it possible it was intentional? Some kind of bomb?"

Alia's eyes flew open. "What are you talking about?"

"Could the wreck have been deliberate?"

"No, of course not, it . . ." Alia hesitated. All of Jason's paranoid warnings came back to her. *We're targets, Alia. Our money. The Foundation. We have to be smart.*

Smart meant trained bodyguards on staff at the penthouse. It meant an armed driver to take her to school every morning and drop her off every afternoon. It meant no class field trips, schedules that accounted for every minute of her day so that Jason always knew where she was, summers spent in the same place each year, seeing the same people, staring out at the same view. It was a good view. Alia knew she had nothing to complain about. *But that didn't stop you, did it?* She'd been happy to whine to Nim on every occasion. And she'd pretty much jumped at a chance for something new, a month spent with different people, away from Jason's ridiculous rules.

Maybe not so ridiculous. Could someone have put a bomb

aboard the boat? Could one of the crew have blown up the *Thetis* on purpose?

Her fears must have shown on her face, because the girl leaned forward and said, "Speak. Is it possible?"

Alia didn't want to believe it. If someone had been willing to blow up her boat, to murder innocent people just to get at her and the Foundation, then Jason had been right about everything and she'd been the biggest fool alive.

"It's possible," she admitted reluctantly. "I'm a Keralis."

"A Greek name."

"My dad was Greek. My mom was black, from New Orleans." People always wanted to know where the color came from. Alia reached for the water. She really did feel a little better, though her hand shook as she lifted the skin to her lips. The girl steadied Alia's arm as she drank. "Thanks. You've never heard of the Keralis Foundation? Keralis Labs?"

"No. What does that have to do with the explosion?"

Alia felt suddenly wary. "Who are you?"

"I'm . . . My name's Diana."

"Diana what?"

"Why does my name matter?"

Why? Because even if this girl lived on a remote island, *everyone* knew the Keralis name. That was part of the problem.

How had Diana gotten to the wreck site so quickly? What if she'd known about the bomb on the boat? Alia gave her head a little shake and was rewarded with a stomach-churning wave of dizziness that left her panting. She pressed her head against the cave wall and waited for it to pass. She wasn't thinking straight. There was no reason for a girl to try to kill her, then save her life and stuff her in a cave. "People hate my parents; now they hate me."

"I see," said Diana in understanding. "Did your parents slay a great many people?"

"*What?*" Alia cast her a sidelong glance. "They were biologists.

Bioengineers. People get weird about some of the work they did in genetics and the Foundation's politics."

Diana's brow furrowed, as if she was attempting to parse all of this information. "You think that's why someone attempted to take your life?"

"Why else?"

The girl said nothing. Alia felt another tide of nausea roll through her. A cold sweat broke out over her body. "I need a doctor."

"There's no one on the island who can help you."

"A clinic. A boat back to Istanbul or the nearest port."

"It's just not possible."

Alia stared at Diana, feeling her panic slip free of its leash. "Then what's going to happen to me?"

Diana looked away.

Alia pressed her palms to her eyes, humiliated to find tears threatening again. She didn't understand what was going on, only that she'd never felt more tired or scared. Not since she was a kid. How had things gone so wrong so quickly?

"I never should have left home. Jason said to stay in New York. He said it was safer. But I wanted this so much."

Diana drew another blanket from her bag and tucked it around Alia. It smelled of sage and lavender. "What did you want?"

"It's stupid," Alia said.

"Please. I'd like to know."

Alia closed her eyes again. She felt too weak to talk, but the guilt and shame were stronger than her fatigue. "There's this summer-at-sea program for biology students. You get college credit. It's really hard to get into, but I thought, I'll just apply and see what happens. But then they accepted me and I realized—"

"How very much you wanted to go."

"Yeah," Alia said with a small smile. She felt it fade from her lips. "I lied to Jason."

"Who is this Jason?"

"My older brother. He's a great brother, the *best* brother. He's just overprotective. I knew he'd say no to the trip, so I told him I'd been invited to Nim's parents' place in Santorini. You don't know how hard it was to keep everything secret. I had to get a visa, get all of these medical approvals, but then I was just doing it. I ditched my bodyguards at the airport, and I didn't call Jason until I was about to board the *Thetis* in Istanbul." Alia released a sob. "He was so angry. I swear, I've never heard him raise his voice, but he was yelling. He forbade me—*forbade* me from going. I hung up on him."

"Does he command you frequently?" Diana asked. "Many men enjoy having authority over women. Or so I've been told."

Alia snorted, but Diana looked serious. "Well, sure, but Jason's not like that. He was just worried about me, trying to keep me safe. I thought if I could show him that I could handle this on my own, he'd have to stop babying me."

Diana sighed. "I understand. My mother doesn't think I can handle anything on my own, either."

"Are you kidding? You saved my life. You carried me to a damn cave *on your back*. You seem pretty capable."

"In my family, among . . . my friends, I'm the weak one."

"You don't seem weak to me."

Diana gazed at her for a long moment. "You don't seem weak to me, either."

Alia blew out a breath. "But Jason was right. If I had stayed in New York, if I'd just listened to him, no one would have died. I should never have left home."

Diana frowned. "If you'd stayed home, maybe others would have been harmed. Your friends or your family."

"Maybe," Alia said, but the thought brought her little comfort.

"And you had this dream," continued Diana, "to study, to garner accolades."

"Well, college credit, at least."

"How could it be wrong to wish to prove yourself?" she asked, a fierce light in her eyes. "You were not wrong to dare."

"Jason—"

"Jason cannot protect you forever. We cannot spend our lives in hiding, wondering what we might accomplish if given the chance. We have to *take* that chance ourselves. You were brave to board that boat."

"I was stupid. Everything that happened just proved Jason right."

"No. You survived the wreck. When the waves came, you held on. Maybe you're stronger than you think you are, than anyone thinks you are." Diana stood. "Maybe I am, too." She offered Alia her hand. "We have to get you out of here."

"I thought you said—"

"I know what I said. Do you want to get off this island or not?"

Alia had no idea what had caused this turnaround, but she wasn't going to look a gift giant in the mouth. "Yes," she said eagerly. She took Diana's hand and rose slowly, trying to fight the surge of dizziness that overtook her. "What do we do? Do you have a boat or something?"

"It's more complicated than that. I'm going to need you to trust me. The people here . . . There are terrible risks, and the things you see . . . well, if we make it out of this, you can never speak of them again."

Alia raised her brows. Was this girl messing with her, or was she a little nuts? "Okay, sure."

"Swear by what is most dear to you."

Maybe more than a *little* nuts. "I swear on Jason and Nim and my shot at an Ivy League school."

Diana cocked her head to one side. "It will have to do." She turned her back to Alia and said, "Climb on."

Alia groaned. "Do we really have to do this again?" She wasn't feeling particularly spry, but there was something humiliating about jumping on someone's back like a five-year-old.

Diana shrugged and said, "See for yourself."

After her first terrifying glance down, Alia had deliberately avoided the entrance to the cave, but now she gathered the blankets around her shoulders and peered over the edge again. The drop to the rocky boulders below looked even steeper than it had that morning.

Holding tight to Diana's hand and the ragged rock of the cave mouth, she looked *up*. Somehow the sheer cliff rising into the stormy sky seemed twice as terrifying as the drop.

"We're going to climb that?" she asked.

"*I'm* going to climb that."

"With me on your back?"

"You're very light. I wonder if you have a calcium deficiency."

"My calcium's just fine."

"Your muscle tone is poor, too."

"I prefer the pursuits of the mind," Alia said loftily.

Diana looked doubtful. "Most philosophers agree that mind and body must be in accord."

"Is that like four out of five dentists?" Alia asked. Besides, she doubted most philosophers ever had to play dodgeball in the Bennett Academy gym.

She sighed. Even at her best, the climb would have been close to impossible for her, and she was definitely not at her best. She eyed Diana warily. Alia had never thought of herself as short, but next to this person, she felt about as statuesque as a miniature schnauzer. It wasn't just that the girl was tall; she was sort of majestic. Like a skyscraper. Or Mount Rushmore, but less craggy.

Alia straightened her spine. "Okay, we do it your way."

Diana nodded and turned, gesturing for Alia to clamber onto her back. Alia hopped on, and the girl hooked her hands beneath Alia's knees, shifting her into place like an oversized backpack. So much for dignity.

"Giddyup," Alia said sourly.

"Pardon?"

"On, you huskies?"

"I am not your steed," Diana said, but she trotted—*jogged*—to the mouth of the cave. Without warning, she dug her fingers into the rock and swung outside. Alia squeezed her eyes shut and held on tight, trying not to think of the unforgiving boulders below.

"So," she said, chin tucked over Diana's shoulder, attempting to distract herself. "Now that we're hanging off the side of a cliff together . . . any hobbies?"

"My mother is trying to get me to take up the lyre."

"Interesting choice. Siblings?"

"No."

"Any nicknames?" Alia felt the girl's muscles tense beneath her.

"No."

Maybe that was enough small talk.

Diana's body moved in stops and starts as she searched for holds, making steady progress up the cliff. Occasionally, she would grunt sharply or mutter, but she wasn't panting or grumbling the way Alia would have been.

Just as Alia was wondering how much cardio this girl did, the cliff shook with a tremor. Diana's foot slipped. They dropped.

A cry escaped Alia's lips as her heart lodged in her throat. They jerked to a rough halt, dangling in the air, supported by nothing except Diana's right hand jammed into the rock. Alia could see blood trickling from somewhere between her fingers.

The urge to look down, to see how far they'd come, how far there was to fall overtook her. *Don't do it*, her logic centers commanded. But the rest of her nervous system was in full flight-or-fight mode. She looked down. Dizziness washed through her. There was nothing below but roiling sea and hulking black rocks, whitecaps smashing to foam on the humps of their backs.

Alia looked up at Diana's bleeding fingers slipping slowly from their hold. Her own hands felt sweaty; her body was sliding. She wriggled to keep her grip.

"Stay still," barked Diana. Alia froze.

Diana released something between a roar and a grunt and shoved her body upward, swinging her left arm overhead. For a moment, Alia thought they were falling. Then Diana's fingers found purchase, her toes dug in, and they were wedged against the rock once more.

Alia felt the tension in Diana's back, the contraction of her muscles. They were moving again, higher and higher. Alia didn't risk another glance down. She shut her eyes and, long moments later, Diana was hauling them over the top of the cliff. Alia rolled off her, and for a moment they just lay there.

Diana leapt to her feet, dusting herself off. She offered Alia a hand.

"Give me a minute," said Alia, trying to get her heart rate to return to normal.

"Why are *you* tired?"

"We almost died!"

Diana cocked her head to one side. "Do you think so?"

"Yes." What was wrong with this girl?

Alia took the offered hand and they stood. The clouds above them were knotted with thunderheads, and the wind tore at their hair. She touched the braids at her scalp. They were uncomfortably stiff with salt and sand.

The beginnings of another storm, or maybe the same storm that had caught the *Thetis* was moving in. She peered along the coastline but could see no lighthouse or harbor, no signs of civilization at all. This place really was isolated.

Alia didn't want to look at the sea, but she did anyway, searching for some sign of the *Thetis* and its crew. Jasmine, Ray, Luke, Dr. Ellis—*Just call me Kate*, she'd said. But they'd called her Dr. Ellis anyway. What had Ray and Jasmine been arguing about when the winds had picked up? They'd been blown off course, their instruments giving readings that made no sense, and everyone seemed to be blaming everyone else.

The crew had been sniping at one another since they'd boarded. Alia had kept to herself, feeling a sinking sense of disappointment. Her month aboard the *Thetis* was supposed to show Jason that she'd be safe on her own, but it was also supposed to give her a chance to make some new friends away from Bennett Academy, and to escape the tension that seemed to follow her everywhere lately. Instead, the trip had been more of the same. Ray and Luke had actually started shoving each other over a playlist, of all things. And now they were gone.

"Maybe we should stay where we are," said Alia. She'd been feeling pretty awful before Diana had shown up, but now that she was out of the cave, her lungs were clearer and she felt a bit less woozy. "They'll send search parties for the ship. Maybe we can find a way to signal from shore."

Diana shook her head. "No one is going to find you here. No one ever does."

Alia raised a skeptical brow. "Is this some Bermuda Triangle shit?"

"Something like that. The island is incredibly hard to reach. It doesn't show up on any maps or charts."

Alia waggled her fingers. "Google knows all and sees all."

"Google," Diana repeated. "Is Google one of your gods?"

"Hey," said Alia. "Just because I spend time online doesn't mean I'm totally brainwashed."

Diana looked at her blankly, then gestured for Alia to follow. "Come on. We're too exposed out here."

"I'm not sure the woods are a good place to be in a thunderstorm," Alia said. Diana bit her lip, as if she hadn't considered that. "I'm guessing you don't get bad weather around here?"

"Never," said Diana. "But it has to be the woods. We can't stay out in the open."

A chill spread over Alia's arms that had nothing to do with the storm or her damp clothes. "What do you mean?"

"The people on this island came here because they don't want to be found."

"Like you?"

"I . . . didn't have a choice. I was born here. But they really don't like outsiders."

Alia shivered. Great, they were one step shy of a dueling-banjos scenario. Dueling lyres? *Keep it together, Alia.* "They're not in some weird militia or something, are they?"

"Actually, a lot of them are . . . uh . . . military."

Better and better. Probably a bunch of paranoid survivalists, with Alia's luck. If they didn't like outsiders, they definitely weren't going to like a brown girl from New York. "And they don't have phones? Radios?"

"No contact with the outside world."

"What if someone gets sick or hurt?"

"That isn't a problem here," said Diana, then added, "Or it didn't used to be."

So Alia had managed to get shipwrecked on Cult Island. Perfect. "Can't we just steal a boat or something?" she asked.

"I considered that, but the docks are full of people. They'll notice someone taking out a craft, especially during a storm. And I think we're going to need more than a boat to get us to Therapne."

"Where?"

"Southern Greece. The Gulf of Laconia."

That made no sense—not if Alia remembered her geography right. The *Thetis* had only been a few days out from Istanbul. Even if they'd been wildly off course, it made no sense to travel that far. Why not Thessaloniki or even Athens? "That's hundreds of miles from here. We can't sail all that way."

"Of course not."

Alia took a deep breath. Her chest hurt as if someone had punched her. Her lungs still felt waterlogged, and her body was covered in bruises. Beyond that, she felt nauseous and bleary. She needed to see a doctor. She needed to get to a real city.

Unless Diana was lying or delusional—both of which were definite possibilities—she was stuck on an island crawling with weirdos, so she needed to be smart. *Play along,* she told herself. *This girl wants to go to southern Greece? No problem.* Alia could nod and smile for as long as it took to get somewhere with a phone.

She steeled herself and followed Diana into the green hush of the forest. It was like stepping into an alien world. Alia's parents had taken her and Jason on a trip to the Brazilian rain forest when she was little, so they could learn about some of the new species of plants being discovered there and the medicines developed from those findings. It had been a bit like this—lush, alive—and yet not like this at all. The trees here were like nothing she'd ever seen, some of them wide enough around that the *Thetis* could have docked in their rings with room to spare. Their roots ran along the forest floor in thick spirals, covered in vines that bloomed with widemouthed trumpet flowers. The air smelled sweet and felt almost silky on Alia's skin, and the raindrops on every surface made the moss, leaves, and branches glint like they'd been hung with gems.

Great place for a cult.

Alia knew she should keep her mouth shut, but she couldn't resist asking, "Why do we need to go to southern Greece?"

"Your expedition wasn't attacked because of your parents' work. You are being hunted."

"Hunted," Alia said flatly. "For my silky pelt?"

"Because you are *haptandra*."

"Say again?"

"A Warbringer."

"I'm not into gaming."

Diana shot her a baffled look over her shoulder. "The Oracle says we must reach the spring at Therapne before the sun sets on the first day of Hekatombaion. It's the site of Helen's tomb, where she was laid to rest beside Menelaus. Once you and your bloodline have been cleansed in the spring, you will be a Warbringer no longer. You will never need fear for your life again."

"Sure," said Alia. "Makes perfect sense."

"Hopefully, your enemies believe you're dead, but we should be ready for anything once we're off the island."

I'm going to be ready to find the nearest police station and get the hell away from you, Queen Loon, Alia thought. But all she said was "Got it."

Diana stopped abruptly and put a finger to her lips. Alia nodded understanding, then crept up behind her and peered over her shoulder through the leaves.

She wasn't sure what she'd expected to see. Maybe a fort or wannabe military encampment, a bunch of rednecks in camo. Instead, she was looking down at a wide road that led into a city cut from golden stone that seemed to glow in the fading light—a fairy-tale city of arches and spires, open porches bursting with cascades of flowers, their domed rooftops and silk awnings held aloft by elegant columns.

Something was happening. Women were hurrying back and forth along the road, a sense of urgency in their movements. Some wore leather trousers and banded tops similar to Diana's, but others were draped in bright silks. They looked less like survivalists and more like a group of performers getting ready to take the stage.

Diana met Alia's eyes and made a gesture.

"That some kind of military thing?" Alia whispered.

"Never mind," said Diana on an annoyed breath. "Just follow me and stay quiet. Try to walk light. For such a little person, you make a lot of noise."

"I am not *little*," Alia protested. And, okay, she wasn't exactly *graceful*, but it wasn't like she'd run into a tree or something.

They continued through the forest, picking their way between the branches. Diana was sure-footed and never stopped to rest, but Alia felt worse with every step. She had no idea how long they'd been walking, but she'd lost her canvas tennis shoes in the wreck, and despite the mossy covering on the forest floor, her feet were protesting every root, bump, and pebble.

At last, Diana came to a halt. This time she got down on her belly and caterpillar-crawled beneath a tree covered in fat green leaves. Alia stood there for a moment. Was she really doing this? She heaved a shrug, then lay down on her stomach and followed. They emerged overlooking a high-walled citadel.

"The walls have cracked," Diana said, her voice full of a kind of miserable awe. "They've stood for nearly three thousand years."

Now Alia knew the girl was nuts. There was no way this building had been around for that long. It looked brand-new, despite the
big crack in one of its sand-colored walls.

As they watched, Alia saw two more women in leather trousers and tops jog beneath an arch. When they reemerged, they
had another woman with them. She had only one arm and it was
tattooed with what looked like—

"Is that chain mail?"

Diana nodded. "Everilde disguised herself as a knight so that
she could fight in the Crusades. The tattoo covers the whole of her
torso."

"Wow. It's like she never has to leave Ren Faire. What's written
on her shoulder?"

Diana blinked, her inky-black lashes dappled with rain. "*Peace.*
In Arabic. She had it done when Hafsah came to the island. Both
of them work in the training rooms, but with the storm and the
earthquakes, they probably need as much help as they can get at
the Epheseum." Diana groaned. "My mother is going to kill me."

"Why?"

"I should be down there, helping. *Taking a leadership role.*"

Alia almost laughed. Apparently, even cult kids had moms
with expectations. "What is this place?"

"The Armory."

It seemed awfully beautiful for an armory.

When the women were gone, Diana led Alia down the embankment and beneath an arch buried in flowers. Alia reached out and
touched a cream-colored rose, its petals tipped with red and heavy
with rain. She'd never seen a more perfect blossom, and it was
nearly as big as her head.

"Gauntlet roses," Diana said. "Jericho lilies, nasturtiums.
They're all plants associated with war or victory. My mother really
loves a theme."

"Doesn't sound weird at all," murmured Alia.

But when they entered the Armory, her jaw dropped. The
room was a vast hexagon topped by an enormous dome. Each wall

featured a different weapon: swords, axes, daggers, staffs, as well as things with spikes and prongs and creepy little barbs that Alia had no name for. The walls seemed to be organized chronologically, the oldest- and most rustic-looking weapons at the top, their sleek, modern counterparts closer to the bottom.

"No guns," she noted.

Diana looked at her like she was daft. "The gun is the coward's weapon."

"*Hmmm,*" Alia said diplomatically. The gun was also the most effective weapon. There was a reason you didn't see cops walking around with double axes. *An anti-gun, horticulture-loving survivalist cult.* Maybe they were just hippies who happened to be weapons collectors?

"What is that thing?" Alia asked, pointing to a staff topped by a giant claw.

"A *zhua.* It's used for robbing a mounted opponent of her shield."

"It looks like the world's deadliest mop."

Diana considered it. "Perhaps you can use it to scare the floor clean."

They crossed the vast room, past padded floor mats and dummies clearly intended for sparring. "You guys just leave all of this lying around? Seems dangerous."

"No weapons are permitted outside the Armory unless they have been sanctioned for exhibitions."

"What if someone steals something?"

"How? These belong to everyone."

Alia silently added *socialist* to her list of cult adjectives. Jason would not approve. But she didn't want to think about her brother or how worried he must be. Or the fact that she might not see him again if she didn't find a way off this island.

They walked through another archway and entered a smaller room. The light was dimmer here, filtered through the blue panels of a stained-glass dome above. The chamber was full of glass cases fitted with clever mirrors that made their contents seem to float in the blue-tinted light. It was like standing at the center of a sapphire.

The cases had no labels or plaques, and each had a different costume in it—a breastplate of pounded bronze and a pair of weathered sandals; the segmented steel and leather of what Alia thought might be samurai armor; heavy furs and beaded saddle-bags; a pilot's jumpsuit that looked like it might be from the twenties—Alia wasn't too clear on the history of military fash-ion, though Nim would know. But when Alia looked closer, she saw the pilot's jacket was riddled with bullet holes. She peered at the heavy plated armor in the case beside it. It had a hole in it, as if it had been pierced by a spear.

There was something else: the armor, the way the clothes were cut, the crowns and bracelets and boots. Alia stopped dead. They'd seen twenty or thirty people on the road into the city—and not a single man.

"Hold up," said Alia. Diana was standing in front of a glass case at the center of the room, larger and brighter than the others, lit by white light piercing the oculus at the top of the dome. "Are there any men on this island?"

Diana shook her head. "No."

"*None?*"

"No."

"Holy shit, are you guys some kind of radical feminist cult?"

Diana frowned. "Not exactly?"

"Are you all lesbians?"

"Of course not."

"It's cool if you are. Nim's gay. Maybe bi. She's figuring it out."

"Who's Nim?"

"My best friend." *My only friend*, Alia did not add. Jason didn't count. And Theo was more "just a friend" than actual friend.

"Some like men, some like women, some like both, some like nothing at all."

"But why no guys, then?"

"It's a long story."

"And how were you *born* here if there are no guys allowed?"

"That's a longer story." Diana turned back to the case and lifted the latch but then hesitated. Tentatively, as if she was afraid the metal might burn, she reached inside the case and took out a slender gold crown, a huge ruby cut like a star at its center.

Alia had seen a lot of big jewels on a lot of Park Avenue socialites, but nothing like that. "Who does that belong to?"

"Me, I guess. My mom had it made when I was born. But I've never worn it."

"Is the ruby real?"

Diana nodded and smiled a little. "Red like the Dog Star. I was named for the huntress, Diana, and born under the constellation of her favor, Orion. The stone was cut from the stone of my mother's crown." Diana gestured to the wide tiara that hung suspended in the case, a far larger ruby at its center. "They're heartstones. They act as a kind of compass."

She popped the star-shaped ruby from its setting and returned the gold circlet to its base. "I hope no one will notice."

"A missing ruby the size of a macaroon? Definitely not."

Diana let her fingers trail over the other items in the case: a wide golden belt set with red jewels and hunks of topaz as big as Alia's thumbnails; an elegant unstrung bow and an embroidered leather quiver full of arrows; a set of what looked like wide iron bracelets; and a long rope, coiled like a snake.

"We'll need this," Diana said, taking the lasso from the case. As Diana fastened it to her hip, it glinted brightly, as if it had been woven from something other than ordinary rope. Diana touched the cuff of one of the iron bracelets. "My mother used to bring me here every week when I was little. She'd tell me the story behind each case, all the women who came here. These are the relics of our greatest heroes. Pieces of the lives they led before they came to the island, and the battles they fought to preserve peace after. She told me all of their stories. All but hers."

They must be heirlooms, Alia thought.

Then the bracelet Diana was touching *moved*.

Alia took a step backward and almost crashed into the case behind her. "What the hell?" It was as if the metal had turned molten. It slid from the case and clasped itself around Diana's wrist. "What. The. Hell," Alia repeated as the second bracelet slithered around Diana's other wrist.

Diana looked just as shocked as Alia felt. She held her hands before her like a surgeon about to scrub in and stared at the bracelets, widemouthed in disbelief.

I have a concussion, Alia's mind babbled. *I definitely have a concussion. In fact, maybe I'm in a coma. I got knocked out during the explosion, and now I'm in a hospital in Turkey. I just need to wake up, because Nim is going to pee her pants when I tell her about the magical island of women.*

"Maybe it's a sign," said Diana.

"Of what?" Alia managed to squeak.

"That my quest is just. That I'm making the right choice."

"To help me get off the island? Absolutely. The justest." Alia considered the rope and bracelets. Regardless of what Diana had said about people carrying weapons, if any of this was real, there could be a whole slew of cult ladies running around with battle-axes and death mops right now. "Maybe we should take something else?"

"Like what?"

"You're the one talking about enemies hunting me. Don't we need, like, a crossbow or a spear? Something pointy, like that sword."

"The other artifacts? That would be stealing."

"What about the bracelets?"

"These are my birthright."

"Can't we *borrow* something from the training rooms, then?"

"We're not going to the spring to start a fight. We're going there to prevent one."

"Yeah, but you know what they say: Sometimes the best defense is a good offense."

Diana raised a brow. "And sometimes the best defense isn't showing up with a giant sword."

"Says the girl who tops out at six feet and can carry me around like a knapsack. No one's going to mess with you."

"You'd be surprised. I—"

Another tremor tore through the floor, making the room swim with blue light.

"Move," Diana said, seizing Alia's arm and yanking her away from the case as it tipped sideways and smashed against the stone floor, sending splinters of glass flying. "We have to get you off this island."

Alia tried to keep pace with Diana as they fled back through the Armory. Her head was pounding, and the nausea had returned worse than before. Chunks of rock dislodged themselves from the vast dome, crashing to the training-room mats as Diana and Alia zigzagged toward the entrance.

Diana held Alia back as they approached the arch, but their path must have been clear, because she grabbed Alia's hand and they ran for the woods. Only when they were up the embankment and hidden by the trees did they pause. Alia felt like her chest was going to explode. She knew she was out of shape. Nim was always trying to make her do yoga, and Jason was basically in a committed relationship with his treadmill, but this was something else. Her head was spinning, the pain pushing against her skull in urgent pulses.

"I need to stop," she said, bending double. Her vision was blurry. She felt something trickling over her lips, and when she touched her hand to her face, it came away bloody. "What's happening to me?"

Diana took a cloth from her pack, moistened it with rainwater from the nearest branch, and gently dabbed at Alia's mouth and nose. At her touch, Alia felt the pain recede slightly, her vision clear. "I told you—we need to get you away from the island."

"The island is a metaphor," Alia muttered to herself. "When we get off the island, I'll wake up."

"It isn't a metaphor," said Diana. "My home is killing you before you can destroy it. We have to keep moving. Do you want me to carry you?"

"*No,*" Alia said, batting Diana's hand away. "I'm fine."

Diana shook her head, but she didn't argue. Alia trailed behind her, leaning on the trunks of trees when she had to, listening to the rattle of the breath in her lungs, squelching her way through soft patches of earth the rain had turned to mud. She was aware of birds taking shelter between the great green leaves, the rustle of their wings. She heard the screech of monkeys, though she saw no sign of them. This place was so alive, brimming with life, drunk on it.

What's real and what isn't? Alia wondered. Maybe the island was real and her perceptions were off. Her brain could have been damaged in the wreck. Her body had definitely been flooded by adrenaline. Or maybe she was lying in a hospital somewhere, being pushed into an MRI machine, and this was all a hallucination. She liked that idea a lot. They'd figure out what was wrong with her misfiring mind and they'd fix it. Science could solve anything given the time and the resources. That was what her parents had taught her and Jason. The world had a beautiful logic to it, hidden patterns that would reveal themselves if you could just learn to see them. What would they think of giant trees and jewelry that acted like a well-trained pet? *They'd say there had to be an explanation. They'd find one.*

Alia staggered after Diana as the woods sloped down. The trees thinned and gradually gave way to a clearing. She had the jarring sense of slipping from one world into another. They'd just left a forest dense with vegetation, crowded with flowers and brightly colored songbirds. Now she was looking at what could only be described as grasslands, long rolling hills of gently shifting reeds, gray and pale green that resolved to the colors of an overcast sky.

Alia tried to catch her breath, acutely aware that she was panting like a tired dog, while Diana didn't seem winded at all. "This doesn't make any sense. This kind of ecology is completely wrong for this climate."

Diana only smiled. "The island is like that. It gives gifts." Alia tried not to roll her eyes. "My mother never talks about life before the island," Diana continued. "But she loves this place. I think it reminds her of the steppe."

Diana stood for a long time, staring out at the grasses. Alia had no desire to start walking again, but she also had the distinct impression that they were supposed to be in a hurry.

"So . . . ," Alia began. Diana shook her head, placing a finger to her lips. "If you're going to shush me—"

"Listen."

"All I hear is the wind."

"Here," Diana said, taking Alia's hand. She squatted down and tugged Alia with her, placing her palm against the damp earth. "Do you feel it?"

Alia frowned but then—a trembling, different from the earthquakes. It was more like the patter of rain, but that wasn't quite right, either.

"Close your eyes," Diana murmured.

Alia gave her a wary glance, then shut her eyes. The world went dark. She could smell the storm in the air, the deep mossy fragrance of the woods behind them, and something else, a warmer smell she couldn't name. She heard the lonely rustle of the wind moving through the grass, and then, so faint she doubted it at first, the softest whinny. It came again, and the sounds began to coalesce with the gentle drumbeat she felt through the earth: bodies shifting together, a snort of breath, hoofbeats.

Her eyes flew open. She felt herself smiling. "Horses?" Diana grinned and nodded. They rose. "But where are they?"

"Here, in the field, the phantom herd."

Diana unhooked the golden coil of rope from her hip and began to move through the tall grass. It came up to her thighs, almost all the way up to Alia's waist, tickling her bare legs in an itchy way that made her think of cobwebs.

"My mother and her sisters were great horsewomen," Diana

said. "They could ride any steed and coax the best from it, land arrows while hanging from a saddle, aim upside down. When Maeve came to the island . . ." Diana's voice wavered. "The phantom herd was a gift from the goddess Epona. A thank-you to Hera and Athena for granting Maeve immortality."

Diana gestured for them to stop, and Alia saw that she had knotted the rope into a loop, forming a lasso. Diana let it swing gently from her hands, building momentum.

Alia could hear those sounds growing closer now, the rumble of hooves that seemed to echo a heartbeat, double it, treble it. The tall grass moved against the wind as if trampled by some unseen force. Alia's mind refused it. *It can't be. It* can't.

Diana's eyes were closed. She stood with her face tilted to the wind, listening, the lasso moving in a lazy, looping rhythm. The rope seemed to glow in her hands as she released it. It cut a long, shining path against the gray sky, then dropped around the neck of a huge white horse that hadn't been there a moment before. It was as if the lasso had caused the horse to appear.

Alia took a step backward, heart slamming in her chest. Diana gave the lasso slack, turning in place as the horse shook its shimmering white mane in frustration, checking its stride. She tugged gently and it slowed, rearing back on its hooves and releasing a high, angry whinny.

"It's all right, Khione," she murmured, her voice low and soothing. "It's just me."

The horse danced back, tossing its mane, and Diana gave another gentle tug, the muscles of her arms shifting beneath her bronzed skin.

She whistled softly, and the horse's ears flicked. Grudgingly, it settled, hooves landing on the grass with a sulky thump, and blew out a disgruntled breath. It walked forward as Diana reeled in the lasso. When it was close enough, she crooked an arm over the horse's neck and patted its flank as it bumped its great head against her.

"She's Maeve's favorite," Diana said, and Alia could hear the sadness and worry in her voice. She waved Alia forward with an encouraging smile. "Go on."

Alia hesitated, then cautiously reached up to stroke the creature's velvety nose. A lot of kids at her school rode, but she'd never seen an animal like this, white as alabaster, marble-hewn, a horse that looked as if it had leapt down from some monument at the center of a plaza. Its lashes were the same snowy color as its mane, but its eyes had no whites. They were the deep purple-black of a pansy.

The horse—*the invisible horse*, Alia's mind corrected, then rejected—bowed its head, and Alia felt some tiny bit of the terror she'd been carrying since the wreck release. Suddenly, she was blinking back tears. She thought of a glass filled to its brim, the tension at its surface that kept it from spilling over. The horse was warm beneath her hand. She could see the long curl of its lashes. It was real in a way nothing else had been since the cold of the waves. If this creature was possible, then *all of it* might be real. It was too much.

Alia shut her eyes and pressed her forehead against the rough silk of the horse's mane. "What did you call her?"

"Khione. It means 'snow.'"

"And she was a gift?"

"Yes. When a rider sits one of the phantom herd and takes hold of its mane, she becomes as invisible as the horse."

"How can we see her now?"

"The lasso. It always shows the truth."

Alia took a shuddering breath that was halfway to a sob. "Can you ask the lasso if I'm going to get home?"

"It doesn't work that way. And, Alia, you can't go home. Not yet. People tried to kill you."

"Because of the Foundation."

"Because of what you are. You're dangerous to a lot of people. We have to get you to Greece, to the spring at Therapne." Diana whispered in the horse's ear and then plucked several strands of

Khione's mane. Khione made a disapproving nicker but remained in place, stomping her huge hooves.

"What are you doing?" Alia asked.

"We need these to get off the island."

Another tremor struck and the horse reared back, yanking the lasso from Diana's hands. Diana stepped in front of Alia, arms spread wide, her expression unruffled. Khione took some skittering steps, then seemed to calm. Diana waited a few more moments before picking up the rope. She patted the horse's flank. "It will be better soon," she said softly. "Promise."

Diana slid the lasso over the horse's head, and Alia watched in wonder as Khione vanished. Magic. She was seeing real magic. The kind of magic in movies. No wands or wizards yet, but maybe if she stayed on the island long enough, a dragon would show up. *It all feels so real*, Alia thought as she followed Diana through the grasslands. But that was probably how delusions worked.

At some point she realized that the terrain was starting to look familiar. In the distance, she saw the sea. They'd returned to the cliffs.

"I'm not going back to the cave," she said stubbornly.

"Not the cave," said Diana. "The cove."

Alia picked her way cautiously to the edge of the cliff and looked down. There was a small sandy beach carved into the coast, like the top of a question mark.

"Okay, but no way am I getting on your back again."

"I can hitch up a sling," said Diana, removing a length of ordinary rope from her pack.

"Not happening. I'm not going over that cliff."

"I won't let you get hurt."

"You know what, Diana? We just met, so maybe you haven't picked up on this, but I'm not made like you. I appreciate that you saved my life—"

"A couple of times."

"Okay, a couple of times, but this day has been a lot. I don't do miles of hiking or any kind of rock climbing that doesn't involve a safety harness, an indoor wall, and some jacked-up guy on the gym floor shouting stuff like 'Good hustle!' I'm trying my best, but I'm about ready to lose it here."

Diana studied her for a long moment, and Alia was pretty sure that the girl could simply throw her over her shoulder if she wanted to. But Diana nodded and gave a small bow. "Forgive me."

Apparently, cult kids had really good manners, too.

"No problem," Alia said, embarrassed by her outburst. At least this meant no more piggybacks. Diana led her along the cliff to the beginning of a steep, narrow path. Alia swallowed and did her best to feign confidence. "Much better."

"My way would be faster," Diana offered.

"Slow and steady wins the race."

"That is almost always untrue."

"Take it up with Aesop."

"Aesop never existed. The stories credited to him were the work of two female slaves."

"That sounds about typical. I'll ponder it on the way down."

Alia started along the path, carefully choosing each step, afraid she'd lose her footing and go right over the side.

"It's going to take you an hour if you do it that way," said Diana.

"I'll get there when I get there. I'm not part goat."

"Could have fooled me."

At that moment another small tremor struck, and Alia pressed her body to the cliff side.

"You're sure you want to take the path?" Diana said.

"Positive," Alia squeaked.

"All right. Wait for me on the sand."

"You aren't coming?"

"I'll go my own way."

Diana tossed her pack over the side of the cliff to the cove below. Then, as Alia watched in disbelief, she sprinted the length of the cliff top. Alia clapped her hands over her mouth. *She can't mean to—*

Diana leapt, silhouetted for a moment against the thunderheads, toes pointed, arms outstretched. She looked like she might sprout wings and simply take flight. *Stranger things have happened today.* Instead, her body arced downward and vanished over the cliff side.

"Show-off," Alia muttered, and continued down the path.

As she shuffled along, she alternated between trying to find the next place to put her foot and gazing out to sea to try to locate Diana in the rocking gray waves. The surf was huge, beating at the cove with ceaseless rage. What if Diana had simply been dragged under? What if she'd cracked her gorgeous head open on a rock?

The farther Alia went, the worse her own head ached and the sicker she felt. By the time she reached the bottom of the cliffs, her thighs were shaking and her nerves had frayed to nothing from fear of the fall. There was no sign of Diana, and Alia realized she had no idea what to do if she didn't return. Climb back to the top? She wasn't sure she had the strength. Hope one of those hippie weapons collectors found her and was friendlier than Diana had suggested? And what about everything Diana had said about Greece and Alia being dangerous?

"Girl is addled," said Alia decisively to no one. "That's what growing up in a cult does to you." *Yeah, and you're the one talking to yourself on a beach.*

Even so, Alia felt the knot of worry in her chest loosen when she looked out to sea and saw Diana cutting through the ocean, her arms slicing through the water at a determined pace. There was something behind her, a massive shape that appeared and disappeared in the spaces between the waves.

When Diana reached the shore, she emerged with water streaming from her dark hair, ropes thrown over her shoulders, feet digging into the sand, every muscle in her body straining as she strode forward. It took Alia a long moment to understand that the ropes were rigging.

Diana had hauled the *Thetis* from the bottom of the sea.

A bone-deep shiver quaked through Alia. One of the masts was still intact; the other had snapped free close to its base. The prow was completely gone. The explosion had left nothing but a jagged line of wood and fiberglass where the rest of the boat should be. *You are being hunted. . . . Because of what you are.*

Diana didn't understand. Alia's family had been targets for so long, first when people accused them of "playing God" with their research, then because of the rules the Keralis Foundation attached to any grant for aid. There was still speculation that the crash that had killed her parents had been an assassination plot. A thorough investigation had proven that there was nothing more to that terrible night than a slippery road and distracted drivers. But every few years, some newspaper or blog ran a conspiracy piece on the deaths of Nik and Lina Keralis. Alia would get an email from some curious reporter, or she'd walk by a newsstand and see her parents' wedding photo looking back at her, and the wound would open all over again.

She remembered sitting in the backseat with Jason, his profile lit by streetlamps, her parents in the front, arguing about which bridge to take home. That was the last memory she had of them: her mother drumming on the steering wheel, her father jabbing at the screen of his phone and insisting that if she'd just taken the Triborough, they'd be home by now. Then the strange feeling of the car moving the wrong way, momentum carrying them across three lanes of traffic as they slid into a skid. She remembered the car hitting the divider, the shriek of tearing metal, and then nothing at all. She'd been twelve. Jason had been sixteen. When she'd woken up in the hospital, she still had the smell of burnt rubber in her nose. It took days for it to dissipate and be replaced by the cloying stink of hospital disinfectant. Jason had been there when she woke, a big slash on his cheek that had been stitched closed, his eyes red from crying. Their godfather, Michael Santos, had come, and his son, Theo, who had put his arm around Jason and held Alia's hand.

Looking at the remains of the *Thetis* felt the same as waking up in that hospital bed, like grief rushing straight at her. *You are being hunted*. Was Alia the reason for the wreck? Was she why Jasmine and Ray and the others were lost forever?

Diana had set about disentangling the rigging and was now tearing the hull apart as easily as if she were digging into a lobster dinner.

"What are you doing?" Alia asked, eyeing her nervously. Maybe the cult members mixed steroids in with their chewable vitamins.

"We need a craft to get out past the boundary."

"What boundary?"

Diana hesitated, then said, "I just meant open sea. The hull is useless, but I think we can salvage part of the deck and the sail and use it as a raft."

Alia didn't want to touch the boat. She didn't want anything to do with it. "A raft? In that surf? Why don't we wait for the storm to pass?"

"This storm isn't going to pass. It's only going to get worse." Diana peered out at the water. "We could try swimming, but if we got separated—"

"It's fine," Alia said, helping Diana brace a piece of the hull against her shoulder and tear it free.

At that moment Diana doubled over in pain.

"What is it?" Alia asked, panicked. Without realizing it, she'd started to think of Diana as invulnerable.

"Maeve," she said. "The others. We have to hurry. Soon it will be too late."

CHAPTER 5

They worked for the better part of an hour. The earthquakes were coming more frequently now, and occasionally bits of the cliff would shake free behind them. Alia had tried to help for a while, but eventually she'd given up and leaned against the makeshift raft, her breath coming in shallow gasps. Diana could see just how ashen she looked beneath her brown skin.

She'd seemed better when they were climbing and Diana had been close to her. *Your proximity may prolong her life, may even soothe her, but it cannot heal her. She will die, and the island will live.* Alia was dying, and though Diana still felt well, she could sense the pain and bewilderment of her sisters through the blood tie that connected all Amazons. What one of them felt, they all felt, and to fight, even to spar, meant to endure the pain of your opponent, even as you dealt the blow. If one of them died . . . No, Diana would not allow it.

"Hold on, Maeve," she whispered.

They lashed together the raft as best they could, and then Diana raised the sail, tying strands of Khione's mane into the knots of the rigging. With each knot, another section of the raft

76

vanished. It would be invisible from the shores of Themyscira and the southern coast of Greece. Diana hoped to put the raft in as close as possible to Gytheio. From there it would be a two-day journey on foot to Therapne. She doubted Alia could make faster time than that in her current state. Perhaps they could acquire one of the machines she'd read about.

"Do you know how to drive an automobile?" asked Diana as she secured the raft's makeshift rudder.

"A car? Nope. No reason to learn in New York."

Diana frowned. "Well, even on foot, we should have plenty of time to reach the spring before the start of Hekatombaion."

"And Hekatombaion is what exactly?"

"The first month in the old Greek calendar. It used to mark the start of the year."

"Got it. Hekatombaion. Party at the spring. All the cool kids will be there."

"Who are the cool kids?"

"Ouch. Okay, you and I will be there."

Diana had the distinct sense that Alia didn't intend to be at the spring at all, but she could worry about that later. She braided a strand of Khione's mane into her own hair and did the same for Alia, then helped her board and bent to grab the edges of the raft.

Diana shoved the raft forward into the water. She leapt atop it, feeling the surf surge beneath her. She let out the sail the barest amount and set her hand to the tiller.

As they raced over the sea, Diana glanced back at the little cove, watching it grow smaller with every passing second. *It's not too late*, she thought. *Turn back. Let the island do its work.* Instead, she told Alia to ease the sail and watched the wind fill the canvas. The raft shot forward over the crest of another wave, sliding down the other side with a stomach-lurching drop.

They passed the rocks that marked the boundary and entered the mists. There was no shift in temperature this time, and Diana wasn't sure she'd know when they'd made the crossing. The waves seemed wilder here, but it was hard to tell. Then Alia tilted her head to the sky and took a deep breath. Diana could see the color in her cheeks returning. Were the earthquakes ceasing on Themyscira? Was Maeve opening her eyes? Or would some sacrifice be demanded to purge the island of Alia's influence?

Diana looked back at her home. She'd never been this far out before, never seen the island from such a great distance. The mists parted briefly and she could see its shape, the curve of its coastline, the towers of the Epheseum at one end and the great dome of Bana-Mighdall at the other, the crests and valleys of its mountains like a green odalisque.

The mists closed. Themyscira was gone. If she tried to return now, would the island know her? Would she be able to find it? Would it welcome her back?

Back to what? a dark voice inside her asked. What if she could return? What if the Oracle didn't tell Hippolyta how horribly she'd betrayed her people? If she remained on the island, she would only ever be Hippolyta's coddled daughter. She would never be allowed to find her way.

Hippolyta could claim that Diana was an Amazon, but before everything else, Diana was her daughter, too precious, too breakable to risk. And that was how the other Amazons would always see her: not as a true sister, but as their queen's child. She would forever be an outsider, a weakness to exploit.

But if she made things right, if she got Alia to the spring, it wouldn't just be a mission; it would be a *quest*, a hero's journey, like those set before champions in times of old. The line of Warbringers would be broken. Alia would live, war would be prevented, and Diana would have proven herself. By then, Hippolyta and Tek would know all about Diana's transgression. She would have to face a trial before the Amazon Council, but Diana had to believe she would be forgiven. To stop the cycle of Warbringers? To prevent not just one war but countless future wars? That was a deed worthy of an Amazon. There would be punishment, but surely not exile. *You will still have to look Maeve in the eye and tell her that you were the cause of her suffering.* That would be the worst punishment, the hardest to endure, and there was no question Diana deserved it.

Of course, she might fail. She might save this one girl and plunge the earth into an age of war, a war that might reach beyond the bounds of the mortal world to her home. Diana remembered the vision of her mother's body lying lifeless on the field, the accusation in Tek's dying eyes, the ground turned to ash, the smell of blood and burnt flesh in the air, that hideous creature with the head of a jackal. Her mistake might cost them everything.

No. There had to be a reason she'd been the one to see the *Thetis* sink, the one to pull Alia from the sea. She'd been given a chance to help bring peace to the world and to end the cycle of war that lived in Alia's blood. She would not fail. And she would not let fear choose her path.

The mist was cold, and the surf bucked beneath them like a living thing. Diana reached into her pocket and took hold of the heartstone. She could feel its faceted edges hard against her palm.

"Alia," she called over the wind. "Take my hand."

Alia lurched across the length of the raft to the stern. She grasped Diana's hand, wet from rain and sea spray, the heartstone tight between their palms.

"Ready?" Diana asked, keeping her other hand on the tiller.

"Ready," Alia said with a firm nod.

Diana felt a grin break over her face. "Destiny is waiting."

She focused on her memory of the map of Greece, the Gulf of Laconia, the divot in its southern shore. *Guide us*, she willed.

Nothing happened.

Diana had the sudden, mortifying thought that maybe she'd misunderstood how the heartstone worked. What if her will wasn't strong enough to direct it? They'd be lost on the sea, stuck on this raft, and she would never see Themyscira again.

Then the raft began to spin, slowly at first, gaining momentum. The waters rose, turning in a spiral, forming a wall around them—a column of gray sea and writhing foam, churning faster and faster, higher and higher until the sky was barely a pinprick of light far above.

With a loud *crack*, the sail ripped free and vanished up the flume. The raft shook, breaking apart beneath them.

"Don't let go!" shouted Diana, holding tight to Alia.

"Are you kidding?" Alia screamed back.

They were soaked through, huddled over the rudder on their knees, their palms pressed together so tightly, Diana could feel the edges of the jewel cutting into her flesh.

Tek was right. The gods are angry. They'd never wanted her on the island. It was the worst kind of hubris to think they'd sent Alia to her as a chance at greatness. They'd sent Alia as a lure, and now she and the Warbringer would die together, consumed by the great mouth of the sea.

The roar of the churning water filled her ears, rattling her skull, the wind and salt lashing at her with such force that she could not keep her eyes open. She huddled against Alia, felt her pulse—or was it Diana's own?—in the press of their palms.

All at once, the world went silent. The roar did not quiet but simply vanished. Diana opened her eyes as the column fell in a great tumble of water, drenching them and sending the raft rocking as the sea sloshed beneath them. Mist clung to the broken stump of the mast as the raft swayed, then stopped, the waters eerily still.

They were shrouded in darkness. Had night fallen in the mortal world? Had they lost or gained time when they used the heartstone?

They were still moving, carried by a strong tide, but the surf had calmed to the barest ripple.

Diana and Alia stared at each other. Alia's hair hung in a wet mass of braids, her eyes wide and round as newly minted coins. Diana suspected she looked just as stunned.

"Did it work?" Alia said.

Slowly, they unclasped their hands. The heartstone was

covered in their blood. Diana wiped it clean on her wet trousers and slipped it into her pocket.

She looked around. The raft was nearly half the size it had been when they left the island. The mast was in pieces, bits of rope and rigging hanging from it limply. Through the mists, Diana saw the first twinkle of lights. They were brighter than the lanterns of Themyscira, steadier than torchlight, hard pinpricks that glinted like captured stars—white, pale blue, gold, silvery green.

"It worked," Diana said, only half believing it herself. "It actually worked." She'd done it. She'd left Themyscira. She'd crossed over into the World of Man.

The lights multiplied around them on both sides, more of them than she ever could have imagined. Diana could hear water slapping at the sides of the raft, and something else, deep and resonant—ships' horns, a sound she'd only ever heard from a great distance on the island.

But the lights were too close, too bright, too plentiful. Had she brought them that near to a city? And why did the Ionian Sea feel flat as a millpond?

The mists cleared, and Diana glimpsed another light burning high in the sky, different from the others, a vibrant yellow torch held aloft by the statue of an Amazon, her stern face framed by a crown like a sunburst, her gown hanging in gray-green folds of weathered copper. Behind her, Diana could see the lights of a vast bridge.

"This isn't right," Diana said, standing slowly. "This isn't Greece."

Alia threw her head back and laughed, a sound of pure exuberance and relief and . . . pride.

"No way," Alia whispered. She spread her arms wide, as if she could take the whole city into them, as if all of these lights had been lit to greet only her. "Welcome to the greatest city in the world, Diana. This is New York." She whooped and turned her face to the sky. "This is home!"

CHAPTER 6

What have I done? The air felt strange on Diana's skin, gritty in her lungs. She could *taste* it in her mouth, dank and ashy against her tongue. The lights onshore seemed less like stars now than the bright reflection of predators' eyes, wolves waiting in the dark.

She whirled on Alia. "What did you do?"

Alia held up her hands. "You were the one steering."

"The *heartstone* was steering. I thought of the spring. I focused on the coast of . . ." Her words trailed off as she looked at Alia's relieved, happy face. The heartstone was supposed to heed the desires of the woman who commanded it. Apparently, Alia's will had been greater. "You were thinking of home." She could not keep the accusation from her voice.

Alia shrugged. "Sorry?"

"I don't think you are."

A horn bellowed, closer this time, as a barge passed, trailed by a rolling wake that struck the remnants of their raft. They stumbled, managed to right themselves, but the raft was taking on water fast. *Think*, Diana scolded herself. The heartstone could only be used to leave Themyscira or return to it. She could use it to take them back to the island, then try again, but could Diana risk bringing the Warbringer back there? Would Alia or the island survive that?

To the east, she saw the beginnings of dawn tipping the sky gray. Her eyes scanned the horizon. New York. The island of Manhattan. Diana knew the maps well enough from her studies, knew she was thousands of miles from Therapne and the spring and any kind of hope.

She released a frustrated moan. "How did this happen?"

Alia smiled slightly. "I've been saying that all day."

Had it only been a day? That morning, Diana's sole worry had been losing a race. Now she had abandoned the only home and the only life she knew, and possibly doomed the world to a bloody age of war. Apparently she had a gift for disaster.

Make a new plan, she told herself. *Soldiers adapt.*

"We need to get to shore," she said decisively. It wasn't much, but it was a start. Of course, they had no mast, no sail, and no way to steer. "We're going to have to swim."

Alia shuddered. "First rule of New York living: Do not swim in the Hudson. Do you know how polluted this water is?"

Diana eyed the river. It was an opaque blue verging on slate. It looked nothing like the clear waters of home. Still . . .

"Water is water," she said, with more confidence than she felt. The wind and sea had torn the strand of Khione's mane from Alia's braids, and Diana's own braid had come loose as well. They would be visible once they left the raft, but there was nothing to be done about it. She wrapped her arm around Alia.

"I can swim!" Alia protested.

"It's dark out. I'm not taking any chances," said Diana. And now that they were back in the mortal world, she wasn't entirely sure that Alia wouldn't just paddle away on her own.

Diana plunged them both into the river, and her whole body recoiled. The cold she had expected, but the water *felt* wrong. It was dense and clammy, like a moist palm clenching around her.

"Hey!" Alia complained, wriggling in her grasp. "Whoa, whoa, head *east*, toward Manhattan. Otherwise we'll end up in Jersey."

Diana kicked hard, eager to get them out of this . . . soup as fast as possible. Suddenly, Alia stiffened in her arms.

"What is it?" Diana asked. "Are the poisons of the water affecting you?"

"I remember."

"Remember what?"

"*This.* You saving me from the wreck."

"That seems unlikely. You were unconscious."

Alia's back was to her, but Diana felt her small shrug. "I remember the water turning warm." She paused. "I remember thinking everything was going to be okay."

Diana could hear the relief in her voice, the conviction that things had turned out all right. *She thinks she's safe now,* Diana realized. *She thinks this is over.*

"There," Alia said, craning her neck. "Straight ahead. That's Battery Park."

In the gray light, Diana could just make out the hulking shape rising from the water, and as they drew closer . . . She squinted. "Are those cannons?"

"They used to be. There's a war memorial."

Her mother had told her the mortal world was pocked with memorials and monuments to loss. *They build with steel and stone and promise to remember,* she'd said. *But they never do.*

"That's the ferry," said Alia as they crossed the wake of a slow-moving ship. "If they see us—"

"Take a breath."

"But—"

Diana didn't wait for an argument. She dunked them beneath the surface, continuing to swim. She wasn't sure how long a mortal could hold her breath, but she counted twenty seconds.

As they reemerged, Alia hauled in a long breath and spat river water. "Oh God, water up the nose," she gasped. "You're lucky I'm so happy to be home."

"I'm glad you're in such a good mood," Diana muttered.

"I'm being crushed by a grumpy giant and I probably just swallowed toxic waste, but, yeah, I am."

Diana eased her hold slightly. It wasn't fair to punish Alia for her desperation to return home. But that didn't change the predicament they were in. Hekatombaion would begin with the rise of the new moon, and it was possible that they'd lost more than just a few hours when they'd broken through to the mortal world.

Diana saw ships moored near the park, their decks and masts still lit by a glittering spangle of lights, but would a ship be fast enough to get them to Greece in time? Diana thought of the planes she and Maeve had sometimes glimpsed above Themyscira. That was what she needed. She just had no idea where to get one.

When they reached the dock, Diana shifted her grip on Alia and grabbed hold of a pylon.

"Hold on to my neck," she instructed. She'd expected an argument, but apparently Alia's happy mood had made her compliant. She locked her arms over Diana's shoulders without a single complaint. Even her grip was stronger away from Themyscira. If she was faring this well away from the island, Diana could only hope Alia's absence would have a similar effect on Maeve.

Diana climbed the pylon and hauled them up to the dock, depositing Alia on the pavement with a thud. Alia flopped onto her back and flapped her arms back and forth.

"What are you doing?" said Diana.

"Making snow angels."

"There's no snow."

"Okay," admitted Alia, "I'm celebrating."

Diana turned her back on Alia and the slate expanse of the river, intending to declare there was absolutely nothing to celebrate about this debacle, when she got her first real look at the city.

Her breath caught. She'd thought Ephesus and Bana-Mighdall were cities, but if that was the case, then maybe a different word was needed for the massive, spiky, dazzling thing before her. It rose in peaks and ridges, a jagged mountain range that should have run a hundred miles, but that had been crammed into a single narrow space, folded onto itself in hard angles and bright reflective planes like some grand formation of mica. And it was *alive*. Even in what should have been the still-sleeping hours of dawn, the city was moving. Motorcars. Electric lights blinking in different colors. People on foot with steaming paper cups in their hands, newspapers tucked beneath their arms.

It was like facing the Oracle all over again—the terror of staring into the unknown. The thrill of it.

"You all right?" asked Alia, pushing herself up from the dock and trying to wring some of the water from her bedraggled yellow shirt.

"I don't know," Diana said honestly.

"You've really never left that island?"

"You saw how easy it is to leave my home."

"Good point."

A man jogged by, wiping the sweat from his brow and singing loudly to himself. He was tall and lean and *hairy*.

"He has a beard!" Diana said in wonder.

"Yeah, that's kind of a thing now."

Diana cocked her head to the side as the man belted out something that sounded like "concrete jungles where dreams tomato" and vanished down the path. "Are males generally tone-deaf?"

"No, but believe me when I say you don't want to hear Jason attempt karaoke."

Diana took a deep breath, trying to clear her mind. She could not let this place overwhelm or distract her. She had a mission to complete.

"Where can we get an airplane?"

Alia limped past her down the running path and into the park. "We don't need a plane. We need a bath, a hot meal." She waved at her bare feet. *"Shoes."*

Diana caught up and moved to block her route. "Alia, you can't go home."

"Diana—"

"The people who tried to kill you believe the Warbringer is dead. We need to make sure it stays that way until we reach the spring." Alia opened her mouth to argue, but Diana cut her off. "I know you don't believe me, but you also know the explosion on that boat was no accident."

Alia paused, then nodded slowly. "I know."

Diana felt a surge of gratitude. She'd feared Alia would try to deny everything that had happened now that she was on familiar ground. "Then you have to know it's safer for everyone if your enemies believe you're dead."

Alia scrubbed a hand over her face. "You're saying if I try to go home I could be putting Jason in danger."

"Yes."

"I can't just let my brother think I'm dead. He could be a target, too."

"Once we reach the spring—"

"Stop talking about the spring. We have no way to get there. We don't have any money, and I'm guessing you don't have a passport."

"What's a passport?"

"Exactly. Let's deal with one thing at a time. I can call Jason—"

Diana shook her head. "Someone knew how to find you on that boat. They could be monitoring your location through your brother."

Diana could see Alia's disbelief warring with her desire to keep her family safe.

"I guess I—" Alia began. A bicycle whirred past them, and Diana yanked her from its path.

"Jerk!" Alia yelled after him.

The bicyclist glanced back once and held up his middle finger.

"Is he an enemy?" Diana asked.

"No, he's a New Yorker. Let's sit. I need to think."

They found the nearest bench, and Diana made herself sit, be still. She wanted to act, not pause to ponder, but she needed Alia on her side if they had any hope of getting to the spring.

"Okay," said Alia, chewing her lower lip. "We can't go to a

bank because we don't have ID. And you're basically telling me I can't go home or to the Keralis offices because everyone thinks I'm dead."

"And we want to keep it that way."

"Right. So I'm home, but if I follow your rules, I'm still completely stranded."

Diana could hear the frustration and fatigue in her voice. She hesitated. She knew she was asking a great deal of Alia, but she had to. The stakes were too high for either of them to flinch.

"After everything you've seen," she said, "after what we just dared, can you at least trust me enough to try to keep you from harm?"

Alia touched her fingers briefly to the bracelet on Diana's left wrist, a thoughtful look on her face. Was she remembering what had happened in the Armory?

"Maybe," Alia said at last. "At least now Jason's going to have something real to be paranoid about." Her head snapped up. "That's it!"

"What's it?"

Alia leapt up from the bench. "I know what to do. And now that I know I'm not going to die, I'm starving."

"But you said yourself we have no money. Do we have something to barter?"

"No, but I happen to know of a bank that doesn't require ID."

"Very well," Diana said. For now, she had little choice but to follow Alia's lead. She would get her bearings, gather her resources. "I'm glad to leave this place. The smell in this part of the city is intolerable."

Alia bit her lip. "Yeah, *this* part of the city. I can't believe I just swam in the Hudson and I'm about to go barefoot on the subway. I'm going to die of something nasty for sure. Come on," she said, offering Diana her hand. "You're on my island now. Let's hop a train."

*　*　*

Diana had read about trains. She'd learned about undergrounds and metros, bullet trains and steam engines, all part of her education, her mother's attempt to give her an understanding of the changing mortal world. But there was a difference between those vague impressions left by long hours turning pages at the Epheseum and the reality of a New York City subway train screaming through the dark.

Alia had led her across the street from the park, past the bronze statue of a bull, and two armed men in military fatigues standing at the top of a long flight of stairs who had given them the barest glance.

"Weird," Alia had muttered. "Maybe there was a bomb threat or something."

They'd descended into the very bowels of the city and entered a large tiled chamber that emptied onto a train platform. Then they'd vaulted a boundary and slipped between the metal doors of a train, and now here they were, sitting on plastic seats beneath lights that seemed unnaturally bright, as the train rumbled and shrieked like some kind of demon.

At each stop, the metal doors opened, letting the balmy air of the platform gust through the train, and more passengers boarded, crowding in against one another. "Commuters," said Alia.

The word meant nothing to Diana. These people were of every size, color, and shape, some dressed in fine fabrics, others in cheaply made garments. Diana noticed Alia kept her feet tucked under her seat, perhaps to hide that they were bare.

Diana and Alia drew a few stares, but most people kept their eyes glued to little boxes they clutched in their palms like talismans or stared off into the middle distance, their gazes blank and lifeless.

"What's wrong with them?" Diana whispered.

"That's the subway stare," Alia explained. "If the first rule of New York is don't swim in the Hudson, the second is do not make eye contact on the subway."

"Why not?"

"Because someone might talk to you."

"Would that be so bad?" The prospect of so many new people to speak to seemed like an unimaginable luxury.

"Maybe not, but you never know in New York. Take that lady," Alia said, bobbing her head very slightly at a woman of middle age with carefully coiffed hair and a large red leather handbag in her lap. "She looks nice enough, maybe a little tightly wound, but for all you know she's got a human head in that purse."

Diana's eyes widened. "Is that common?"

"I mean, not common. She probably just has a bunch of wadded-up tissues and a lot of pictures of her grandkids she wants to show you, but that's bad enough."

Diana considered. "Direct eye contact is sometimes considered an act of aggression among primates."

"Now you're getting it."

Diana tried not to be too confrontational in her gaze, but she took advantage of the other riders' blank looks and distraction to study them, particularly the males. She'd seen illustrations, photographs, but still they were more varied than she'd expected—large, small, broad, slender. She saw soft chins, hard jaws, long, curling hair, heads shaved smooth as summer melons.

"Hey," said a young man in front of them, turning to the bearded, heavyset passenger behind him. "Do you mind?"

"Mind what?" the bearded man replied, his chest puffing out.

The smaller man stepped closer. "You're in my space. How about you back off?"

"How about you learn your place?" He jabbed his finger into the young man's chest.

Alia rolled her eyes. "God, I hate the subway." She grabbed Diana's elbow and pulled her along, yanking a door open at the end of the car so they could find seats elsewhere. Diana looked back over her shoulder. The men were still glaring at each other, and Diana wondered if they would come to blows.

Or would they calm themselves, step away from each other,

and realize they hadn't started this morning looking for a fight? Was this Alia's power at work, or was it just New York?

The new car they entered was a bit emptier, though there were no seats to be had. Near one of the doors, two girls in sheer, shimmery dresses slept slumped against each other, glitter on their cheeks, wilted flower crowns in their tangled hair. The sandals on their feet had high, pointed heels and gossamer-thin straps. They'd painted the nails of their toes silver.

"Where do you think they're going?" Diana asked.

"Probably coming back from somewhere," said Alia a little wistfully. "A party. I doubt they've been to bed."

They looked magical, as if their sleep might be enchanted.

A cluster of young men entered the car, talking loudly, containers of what smelled like coffee in their hands. They wore what Diana realized was a kind of uniform—dark suits and shirts of white, pale pink, light blue. The men were laughing and whispering to one another, casting looks at the glittery girls. *Assessing them*, she realized. There was hunger behind their smiles.

Diana thought of Hades, lord of the underworld. Maybe here he was the subway god, demanding tolls and tribute from all those who trespassed in his territory, his suited acolytes shuffling from train to train in the dark. Did these girls in their flower crowns know to be watchful? Or, lulled into sleep and incaution, might they simply vanish into some deep wedge of shadow?

Diana's gaze returned to the young men, and one of them took notice. "Hey, baby," he said with a grin at his companions. "You like what you see?"

"I'm fully grown," she said. "And I'm not yet sure."

Alia groaned, and the man's companions hooted and jostled him.

"That's cold," he said, still smiling, sidling closer. "I bet I could convince you."

"How?"

"Let's just say I don't get many complaints."

"From your lovers?"

The man blinked. He had sandy hair and freckles on his nose. "Uh, yeah." He grinned again. "From my lovers."

"It's possible they refrain from complaining in order to spare your feelings."

"What?"

"Perhaps if you could keep a woman, you'd have less call to proposition strangers."

"Oh damn," said one of his companions with a laugh.

"You're a little bitchy, huh?" said the sandy-haired man. He ran a finger along the strap of her top, his knuckles brushing her skin. "I like that."

"Hey—" said Alia.

Diana seized his finger and twisted it hard right. The man expelled a high-pitched bleat. "I don't like that word. I can see why you're unpopular with women."

"Let go of me, you—"

She twisted again, and he crumpled to his knees. "Perhaps some classes?" she suggested. She looked to his companions. "Or better advisors. You should keep your friend from embarrassing himself." She let him go and he howled, clutching his finger to his chest. "It reflects poorly on you all."

"Call a cop!" the man wailed.

"Oh, look," said Alia. "Wouldn't you know, this is our stop."

She yanked Diana through the doors and onto the platform. Diana looked back once. The glittery girls were waving.

Then Alia pulled her onto a moving metal staircase and they rose higher, higher, up into the swelter of the sun. Diana squinted, eyes adjusting to the glare and the noise. The extraordinary noise. The city she'd glimpsed from the park had hummed dimly with life, but now morning had arrived in earnest, and they were at the center of the thrumming hive. It was as if the very pavement beneath their feet, the walls around them, vibrated with sound.

There were people everywhere, crowds of them, great packs of them that milled on corners and then surged forward in lowing herds. Every surface was covered in images and signs. They were full of commands and promises: *Act today. Give diamonds. Earn your degree. Low, low prices. Enchant him.* Who exactly? Diana recognized most of the words, and the numbers she knew referred to currency. Other messages were less clear. What exactly was a bar made of salad, and why would one want to pay for food by the pound?

The men and women who stared back at her from the signs looked different from those walking the streets. Their hair gleamed, and their skin was perfectly smooth and unblemished. Perhaps they were meant to be religious icons.

Beside her, Alia hissed, and Diana realized her limp had worsened. "Do you want to rest? Or I could—"

"You're not carrying me through the streets of Manhattan."

"We're already drawing attention," Diana said with a shrug. "I don't see how it could hurt."

"It could hurt my pride."

A young man in a T-shirt and short pants shook his head as they walked by. "Hey, girl, you look wrung out."

"Someone ask you?" said Alia, and the man put his hands up as if to make peace, but he was smiling.

"Is he a friend?" Diana asked as they passed a store window filled with electronics. She was tempted to see if they could stop to go in. Everything had so many fascinating buttons and knobs.

"Who? That guy? No."

"Then why would he presume to make a comment on your appearance?"

Alia laughed. "Guys presume all kinds of things."

"You *do* look tired," Diana noted.

"I didn't ask you, either. You've really never seen a man before?"

"Only in books and from a great distance."

"Well, what do you think?"

Diana watched a man in glasses pass. "Well, they're a bit disappointing. From my mother's descriptions I thought they would be much larger and more aggressive."

Alia snorted. "We'll find you a frat house."

"And why are they so bug-eyed and slack-jawed? Is that an affliction of all males or particular to the men of your city?"

Alia burst out laughing. "That's what happens when a six-foot supermodel walks down the street in a few scraps of leather."

"Ah, so they're *ogling*. I've heard of that."

Alia held up a hand, signaling for them to stop. "We're here."

Diana peered through the window at rows of tiny frosted cakes. "Is this where we'll eat?"

"I wish. As soon as I have cash in hand, I'm going to eat a dozen cupcakes."

"Why not just eat one big cake?"

"Because—" Alia hesitated. "I'm not entirely sure. It's the principle of the thing." She glanced across the street, but Diana wasn't certain what held her attention. There was a large sign that said ENTRANCE, advertisements offering what seemed to be hourly rates for parking, as well as a baffling banner promising special treatment for "early birds." Perhaps they were poultry traders.

"What is this place?" Diana asked.

"A parking garage. It's like a hotel for cars." Alia rolled her shoulders. "Ready?"

"For what?"

"You've been in New York nearly two hours," said Alia. "It's time for some light breaking and entering."

CHAPTER 7

Alia kept one eye on the entrance to the parking garage, trying not to look like she was studying it too closely, and doing her best to ignore the way her stomach was growling. She could have eaten every single thing in that bakery display.

"You intend to steal a car?" Diana sputtered.

"Why would I steal a car I can't drive?" Alia said, hoping she sounded calmer than she felt. At this point she was getting by on bravado alone. It had been nerve-racking enough to hop the turnstiles on the subway—something she'd never done without Nim to egg her on—and now she was basically about to commit a crime. It wasn't as if Jason would press charges, but she wasn't big on the idea of getting caught. Everything in her was screaming, *Go home. Hit reset.*

She was on her own turf now. She should feel calmer, more confident than she had on the island, but she never did well in crowds, and Manhattan was basically one big crowd.

She watched one of the attendants vanish into the recesses of the garage. The other was on the phone in the office, just visible through the glass. This might be their only opportunity to get inside. "Look, you asked me to trust you; now I'm asking you to trust me."

Diana's dark brows lowered, and she huffed out a breath. "Very well."

A huge vote of confidence from the Cult Island delegation. "Good," said Alia, hoping she sounded sure of herself. "First task is to get past those attendants without them noticing us." She loped quickly across the street and then dropped into her best crouch as she slunk along the wall, relieved that Diana followed.

"This feels like law breaking," Diana whispered as they crept up the ramp.

"I mean, we're not *really* breaking any laws. We're just circumventing some bureaucratic challenges."

Alia led them past the booth and to the stairwell, hoping they wouldn't run into the other attendant as they climbed.

When they reached the third floor, she pushed the door open. It was quiet up here, the air cool in the dark. The only sounds were the occasional squeal of tires or the rumble of an engine echoing from somewhere in the cavernous building. She counted the spaces. She'd never actually been to this garage, but she knew the number she was looking for—321. March twenty-first, her mother's birthday.

318, 319, 320 . . . Could this possibly be it? Alia felt a little deflated. She wasn't sure what she'd expected, but the car was a disappointingly dull Toyota Camry. Of course, it was possible she'd gotten this all wrong. What if the space number was her parents' anniversary and not her mother's birthday? What if Jason wasn't using this garage anymore?

She peered through the driver's-side window. The interior of the car was spotless: empty drink holders, a receipt folded on the dashboard, and there, hanging from the rearview mirror, a pendant emblazoned with a fleur-de-lis—the symbol of New Orleans, Lina Mayeux's hometown. Alia's mother had once confided she'd contemplated getting a tattoo of the fleur-de-lis to remind her of home. *What changed your mind?* Alia had asked her. Her mother had just winked. *Who says I have?*

Alia blinked back an embarrassing prickle of tears.

"Okay," she said. "Don't freak out, but we're going to have to break the window."

"Why?"

"We don't have a key, and I need to get into the trunk."

"But it's your car?"

"My brother's."

"Perhaps I can get the trunk open without the key."

Diana gripped the lip of the trunk just above the license plate and yanked upward. Instead of the latch giving, the metal of the trunk peeled upward with a shriek. Diana bit her lip and stepped back. The rear of the car looked like an open coin purse. "Sorry about that."

Alia listened for the patter of running footsteps, but apparently the attendants either hadn't heard one of their cars being torn apart or hadn't cared. She looked at the gaping trunk, then back at Diana. "So you're the weak one in your family, huh?"

Alia and Diana peered into the trunk. There was an industrial-size flashlight, jumper cables, and a gigantic canvas duffel.

"Bless you, Jason, you paranoid loon."

"What is it?"

"A bug-out bag." Alia hefted the duffel from the trunk, laid it on the ground, and unzipped it. "Jason has them stashed all around the city in case of emergency. In Brooklyn, too." Alia ignored most of the gear—a tarp and tent, a water-purification system, rain ponchos, matches, freeze-dried meals. She set aside the first-aid kit. Her feet would be grateful for that later. "It's basically everything you'd need to survive an apocalypse."

"Is he so sure one will come?" Diana asked.

"No, he's just a control freak. Jason is basically the biggest Boy Scout ever. He likes to be prepared for every possibility."

"But that's impossible."

"Try telling *him* that. Aha!" Triumphantly, Alia held up a huge wad of cash. "We're rich!"

"Is it enough for an airplane?"

At least Diana was consistent. "Maybe a model airplane. It's only a thousand dollars, but it's enough to get us a room and something to eat while we figure out what to do next."

Alia didn't miss the troubled expression that crossed Diana's face. She knew Diana truly believed in all of this Warbringer stuff, an age of bloodshed, the magical spring. Alia wasn't sure what she thought. She couldn't deny the bizarre things she'd seen over the last twenty-four hours, or the fact that they had somehow traveled all the way from the Aegean to the Hudson River in what had felt like the blink of an eye.

Part of her still wanted to believe it was all a vivid dream, that she would wake up in her bedroom on Central Park West having never left for Istanbul at all. But that part of her was growing less and less convincing. Being back in Manhattan should have made Diana's island seem more like a fantasy, but there was something about seeing this girl walk and talk in such an ordinary place that made everything that had come before feel even realer. It was like looking out a familiar window and seeing an entirely new view.

Alia pulled a small red nylon backpack from the larger duffel. She could sort through what had happened on the island later. Right now, she was too tired and hungry to form a rational thought.

"Could you . . ." She gestured to the duffel. As Diana hefted the bag into the trunk and crushed the metal back together, Alia opened the red backpack and stuffed everything she needed inside. The car's rear end was a lumpy mess, but at least no one walking by would know it had been pried open.

They took the stairs back down to the ground floor and then strolled casually past the attendant at the entrance. He stared, but it wasn't as if they were leaving with a car.

"What now?" said Diana.

"First stop, shoes," replied Alia, though she was dreading

walking into a store with her grubby bare feet. After that, she really didn't know what to do. And there was something else bothering her. They'd seen soldiers on all the major street corners and at the entrance and exit to the subway. It reminded her of the images she'd seen of New York after 9/11 when the National Guard had been stationed in the city. Had there been some kind of attack while she was away? Her fingers itched for her phone. Once they were settled, she needed to get online or at least find a newspaper.

There was a Duane Reade on the corner, and as they entered the drugstore, Diana heaved a great sigh, holding her arms out to her sides. "The air is so much cooler in here."

The clerk behind the counter raised her brows.

"Um, yeah, the wonders of technology. Fantastic." Alia cleared her throat, grabbed a shopping basket, and pulled Diana down the nearest aisle.

"Look at this place," Diana marveled. "The lights, the profusion of plastic. Everything is so *glossy.*"

Alia tried to restrain a grin. "Stop fondling the deodorants."

"But they look like jewels!"

"Now I'm picturing you wearing those as earrings. Let's keep moving." In her peripheral vision, she could see a security guard tracking them through the store.

She wasn't really surprised. Diana looked like she'd gotten lost on her way to work at the barbarian strip club, and Alia was a black girl in dirty clothes with no shoes. She was a perfect magnet for a shop cop. She could almost hear her mother's voice warning her and Jason to be careful, not to draw attention. *Don't get into a situation where you have to explain yourself.*

Lina, their father would say, *you're teaching them to imagine snubs where there are none. You're making them afraid.* It was the one thing their parents had never managed to see eye to eye on.

At least she had a pocket full of cash. Alia found her way to a sign that said SUMMER FUN and plucked the most comfortable-looking pair of flip-flops she could find off the shelf, then herded Diana down the hair care aisle.

"How can there be so many kinds?" Diana asked, running her fingers over the bottles of shampoo.

"What do you use to wash your hair at home?"

Diana shrugged. "We make our own soaps."

"Of course you do," said Alia.

Alia scanned the rows for a deep conditioner that she hoped would get her braids back in shape and a leave-in to go with it. As a kid, she'd insisted on using strawberry oil every single day until her mother had refused to buy her more.

"I thought we were just here for shoes," Diana said as Alia tossed the bottles into her basket.

"And other necessities."

"But—"

"Trust me, these are necessities." At least the shop cop seemed to be keeping his distance, but she could see him in the mirror, tracking back and forth down the neighboring aisle like a circling shark, just waiting for her to make trouble or step to the register without enough money.

As they made their way to the checkout, Alia filled their basket with candy, chips, and soda, making it clear they were here to spend.

"You don't want anything?" she asked. "It's on me."

Diana's even white teeth worried her lower lip. "I wouldn't know where to begin."

"If Jason were here, he'd try to get you to eat protein bars and squirrel food. Do you know one Halloween he gave away raisins to all the kids in the building? He said they were *nature's candy*. I was getting dirty looks from the kids downstairs for months."

"Nature's candy?" said Diana. "Dates maybe, but not raisins. Perhaps beets. They have a very high sugar content."

"It was even worse the next year. He gave away toothbrushes." Alia shook her head. Sometimes it was hard to believe they came from the same parents. "Lucky for you, I'm a junk-food aficionado. We shall have only the finest of gummy bears and the fieriest of Doritos. Once you've truly experienced the sodium and high-fructose corn syrup America has to offer, you'll never want to go home." This time Alia couldn't ignore the worried expression on Diana's face. "What is it?"

Diana fiddled with a bag of yogurt pretzels. "I'm not sure I *can* go home after what I've done."

"I know you guys are all no contact with the outside world, but . . ." Diana looked up at her with those steady dark-blue eyes, and Alia's words trailed off as realization struck. "You mean saving me. You might not be able to go back because you saved my life."

Diana turned her attention to a tin of almonds. "There's a great deal at stake. Not just for me."

Alia felt a tide of guilt wash through her. Diana had saved her life not once but twice. As much as she wanted to just find a way home and spend about a week sleeping, watching TV, and forgetting she'd ever met this girl, she owed her. She knew she should say something, but instead she tossed a T-shirt at Diana and headed toward the register.

Diana held it up. " 'I heart NY'?"

"I love New York."

"That much is apparent."

"No, the shirt is for you."

"It's a very strong statement. The city is enticing, no doubt, but—"

"It's so idiots will stop staring at your boobs," Alia said loudly as a couple of boys who couldn't be more than thirteen craned their necks over the aisle.

"You wish me to cover myself?"

"I'm not going all puritan on you, but you're the one who said we should avoid attracting attention. No one seems to be able to resist the magical combination of cleavage, leather, lots of bronze skin, and bed head."

"Bed head?"

"It means— Oh, never mind. Let's just say you look like some nerdy wet dream."

Diana glanced at the boys who hadn't stopped gawking. "Surely they've seen breasts before."

"On a real live girl? Who knows? But the novelty never seems to wear off." Alia tossed two pairs of sweats and another T-shirt into the basket. Sweatpants during a New York summer made her skin crawl, but they were low on options.

"More clothes?"

"Trust me, if you really want my help getting us to Greece, I'm going to need better clothes than these."

"Why?"

"You can get away with . . ." Alia waved vaguely at Diana's ensemble. "Whatever this is. But I can't walk around looking like a tennis-playing hobo."

"Why?"

Alia bristled. "Because people see different things when they look at me."

"Because you're so short?"

"I'm not short! You're just a giant. And, no, because I'm black." She tried to keep her voice light. She didn't want to talk about this stuff. It was bad enough when one of her teachers thought they should have "a forum on race" and she had to deal with a bunch of Bennett kids debating affirmative action, or worse, coming up to her to apologize after class.

Diana frowned as Alia walked them to the register. "I've read about the racial conflicts in your country's history. I was given to understand they'd ended."

That was what her father had wanted to believe, too. But he'd never had to live in his wife's skin, or his daughter's, or his son's.

"They haven't. They happen every day. And if you don't believe me, check the security guard breathing down our necks. When people look at me, they don't see Alia Keralis. They just see a messed-up brown girl in ratty clothes, so let's get out of here before he comes by with a *'How you ladies doing today? Mind opening up that bag for me?'*"

They plunked their items down at the register.

"You doing cosplay or something?" the girl behind the counter asked, cracking her gum. "You a warrior princess?"

Diana flinched. "Is it that obvious?"

"You look good," said the clerk. "I don't like that fantasy stuff, though."

"How about when you can't tell the difference?" Alia muttered.

"Huh?"

"Nothing. Just been a long day."

Once they had paid with a few bills from Alia's giant wad of cash and the security guard had stopped giving them the fisheye, Alia slipped the new flip-flops onto her feet, gratified by their loud slap on the linoleum.

Laden with plastic bags, they headed outside and crossed the little park. Then Alia pointed them toward Alphabet City and the Good Night hotel. She knew there must be hostels or hotels that were closer, but she didn't have her phone, and she didn't want to wander the streets asking for directions. That voice inside her telling her to just go home was getting louder and louder.

"You've stayed here before?" asked Diana doubtfully when they arrived in front of the hotel's grubby facade.

"No," Alia admitted. "But my mom and I used to pass by this place all the time."

They were some of her happiest memories, sitting with her mother in Ebele's salon on Avenue C, reading or just listening to the ladies talk, watching hour after hour of true-crime shows. After her parents had died, Alia hadn't been able to bear the idea of returning to the little salon without her mother, but eventually her hair was in such a state that she'd had to. It was that or go somewhere new, and Alia wasn't big on "somewhere new."

She hadn't talked to Jason about it. She'd just asked their driver, Dez, if he knew where to go, and he'd taken her to Ebele's without a word. Alia thought she was ready to walk through that familiar door, and she'd been fine when she saw its cheerfully painted awning, even when she glimpsed Ebele through the window. But when she'd walked inside and that bell had jingled, the smell of sweetness and chemicals had just about knocked her down. She was crying before she knew it, and Ebele and Norah were hugging her tight and handing her tissues.

They hadn't fussed or asked questions Alia didn't want to answer. They hadn't spouted useless crap like "everything happens for a reason." They'd just turned on the TV, plopped her in a chair, and set to work as if nothing terrible had ever happened, as if Alia's life hadn't been torn in two. Ebele's had become a kind of refuge. In fact, Alia had been there less than two weeks ago, getting her hair braided before the trip. They'd watched a billion episodes of *Justice Served* because Norah was on a serial-killer kick, and by the time Alia left, her scalp felt as if it had been winched tight to her skull.

Alia had passed beneath the sign of the Good Night with its sleeping moon as she always had, made a wish as she always had, her mind trained only on preparing for her trip aboard the *Thetis* and escaping New York. Now she looked up at that sign and scowled. "Stupid moon."

The hotel was just as miserable on the inside, the lobby walls water stained, the linoleum chipped in places.

The guy slouching at the front desk didn't look much older than Alia, and he had one of those chin-burp goatees that always made her want to offer up a napkin. This was the part Alia had been the most nervous about, but she did her best to sound calm and beleaguered as she explained that they'd had their luggage stolen at Port Authority.

"I don't know," he said in a heavy accent. Russian maybe. Definitely Eastern European. "Lots of bad stuff happening. Must be careful."

"Come on," Alia said, attempting some measure of the easy charm her father had possessed in such abundance. "Do we look like trouble?"

The guy looked up, up, up at Diana.

"Nie ne sme zaplaha," she said, looking solemn.

Alia stared. Diana spoke Russian?

The man's flat expression didn't change. "Cash," he said. "A full week. Up front."

A full week? Even at a dump like the Good Night, that cut deeply into their funds. *It's fine,* she told herself as she counted out the bills. *You'll figure out a safe way to contact Jason, and then money isn't going to be an issue.*

And what if you didn't have the Keralis name and fortune to back you up? She'd save that question for another day.

"Rooms are cleaned every afternoon," said the clerk as the money vanished beneath the desk. "No cooking in rooms. No tampering with thermostat." He slapped a metal key on the counter. It had a pink plastic tag with "406" written on it in black marker. "You lose key, pay one-hundred-dollar fine." He narrowed his eyes at Diana. "I watch you."

"Geez," Alia said as they headed up the stairs. "What did you say to him?"

"I simply told him we weren't threats."

Alia rolled her eyes. "Not suspicious at all. How did you learn to speak Russian?"

"It was Bulgarian, and . . . I'm not entirely sure."

"How many other languages do you speak?"

Diana paused as if calculating. "I think all of them."

A day ago, Alia would have said that was impossible, but now it was just one more weird thing to add to the list. "Where were you when I had two hours of French homework?" she grumbled.

Naturally, the Good Night didn't have an elevator, so they trudged up four flights to their floor. Well, Alia trudged. Diana scampered up the stairs like the world's most beautiful goat. They followed a long, dank hall to their room, but the old-fashioned lock beneath the doorknob didn't want to cooperate at first.

After a few minutes of swearing and key jiggling, the door popped open. The room smelled of old cigarettes and was carpeted in a color that might have started life as emerald but had faded to what Alia would have described as "Summer Swamp." A cramped passage led past a tiny bathroom tiled in grubby white to a room with a low ceiling and two narrow beds, a battered nightstand between them. No phone, no television, just a radiator against the wall and an air conditioner in the window. Alia set her bags down and pressed one of the buttons. Nothing.

"Don't tamper with the thermostat, my butt." She was already sweating.

Diana stood in the center of the room, arms still laden with plastic bags. "Do you really live in such places? No view of the sky? So little light and color?"

"Well, yeah," Alia said, feeling defensive, despite the fact that she'd been composing a list of the room's shortcomings herself. "Some people have to."

Diana placed her cargo carefully on the bed. "This must be why everyone looks so tired. You travel in tubes underground, live crammed into warrens not fit for rabbits."

"We manage," Alia said, extracting the clean clothes and toiletries they'd purchased.

"I didn't mean to offend," Diana said. "It looks mostly tidy."

"Hmm," Alia said, and left it at that. She could defend New York all day, but one of the unhappy perks of loving biology was knowing exactly how resilient germs were and exactly where vermin liked to hide. They'd both probably end up crawling with bedbugs. "Let's shower and then find something to eat."

"I'm not sure it's safe for you to go back out."

Alia popped open the bag of Doritos. "You saw how crowded this city is. We'll be fine. And if anyone is looking for Alia Keralis, they're not going to start here." She crammed a handful of chips into her mouth.

"I thought we were going to get a proper meal."

"Appetizers," Alia said with her mouth still full. When she managed to swallow, she snatched up the toiletries and clothes. "I'm taking first shower. Don't, uh . . . wander off."

In the bathroom, Alia spared herself the briefest glance in the mirror as she stripped out of her clothes. One glimpse of her bruises was enough. She shoved her Learning at Sea polo shirt into the trash. She never wanted to look at it again.

The pipes creaked as she turned on the shower, but the water pressure wasn't terrible. Miserably hot and sweaty as she was, Alia set the water to scalding and tried to scrub all the grime and salt from her body. She had bumps and bruises everywhere. One thigh was almost all scratches and abrasions, and one of her toenails was cracked and nearly black with blood beneath the nail. But she was alive. After all of it, she was alive.

Panic and grief came roaring toward her again, and this time she didn't fight it. She braced her back against the plastic shower door and let the tremors shake her in heavy, tearless sobs. It wasn't the cry she wanted. It wasn't the comfort of being in her own bed, Nim telling some stupid joke beside her, a pint of ice cream close at hand, but it would have to do. She turned the water to cold to cool down her body, and when she emerged a few minutes later, dried off with one of the scratchy white towels, and pulled on her cheap drugstore sweats, she felt almost human again.

"You're up," she said to Diana.

As soon as Diana disappeared into the bathroom, Alia hooked the red backpack over her arm and headed for the door. She knew Diana didn't think it was safe to get in touch with Jason, but she needed to reach her brother. If she had been targeted, Jason could be targeted, too—and if someone on his team had tipped off the Foundation's enemies to Alia's whereabouts, then maybe Jason was putting his trust in the wrong people. She had spotted the burner phone in Jason's duffel at the parking garage and managed to slip it into the backpack while Diana was turned away. Now she'd just step outside, call Nim, and figure out how Nim could set up a meeting with Jason without revealing that Alia was back in town.

But when Alia reached for the doorknob, she stopped short. It was gone. The lock was still intact, but the doorknob above it had been snapped clean off its base. *Diana.* She must have done it while Alia was in the shower. So much for trust. Then again, Alia *had* been planning on leaving.

"That's beside the point," she mumbled, tearing open a bag of sour gummy worms with her teeth. "When that girl gets out of the shower, we're going to have words."

"What would you like to discuss?" Diana called over the sound of running water.

"You can *hear* me?" Alia asked incredulously. Then she flopped back on the bed in defeat. "Never mind. Of course you can."

Alia had every intention of staying awake to tell Diana exactly how she felt about doorknobs going missing, but she must have fallen asleep, because the next thing she knew, Diana was shaking her awake. Her hair was damp, and she'd changed into the "I ♥ NY" T-shirt and gray sweatpants.

"Wha—" Alia began, but Diana clapped a hand over her mouth and placed a finger to her own lips.

"Someone's trying to get into our room," she whispered.

Alia felt her heart start to pound. "The maid?"

"The maid would have a key. And the tread is too heavy. Alia," Diana said, "they've found us."

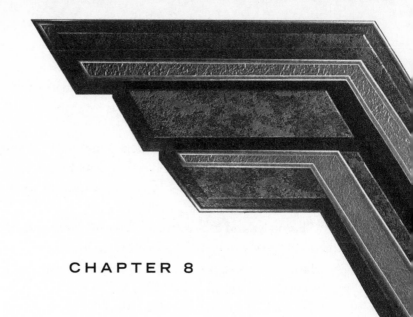

CHAPTER 8

"Stay here," said Diana, wishing that she hadn't taken quite as hard a stance on weaponry back on Themyscira.

"But how could they have found me?" Alia protested in hushed tones.

"We don't know what forces are working against you. Be silent and be still. And if anything happens to me . . ." Diana trailed off. She didn't know how to finish that sentence. She supposed she should try to extract a promise from Alia that she would attempt to reach the spring on her own. But there was no time for oaths. "Run." Alia nodded, her eyes wide.

Diana's feet were bare from the shower. She padded silently down the narrow passage that led past the bathroom, the feel of the carpet's rough fibers strange against her skin. She crept the last few feet, her heart thudding hard in her chest. This would be a fight—a real fight, not a sparring match in the Armory.

She paused, waiting. Silence. Had she imagined the whole thing? Had her overstimulated mind fabricated an intruder? Another guest might have simply mistaken their room for his, tried his key, and, realizing his mistake, moved along.

The door rattled slightly again. Someone was trying to tamper with the lock. She heard a click as the tumblers gave way. There was no time to think.

Diana bent her knees and kicked, her foot connecting hard at the very center of the door. It flew off its hinges, and she heard a surprised cry as the door crashed into the intruder, driving him back against the wall.

She registered a large form—a young male, about her height, broad in the shoulders. Good reflexes. He recovered quickly, shifting into fighting stance, and they faced each other in the dim light of the hallway, circling.

He lunged toward her. She seized his shoulders, twisting to the side to bring him down, using his momentum, but he adjusted his stance—*very* good reflexes—and regained his balance. He was strong, too, surprisingly so. Diana found it was a bit like reaching for a pitcher and discovering it full instead of empty—unexpected, but no great challenge.

She shifted her grip. The fabric of her attacker's shirt bunched in her hands as she slammed him against the wall. The plaster splintered. He groaned, and she shoved him to the floor, pinning him facedown, one arm extended, the tendons bending as she applied pressure.

"I'll break it," she said as he struggled against her. "Be still."

"Diana!" Alia was standing beside the destroyed door, staring down at them in shock.

"I told you to remain in the room."

"Diana—"

"The situation is under control. Whoever dispatched this assassin sent a weakling."

The young man beneath her grunted, trying to wriggle free.

She gave a tug on his arm, and he froze. "Who sent you?" she growled.

Alia clapped her hands over her mouth. She bent double, shoulders shaking, and for a moment, Diana thought she was weeping—but she was laughing. Was she having some kind of hysterical fit?

"Diana," she gasped, "that weakling is my brother."

Diana looked down at the male in her grip, his face planted in the hallway's dirty green carpet. "Are . . . are you sure?"

Alia barked a laugh. "Pretty sure, yeah."

Diana changed her hold, flipping the intruder so that he was pinned by her knees, and peered into his furious face. His gaze blazed with anger, a muscle twitching in his jaw. Now that she looked, she supposed he wasn't dressed like an assassin. He wore a clean white shirt of fine cotton unbuttoned at the throat, the sleeves rolled up to his elbows. His head was shaved, though not quite smooth, and he had the same dark liquid eyes and brown skin as Alia. In fact, now that she was looking at him properly, the resemblance was striking.

"Why did you attack me?" she said.

"You attacked *me*."

Diana winced. So she had. "Well, why were you trying to break into our room?"

He bucked once beneath her, and she used her body weight to shove him back to the floor. Brother or not, she didn't know his intentions. "I was looking for my sister," he snarled. "Who the hell *are* you?"

Alia cleared her throat. "Maybe you should let him up."

"He's in no danger. I'm not hurting him."

"I'm pretty sure his ego is permanently bruised, and I don't know what might be hiding in that carpet."

"We should search him for weapons."

"Diana, he's my *brother*. Let him up."

Reluctantly, Diana rocked back on her heels and stood, releasing him. She offered him a hand, but he ignored it, making what she thought was an unnecessarily dramatic show of shaking out his arm.

He came up to his knees and, in a single swift movement, yanked a gun from a holster near his ankle as he leapt to his feet. "You should have searched me for weapons."

"Jason!" Alia yelped.

"I'm just making a point. If—"

Diana had never seen a gun outside of the pages of a book, but she'd been trained to disarm an assailant. Her hand snapped forward, striking the pressure points of his wrist. The gun dropped from his grip, and in the next breath she had him up against the wall, cheek pressed to the plaster.

"I was just making a point!" Jason said. "I was agreeing with you . . . whoever you are. Alia, will you call her off?"

"I'm not sure I should. What are you doing with a gun, Jason?"

"I have it for protection!"

"How's that working out for you?"

Diana gave him a little shove. "Alia hasn't been out of my sight once. How did you find us?"

"The trunk with the go-bag is equipped with an alarm in case of theft," he said. "You triggered it when you broke in, although I have no idea what you did to that poor car. I asked the attendants if they'd seen anyone coming or going with a red backpack, and they remembered you two."

"But how did you find the hotel?"

"The cell phone in the backpack."

"A phone?"

"Yes," he grunted. "There's a burner phone in every go-bag. I followed the signal here."

"Did you know this?" asked Diana, but the guilt on Alia's face told her all she needed to know. She remembered how Alia had asked her to put the duffel back in the trunk. Had she done it deliberately so Diana would turn her back? She was surprised at how much the betrayal stung.

"Diana, I need to ask you to unhand my brother. Again."

Grudgingly, Diana released him, but this time she patted him down. She decided not to think too much about the fact that she was in such close proximity to a male—friend or foe—and ignored his sharp "Hey!" when she ran her hand up his thigh.

"You pulled a gun on us," she said. "Your discomfort is your own doing."

"I'm trying to teach Alia to be more cautious," he complained.

"Lesson learned, big brother. Was it worth it?"

Diana stepped back and Alia's brother turned, straightening the collar of his shirt.

"Happy?" he asked.

"Reassured."

She expected another round of recriminations, but instead Jason turned to Alia. He crossed the short distance between them and pulled her into a tight hug. "I thought . . . We had word the *Thetis* had lost contact. I didn't know what to think."

"I'm okay," Alia said, but Diana could hear the wobble in her voice.

Diana was embarrassed by the acute pang of envy she felt. She would have liked someone to lean on, to tell her she hadn't made a terrible mistake, that she wasn't in this alone.

Then Jason broke the hug and held Alia at arm's length. "How could you be so stupid?"

"I'm not stupid," she said, knocking Jason's hands away and folding her arms.

"Do you have any idea how worried I've been? The *Thetis* lost radio contact almost a week ago."

"A week?" said Alia.

Diana's heart lurched. A week gone? They must have lost time when they left the island. Hekatombaion began with the rise of the first visible new moon after the summer solstice—the slender white scythe of the reaping moon. How long did they have?

"When was the last full moon?" said Diana.

Jason stared at her as if she'd gone mad. "What?"

"I need a calendar."

He scowled and handed over the boxlike device she realized was his phone.

She touched the screen tentatively. "I don't—"

He snatched it from her and jabbed at it a few times before holding it up. They'd reached the end of June. According to the screen, the last full moon had been on June twentieth, and that meant Hekatombaion would begin on July seventh. They had less than a week to get to the spring.

Jason shoved his phone back in his pocket. "You disappeared," he said to Alia. "They sent out search parties. I thought . . ." His voice broke. "For God's sake, Alia, I thought you were dead."

"But I'm not, Jason. I'm here."

"How is that even possible? They said you boarded the boat in Istanbul. Did you change your mind?"

"I—"

"Everything okay up here?" The Bulgarian from the front desk stood panting at the end of the hall. It had taken him long enough to come investigate.

As one, they moved to block his view of the demolished door. "Everything's great!" said Alia.

"You bet," said Jason.

"Vsichko e nared. Molya, varnete se kam zanimaniyata si," said Diana as reassuringly as she could.

The Bulgarian made an unconvinced "huh" sound and started back down the stairs.

"Should I even ask?" said Alia.

"I just told him that all was well and instructed him to return to what he was doing."

"Not suspicious at all," said Jason. Diana saw Alia bite back a smile.

She bristled. "It was a perfectly reasonable thing to say."

"Let's get inside before he changes his mind and comes back to take a closer look," said Jason. "Help me with the door."

"Diana can just—" Alia began, and Diana gave a frantic shake of her head. It was one thing for Alia to know how strong she was, but the less Jason knew about where she was from or what she could do, the better.

"Just what?" said Jason, already hefting one side of the door.

"Just help," Alia finished weakly.

They shuffled into the passageway and got the door wedged

shut behind them. Somehow the room looked smaller and shabbier with Alia's brother standing inside it. Despite the fact that he'd just been in a fight, he looked unrumpled and immaculate, the white of his shirt unsullied, a heavy watch glinting at his wrist. Could she convince this boy of her cause? Could she convince Alia? She'd thought she would have time to make her case and get them to Greece. Now she had only a few days.

Jason turned a slow circle, taking in the room's bleak furnishings, the plastic bags of candy. "I've been trying to call in favors with the Turkish government, and you're having a slumber party."

"That's not what this is," Alia objected.

Jason threw his hands up in exasperation. "Then what is it? What are you doing in a place like this, Alia? And how did you get here?"

Diana sat down on the bed. Alia had lied to her. "You said you wouldn't call him."

"I didn't," said Alia.

"But you knew he would trace you."

"I thought he *might*."

"What difference does it make?" asked Jason irritably. He turned to Diana, touching his hand to his shoulder as if it still pained him. "*Who are you?* And what right do you have to keep my sister from contacting me?"

Diana felt her temper rise. "It was for her own protection. Gods," she said shooting up from the bed as realization struck. "You could have been followed. We should leave this place immediately."

"*Gods?*" said Jason. "Plural?"

"No one is looking for me," insisted Alia. "They think I'm dead."

Jason released a growl. "Will someone tell me what the hell is going on?"

Alia bounced nervously on her heels. "Can we all just . . . sit down for a minute?"

Jason glanced at the nearest bed, his lip curling slightly. With a disdainful flick, he shoved a pile of sweets away and sat down at the edge of the bed. He glanced around. "Do you have anything to drink?"

"Warm soda?" Alia said, offering him a bottle of cola.

"I was hoping for something stronger."

Alia raised a brow. "Seriously?"

"I'm twenty-one—"

"Barely."

"And I just got pounced by this . . . *person*."

"My name is Diana."

Jason took the soda bottle from Alia. "Diana what?"

She answered without thinking. "Diana, Princess of—"

"Diana Prince," Alia said hurriedly. "Her name is Diana Prince."

"Yes," said Diana, grateful for the rescue, even if she was still angry at Alia. "Diana Prince."

Alia sat down on the other bed and gestured for Diana to join her. Reluctantly, Diana settled on the farthest corner.

Jason took a gulp of soda. "Start talking, Alia."

"There was an accident."

Diana held Alia's gaze. They couldn't afford this pretense. "It wasn't an accident."

Alia took a deep breath. "Okay, there was an explosion aboard the *Thetis*. Someone . . ." She hesitated, and Diana realized this was the first time Alia had spoken the words out loud. She'd let Diana make the claim, agreed with her as far as she was able, but she'd never acknowledged the fact of what had happened herself. "I think someone tried to kill me."

Jason set down the bottle with a loud clunk. "I told you not to go. You know what kind of threats the Foundation gets. I told you how dangerous it was for you to be without security."

Alia dropped her eyes. "I didn't think—"

"No, you didn't. You could have been killed."

"I would have been. But Diana saved me."

"How?"

"I saw the explosion from shore."

"And you brought her all the way back to New York?"

"It seemed the safest thing."

Jason's expression was sour. "Well, at least someone was thinking."

"That isn't fair," Alia said quietly.

"Fair?" Jason leaned forward. "You almost died. I almost lost you. After what happened to Mom and Dad—"

"I—"

"If you wanted to go so badly, you should have talked to me. We could have arranged an expedition."

Alia sprang to her feet. "I didn't *want* a Keralis expedition," she said, pacing back and forth in the tiny room. "I wanted to be a student. Like a normal kid. Like everyone else."

"We aren't like everyone else, Alia. Our family doesn't have that luxury."

Diana hadn't meant to speak. This wasn't her battle. But she still found herself saying, "She was right to try."

"Excuse me?" said Jason.

"It's not just to ask someone to live half a life," Diana said. "You can't live in fear. You make things happen or they happen to you."

Jason turned his cold, angry gaze on her. "People died. Alia could have been killed."

"And if she'd remained in New York, she might have been targeted here."

Now Jason was on his feet. "I don't know who you think you are, but I've had about enough of being scolded by a teenage girl."

Diana rose and met his eye. "I could be a man of fifty and you'd still be just as wrong."

Jason snatched up the red backpack and started toward the door. "We're leaving, Alia."

Diana stepped into his path. "No."

A muscle ticked in Jason's jaw. "Get out of my way."

"You said yourself that she's in danger. If people are watching you—"

"I can keep my own sister safe. We have an extensive security team of trained professionals."

"And you trust these people?"

"More than I trust a stranger in sweatpants who slammed me against a wall and speaks Bulgarian."

"Tell me," said Diana. "When Alia called you from Istanbul, did you relay her location and the details of her situation to your security team?"

"Of course. I—" Jason stopped and his face turned ashen. He rubbed a hand over his mouth, then paced slowly back to the bed. He sat down heavily, his gaze stunned.

"Jason?" said Alia.

"It's my fault. There must be someone on staff . . . But I don't get it. Why would they go after Alia? I'm closer to the company. Why didn't they come after me?"

Diana almost felt sorry for him. "You're fighting the wrong battle," she said gently. "I know you think this is about your family's business, but Alia is the real target."

"Diana—" Alia said warningly.

"What are you talking about?" said Jason.

Alia tugged on Diana's wrist. "Just leave it be."

"Why?"

"Because you sound insane when you talk about that stuff," Alia whispered furiously. "Oracles, Warbringers, magic springs—"

Jason's head snapped up. "What did you say?"

"It's nothing," said Alia. "Just some goofy new age stuff Diana got from . . . her weird family."

"What do you know about Warbringers?" Jason was on his feet again, and his face was deadly serious.

Alia cut her brother a baffled glance. "What do *you* know about Warbringers?"

"It's . . . it's something I found in Mom and Dad's papers. After the accident."

The information seemed to strike Alia with physical force. She took a half step backward. *"What?"*

"I had to go through all of their documents. There was a safe in the office. I can show you."

"Why didn't you show me before?"

"Because it was all so out there. I didn't . . . There was enough to deal with after they died. I had my hands full. And this was just so wild, all of this bizarre stuff about Dad's Greek ancestors. I didn't want to put that burden on you."

"What *burden?*" Alia said, her voice rising, panic creeping in.

"The burden of your bloodline," said Diana. She wasn't angry anymore. If anything, she felt only regret. She remembered visiting the Soldiers' Pantheon at the Armory, walking hand in hand with her mother past the glass cases, surrounded by blue light, listening to the stories of the Amazons, the courage they'd shown in battle, the greatness of their deeds, their homes, their families, their people, their gods. *What's my story?* she'd asked her mother. *It hasn't been written yet,* Hippolyta had said with a smile. But as the years passed, Diana had started to hate that memory, the knowledge that her story had been flawed from the start.

"Jason?" Alia asked, her fists clenched.

"It's just a bunch of legends, Alia."

"Tell me," she demanded. "Tell me all of it."

CHAPTER 9

Jason looked to Diana almost helplessly. "I don't know where to start."

Alia ground her teeth together. She wasn't mad exactly—no, that wasn't true, she *was* angry, off-the-charts angry that Jason had kept this from her—but more than needing to punch him in the face, she needed to know what he knew.

"Just *start*," she said, leashing her rage.

But it was Diana who spoke. "Warbringers are descendants of Helen of Troy."

Of all the things Alia had been expecting, that wasn't one of them. "Helen," she said skeptically. "As in 'the face that launched a thousand ships'?"

"It wasn't her face," said Diana. "Helen's power lay not in her beauty but in her very blood. The birth of a Warbringer signals an age of conflict. If the Warbringer dies before Hekatombaion in her seventeenth year, no war will come. But if her powers are allowed to reach maturity—"

Alia held up her hands. "I know *you* believe this stuff, but Jason—"

Only Jason didn't look scornful. He wasn't scoffing or curling his lip in that contemptuous way that made Alia want to smack him. Instead, he was looking at Diana with deep suspicion. "How do you know all of this?"

Diana shifted uncomfortably. "It's a story . . . a legend among my people."

"And just who are your people?"

Why did it matter? Why was he asking these questions? "Jason, you can't possibly believe any of this."

"I don't know what I believe. Mom and Dad had references to what your friend is describing, these Warbringers. They also called them hap . . . hap-something."

"Haptandrai," Diana finished.

"That's it. There were other names, too, in almost every country."

"Mom and Dad were *scientists*," protested Alia. "We're scientists. This is . . . this is a bunch of superstition. Bedtime stories."

Diana shook her head, but she didn't look frustrated, just sad, almost pitying. "After all you've seen, how can you still say that?"

Alia's eyes fastened on the metal bracelets at Diana's wrists. She remembered the feel of the metal beneath her fingertips earlier that day, cool and solid. Real. But she'd seen that same metal move. She'd seen palaces that shouldn't be, phantom horses. She'd traveled through the heart of a storm. "There's an explanation," Alia said. "There's always an explanation. Even if science hasn't found it yet."

"It was the science they were interested in," said Jason. "They'd traced the Keralis line all the way back to ancient Greece; other families and offshoots of Helen's bloodline, too, charting the lives of Warbringers, linking them to world events."

Alia shook her head. "No."

"They thought they might be able to help you with the right science."

"And you believe all of this?"

Jason threw his hands up. "Maybe. I don't know. Have you looked outside, Alia? Have you watched the news?"

Alia planted her hands on her hips. "We've been in the city less than twenty-four hours. Running for our lives. I haven't been keeping up."

"Well, something is happening and it isn't good. You must have seen the soldiers on street corners."

"I thought there'd been a bomb threat, a terrorist attack."

"Attacks. Plural. All over the world." He took out his phone and poked at the screen, then handed it to her.

She flicked through the headlines, one after another, Diana peering over her shoulder. *Coup Attempt. Civil War Erupts. Bombings Increase. Talks Break Down. Twenty Believed Dead. Hundreds Believed Dead. Thousands Dead.*

A fistfight had broken out in the middle of the UN General Assembly. Emergency meetings of Congress had been called.

"It's beginning," said Diana, gazing at the screen, her eyes wide. "It will only get worse. If we don't reach the spring by Hekatombaion, the tipping point will be reached. World war will be inevitable."

The images slid by: bombs exploding in cities she did not know, homes reduced to rubble, bodies on stretchers, a man standing in a field with a gun raised over his head, stirring up an audience of thousands. Alia clicked on the next image—a video—and heard people shouting in a language she didn't understand, screams. She saw a crowd surge past a barricade, police in riot gear opening fire.

"You're saying"—she cleared her throat—"you're saying I did this."

"It isn't something you did," said Diana.

Alia choked out a laugh. "Just something I am?"

Neither Diana nor Jason seemed to know how to respond to that.

"It's the way of men to make war," Diana attempted. "You're just . . ."

"There was another word in the records Mom and Dad left," said Jason. "*Procatalysia.*"

"Precatalyst?" Alia asked. It sounded like a scientific term.

"It refers to the original meaning," said Jason. "From the Greek. To dissolve. To break apart."

"*Procatalysia,*" Diana murmured. "She who comes before the world dissolves."

Alia clamped her lips shut. A cold sweat had broken over her skin, and her clothes suddenly felt too tight. She thought she might be sick. Her eyes registered the horrors on the screen, but her mind was full of other images, too. The riot in Central Park when she and Nim had gone to that free concert. The brawl that had broken out at the junior dance. Nim and Theo, usually so cheerful and easygoing, screaming at each other in the backseat when they'd all tried to drive up to Maine together. The arguments—so many arguments and breakups and accusations that had seemed to come from nowhere. Class debates that turned nasty. Teachers who suddenly went into a rage. Mr. Kagikawa had *slapped* Kara Munro. They'd all been shocked. He'd been fired. But then they'd forgotten, gone on with their lives.

Alia had never thought to question it. That was just the way life worked. It was why she liked being home, why she didn't like crowds. The world was a hostile place. Maybe she'd been sorry she and Nim didn't seem to be able to hold on to friends, told herself it would get better when she went to college. She'd spent more time on her own and convinced herself that was a choice. But had she ever added it up?

Recently, she'd felt the tension rising around her, and she'd hoped that a change of scene, getting out of New York, would help. Then things had been just as bad aboard the *Thetis*. In fact, even on the flight to Istanbul, the passengers had been snapping at one another. Again that voice in Alia's head had clamored, *Go home. Hit reset.* Things got loud and ugly out in the world. But what if that wasn't the case? What if things had only been that way in *her* world?

On the screen, a woman ran from a burning building. She held the limp body of a child in her arms. Her clothes were smeared with blood, and her mouth was open in a silent howl. *I did that.*

Alia stumbled past Jason and Diana, bolting for the bathroom. Her knees knocked painfully against the tiles as she collapsed to the floor and vomited a sludge of candy and bile into the toilet.

Warbringer. Procatalysia. Haptandra. They could call it whatever they wanted. It sounded a lot like *monster*. She couldn't remember much about the Trojan War. She'd thought it was all mythology, old poetry. She'd thought Helen was just a character from a story. Maybe she was. And maybe Alia was a character in a story, too. The kind that got people killed. The monster that had to be put down.

"Al?" Jason asked quietly from the doorway.

"Don't call me that," she muttered into the bowl, flushing away the mess she'd made.

"Alia—"

She didn't look at him when she asked, "Do you believe I'm . . . do you think it's true?"

He was quiet for a while. "I think it might be," he said at last. "Yes."

"Because Mom and Dad believed it?"

"That's part of it. Some of the work they were doing . . . They had a team searching out ancient battlegrounds, looking for the blood of ancient heroes and kings, extracting biological material. They believed, Alia. They thought they could do good with the knowledge. And they wanted to protect you. I wanted to protect you."

"So all this time—"

"The threats to our family have always been real. But—"

"But you knew people might come for me, try to kill me before I could, y'know, destroy the world."

"Yes."

Alia pressed the heels of her hands against her eyes. She felt ridiculous sprawled there on the bathroom floor, elbows resting on the edge of a toilet bowl, but she couldn't bring herself to move. She kept seeing that woman running from the flames. She could feel the limp weight of the child clutched in her arms. "Maybe that wouldn't be such a bad thing."

She heard footsteps, and then Jason was crouching beside her. He put his arm around her shoulders. "Yes, it would. Wars happen, Alia. Even in generations when no Warbringer was born, people still found plenty of excuses to kill each other. And you know what? Humanity survived it all. Maybe Mom and Dad were right, or maybe it's all just a legend, but the one thing I know is they told me to keep you safe, and that's what I'm going to do."

Alia shrugged him off, forcing herself to her feet. "What makes you so sure you can?" She picked up her toothbrush and squirted a huge dollop from the travel-sized toothpaste they'd bought, scrubbing the sour taste from her mouth. "Someone blew up my boat. They killed innocent people to get to me."

"The company owns a cabin up in Canada. It's isolated, secure. We'll go there, try to figure out what's happening, if there's a way to fix this."

"I'm sorry," Diana said from the hall. "I can't allow that."

Jason whirled on her. "If you try to hurt her—"

"I risked my life to save her," Diana said. "I risked everything."

"Then you should know the safest place for her is far away from all of this."

"There's a spring in Therapne, near the boundaries of ancient Sparta. If Alia bathes in its waters before the sun sets on the first of Hekatombaion, the world need not suffer an age of bloodshed, and the cycle of Warbringers will be broken."

"Therapne?" said Jason. "In Greece? Are you out of your mind?"

"Alia," Diana said softly. "Please."

Alia met Diana's gaze in the mirror. She'd pulled her from the waters. Brought her back to life. *I risked everything.* And what if Diana was right? What if there was a way to stop this? What if Alia could fix this instead of letting the world descend into war?

As if sensing her thoughts, Jason said, "No. Absolutely not. I've never even heard of a spring. It wasn't in any of the files Mom and Dad left."

"The spring is real," said Diana. "It's near the Menelaion, where Helen was laid to rest."

"I'm not dragging Alia halfway across the world and betting her life on a magical spring."

Now Alia raised a brow. "You think I'm a walking, talking teenage apocalypse, but you draw the line at a magical spring?"

"It's too big a risk."

He didn't believe Diana; why should he? He hadn't witnessed what Alia had. Alia didn't know what was real or imagined anymore, what was fiction or fact. And it didn't matter. This was her reality now. "It's a risk," she said. "But it's my risk to take."

"How much do you even know about this girl?" Jason said, waving at Diana. "We have to be careful. People—"

"She doesn't want our money, Jason. She isn't a reporter. She isn't a gold digger. She saved my life."

"That doesn't mean you get to go traipsing off to Greece with her. I forbid—"

Alia turned and jabbed a finger at his chest. "You do not want to finish that sentence. Jason, you're my big brother and I love you, but this is on me. I'm the one who has to live with being the biggest mass murderer of all time if this plays out the way you seem to think it will. You can't expect me to just go hide in the wilderness."

"Alia," he said desperately, "this isn't your responsibility. We go to Canada. Wait it out. We—"

"Correct me if I'm wrong, Diana, but we only get one shot at this, right?"

"Yes," said Diana. "You must reach the spring before the sun sets on the first day of Hekatombaion. After that—"

"After that a lot of people die."

"That's less than a week away!" Jason said.

"You weren't on that boat. Those people would be alive if it wasn't for me. I'm going to have to live with that forever. I'm not going to have Armageddon on my conscience, too. You can lock me up. You can try to stop me, but I'm going to do this."

"No," Jason said, hands cutting through the air in a decisive gesture. "I made a promise to Mom and Dad. You don't know—"

"Are you so sure you can stop us?" said Diana.

"Beg your pardon?"

Alia almost laughed at the indignant look on his face.

"Diana *did* just put you on your butt," she said. "I'm pretty sure she can do it again."

"You cannot make this kind of decision," he said. "Go off with someone you barely know. You're *seventeen*."

"And you're the guy who got drunk on eggnog last Christmas and danced to 'Turn the Beat Around' in Aunt Rachel's wig, so stop acting like you're in charge."

"We agreed not to mention that ever again," Jason whispered furiously.

"Jason, I'm doing this." For the first time since the bomb had exploded aboard the *Thetis*, Alia felt like she was making a choice, not just being cast about by the sea. But the truth was that they needed Jason's help if they were going to get to Greece in time. She reached out and took his hand, squeezing it tight, trying to make him understand. "Mom and Dad would want me to try. I know they would. You know it, too."

She could feel the grief they shared around them like an unwanted shield, an invisible wall that separated them from the world. Sometimes it felt unbreachable, as if no one would ever know what they'd been through, what it was to have your world crack down the middle.

At last he squeezed back. "Okay."

"What?" The word leapt from her lips. Jason never changed his mind. Mules could take lessons in stubbornness from him.

"You're right," he said with a sigh. "Mom and Dad would never hide from doing the hard thing. Not if it could save lives. We'll take the company jet."

"You have an airplane?" Diana said.

Alia suppressed a small smile. "This girl really wants an airplane."

"Yes," said Jason. "We can bring the security team as an escort."

"You don't know which of them may be trustworthy," said Diana.

"We can trust the security detail from the penthouse. If they'd wanted us dead, we'd be dead. They've literally watched over us while we sleep."

"I can protect Alia," said Diana.

"Of course," Jason said with a scowl. "A teenage girl protecting another teenage girl. Look, I appreciate what you did for my sister, but you're basically a stranger. I'll take it from here."

"I can't agree to that."

"I didn't ask. My team is former special ops. They're the best in the business, and they're nonnegotiable." He turned back to Alia. "You want to go to the spring, my security team travels with us."

"Fine," Alia said, considering the implications of what they were about to do. "But Diana goes, too."

Diana blinked, and Alia could see the surprise on her face. *My mother doesn't think I can handle anything on my own, either.* Maybe they'd both had their fair share of feeling underestimated.

Jason narrowed his eyes. "Where are you from exactly, Diana Prince?"

"An island. In the Aegean. You wouldn't have heard of it."

"And you don't find this at all shady?" he said to Alia. "A girl with a sketchy background happens to save you, happens to know about the Warbringer, happens to know about a spring that can mystically cure you?"

"Jason, she could have just let me drown. Like you said, if she wanted me dead, I'd be dead. And *she's* nonnegotiable."

Jason rolled his eyes. "Fine. Get your things together. We're moving you and your bodyguard to the penthouse. We'll leave for Greece tomorrow."

"We should leave now," said Diana. "Immediately."

"Do you have a jet?"

Diana crossed her arms. "No."

"Then you don't get to decide when we leave."

"I can see why Alia left the country to avoid you."

Alia winced.

"She did *not*," Jason snapped.

"Let it go," Alia pleaded.

"Just get your things together," Jason growled, and stormed past Diana.

"Don't forget the door—" A crash sounded, followed by a string of angry swearing.

Oops.

"He's just as you described him," said Diana. "Domineering, imperious, used to having his way."

"He's not *really* like that, not when you get to know him." Diana shot her a doubtful glance as they returned to the bedroom to pack up their few belongings. "Okay, he's exactly like that. But he wasn't always."

Diana tucked her leathers and the coils of her golden lasso into one of the plastic Duane Reade bags. "Thank you for not saying anything to Jason about my home. My people . . . You know they value isolation."

Alia nodded. She didn't really understand the rules of Diana's world, but she owed Diana her life. Keeping quiet on some of the stranger details of her background was the least she could do.

"And thank you for insisting that Jason allow me to accompany you," Diana continued. "I would have found a way to come regardless, but it meant a great deal to me."

Alia twisted a braid around her finger. "Yeah, about that." She took a deep breath. "If we don't make it to the spring in time—"

"We will."

"But if we don't, I'm going to need you to kill me."

CHAPTER 10

Kill me. Diana wanted to drive those words from her mind the second Alia spoke them. And she'd said them so easily. *Too eas-ily*, Diana decided. Alia was just frightened, shaken by what she'd learned. None of it would matter when they reached the spring.

Jason made a quick phone call and ushered them out through the hotel's back entrance in case anyone was watching the prem-ises. Diana could at least appreciate that he'd taken some of her warnings seriously.

The alley behind the hotel was pungent with smells Diana's mind could barely make sense of—a rotting vegetable stink cou-pled with what she thought might be urine and human feces, all of it made worse by the summer heat.

They passed through the back of a cleaning facility, crowded with moving racks of clothing packed in plastic, the cloyingly sweet steam welcome after the alley. Then they crossed the street and raced down the sidewalk to another alley, where a sleek black car was idling.

"Hey, Dez," Alia called to the driver as they climbed inside.

"Hey, Al."

Diana noticed Alia didn't correct the driver's use of the nick-name the way she had with her brother.

The air inside the car was crisp and fresh, and Diana allowed herself a small, contented sigh as the sweat cooled on her skin. She was surprised at how pleasant the vehicle was inside, spacious and dark as a cave, its black seats stitched with a precision that could never be accomplished by hand. Jason poured himself a drink from a bar tucked in the car's paneling, and Diana watched the streets slide by slowly through glass tinted dark as smoke, the sounds of the street muted in a heavy, comforting hush. She inhaled deeply, breathing in the scent of leather and something she couldn't quite identify.

"What are you doing?" Jason said abruptly. He was seated across from Diana, watching her closely.

"I did nothing."

"You were smelling the car." He turned to Alia. "She was *smell-ing* the car."

Diana felt her cheeks color slightly. "It has a pleasing aroma."

"It's new-car smell," Alia said, a smile twitching her lips. "Everyone loves that. And Jason is so uptight about keeping the car clean, Betsy never lost it."

"Betsy?"

Jason rolled his eyes. "Alia insists on naming every car. How has Diana Prince, Origins Unknown, never smelled a new car?"

"They don't drive where she's from," Alia said smoothly. "They're almost Amish."

"Amish with combat training?"

Diana ignored the jab. "Why can't we leave for the spring immediately?"

"The annual board meeting for Keralis Labs is tonight, fol-lowed by the reception for the Keralis Foundation's donors. We'll leave as soon as it's over."

Diana sat forward, the appealing smell of the car forgotten. "You want us to stay in New York for a *party*?"

"It isn't a party; it's a reception. Our family is the face of the

Foundation. And if we want to keep it that way, I need to be there. Alia should attend, too."

"A public event?" Diana could hear her pitch rising, but she simply couldn't believe what he was saying.

"It's hardly public. It's a private event at the Temple of Dendur."

Diana frowned. "So it's a type of holy rite?"

Jason took a long sip of his drink. "Where did you find her? It's a permanent exhibit in the Metropolitan Museum of Art. People throw galas there all the time."

"Galas," said Diana. "I believe that's another word for *parties*."

"Hold up," said Alia. "What do you mean, '*if we want to keep it that way*'? How can there be a Keralis Foundation without Keralises?"

Jason leaned back in his seat. Diana knew that he was only a few years older than Alia, but there was a weariness in him that made him seem older. "You don't go to the board meetings, Alia. You don't read the reports. The Foundation's been taking a beating in the press recently. The company's profits have slowed. The board doesn't take us seriously. If we want to be a part of our parents' legacy, we have to step up."

"You're saying the board is going to try to keep you from taking control?" Alia said.

"Michael is worried," Jason admitted, his gaze troubled. "It's one thing for me to be involved with a charity, but no one is that excited about a twenty-one-year-old taking over a multibillion-dollar corporation."

"Who's Michael?" asked Diana.

"Michael Santos," said Alia. "Our godfather. He's been running Keralis Labs since our parents . . . since the accident. But now that Jason's coming of age—"

"He wants me to take more responsibility."

Alia fiddled with the hem of her T-shirt, then said, "Would it be such a bad thing for you to let Michael run the company awhile longer? You could finish up at MIT, go to grad school—"

"I don't need a degree," Jason said sharply. "I just need a lab."

Diana wondered if he was trying to convince Alia or himself. "And I can't miss the meeting tonight," he continued. "It would mean a lot for us to present a united front at the reception."

"This is absurd," said Diana. "Alia can't possibly attend."

To her surprise, Alia said, "Agreed. One hundred percent."

Jason pursed his lips. "You're only saying that because you hate getting dressed up."

"I feel like death threats are a totally legitimate reason not to put on a gown."

"No one would know you're going to be there," said Jason. "I thought you were going to be on that stupid boat trip—"

"Not stupid," grumbled Alia.

"So everyone else still thinks you're abroad. And the people who attacked the *Thetis* believe you're at the bottom of the sea. They won't expect you to be at a party in New York tonight. No one will."

"But if she's spotted—" Diana began.

"Then that can only work for us. By the time word reaches anyone that she's been seen in New York, we'll be on a plane bound for Greece and they'll be chasing their tails in Manhattan. The security will be top rate." He leaned forward. "Alia, if it wasn't safe, you know I would never suggest it."

"That's true," Alia conceded reluctantly. "He's really uptight."

"Cautious," Jason corrected.

Diana considered Jason's bunched shoulders and clenched jaw. "He does seem highly strung."

His eyes narrowed. "Maybe it's because WNBA players jump me in hotel rooms."

Diana shrugged. "If you try to break into a woman's chambers, you should expect to be trounced."

"Trounced?" he said indignantly. "You took me by surprise."

"I had you facedown on the floor."

"Would you two quit it?" said Alia. "I need a minute to think."

Diana crossed her arms and stared through the window, telling herself to take note of her surroundings, biting her tongue against the flood of words that wanted to break free. The *arrogance* of this boy, so sure in his power, buttressed by the trappings of his wealth. It was possible Alia's power was increasing her irritation toward him. *Or maybe he's just irritating.*

The car turned off of the street and entered a dark corridor that led underground. If this was where Alia and her brother lived, she supposed that with the vehicle's tinted windows, someone observing Jason's comings and goings from afar would have no way of knowing he hadn't returned to the building alone. They passed row after row of gleaming automobiles far sleeker than those they'd seen in the other parking garage.

"Home, sweet home," Alia said, her face melancholy.

"You may not be glad to be here," said Jason quietly. "But I'm glad to have you back."

Alia looked down at her hands, and Diana thought she understood her sadness. Alia had sought adventure and independence but had found only failure and suffering. Diana wondered if she would feel that same sadness returning to Themyscira. If she ever could return. She didn't want to think about that possibility. She'd hungered for the chance at a hero's quest, and heroes didn't get homesick. Better to focus on the task at hand: ensuring Alia's safety and getting to the spring.

The driver pulled the car around to an unobtrusive-looking set of metal doors.

"Is this secure?" Diana asked as they exited the vehicle and Jason pushed a button.

"This elevator is reserved for the penthouse," said Jason. "No one else has access."

Diana looked around warily as the doors slid open and they entered the little room. They had elevators on Themyscira that were operated by pulleys and used for moving heavy or unwieldy cargo. Aside from the panel of buttons to the right of the door, she supposed this was no different, even if it was more luxuriously appointed. Its floor was carpeted, its walls mirrored. She caught a glimpse of her reflection, dark hair still damp from the shower, rumpled T-shirt, blue eyes a bit dazed. She looked like a stranger. Jason's gaze met hers in the mirror, and she realized he'd been watching her again. He took a key from his pocket, inserted it into a lock beside the panel, and pressed *P*.

The elevator lurched, and Diana attempted to keep her face neutral as they shot upward, leaving her stomach somewhere near her feet. This was *not* like the elevators on Themyscira.

She took a deep breath through her nose and tried to keep her mind off the horrible sensation in her gut and instead concentrate on what Jason had said about the elevator's security. So what if access to the penthouse was restricted? There had to be stairs somewhere. And if someone was determined enough, they could simply take down the whole building with explosives. What were a few more lives lost if a world war could be prevented?

A moment later, the elevator jounced to a halt, and the doors opened into a cavernous hallway, two stories high. Sunshine streamed in through a skylight, illuminating a staircase of polished wood that swept up one paneled wall, and floors set in a spiral mosaic of black and white tiles.

Diana tensed at the sight of two large men in dark suits standing by the doors, but they simply greeted Jason and Alia with a nod.

"This is Meyers, and this is Perez," Jason said to Diana as they passed. "They're both former Navy SEALs and have been with my family for almost ten years. They're either trustworthy or the slowest assassins ever."

Diana said nothing. If her reading on politics had taught her anything, even a loyal man might be swayed under the right circumstances.

They entered a large dining room and a living area that opened onto a terrace of gray stone squares separated by manicured hedges, and beyond that, a swath of open blue sky that made her heart lift. Colored spheres of blown glass spread over the living room ceiling so that it looked as if an underwater garden had bloomed above them. These were considerably nicer lodgings than the Good Night.

Jason continued on to the kitchen, set his keys down on the counter, and opened what appeared to be a refrigerator.

"Juice?" he said.

Alia nodded, and Jason set three glasses on the counter, along with a pitcher of juice and a jug of milk. Alia filled her glass with orange juice, added a splash of milk, and pushed the mixture over to Diana.

"Try it," she said. "It's delicious."

"It's disgusting," said Jason, pouring himself a glass of plain orange juice.

Diana had the feeling they'd done this a thousand times, a homecoming ritual. She accepted the glass Alia offered and took a sip. Sweet Demeter, it *was* disgusting. But she forced herself to drink the rest and smile rather than agree with Jason.

"Refreshing," she managed.

Jason lifted a brow. "You're not fooling anyone." He leaned back against the sink. "Give me an hour at the party," he said to Alia. "We'll shake hands, put a good face on everything, then we can take a helicopter straight to the airport and see about this spring of yours."

"How long is the flight to Greece?" Diana asked.

"About twelve hours, give or take. I've texted our pilot, Ben. We can fly into Kalamata. That's about a two-hour drive from Therapne."

If he was right, they could be at the spring in less than twenty-four hours—with days to spare before the reaping moon.

"Alia, we need this," Jason said. "There are people on the board who have their own ideas about the direction Keralis Labs should go. The only reason they haven't moved against me is because they know how bad the PR would be. We need to keep it that way. Show them we're continuing in the tradition Mom and Dad began. Show them . . . we're still a family."

Alia turned the glass in her hands. Diana could see the effect Jason's words had on her. She supposed she could respect how seriously he took his responsibilities. Even if he was a domineering ass.

"What do you think?" Alia asked Diana.

Diana pressed her lips together. She knew attending the party wasn't a wise choice, but she also understood the stakes were different for Alia and Jason. They had a life they wished to return to when this journey was over. No one would know Alia was attending until she was mingling with the guests, and if any spies relayed that information onward, they'd be gone from the party before Alia's enemies could act. "An hour," she said at last. "No more."

"Okay, then," Alia said. "I'll go."

A broad smile broke over Jason's face, carving a dimple into his left cheek and transforming his features completely. "Thank you."

Alia returned the grin. "See, Jason? You'd get your way more often if you just made your case like a human instead of resorting to 'Obey or face the consequences.'"

He shrugged, still smiling. " 'Obey or face the consequences' is just so much more efficient."

"Can I bring Nim?"

Now the smile vanished. "Alia—"

"Nim comes, or I'm wearing sweats."

Jason blew out a breath. "Fine."

Alia pumped her fist. "Cell." Jason slapped his phone into her palm with a resigned expression. "Come on," Alia said to Diana, already heading back toward the entry, her attention focused on the phone, thumbs moving in a blur.

But as Diana made to follow, Jason stepped into her path. All the warmth he'd exhibited the moment before had vanished.

"Who are you, really?" he said, voice low. "You'd better believe I'm going to have my people digging up every bit of information on you they can find, Diana Prince."

"They're welcome to."

His scowl deepened. "If you hurt my sister—"

"I would not harm Alia. I risked a great deal to bring her here."

"So you keep saying. What I want to know is what's in it for you?"

How could he ask that, knowing so much was at stake?

"A future," she said, though she knew that wasn't the whole story. *I see you, Daughter of Earth. I see your dreams of glory.*

His laugh sounded hollow as a drum. "I'm not sure if you're a fanatic or a scam artist—and I'm also not sure which is worse."

"Is it so hard to believe I'm trying to do the right thing?"

"Yes."

Diana frowned. What kind of life had this boy led that he'd grown so cynical? "I want nothing from you or Alia except the chance to set this world to rights."

"Being a Keralis means everyone wants something from you. Always. Alia is the only family I have. If—"

"Then maybe you should stop bullying her."

"I never—"

"Since I've met you, all you've done is dictate her behavior, call her stupid, and sneer at her attempts to pursue her dreams."

"I'm letting her chase after this ridiculous spring, aren't I?"

"*Letting* her."

Jason cut his hand through the air dismissively. "She's not equipped to deal with the world. Alia has had a very sheltered life."

"Whose fault is that?" Diana felt her temper quicken. "You can't even imagine the courage and resilience I've seen her show."

"In your long acquaintance?"

"Maybe if you saw more truly, listened more closely, she wouldn't have felt the need to lie to you."

Jason's jaw hardened. He took a step closer. "You don't know anything about me or Alia, so just stay quiet and don't get in my way."

"You wouldn't even know your way without me."

"If you make one move that seems—"

Diana leaned in. She was tired of threats from this boy. They were almost the same height, and she met his gaze easily. "What will you do?"

"I'll end you."

Diana couldn't help it. She laughed.

"What's so funny?" he growled.

How could she possibly explain? She'd faced the death of her mother and friends in the Oracle's vision. She'd braved exile and nearly drowned to come here. Besides, when you'd stood toe-to-toe with the great Tekmessa, general of the Amazons, and endured her derision, it was hard to fear a mortal boy—regardless of his well-made frame.

"You're pretty enough, Jason Keralis. But hardly intimidating."

His eyelids stuttered. *"Pretty?"*

"Is Jason being a jerk?" Alia called from somewhere in the penthouse.

"Yes!" Diana called back without breaking Jason's gaze. "If you'll excuse me?"

She bracketed his shoulders with her hands, and he emitted a squeak as she picked him up and moved him out of her path.

Diana strode past, not bothering to look back. From behind her, she heard Jason mutter, "Pretty *enough?*"

CHAPTER 11

Alia hovered halfway up the stairs in the entry as Diana strode from the kitchen. How did she manage to make a crappy drugstore T-shirt look regal?

"What did Jason say?" she asked. "Was he horrible?"

"Yes," said Diana as she followed her up the steps. "I suppose his motives are good, but his manner makes me want to—"

"Stab him with a pencil?"

"Not exactly that," said Diana. "But he's certainly irritating."

The phone buzzed, and Alia bounced on her toes with a happy whoop. "Nim is on her way!"

"It would be best if she wasn't seen entering the building."

Alia paused, her foot on the stair above her. It was too easy to slide out of the reality of her situation. It was like her mind couldn't accept what was happening, so it just kept defaulting to the ordinary.

She sent a text to Nim telling her to take a car and use the private elevator. They could send Perez down with a key.

"Can she be trusted, this Nim?" asked Diana.

"Definitely. But let's spare her all the Warbringer talk, yeah?"

At the top of the stairs, Alia hesitated. She longed for her room, her clothes, a good long nap. Instead, she made herself turn right and follow the hallway, the skylights casting squares of sunshine on the black-and-white paneled floor.

"The pattern is different here," Diana noted.

"Yeah, the tiles in the entry hall make a fractal. This is a DNA sequence." Alia shrugged. "That's what happens when you give nerds money."

She stopped before the double doors to her parents' office, her hands resting on the handles, then took a deep breath and pushed them open.

There was a time when this had been her favorite room in the apartment. Its walls were lined with bookshelves paneled in the same warm wood as the staircase, and a huge fireplace took up half of one wall. A small table and two chairs had been positioned in front of the cold grate, and a paperback lay open on one of the armrests, just where Lina Keralis had left it. *Death in the Air*, by Agatha Christie.

"Mom loved mysteries," Alia said, touching the cracked spine of the book lightly. "And thrillers. She liked puzzles. She said they helped her relax."

Diana ran her hand along the stone mantel, pausing to pick up a photograph. "Are these your parents?"

Alia nodded. "And Neil deGrasse Tyson in the middle."

Diana set the frame down gently. "This room is so different from the rest of your home."

It was true. Her parents had kept the rest of the penthouse light and airy, but the office looked like they'd stolen the library from some English manor house. "My parents loved this kind of old-world stuff."

"Well, old is relative," Diana murmured, and Alia remembered her claim that the walls on her island dated back three thousand years.

"They said they worked in a sterile white lab all day; they wanted to feel like they were escaping when they came home."

Again, Alia touched her hand to the spine of the book on her mother's chair. A decanter with two glasses beside it sat on a low table. It all felt so immediate, as if they might return at any moment. Alia knew it was a little creepy, definitely depressing, but she couldn't quite make herself close that book.

"I just can't believe my mom would have kept such a huge secret from me," she said.

"Maybe she didn't want you to feel different," Diana said. "Maybe she wanted you to have a chance at being like everyone else."

Alia snorted. "Not much hope of that." She crossed to the double desk where her parents had liked to work across from each other.

"Why?"

She plunked herself down in her father's old chair and used the edge of the desk to give herself a shove, sending herself spinning. "Well, Nim and I are the only brown girls in my grade, and two of about ten in the whole school." She switched directions, launching herself into another spin. "I'm a complete science nerd." She spun again. "And I'm more comfortable reading than at parties. So, yeah, not much chance at normal. Besides, you should have seen me when I had braces."

"Braces?"

"For my teeth?" Alia bared her teeth. "Let me guess, yours are just naturally straight and pearly white." She tapped her fingers over the desk. "I know Mom had a safe for her jewelry and stuff, but I don't know where it is."

"There's a panel beside the Faith Ringgold," Jason said from the doorway.

He strode behind the desk and slid open a panel next to the framed quilt, revealing a heavy-looking safe set into the wall. He entered a long combination into its keypad, then pressed his fingertip to a red screen. Alia heard a soft metallic whir and a click. He pulled open the safe's door.

"Here," he said, handing Alia a flash drive. "Most of the files are on this. They kept hard copies, too, if you want them. And this." He drew a slender metal case from the safe and set it on the desk.

Alia cast a wary eye at the box. "What is it?"

"A record of all the known Warbringers. I don't know where they got it or how it's passed from one family to another."

Alia flipped the latch and lifted the lid. There was a scroll inside, yellowing parchment wrapped around a spool of polished wood. She touched her fingers to it briefly, then drew her hand back. How much did she want to know?

But that wasn't the way a scientist thought. It wasn't the way her parents had taught her to think.

She lifted the scroll from the box and began to unroll it. She'd expected some kind of family tree, but it was more like a time line. The inscriptions were made in several different languages, names and dates scrawled in different hands, different inks, one a rusty brown that might be blood.

The first words were written in Greek. "What does this mean?" Alia said, fingers hovering over the entry.

"Helen—" Diana and Jason began at the same time.

"Daughter of Nemesis," Diana continued. "Goddess of divine retribution, born with war in her blood, first of the *haptandrai*."

"Wait a minute," Alia protested. "I thought Helen was supposed to be the daughter of Zeus and Leda. You know, the swan?"

"That's one story. In others, Helen and her brothers were the children of Zeus and Nemesis and were only fostered by Leda."

"Divine retribution," said Alia. "That's . . . cheerful."

"She was also known as Adrasteia."

"The inescapable," said Jason.

"I bet she's fun to have around." Alia furrowed her brow. "You said that word before. *Haptandrai*."

Jason nodded. "The meaning is a little cloudy. The root can mean to ignite or to assail, but also just to touch."

"The hand of war," murmured Diana.

Alia stared at Jason. "Did you brush up on Greek because Dad was Greek or because of this Warbringer thing?"

"A little of both," he admitted.

Alia wasn't too surprised. Jason had always been more interested in their Keralis side than their Mayeux side.

"Your translation isn't entirely accurate, though," Diana said. "The root can mean other things. To grab, to grapple with, to couple with."

"*Couple with?*" squeaked Alia.

"I did not need to know that," said Jason.

Diana shrugged. "It makes a kind of sense. Helen wasn't just one thing, and there can be many reasons for war."

Alia didn't want to ponder that too deeply. She turned her focus back to the scroll, unfurling it a bit more. She was wrong; it looked less like a time line than a cross between a seismograph and an EKG. Each girl's name was followed by a series of peaks tagged with incidents of conflict, each peak larger than the last, like foothills rising to mountains, culminating in a sharp apex of violence that ran in a spiky range across the top of the scroll until at last it dropped off again.

"Evgenia," Alia murmured, touching her finger to one of the names inscribed on the parchment. "The Peloponnesian War. It looks like it lasted nearly sixty years."

"Longer," said Jason. "It was the beginning of the end for Greek democracy."

"Livia Caprenia," she said. "The Sack of Rome. Angeline de Sonnac, the Seventh Crusade." Her fingers jumped from era to era in no particular order, from girl to girl, tragedy to tragedy. "The Hundred Years' War. The Wars of the Roses. The Thirty Years' War. Did they know?" Alia's voice sounded shaky to her own ears. "Helen knew she was the cause of the Trojan War, but did these girls know what they were? What they caused just by breathing?"

"Maybe," said Jason. "I don't think so. How could they?"

"Someone was keeping these records," Diana said.

Alia kept her eyes locked on the scroll. "Oh God. World War One. World War Two. You're telling me we were the cause of that?"

"*No*," said Diana. She braced her hand against Alia's shoulder. "The Warbringer is a catalyst. Not a cause. You cannot take the blame for the violence men do."

Alia drew in a sharp breath. "Look," she said, jabbing her finger at the year 1945. Next to it was an annotation: *Irene Martin. B. December 1.* A series of small peaks followed in the same pattern as the other entries, moderate at first, widely spaced, then rising in irregular lines, each closer to the next. They reached an apex in 1962 and then abruptly dropped off. The inscription there read *Irene Martin. D. October 27.*

Alia frowned. "What was happening in 1962? I don't remember—"

"I didn't, either," said Jason. "I had to look it up. It was the Cuban Missile Crisis. The Soviets and the Americans came to the brink of nuclear war."

"But then the Warbringer died?"

Neither Jason nor Diana met her eyes.

"Oh," said Alia quietly. "She didn't die. She was assassinated." Alia touched her fingers to the date again. "She never got to turn seventeen. They found her and they killed her because they knew it would just keep getting worse."

"Alia, there were still wars after the Warbringer died," said Jason. "Vietnam, Cambodia, the Balkans, countless wars in the Middle East and Africa."

"But who knows how much worse it would have been if Irene Martin had lived?" Alia brushed hastily at her cheeks. When had she started crying?

Diana squeezed her shoulder. "Listen to me," she said. "We're going to reach the spring. We're going to change all of this."

"You don't know that."

"Yes, I do. We'll reach the spring. We'll break the line. And there will never be another Warbringer. No girl will have to bear this burden again. Including you."

"That's right," said Jason.

"You don't even believe there's a spring," Alia said, sniffling loudly.

"I believe . . . I believe that if there was a start to this, then there has to be an end."

A buzzing sound broke the quiet of the room. Alia looked down at the phone. "Nim's here."

"Go wash your face," said Jason, taking the phone from her. "Perez will let Nim up. I'll have the files put on the jet, and we can look them over during the flight. Both of you should pack a travel bag, too." He put his arm around her. "Alia, we—"

She shook him off and stepped away from Diana. "Don't," she said, ignoring the flash of hurt that crossed Jason's face as she headed for the door. She couldn't bring herself to let him comfort her. He couldn't fix this. The only thing that would make this right was the spring.

She closed the door on Jason and his files and the long shadows their parents had left behind.

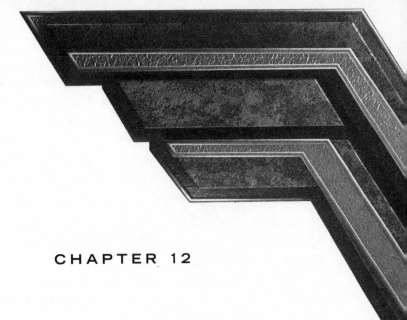

CHAPTER 12

Diana found Alia flopped on a canopy bed heaped with snowy linens in a large chamber at the other end of the hall. This room had a floor inlaid with wood in the pattern of a huge sunburst, and one wall was painted with a misty view of a lake dappled with pale pink water lilies.

"Monet," Diana said, finding the name in a memory of one of her art history lessons.

"I was really into that story 'The Frog Prince' when I was a kid," Alia said to the ceiling. "Mom wasn't big on princesses, so we compromised with a lily pond."

But the wide windows that overlooked a vast swath of parkland had already captured Diana's gaze. From this height, the city was transformed. It was like looking into her mother's jewel case—a city of silver spires and mysterious ironwork, windows that glinted like gems in the afternoon light. The park was rigidly symmetrical in its boundaries, hard lines demarcating where it began and the city ended. It was as if someone had set a door into another world at the center of the city, someplace lush and green, but contained on all sides by strong magic.

Alia's room seemed full of small magics, too. Her desk was stacked with textbooks and a little hourglass sat beside the lamp, but the sand in it seemed to be lodged at the top. Diana shook it, then flipped it and gasped.

"Is the sand in this flowing upward?"

Alia rolled her head listlessly on the pillow. "Oh. Yeah. It's because of the density of the liquid inside it instead of air."

A framed photograph sat on the corner of the desk: a young Alia and Jason on a boardwalk, their hair braided into tight rows, Alia's head studded with plastic barrettes. Behind them stood the same couple Diana recognized from the photo in the study—a man with a craggy, friendly face, his blue eyes sparkling, his cheeks reddened by the sun, and a woman with dark-brown skin and a soft cloud of hair held back from her face by a cheerful red headband. They were all striking a silly pose, flexing their muscles like comic strongmen. Jason's smile was broad and open, his dimple carved deeply into his left cheek. Maybe Alia was right about how much he'd changed.

"And what are these?" Diana asked, pointing to a shelf of neatly stacked patterned boxes.

Alia groaned. "It's super nerdy."

"Tell me."

"I'm trying to collect the element that corresponds to my age every year for my birthday, like Oliver Sacks. He was a neuroscientist."

"I know. We have his books."

Alia lifted her head. "You do?"

"We try to keep up with the outside world."

Alia flopped back against the pillows. "Yeah, well, here's hoping I make it to argon."

Diana heard footsteps on the stairs and tensed, preparing herself. Alia might trust Nim, but Diana couldn't afford to.

The bedroom door banged open and a girl stormed through—though she was less like a girl and more like a human whirlwind. She wore open-toed boots that laced up to her dimpled knees and a smock dress that sparkled. The side of her head was shaved and the rest of her hair fell forward in a slick black sheaf that flopped over one eye. The other eye was black as jet and rimmed with gold, and her visible ear was studded with silver and gems all the way from lobe to top.

"I cannot *believe* you lasted all of what? A *week* in Turkey? I thought this was supposed to be the big adventure, Alia. The moment when you cast off your chains and—" The girl's voice broke off as she caught sight of Diana standing by the window. "Sweet mother of apples."

"Pardon?"

"Nim—" Alia said, a note of warning in her voice.

The girl strode forward. She was round cheeked, round shouldered, round everything.

"Poornima Chaudhary," she said. "You can call me Nim. Or whatever you like, honestly. God, how tall are you?"

"Nim!" snapped Alia.

"It's a totally reasonable question. All in the name of research. Your text said we need clothes." Nim hooked her hand around one of the bedposts and muttered, "Please tell me this girl is less of a pill than the last one you forced me to hang out with. No offense," she said to Diana. "But, excluding me, Alia basically has the worst taste in people ever." Her one visible eye narrowed. "Are those bruises? What the hell happened in Turkey?"

"Nothing," said Alia, fluffing her pillows and propping herself against them. "Boating accident. They had to cut the trip short."

Diana was surprised at how easily Alia delivered the lie. But how many tears had Diana hidden from Maeve? Some sorrows had to be borne alone.

Nim crossed her arms, bracelets jangling. "You look like you've been crying."

"The jet lag is just messing with me."

"You weren't *gone* long enough for jet lag."

"I—"

Nim held up her hands. "I'm not complaining. Summer in this

dump of a city sucks without you." She cast Diana an assessing glance. "And you definitely know how to bring back a souvenir."

Alia tossed a pillow at her. "Nim, quit flirting. You are here for style-emergency purposes."

"Your life is a perpetual style emergency. So much money, so little chic. Am I right?" She turned to Diana. "Who are you exactly?"

Diana took in Nim's bright, inquisitive eyes, her head cocked to the side. She looked like a sparkly, round-cheeked sparrow. "Diana," she said, and smiled. "But you can call me Diana."

"Are you going to help us or not?" said Alia.

"Of course I am. I love spending your money. But how did Jason convince you to go to a party?"

"Guilt bomb."

"Typical. All right, my females," Nim said, whipping out a measuring tape and flipping open what Diana realized was a computer on Alia's desk. "Let's go shopping."

"We can't go out," said Diana, though she hated to dampen Nim's enthusiasm. "We're already taking enough risks."

Nim pulled out a pair of green plastic glasses and plunked them on her small nose. "What's that, now?"

"Jason's being strict on security again," Alia said hurriedly. "We've had some threats."

"Crazy, right?" Nim asked Diana. "Can you imagine living on lockdown?"

"Come on, Nim. It's not like I have that many places to go."

Nim waved her hand dismissively. "Someday, Alia, we will have all the places to go and all the clothes to go there in. And don't worry," she said to Diana. "The shopping comes to us."

They gathered around the computer on Alia's desk—Nim at the keyboard, Alia and Diana huddled behind her—and the next hour was a blur of confusing talk and images flying by on the tiny screen. Nim knew a great deal about textiles and design, and apparently, she'd helped Alia shop this way before. She took

Diana's measurements, all while catching Alia up on how she'd spent the last two weeks, the course she'd just finished at some place called Parsons, and how disgusting the heat in the city had been.

Diana mostly listened and nodded, enjoying their chatter. Nim was a little like Maeve, but her cheer and boldness were somehow more vivid. It reminded Diana of the bright shelves of the drugstore, everything noisy with electric color, even the candy. *You dance differently when you know you won't live forever.* Was this what Maeve had meant? There was something reckless in mortal joy that Diana liked. It held nothing back.

"You're awfully quiet," Nim said, looking up at Diana suspiciously. She pushed back from the desk in her chair. "You're not silently seething over something I said, are you?"

Diana startled. "Not at all. Why would you think that?"

Nim shrugged, taking out her phone and sending another text to someone Diana thought she'd called Barney Buyer. "Nothing personal. I just never get along with Alia's friends. We tend to do better on our own."

"It's true," Alia said thoughtfully, leaning against her bookshelf.

"And we're delightful!" said Nim. "Even though Alia is a total jinx. If something can go wrong around her, it will. I swear, she's a drama magnet."

Alia gestured at the screen. "Focus." But Diana knew she was thinking about all of those tense moments, those disagreements, those broken opportunities for friendship in a new light.

Diana peered at Nim, whose head was cocked to the side as she sucked thoughtfully on her lower lip and tapped at the screen of her phone. *Did* Diana feel hostile toward her? She didn't think so. She'd wondered if her conflict with Jason had been influenced by Alia's powers, but she and Nim seemed to be getting along just fine. The Oracle had said Alia would not cause her to sicken; maybe her powers had no effect on Diana at all. "Nim, do you and Jason get on well?"

"As well as anyone can get along with that pill." Nim whirled in her seat and clutched a hand to her chest. "Don't tell me you're into him."

Alia banged her head against her bookshelf. "Can we not?"

Nim fluttered her fingers as if casting a spell. "Girls lose all sense around Jason Keralis."

"It's the billionaire factor," said Alia.

"It's not just the money: It's the cheekbones, the icy disposition. I had three kinds of a crush on your brother before I matured enough to realize he's a total bore."

"That isn't a secret, Nim. You used to steal his T-shirts."

Nim folded her arms, but her brown cheeks pinked. "So?"

"His *dirty* T-shirts."

Diana grimaced, but Nim didn't seem deterred.

"All I'm saying is most guys who are that rich and that young are either awful legacies with 'the third' after their names or gross Internet entrepreneurs. Jason's mad-science angle is hot."

Alia scoffed. "Could have fooled me."

"Totally different standard for girls. Guys don't care if you have a sexy brain."

Diana recoiled. "You can't mean that."

Alia tossed a pillow at Nim. "She *doesn't* mean it. Nim, you're the worst."

"I'm the best. And I can't help it if we live beneath the thumb of the patriarchy. Why don't you go yell at your brother for being a tool and only dating supermodels and socialites?"

"What's a supermodel?" Diana asked.

Nim stared at her.

"Uh, Diana's homeschooled," said Alia.

"Under a rock?" asked Nim.

"Her parents are just super weird. Hippies, kind of. You know, no TV, only public radio."

Nim took Diana's hand in both of hers. "I am so deeply sorry."

Diana raised a brow. "I manage."

"Do you?" Nim asked with a sincerity so profound Diana

couldn't help laughing. Nim grabbed her other hand, holding Diana's wrists out. "Wow, cool bracelets. Are these soldered on?"

"Um, yes."

"I can't even see a seam. That is some amazing craftsmanship. What are they? It's got to be an alloy, but—"

"Nim makes jewelry," Alia explained.

Nim dropped Diana's hands. "Don't say I make jewelry. That sounds like I'm someone with a BeDazzler and an Etsy shop. I make *art*."

Alia rolled her eyes. "Okay, how about this? Nim is really good with textiles and just about everything else visual, and that's why I invited her over to berate us."

"Also I'm great company."

Alia grinned. "That, too."

"What makes these models super?" inquired Diana, still curious. "Do they have powers?"

Nim burst out laughing. "I *love* this girl. Yes, supermodels have the power to make you buy things you don't need and feel terrible about yourself."

Could that be true? "You used that word to describe me," Diana said to Alia. "It doesn't sound like a compliment."

Alia hurled herself onto the bed and said, "It *is* a compliment. Nim just thinks she's being clever."

"Speaking of which," Nim said, consulting her phone. "Marie pulled a bunch of clothes for us. They should be delivered in a couple of hours." She hopped up on the bed and settled next to Alia. "Prepare for perfection."

"I don't need to be perfect," Alia said. "Just passable."

Nim held up her pinky. "Bubble, bubble."

Alia sighed and hooked her pinky into Nim's. "Make some trouble." She cast a glance at Diana. "This all probably seems really silly to you, right?"

Diana wasn't entirely sure what ritual she'd just witnessed, so she said, "The dresses? Attire is important. It sends a message to everyone you meet."

"Yes!" Nim declared, fists held aloft in victory.

"*Nooo,*" wailed Alia, burying her head in the pillows. "Now there's two of you."

"You said as much in the drugstore," Diana pointed out, leaning against the desk.

"But there's a difference between looking respectable and saying, *Look at me!*"

"Perhaps you should think of it as armor," suggested Diana. "When a warrior readies herself for battle, she doesn't just worry about practicality."

Alia rolled onto her side and propped her head on one hand. "I'd think not dying would be the big concern."

"Yes, but the goal is also to intimidate. A general wears her rank. The same is true of athletes when they compete."

"That's true!" said Nim. "I read that football players play more aggressively when they're dressed in black and red."

"Nim loves trivia," said Alia.

"I love *information.*"

Diana lifted Nim's measuring tape from the desk and curled it over one finger. "Where I'm from . . . I get a lot of attention because of my mother."

"Who's your mom? Is she famous?"

"Um . . ."

"Only locally," interjected Alia.

"Anyway," said Diana, "I know people will be judging, so I have to think about what to wear. My mother does, too. She's really good at it. And it isn't just about battle. Sometimes everything feels like a fight. You know, like just sitting through a dinner."

"Or walking down the street," said Nim.

"Or making it through an hour at a party," Alia said.

Diana found herself smiling. "It's just an hour. We'll manage it." And when that hour had passed, they would be on their way to the spring, on their way to changing the future.

A knock came at the door, and Jason ducked his head inside. "I need to head over to the meeting soon. Traffic's heavy."

"Tell me you're not wearing that to the party," said Nim.

Jason had donned a suit similar to the ones worn by the businessmen on the train.

He tugged at his cuff a bit self-consciously. "I'd planned to change into my tux at the office. And hello, Nim. So glad you can join us tonight."

"Wouldn't miss it for the world, Jay-jay."

"Meyers and Perez will escort you to the party. Dez will drive, but I got him to pick up a new car. If anyone's tracking our fleet, they're going to miss him coming and going." Jason held out a piece of paper that Nim snatched from his hand. "If you need to reach him, use this number. I got him an encrypted burner cell."

"An encrypted burner cell?" Alia repeated. "You just had one lying around?"

"Alia, what do I always tell you?"

"That you only watch reality TV as an anthropological exercise."

Nim cackled, and Jason rolled his eyes.

"No," he said. "Enjoy the best, but prepare for the worst."

"Wise, Jason," said Nim. "So wise. Ever notice how hard it is to enjoy something when you're preparing for the worst?"

He ignored her. "Theo and I will meet you at the party at eight thirty. Don't be late."

"Oh lord, *Theo's* coming?" said Nim. "Talk about preparing for the worst."

"And what about . . ." Diana hesitated. "Our ride home?"

Jason gave a single grim nod. "It will be ready to go." He shut the door.

"Thanks for the invite!" Nim called after him.

Jason's voice floated back through the door. "Just don't set fire to anything."

Nim pirouetted and struck a pose. "Nothing but the dance floor. Who's hungry?"

* * *

A cold supper had been laid out for them in the kitchen, and Diana realized there must be staff here, servants who came and went barely seen. She hoped Jason's faith in their loyalty was justified, and that both he and Alia were right about the party being a worthwhile risk. Even so, she was glad that they weren't leaving for Greece right away. Once they'd broken the Warbringer line, Diana would have to return home to whatever consequences might be waiting. With Jason's jet at the ready, she could at least enjoy a few more hours to observe the mortal world. There was so much to see, and if she was honest with herself, she could admit there was something to be said for being Diana Prince, something freeing about being judged on her own words and actions, instead of her origins or her mother's choices.

As they hovered around the kitchen counter, piling food onto their plates, Diana wondered if Alia and Jason ever used the huge dining room or threw parties on their grand terrace. Or was it always just the two of them and the occasional trusted friend, sharing this huge home with the ghosts of Alia and Jason's parents, eating standing up at their counter, looking out at the beautiful view?

Diana had felt so alone on Themyscira, but Alia was just as isolated in this massive city—maybe more so. The palace at the Epheseum was large, but it had been built as a communal space, one where people came and went to seek audience with their queen, where classes were taught. The women who served Diana and her mother were also their friends, the same people with whom they ate and trained. Everyone served Themyscira in some way, but they were all warriors, all equals. It was one of the reasons many believed there should be no queen at all, just an elected council. Maybe this quest would free both Diana and Alia. Maybe it would give Diana a chance to truly belong among her sisters and Alia the opportunity to live her life with some measure of peace.

"Funny how you neglected to mention that Theo Santos is going to be there tonight," Nim said as she stuffed her mouth full of cheese.

"I didn't know," said Alia.

"You should have told me so I could better gauge how much cleavage you wanted to show."

"First you'd have to find me some."

"Who's Theo Santos?" Diana asked, selecting a cluster of grapes from a bowl.

"Jason's junior sidekick."

"He's a family friend," said Alia.

"Hot in a gangly, not-hot-at-all way."

"He's objectively attractive," Alia protested.

"He's a complete loser. He spends all his time over here or in some dark room gaming and avoiding actual human contact."

Alia tossed a carrot at Nim. "Actual human contact is overrated."

When the dresses arrived, Perez went down to retrieve them with Nim in tow. They returned with two metal racks laden with large dark bags dangling from hangers, which Meyers helped carry upstairs. Diana felt a bit guilty watching them struggle up the steps, but she thought it best to let them manage on their own.

Back in Alia's room, Nim immediately began unzipping the bags and yanking them off to reveal swaths of shimmering fabric and beading. There were several smaller bags filled with just shoe boxes and sheer wraps.

Alia sighed. "Let's get this over with."

Diana nudged her with her elbow. "Armor, remember?"

Alia squared her shoulders and took her pile of dresses into the bathroom. "Those who are about to die salute you."

"I don't know why I even bother," grumbled Nim as they perched on Alia's bed to wait. "She always picks the most boring thing on the rack, always in basic black. If it's shaped like a sack, even better."

"Maybe it feels easier that way, just being invisible instead of always worrying what people think of you."

Nim's voice was surprisingly emphatic. "But that's a choice, too, right? Because people are always going to look. They're always going to judge, so you can say nothing or you can at least answer back."

Diana had the sense that Nim wasn't talking about Alia at all. The tiny girl's clothes were distinctive, her manner of speech decisive. But her confidence was vibrant and spiky, like a bright flower guarded by thorns.

"What do you think people see when they look at you?"

Nim turned to her. "What do *you* see?"

"A bold girl. Talented and audacious."

Nim dropped backward in an exaggerated swoon. "Could you just stay forever?"

"What was that thing you and Alia did?" Diana said, trying to remember. "Bubble, bubble. . . . It was a play on Shakespeare, wasn't it?"

Nim propped herself up on her elbows. "I know it's goofy."

"What does it mean?"

Nim slid off the bed and crossed the room to where a collage of her and Alia was propped on a dresser. She plucked a photo from the frame and held it up: three girls in shredded black robes with pointy hats. "When Alia and I were freshmen, we both got cast as witches in *Macbeth* along with this Thai kid, Preeda. That's right, out of the whole school, they cast the three ethnic kids as witches. People would see us in the hall and pretend to shriek and cry. They thought it was hilarious."

Diana had always regretted not growing up with other children, but that sounded awfully cruel. "What did you do?"

Nim tucked the photo back into the collage. "We just went for it. We cackled and went berserk every night and made sure to always get our lines wrong. Bubble, bubble."

Diana smiled. "Make some trouble."

"Come on, Alia!" Nim shouted at the closed bathroom door. "You have to pick one, and we all know it's going to be the black dress with the long sleeves so you can schoolmarm it up—"

The door opened, and Nim's jaw dropped.

"She didn't pick the black one," Diana observed.

"No shit," breathed Nim.

Alia wore a dress of shimmering gold scales that moved like light glinting off water—no, like the sun off a warrior's helm.

"Did you hit your head in Turkey?" Nim said in disbelief.

Alia grinned at Diana and cocked her hip. "Armor."

CHAPTER 13

They were more than a little late. Nim pinned up half of Alia's braids in a crown and wove a gold chain through them, then chose a garnet-colored jumpsuit for herself that she paired with terrifyingly high heels. She picked a strapless, midnight-blue gown for Diana. The fabric was of a fine quality, but it felt stiff around the waist and hugged her hips too tightly, as if it had been constructed with little thought to comfort.

"It looks good," said Alia. "Elegant."

Diana frowned. "I wish it had another slit up the side."

"One is classy, two is trashy," said Nim.

"One is pointless," replied Diana, wondering what refuse had to do with it. "Two would make it easier to run in."

"Pretty sure there's no red-carpet obstacle course," Alia said as Nim tossed Diana a slim silver bag.

"I'm going to need something larger."

"Why?" said Nim. "That clutch is perfect."

Diana removed the lasso from the plastic bag. "I need something for my things." Meyers and Perez would transfer the rest of their belongings, including her leathers, to the jet, but there was no way Diana was parting with her mother's lasso or the heartstone.

"What *is* that?" Nim said, reaching for the golden coils. "What is it made out of?"

Diana hesitated, then let Nim run her fingers over the glimmering fibers. "It's kind of an heirloom."

"I mean, it's gorgeous, but you can't carry it around like you're going to hog-tie the DJ."

"It will definitely attract attention," said Alia.

"Wait," Nim said. "Give me that."

Diana frowned, hesitant. "What are you going to do?"

"Eat it," Nim said with a roll of her eyes. "I'm not going to hurt it; just trust me." She laid the rope on the desk and turned her back to them, making little humming noises as she worked. A moment later, she hopped onto the desk chair and held up an open-work capelet of shimmering knots. It was somewhere between a shawl and a shrug. "Turn around, you magnificent tree."

Diana let Nim help her into the glittering creation and looked at herself in the mirror on the back of Alia's closet door. The lasso felt cool against her skin, its weight light over her shoulders, but it glinted like gold when she moved, as if her arms had hooked a field of falling stars.

"Perfect," said Nim with a happy sigh.

And it was. Bolder and more whimsical than anything she'd ever worn before. It was *fun*. She had always let her mother dictate what she wore, let her desire to belong, the wish to look like an *Amazon* make her choices. But tonight she could look like anything she wanted. A laugh rose in her throat, and she spun in a circle, arms out, watching the gold flash at the corner of her eye. She felt transformed.

"Nim," said Diana happily. "You're a genius."

"Guilty as charged. But the hair is going up. This look needs more neck."

Nim pinned Diana's hair into a twist, and then they were racing down the stairs.

Meyers and Perez were waiting to escort them to the car and rode in the backseat with them the short distance to the museum.

"There it is," Alia said, pointing through the dark glass.

Diana glimpsed the outlines of windows, high and arched, glowing with light in the gathering dusk.

Dez continued on, and Diana realized he was circling the building so they could enter away from the main doors. When they stopped, Meyers and Perez spoke briefly into their sleeves. It took a moment for Diana to understand they were wearing communication devices. They exited the car first, and Diana saw more guards at the door, but she kept close to Alia anyway. She wasn't about to trust these men just because Jason did.

They entered a shadowy, high-ceilinged hall. In the distance, Diana could hear voices, the swell of music. She remembered being a little girl in the palace, falling asleep as the sounds of Amazon revels continued in the courtyard below. The museum felt a bit like that now, as if the adults were having a party while the rest of the building had been put to bed.

She saw two men approaching and shifted her stance so she could block their path to Alia.

"I said eight o'clock," said Jason's voice as he stepped into a well of light. "You—" His voice broke off abruptly as his eyes locked on Diana. There was that strange look she'd seen on male faces all morning: gaze stunned, mouth slightly ajar.

"What did I tell you?" murmured Nim. "I know what I'm doing."

Jason had changed since they'd seen him that afternoon. He still wore a suit, but it was sleek and black, and its lapels looked almost like burnished metal. He seemed to remember himself. A scowl broke over his face. "You're late."

Nim shrugged. "It takes time to look this good."

"You can work as hard as you want," said Jason's companion, a gangly boy with dark brown skin and hair that stood up from his crown in exuberant twists. "You'll never be as fine as me."

"What a surprise," said Nim. "Theo is with Jason. It's almost like he doesn't have something better to do with his time."

"Can we not start this tonight?" said Alia.

"That's right, Nim," Theo scolded. "Show some maturity. I don't want you poisoning the new girl's mind against me. Hi, New Girl."

"Theo," Jason said warningly.

"I just said hi! Not even hello! I kept it to one innocent syllable."

Theo Santos was a little shorter than Jason, and far leaner. He wore a snug suit of dark-green fabric with a showy sheen, and an open expression that made him look far younger than his friend.

"I stand corrected," Theo said, jamming his hands into the pockets of his trousers and rocking back on the heels of his pointy-toed shoes. "You guys are almost as gorgeous as I am."

"Weak," said Nim. "We're going to need a higher caliber of compliment."

"If I must," Theo said as they started toward the noise of the party bracketed by Meyers and Perez. "Nim, you look like a delicious confection, a walking, talking—probably poisonous—petit four."

"In that case," said Nim, "bite me."

"And you—" he said, looking at Diana. "You look like a star-spangled slice of hell yeah. Who are you, anyway?"

"She's one of Alia's friends, so leave her alone," said Jason.

"Don't mind him," said Theo. "He's just bitter because he got stuck with me as his date."

"I'd think he would be pleased to escort the most gorgeous among us," said Diana.

Theo barked a laugh. "Oh, I like her plenty."

"What about Alia?" said Nim.

"Shut up, Nim," Alia said under her breath.

Theo glanced over his shoulder and gave a cheerful thumbs-up. "Alia looks really nice, too!"

"Gosh, thanks," Alia muttered.

They entered a vast room teeming with people and echoing with sound. It was an extraordinary chamber. The far wall tilted at an angle like the side of a pyramid and was comprised entirely of windows that showed night falling over the park beyond. Partygoers sat at the edge of a rectangular reflecting pool bordered in slate stone, and others clustered around tables set with white orchids and glimmering candles. But the focus of the room was what Diana realized were ruins: a vast stone gate that she suspected had once led to a courtyard and the columned temple itself, covered in hieroglyphs.

My mother is older than these stones, she thought as they joined the swarm of guests. *In the mortal world, my people are the stuff of museums and myth. Legends. Artifacts.* Hippolyta and the first Amazons had vanished from the world long before this temple had been built. Diana looked at the partygoers, drinking, laughing, lifting glasses of wine to their lips. *Lives like the wing beat of a moth. There and then gone.*

"This room was designed to mimic the place where the temple was originally located," said Nim, eyes sparkling, as they made their way to one of the tall tables. Heads were already turning at the sight of Jason and Alia, hands lifted in greeting, beckoning them over. "The pool represents the Nile, and the windowed wall echoes the cliffs."

"You know what no one asked for?" Theo said. "Trivia."

Jason glanced at Theo. "Go find yourself some champagne."

Theo saluted. "That's my kind of ultimatum."

"Good riddance," Nim said as he loped off. "I don't know what it is about that guy, but I constantly want to shove him down a flight of stairs."

"I have a pretty good guess," murmured Alia.

"And he couldn't even be bothered to pay you a proper compliment," said Nim, her glare tracking Theo as he wended his way through the crowd.

"It's fine," said Alia, but Diana didn't think that was true.

"I appreciate that you made an effort," Jason said stiffly. His gaze touched briefly on Diana. "You look nice. All of you."

"Very smooth," said Nim. "You're lucky you're rich, or you'd never get any action at all."

Diana waited for Jason's sharp retort, but instead that broad grin reappeared, his dimple flashing. "You're forgetting how good-looking I am."

Alia rolled her eyes. "Can we just get this over with before I have to find a potted plant to throw up in?"

Jason straightened his cuffs, his sober demeanor returning as quickly as it had vanished. "Yes. But that's the last eye roll for the next hour, deal?"

"Wait, I need one more. You can't just cut me off like that." Alia rolled her eyes theatrically. "Okay, I'm good."

Jason's mouth pulled up at one corner, as if he was fighting not to grin again. "I expect smiles and an attempt to look like you're happy to be here."

"That wasn't part of the deal."

"Alia—"

Alia threw her shoulders back and pasted a cheerful smile on her face. "Better?"

"Slightly terrifying, but yes."

"Hold on," said Nim. "You need powder."

As Nim touched up Alia's makeup, Diana took the opportunity to murmur to Jason, "I saw the armed guards posted at the eastern and southern doors, as well as the entry."

"But—"

"They're spaced too evenly against the wall."

"I'm not a fool," said Jason. "There are members of the security team dressed as partygoers as well."

"Two by the buffet, one by the musicians, and at least three near the western perimeter."

Jason started, his surprise evident. "How the hell did you spot them?"

Diana frowned. It was obvious, wasn't it? "I can tell they're carrying weapons by the way their clothes hang. And they hold themselves differently than the other guests." Jason's eyes scanned the crowd, and she wondered if even he could tell where his people were. "Just stay alert," Diana said. "If I can spot them, our enemies may be able to as well."

She was prepared for a rebuke, but Jason simply nodded.

"Um, and you guys may want to keep moving," Diana said as a nearby waiter shoved another waiter, knocking his tray of food to the floor. "Don't stay in any one spot for too long."

She still didn't understand the limits of Alia's power or how it worked. It could reach across worlds, but proximity did seem to matter.

"Understood," said Jason.

"Are we doing this?" said Alia. "'Cause I'm thinking about drowning you in the punch bowl and just making a break for it."

Jason nodded and offered her his arm. Under his breath, he said to Diana, "Keep us in your sights."

"I'll try not to get in your way," she murmured.

He stiffened and then she saw the corner of his mouth twitch again. Still an imperious bully, but at least he could laugh at himself—and maybe he'd begun to realize she was an asset. She didn't want to fight him every step of their journey to the spring.

Diana spent the next half hour drifting through the party-goers with Nim, making sure to keep Alia and Jason within view. It wasn't easy. The room was crowded, and the way voices bounced off the stone set Diana's teeth on edge. She also felt like she was trying to read too many signals at once. She'd successfully picked out most of Jason's security team, but the party itself felt unwieldy.

On the surface, it didn't look radically different from the celebrations on Themyscira. Though the clothes might be cut differently, it was still a collection of people in silks and satins, glasses in hand, some bored, others eager. But there was something odd about the way the crowd separated and then re-formed. The men would step forward to greet each other as their female companions hung back, then a moment later the women would engage, shake hands, possibly embrace. Power moved in its own way here, driven by unseen currents, and it eddied and flowed primarily around the men.

I don't belong here. The thought echoed loudly through her head, but she wasn't sure if it was her voice or the Oracle's that spoke with such conviction. She shoved the thought away. In an hour, she'd be on her way to Greece. By this time tomorrow, they'd have reached the spring and her quest would be at its end. For these few moments, she could let herself enjoy the newness of this place.

She noticed Nim murmuring names under her breath. "Do you know everyone here?"

"No, but I know who they're wearing." She reeled off a series of Italian-sounding names.

"More trivia?"

"*Information.* Design is all about conveying information. This whole room was built to convey messages you don't even know you're receiving. The sightlines, the way the tiles are laid into the floor."

"You see the world differently."

"Seeing is easy. The hard part is being seen. It's why I'm always trying to get Alia to go out more." Nim plucked a skewered shrimp from a passing server. "When I started at Bennett, it felt like everywhere I went people weren't seeing me. I mean, they *saw* me. Boy, did they see me. But I was just the short, fat Indian kid who brought weird food for lunch."

"What changed?" asked Diana.

"Alia. She was the first person to look at my designs and tell me they were good. She even wore one of the first dresses I made to a dance. It was truly hideous." Diana had to laugh, but that did seem like something Alia would do. "She's always been the one to prop me up," said Nim, "and make me stick with designing."

"What about your family?"

"Please. They *have* to tell me I'm a good designer. That's their job."

Diana thought of her mother saying, *I didn't expect you to win.* "Not necessarily."

"Oh man, do you have one of those tough-love families? I just don't buy into that."

"Why not?" Diana asked cautiously.

"Because the whole world loves to tell us what we can't do, that we aren't good enough. The people in your own house should be on your side. It's the people who never learn the word *impossible* who make history, because they're the ones who keep trying."

The very air seemed to crackle around her as she spoke. Diana considered telling Nim she'd make a great general, but opted for "Alia is lucky to have you as a friend."

"Yeah, well, we're both lucky. I don't know many people who would put up with me."

Alia caught sight of them by the reflecting pool and separated herself from the couple she and Jason were speaking to, scurrying over to them as if afraid Jason would snatch her back.

"Please kill me," she moaned. "My cheeks ache from smiling, and my toes are throbbing in these shoes. I swear this is the longest hour of my life."

"Boohoo. Big party where everyone wants to meet you," said Nim. "And don't you dare speak ill of those shoes. They're perfection."

"I can't tell if your brother is pleased," Diana said, glancing over at Jason, who was listening intently to someone and nodding his agreement. He seemed at ease, his posture relaxed, but Diana could see the tension in his shoulders. He held himself as if on guard, unsure of where the attack might come from, but certain it would come nonetheless. "He doesn't like these parties, either, does he?"

"You noticed?" Alia said, scanning the crowd. "I hate who he becomes at these things. It's like he's an actor in a play. He smiles and chatters, but I know he hates every minute of it."

"Speaking of hating every minute," Nim said, her expression turning sour. Theo was headed their way. "I cannot take his nonsense right now. I'm going to go ask Gemma Rutledge to dance."

"Is she gay?" asked Alia.

"Who cares? She's wearing Badgley Mischka. I just want a better look at the dress."

"Aw," said Theo as he approached with two full flutes of champagne, "I chased Nim off. Such a shame. I swear that girl gets worse and worse."

Alia pursed her lips. "Leave Nim alone."

"Will do. All alone."

"And what are you doing with champagne? None of us are old enough to drink."

Theo took a big gulp from one of the glasses. "Don't tell me you're going to send me packing, too."

Diana followed Theo's gaze to where Jason had moved on to a group of young men, all of them with summer tans and artfully shaggy hair. Their raucous laughter, the way they took up the space around them, reminded her of the businessmen on the train. And there was something in the way they surveyed their surroundings. . . . "They look at the room as if they own it."

"You don't say," said Theo.

"Some of their fathers are on the board," said Alia. "Jason's just doing his job."

"By joining the Legion of Bros?"

"Are they a club?" asked Diana.

"Pretty much," said Theo. "And Jason's hoping if I'm not around they'll forget he's black and teach him the secret handshake."

Diana took a longer look at Jason, remembering what Alia had said about how the world saw her. Maybe Jason had good reason for the wary way he carried himself.

"Think of it like this," Alia said. "If Jason waved you over, you'd actually have to make conversation with those guys."

Theo shuddered. "They'd probably make me talk American football."

169

"And how much they love the Red Hot Chili Peppers."

Theo hissed. "Stop it."

"And Dave Matthews," Alia said ominously.

Theo threw his arms over his head. "You monster."

Alia waggled her fingers at him. "And how they once saw Jimmy Buffett live at Myrtle Beach!"

Theo flopped across the table as if he'd been grievously wounded. "Save me, New Girl," he rasped. "You're my only hope."

Diana had no idea what they were talking about, or the names of the demons Alia was invoking, but she moved one of the candles out of the way so Theo's sleeve wouldn't catch fire. "There," she said. She nodded toward Jason, who had detached himself from his friends and was heading toward them. "I'm afraid your reprieve may be over, Alia."

"Quick," she said, "stuff me under the buffet."

"Too late," Theo said, righting himself and taking another gulp of champagne.

"Have you come to drag me back already?" Alia asked Jason.

"You made a commitment."

"Alia!" said a booming voice, and Diana saw Theo flinch. A barrel-chested man with a salt-and-pepper beard approached the table, with another man in tow. He swept Alia into a hug, then stepped back to look at her. "It's been too long. Jason said you had summer travel plans."

Alia smiled. "I didn't want to miss the chance to meet some of the Foundation donors."

Diana was impressed with how smoothly Alia lied, even as she realized how easy it must have been for her to pretend she intended to visit the spring with Diana or to toss the cell phone into the bag, knowing her brother would use its signal to track them. *Remember that*, she warned herself. *For all the dresses and the laughter and the ease you feel, remember how little you know these people, how easily deception comes to them.*

"I'm delighted you're here and taking an interest," said the bearded man. "You should have seen your brother at the board meeting earlier. He's a natural."

"I had a good teacher," Jason said, though he looked pleased.

"Dad has always been great at telling people what to do," said Theo, taking a swig of champagne. *Dad.* So the bearded man was Michael Santos, Theo's father and Alia and Jason's godfather. Next to him, they looked impossibly young.

Michael chuckled easily, but the mirth didn't reach his hazel eyes. "I can always count on Theo to keep my ego in check." He turned away from his son. "Alia, Jason, this is Dr. Milton Han. He's doing fantastic work in environmental remediation, and I think he could take Keralis Labs in some interesting directions."

Dr. Han shook Jason's hand. "I knew your father at MIT. He was one of the smartest and most creative thinkers I ever met."

"I can assure you we're continuing in that tradition."

"I was just reading about some exciting work in biofuels," said Alia. "Is your research focused primarily on the use of bacteria for waste disposal or conversion?"

Dr. Han seemed to startle, as if he was actually looking at Alia for the first time. "Ideally conversion, but that may be a long way off."

Theo laughed softly and said under his breath, "Do *not* test Alia Keralis, Girl Genius."

Diana remembered what Nim had said: *The hard part is being seen.* She wasn't sure what Theo saw when he looked at Alia, but he was certainly paying attention.

As Alia and Jason fell into conversation with Dr. Han, Diana heard Michael mutter to Theo, "Getting a quick start, I see." He glanced at the two glasses in Theo's hands.

Theo's smile faltered, but he just said, "Aren't you always telling me to apply myself?"

"What are you doing here? This is an important night."

Theo downed the glass. "Jason wanted me here, so I'm here. Shocking, I know."

"You will not embarrass us tonight," Michael whispered furiously. "Not when so much is on the line."

"Have you met Diana?" Theo said. "Diana, this is my father, Michael Santos. The savior of Keralis Labs. He's quite the strategist, but not what I would call a lot of fun."

Michael ignored him and offered Diana his hand. "A pleasure. Are you one of Alia's friends from Bennett? She's usually with that pudgy little Indian girl."

"I'm not sure who you mean," said Diana, feeling her anger prickle. "I've only met her friend Nim, the brilliant designer."

Theo beamed and held up his remaining glass of champagne. "How about a sip to wash the taste of your foot from your mouth?"

"Just make yourself scarce," hissed Michael.

"I would," said Theo loudly, stepping past his father. "But I promised Alia a dance."

Alia looked over. "You did?"

Theo snatched her hand and bowed theatrically. "You're not going to change your mind, are you?" He dragged her after him to the dance floor. "My fragile heart couldn't take it."

With a nervous glance at Dr. Han, Michael laughed again. "Spirited boy. If he would just apply himself the way Jason does."

But Diana wasn't listening; her attention was focused on Alia vanishing through the crowd. Her gaze met Jason's, and he held out his hand. "I'm so sorry, Dr. Han," he said. "But I have the uncontrollable urge to dance."

Diana's brows shot up. Maybe not all mortals excelled at subterfuge.

She took Jason's hand, and they wended through the partygoers to the dance floor. Diana allowed herself a small sigh of relief when she spotted Alia and Theo swaying together in the spangled light. Alia was laughing and seemed to be all right, but Diana didn't intend to lose sight of her, no matter how many guards Jason had posted.

Jason led her onto the dance floor, sliding his hand beneath the golden fall of the lasso shawl as he drew her closer, his fingers brushing the bare skin of her back. She stiffened, then flushed when she realized he'd noticed.

"I have to touch you if we're going to dance," he said, sounding bemused.

"I know that," Diana replied, bothered by the edge to her voice. "We don't dance like this where I'm from." Alia laughed again, and Theo spun her beneath his arm and into a dip. "Or like that, for that matter."

It was comforting to focus on Alia and Theo instead of the scrap of distance between her body and Jason's. Why should standing so close to someone make her pulse jump? Was it simply because he was a male? *It's a novelty*, she told herself. Or maybe it was because, poised this way, her hand clasped in his, their bodies separated by a breath, felt almost like the moment before an embrace. Or a fight. Why couldn't they just wrestle again? That had been easier. And she would win.

Jason pressed his hand firmly to her back, and she nearly lost her footing.

"What are you doing?" she asked, more irritably than she'd meant to.

"I'm trying to lead."

"Why?" It was hard enough to manage these strange movements in new shoes and a borrowed dress without him jostling her around.

"Because that's the way it's done."

"That's a lazy answer."

He huffed a small, surprised laugh. "Maybe it is," he said. "This is how I learned. I guess I don't know how to do it any other way."

Diana felt something in her relax. "I like it when you're honest," she said, realizing the truth of the words as she spoke them.

"When I make my case like a human?" he said, a grin in his voice.

She let herself yield to the pressure of his hand, the tilt of his body—for now. Dancing might not be quite like fighting, but you still had to be careful when someone stepped into your guard.

"Better," he murmured. "Next time, you can lead."

What next time? she wanted to ask.

Alia's laugh floated over the crowd, and Jason swung Diana around gracefully, cutting through the other couples so they could keep Alia and Theo in view—they were laughing, breathless, hands clasped, spinning in a tipsy circle. Theo's style of dancing was definitely more theatrical than Jason's.

"I don't hear Alia laugh enough," Jason said.

"I suspect she'd say the same of you."

His shoulders lifted slightly in a shrug. "Maybe. She needs to meet more people, have more fun, but with the danger . . ."

"She's having fun now."

"Well, I don't want her having too much fun. Not with Theo."

Given the display with his father, Diana wasn't sure Theo was the best thing for Alia, either. Even so, it was hard not to think of what Theo had said about Jason not wanting him around. "I thought you were friends."

"We are. But Theo isn't exactly . . . steady. He falls in and out of love like a kid on a waterslide. Falls hard, hits bottom, wants to go again."

"His father seems to agree."

Jason winced. "I know. He's too rough on Theo, but I understand his frustration. Theo's brilliant. He can write code, hack pretty much any security system. He just seems to want to spend all of his time gaming."

"Is that so bad?"

"He could make a lot of money at it, if that's what you mean."

"It isn't," Diana said, annoyed.

"I just think he could do a lot of good, if he wanted to." Jason lifted his arm, his other hand pressing at Diana's back so she spun in a tight circle, the lights of the room whirling past. "But Theo doesn't want to listen to me any more than Alia does."

"No one likes to be told what to do. You've chosen a future. Alia deserves the same chance."

"She isn't ready. She trusts too easily. Case in point, you."

This again. Jason's wariness was understandable, but his assessment of his sister was so wrongheaded. She pulled back a little so that she could look at him. "Alia didn't trust me because she's naive. She leaned on me because she had to."

"And now you've conveniently gained access to our home and a party full of some of the most powerful people in New York."

"There is nothing convenient about this for me."

Jason hissed in a breath and Diana realized she was clutching his hand like a vise as her anger rose. His hand gripped her waist, drawing her closer, his gaze fierce.

"What brought you here, Diana Prince? How do you fight the way you do? How did you identify my security team?"

Part of her wanted to pull away, but she refused to retreat. Instead, she leaned in, so close their mouths were almost touching. His eyes widened.

"Do you really think you'll get the answers you want by trying to bully me?" she asked.

He swallowed, then seemed to regain his composure. "I tend to be very good at getting what I want."

Diana's chin lifted. "I think you've grown too used to people saying yes to you."

"Have I?"

"But you have no idea how much I enjoy saying no."

The corner of Jason's mouth curled, his dimple flashing briefly, and Diana felt an unexpected surge of triumph.

"You think I'm a bully," he said, shifting his weight with ease, using his momentum to guide her.

"Yes."

"A jerk?" He took another smooth, sure-footed step, his thigh brushing hers as they glided through the crowd.

"Yes."

"A budding tyrant?"

That seemed a bit extreme, but she nodded anyway.

Jason laughed. "You may be right." He took advantage of her surprise to spin her. The lights of the room whirred around her, and she felt the swell of the music rise up through the floor as he drew her back into his orbit. "I know what people think of me. I know I'm not fun the way Theo is or charming the way my parents were. None of this comes easy to me. But I also know I'm fighting for the right things."

She envied his certainty, the conviction in his voice.

"How can you be so sure?" she asked.

"Because I know what it would mean to lose them. Alia wants me to let Michael do more of the work, enjoy myself. She doesn't understand how fast we can be on the outside of what our parents created, with no way back in."

Diana thought of her mother sitting at the table in the Iolanth Court, speaking to one Amazon after another, the long meetings and debates and dinners, Diana waiting, always waiting for a moment of her time. *I can never be seen to be shirking my duties,* she'd said. *To the Amazons, I must always be their queen first and your mother second.* Diana hadn't really understood, hadn't wanted to. *Can't Tek do it?* she'd asked. But Hippolyta had only shaken her head. *If Tek does the work, then the Amazons will begin to see her as their queen, and rightly so. It must be me, Diana. And one day, when I grow weary of this work and this crown, it will be you.*

"What?" said Jason. "I can see you want to say something, so spit it out."

Diana met his eyes. "When you ride, your mount learns the feel of the hands that hold the reins; it gets used to responding to those commands. There's danger in letting someone else take the reins for too long."

A troubled expression passed over Jason's face. "That's it exactly." He spun her again, and this time, when he drew her back to him, there was a hesitancy she hadn't sensed before.

"What is it?" she asked, looking over her shoulder at Alia. "Is something wrong?"

"She's fine," said Jason. "Everything's fine. It's just, you're the only . . ." The muscles of his shoulder bunched beneath her hand, and he gave an almost-irritated shrug. "Everyone always just tells me to relax."

Uptight. High-strung. Alia and Diana had both used those words to describe Jason. But maybe he was so focused because he couldn't afford not to be.

"Michael must understand," she ventured.

But Jason's frown deepened. "My parents trusted Michael implicitly. Sometimes I worry they trusted him too much." He cast her a guilty glance, and she realized how dangerous a dance could be. The music, the glow of the lights, this half embrace. It was too easy to speak secrets, to forget the world waiting beyond the last note of the song. "That isn't fair. He's done a lot for our family. Still . . ."

Diana looked over at Alia and Theo and saw him give her another wild spin. "Still?" she prompted.

"There were a lot of people with a lot to gain from my parents' death. Michael didn't buy into the conspiracy theories. He made sure there was a full investigation, and there was nothing suspicious. The roads were wet. My parents were arguing."

"But you think there's more to it."

"You don't understand." He took a long breath. "They'd been arguing more and more."

Despite the heat of the room, a chill settled over Diana's shoulders. "You think that Alia was the reason?"

"I don't know. If her power—"

"You seem immune to it," Diana protested. "Your friendship with Theo has thrived. You and Nim spar, but you seem genuinely fond of each other."

"But what if our mother and father weren't immune? What if . . . what if they weren't fighting because of problems at the lab or because they'd fallen out of love? What if . . . I don't know."

"Sure you do," Alia said. She was standing right next to them in her dress of gold scales, Theo beside her, his hand still at her waist. Her dark eyes were wide and startled, the pain in them a palpable thing. "You think I killed them."

"Alia, no, that isn't what I meant—"

"Then what *did* you mean, Jason?"

Diana hated herself for being so thoughtless, for losing herself in the questions Jason had posed.

"I—I only—" Jason stuttered. "I didn't—"

"That's what I thought."

Alia turned on her heel and fled through the crowd.

Theo shook his head, looking at Jason as if he were a stranger. "Why would you say something like that?"

"It's complicated," Jason bit out. "You wouldn't understand."

Theo flinched as if Jason had struck him.

"Probably not," he said with an attempt at a disinterested shrug.

"I need to go find her," Jason said. "She's not—"

"No," said Diana. "I'll go."

"I'm her brother—"

And I understand what it's like to feel like your crime is just existing. Diana turned and hurried through the crowd before Jason could finish.

"Alia!" she called, wending through the partygoers.

Alia stumbled but kept moving. When she reached an empty corner near the back of the room, she leaned against the wall and shucked off her shoes, collecting them in one hand. With the other, she batted at the tears that had begun to fall.

Diana thought of Alia emerging from the bathroom in her golden mail, shoulders back, head held like a queen, and felt that something lovely had been lost.

She approached slowly, afraid Alia might take off running again. She said nothing as she took up a place against the wall beside her, and for a long while, they stood in silence, looking out at the partygoers, hidden by shadows broken by slices of colored light. She hesitated, unsure of where to start, but Alia spoke first.

"Why didn't they send me away?" she said, a flood of fresh

tears coursing over her cheeks. "If my parents knew what I was, why didn't they send me somewhere I couldn't hurt them?"

This at least was a place to begin. "You don't know that you caused the accident."

"Jason thinks I did."

"Jason was just talking, trying to ease his own mind. He doesn't blame you. He loves you."

"How could he *not* blame me?" A sob caught in her throat. "I blame me."

Diana struggled for words that might soothe her, and the only ones she found were those she'd whispered to herself when the island had felt too small, when Tek's barbs had felt too sharp. "We can't help the way we're born. We can't help what we are, only what life we choose to make for ourselves."

Alia gave an angry shake of her head. "Tell me some part of you doesn't wish you had never saved me," she said. "You and I both know I should have died in that shipwreck."

Hadn't the Oracle said much the same thing? Diana had almost believed it then, but she refused to believe it now. "If you'd drowned that day, if you died now, it would only be a question of time until a new Warbringer was born. If we reach the spring—"

"So what if we reach the spring?" Alia said furiously, then lowered her voice as a woman in a black taffeta gown cast her a curious glance. She pushed off the wall and turned to Diana, dark eyes blazing. "So what if it fixes me or purges me or whatever? It won't bring Dr. Ellis or Jasmine or the crew of the *Thetis* back. It won't bring my mom and dad back."

Diana took a breath and placed her hands on Alia's shoulders, desperate to make her understand. "My whole life . . . my whole life people have been wondering if I had a right to be. Maybe I don't. Maybe neither of us should exist, but we're here now. We have this chance, and maybe that isn't a coincidence. Maybe we're the ones who were meant to break this cycle. Together." Alia held her gaze, and Diana hoped her words were reaching her. "Your parents thought there might be a way to turn your power, the legacy of the Warbringer's blood, to something good. By going to the spring, you're fulfilling that promise in a different way."

Alia pressed the heels of her hands to her eyes as if trying to shove back her tears. "Diana, swear to me that if we don't make it, that if something happens, you'll end this. I can't be the reason the world goes to hell."

Diana dropped her hands. *I'm going to need you to kill me.* She'd hoped those words had been spoken in haste, that they were the result of shock and Alia would abandon such thoughts. "I can't do that. I . . . I won't commit murder."

"You pulled me from the wreck," Alia said, her voice hard with resolve. "You took me off that island. You can't ask me to live with all the rest."

A sick sensation settled in Diana's gut. Making this vow would mean turning her back on everything she'd been taught to believe. That life was sacred. That when it seemed violence was the only choice, there was always another. But Alia needed strength to continue, and maybe this grim excuse for hope was the only way to give her that.

"Then we make a pact," Diana said, though the words felt wrong in her mouth. "You agree to fight with everything you have to make it to that spring."

"All right. And if it isn't enough?"

Diana took a deep breath. "Then I will spare the world and take your life. But I want your word."

"You've got it."

"No, not a mortal vow. I want the oath of an Amazon."

Alia's eyes widened. "A what?"

"Those are my people. Women born of war, destined to be ruled by no one but themselves. We make this pact with their words. Agreed?" Alia nodded, and Diana placed her fist over her heart. "Sister in battle, I am shield and blade to you. As I breathe, your enemies will know no sanctuary. While I live, your cause is mine."

Alia placed her own hand over her heart and repeated the words, and as she did, Diana felt the power of the oath surround them, binding them together. It was a vow Diana had shared with no one else, one that might make her a killer. But she did not let her gaze falter.

"All right," said Alia on a shuddering breath. "Let's find Jason and get the hell out of here."

That was when the air tore open around them. A loud, staccato clamor filled Diana's ears. She knew that sound; she recognized it from the vision she'd glimpsed in the Oracle's waters. Gunfire.

CHAPTER 14

Diana covered Alia's body with her own, hurling them both to the ground as the ugly cacophony of gunshots filled the gallery, battering her senses. It was so much *louder* than in the vision.

"Alia—" she began, but her words were smothered by a thunderous *boom*.

The vast wall of windows shattered, dropping to the floor in a cascade of glass.

Diana kept Alia's body shielded, jagged bits of glass peppering her back and shoulders like wasp stings as people cried out around them.

Men in black body armor were rappelling in through the huge hole where the windows had been. They dropped to the floor near the reflecting pool as party guests scattered, screaming and racing for the doors, gunshots echoing through the room.

Diana dragged Alia behind the shelter of a table. "We have to get out of here."

"The others—" protested Alia.

The men were advancing from the opposite side of the gallery, tossing guests out of the way as they shone lights in the faces of the bodies that had fallen, examining their features.

They were clearly looking for someone—someone they didn't intend to take alive—and Diana knew she and Alia didn't have long.

She could smell the fear-tinged sweat of the partygoers, feel her heart racing in her chest, as if she'd woken suddenly from sleep. She tugged at the knots in the shawl Nim had made of her lasso. There wasn't time to untangle them all. The one weapon she had was useless.

"We can't just stay pinned down here," Diana said, shrugging off the knotted rope and tying it around her waist to keep it from constricting her movements. "We have to make a break for the doors."

"I don't see the others," Alia said, peering around the table. "We can't leave without them."

Though Diana's heart was pounding, her thoughts were clear as she adopted and discarded strategies, her mind turning over the layout of the room, calculating the positions of their assailants. The other guests were trying to crowd through the room's two doorways, shoving and pushing at one another in their panic, but she suspected the soldiers would have already barricaded the hallways and would move to seal the doors. Any time someone tried to escape through the shattered glass wall, a bullet struck them down. Diana scanned the shadows of the wide balcony above the reflecting pool where she knew snipers must be lurking.

A bullet struck the slate floor beside the table, sending up a puff of pulverized stone. Diana wondered what a gunshot might do to her, but there was no time to worry about it. She had to get Alia to safety.

"Diana!" The shout came from the other side of the temple, barely audible in the chaos. Jason and Theo were crouched behind another table. She met Jason's eyes and gestured toward the rear of the temple. It was the one spot in the room that provided a defensible position with any kind of real cover. If Diana could get Alia there, she would have time to locate Nim and maybe figure out an escape plan.

"I'll find Nim," she said. "But we need to get you behind that temple. We can't just sit here and wait for them to flank us."

"Okay," Alia said, "okay." But Diana wasn't sure how much of what she was saying was getting through. Alia was breathing hard, her eyes wide, her pupils dilated.

"When I count three, I want you to roll right and get behind the next table, understand? That's how we're going to do it. I count three, you move, no time for hesitation. We're going to get you to Jason and Theo."

"Promise me you'll find Nim."

"Your cause is mine," said Diana.

Alia blinked as if her terror had driven the meaning of the vow from her mind. "All right," she said, then clutched Diana's wrist. "Be careful."

Diana felt a grim smile on her lips. She was afraid, but swelling against that fear was a tide of exhilaration. Her fight with Jason in the hotel hallway had been a tussle. This was a battle. Suddenly, she didn't feel like being careful at all. Was this what it meant to be an Amazon? A sword's edge went dull if left unused too long. She was ready to hone her blade.

"On three." She slid into a crouch. "One." She braced her hands against the table's legs. "Two." She nodded to Alia. "Three!"

She waited only long enough to see Alia drop and roll, then flipped the table on its side in a clatter of dishes. Gunfire rattled off its surface. She ripped the metal legs from the table, seized it by its edges, and hurled it with all her might.

It spun through the air like a huge discus and crashed into the phalanx of soldiers, but she didn't stop to watch them topple. She leapt behind the next table, slamming gracelessly into Alia as a spate of bullets followed her.

"Again!" she yelled.

Alia rolled and Diana tossed the table, diving to the ground as gunfire chased her tumbling form. She hissed as a bullet grazed her shoulder—more like a burn than a sword slice.

Diana heard boots thundering over the ground. "They're coming around. Keep moving!" she commanded Alia.

But it was too late—a soldier had flanked them on their left. She saw him raise his gun, fire. She threw her body in front of Alia's and felt the bullets strike her arm, her side. Pain like she'd never known hammered at her body in sharp, reverberating jabs, each gunshot a fist of fire that drove the breath from her lungs. She heard a loud *ping* as a bullet struck the bracelet on her arm and looked down. It hadn't even made a dent. But the ricochet . . .

"Are you hit?" Alia gasped from beneath her. "Are you hurt?"

"I'm fine," she said. But that wasn't quite true. Though she wasn't bleeding, her skin was covered in red welts, and her body ached as if she'd taken the worst beating of her life. Maybe bullets would have glanced off an Amazon at the height of her strength. Diana just knew she didn't want to get shot again.

With a click, the soldier on their left slammed home a second clip and readied to fire again. A shot sounded and a circular black wound appeared on the soldier's thigh. He screamed and crumpled to the ground, clutching his leg.

Jason peeked out from behind the temple, the gun from his ankle holster in hand, and gave her the briefest nod.

"Alia, I need you to run for the temple. Get to Jason. I'll cover you."

"How?" Alia cried. "You don't have a weapon."

I am the weapon, she thought. "Just go."

"I'm not going to leave you to be slaughtered."

"Alia, now!"

Alia ran. This time when Diana threw the table, she stood her ground. *This is madness*, railed a voice in her head, but by then ten soldiers were opening fire.

She didn't stop to think, just let herself react. Time seemed to slow as the air came alive in a hail of bullets. This was like no sparring match or staged skirmish, and some part of her knew it.

Her muscles responded with effortless speed, instinct guiding her movements. She forgot her pain as she barreled toward the line of men facing her down, deflecting their gunfire as she ran. The bullets made silver streaks in her vision, strange music as they clanged against her bracelets, their impact like the hard patter of rain on a metal roof.

She rolled into a somersault, came up, glimpsed sparks glinting from her wrists as another shower of bullets flew. She could hear triggers being pulled, the jangle of the metal casings hitting the floor, smell an acrid heat that she knew was gunpowder.

"What the hell?" she heard someone cry as she crashed into the row of men, breaking their ranks, sending them flying into the remaining tables. She felt hands seize her as the soldiers who hadn't been knocked down fell upon her in a wave, trying to wrestle her to the ground. They were kindling in her hands, insubstantial. She threw them off, and one struck the temple's gate hard enough to buckle the stone pillar.

Is this all you are? something inside her demanded. *Cowards clutching your guns? Give me a challenge.*

Diana heard a high, whining sound, like the rising shriek of a firework. From across the reflecting pool, another man was aiming something at her. It was far larger than the other weapons, its barrel terminating in a wide, ugly mouth.

"Diana, get down!" screamed a voice.

Nim. She was on the floor where the musicians had been gathered, their instruments now abandoned. Her face was tearstained, the heavy kohl that lined her eyes trickling down her cheeks, and Diana saw a pretty blonde in an elaborate gown lying motionless beside her.

Panic flooded Diana's body as that high whine reached a crescendo. Her muscles itched to dive, evade, run. Instead, she listened to the fighting instinct that had been trained into her over countless hours in the Armory, that had flowed into her with her mother's blood and the blessing of the gods—the warrior's call that refused to let her flinch. If she didn't have a shield, she would make one.

The floor was set with huge slate tiles. She flattened her palms and drove her fingers into the narrow space between two of them, ignoring the pain, and yanked the slab upward.

The man with the big gun fired. Diana glimpsed a flash of glowing blue light and a wall of pressure slammed into her, knocking her off her feet and hurling her backward, the slab blown to dust in her hands. She struck the wall, breath releasing in a grunt, and slid to the floor. Then she was back on her feet, shaking off the force of the impact. What *was* that thing?

Diana heard that electrical whine begin again as the weapon repowered—but this time the soldier was aiming toward the temple. Her mind registered Jason trying to herd partygoers to shelter, her ears plucking the steady command of his voice from the chaos. She couldn't see Alia, but she had to be behind the temple with Theo.

Diana knew she wouldn't reach the gunman in time to stop him from firing. She looked down at the tiles fitted together on the floor. She needed reinforcements. Maybe they could be her army. She took a running leap toward the soldier and came down hard, foot and fist connecting with the ground at the same time. The tiles lifted in a rippling wave, and the man with the pulse gun screamed as the floor heaved beneath his feet. He toppled.

Diana sprang toward him, seized the weapon from his arms, and snapped it in two. He skittered backward in a crouch, his eyes wide and terrified.

He drew his sidearm and fired, but her mind had registered his intention in the shift of his shoulders. Her wrists were already moving to deflect the bullets, bracelets clanging like finger cymbals in some bloody dance. One of the bullets pinged off her right wrist and struck his thigh. He yelped. She grabbed him by his collar.

"What are you?" he gasped.

A hundred answers came to mind, but she opted for the easiest one. "A tourist."

She tossed him into the reflecting pool.

Diana wrenched two more slate slabs from the edge of the pool, stepped back, and hurled them at the snipers on the balcony. It was a bit like trying to knock down ceramic targets with her Amazon sisters. Except these targets grunted or whimpered instead of exploding into pieces.

The other soldiers around her were recovering, getting to their feet. Diana raced toward Nim and grabbed her under one arm.

Nim squeaked but thankfully didn't fight her. Diana wasn't sure how much she'd seen, how much any of them had seen of what she could do—what she hadn't even known she could do— but she couldn't think about that now.

Again, she heard weapons being cocked. This time she was ready for the gunfire that would follow. She dove to the floor, protecting Nim's body from the fall, and rolled until they were at the back of the temple. Alia grabbed hold of Nim and hugged her tight as they both sobbed and another round of gunfire erupted through the air.

"You made it," said Jason on a grateful gasp. He squeezed out a couple of shots from behind the additional cover he'd constructed from a stack of tables, and Diana saw that he'd managed to get a fair number of guests behind the temple. Some were still crowded against the room's exits, trying to push through the doors, but at least snipers were no longer picking them off.

Diana and the others crouched in a knot against the temple wall. They didn't have much time. She could see the fear in their faces as Alia held tight to Nim and Theo. Jason's eyes were bright, his jaw clenched. Only he looked ready for a fight.

"They're going to blow the temple," Diana said as loudly as she dared over the roar of gunfire.

"The helicopter—" Alia began.

Jason shook his head. "It was on the roof." The men had rappelled down from above. The roof must be compromised.

The gunfire stopped.

In the eerie silence, Diana could hear the soldiers' murmurs and shouts. They were speaking a language different from Alia and Jason's, but Diana understood it. *German*, she realized, and they kept repeating the same word: *Entzünderin*. Igniter. They might have been talking about the bombs, but Diana had a feeling they were referring to Alia.

"They're setting explosives," she said.

Nim's eyes were dazed. "They're going to blow up the museum?"

Theo gave his head a sharp shake. "What is all this? What do they want?"

"We'll explain when we're out of here," said Jason.

"*If* we get out of here," said Alia. "There's no helicopter—"

Jason's brow furrowed. "What if I can get the jet here?"

"Where would it land?" said Theo. "You can't put that on the roof. We need a runway."

"The Great Lawn," offered Nim.

"It's a long sprint to the park," said Alia.

Jason bobbed his chin toward the blocked doors. "First we have to get out of this room."

"You'll get out," said Diana. "I'll make sure you do."

Jason jabbed at his phone and spoke rapidly into it.

Diana had no idea how feasible a landing was, but she had to believe there was a way out of this, not just for Alia but for the people who had put on their best finery and come here to drink and dance tonight. She could sense their mortal lives flickering, fleeting as the shine of fireflies under glass.

"Ben's coming," said Jason. "We need to get to the park."

Thank all the gods. They had a chance. But the only way out was the wall of shattered windows to their left, and it was far too exposed. Diana couldn't be a shield for everyone, and all it would take was a single stray bullet, the right moment, the right angle. She couldn't let that happen. They needed cover. A lot of it. She touched her hand to the temple stone and wondered if she was strong enough to do what she was imagining.

"I can give you enough cover to make a break for the glass wall. I'll meet you below."

Alia gripped her arm, her eyes bright with fear. "You're not coming?"

"They're barricading the rest of the guests in. I won't leave innocent people here to die."

"Diana—"

"Stay with Jason; he'll keep you safe."

"They're too well armed," said Theo. "You won't make it."

"Stay low. When I give the signal, you bolt for the closest corner of the window wall."

"How will we know—" Alia said.

"Trust me, you'll know. This temple is coming down, and you need to be on the other side of it when it does."

Jason offered her his gun. "At least take this."

She lifted a brow. She was not afraid of these men, only of the harm they might do others, and she would not resort to playing with their ugly toys. "I'm going to choose to ignore this insult, Jason Keralis. Now *go*."

As soon as they were moving, Diana wedged her shoulder against the wall of the temple. She thrust her weight against the ancient stones, her battered muscles straining, feeling every aching spot where a bullet had struck. She dug her feet into the slate floor, reaching for strength that seemed just out of her grasp. What if she'd reached the limits of her might and she couldn't protect them? *No.* She refused that thought. She sucked in a breath and doubled her effort, grunting with the strain, the threads of her dress popping.

"I am never wearing anything without straps again," she growled.

Something in the temple creaked. Diana whispered a quick prayer to the goddesses, begging that they would seek Isis's forgiveness on her behalf, and *pushed*. The stone beneath her palms shuddered.

"Now!" she shouted.

The temple collapsed with a thunderous roar, sending a huge plume of dust into the air. She drove her legs forward, and the wide heap of stone groaned as it slid into place, blocking off the northwest corner of the window wall—the perfect barricade to keep the soldiers at bay as Alia and the others escaped.

But now the party guests were shouting and running, crowding up against the sealed doorways. She needed a battering ram. Her eyes lit on one of the fallen pillars of the temple. It was huge and unevenly weighted, the stone rough beneath her palms, but she managed to balance the column in her arms. She didn't know what the soldiers had erected to keep the exit doors shut, but she was going through.

"Move or be crushed!" she commanded as she launched herself toward the exit, surprised by the authority that rang through her voice. *Well*, she thought, *all those years listening to Tek give orders ought to be good for something.*

It seemed to work because the crowd scrambled to get clear.

She tightened her grip and drove the pillar into the doors. They gave way with a terrible crash, scattering the wall of sandbags the men had erected behind them. Diana's momentum carried her into the hallway, past stunned men in body armor. She released the pillar, and it slammed into the wall.

Partygoers poured toward the confused soldiers as Diana tried to fight the tide back to the temple room. One of the men stepped into her path, gun raised.

"Who do you fight for?" he demanded. His hair was so blond it was nearly white and cropped close to his head. She grabbed him by the throat and the wrist and shoved him against the wall, knocking the weapon from his hands.

"Get out of my way."

She strode past him, but he seized her arm. "Our cause is just," he said pleadingly. "Stop her. The Warbringer must die before the reaping moon. You cannot know the horrors that will be unleashed."

"She's a girl, and she deserves a chance," Diana said, and wondered if she was pleading her own case, too.

"Not at this price."

"Who are you to make such a calculation?"

"Who are *you*?" said the soldier.

Diana gazed into his determined blue eyes. He was right. She was gambling with the future of the world. Under other circumstances, they might have been allies.

"Whoever your leader is," she said, "tell him there's another way. There's a cure, and we're going to find it."

"You're mad," he said. "The Warbringer must be stopped."

Maybe she was, but her choice was made. Diana slammed the soldier back against the wall. "Then try and stop us."

She ran past him, racing toward the window wall. She heard him shout, "Blow it! If we can't get the Warbringer, we can get her bodyguard."

From somewhere, she heard a tiny click, a button pressed, a fuse catching. She vaulted over the ruins of the temple, launching herself through the window wall. From behind her she heard an earsplitting explosion and felt a wave of heat at her back. It thrust her forward through the air. Her arms pinwheeled at her sides as the force of the bomb carried her too far too fast.

CHAPTER 15

Alia's lungs burned as she stumbled across East Drive, dodging the Saturday-night traffic, the screech of brakes and blaring car horns registering in rapid flashes as panic careened through her. She was aware of Nim's hand in hers, of the painful slap of her soles against the pavement. Then they were on the other side of the road and tumbling into the park. She tripped and fell as her feet struck the softness of green grass.

A *boom* sounded behind them, and Alia turned to see a cloud of flame blooming like an angry flower from the museum's flank before the petals curled in on themselves and the explosion receded.

Diana.

Nim was pulling on her arm. Jason was shouting. She told her feet to move, but she couldn't stop staring at the flaming wreck of the room where they'd just been, still lit by the museum's outdoor floodlights, as if no one had yet realized what was happening. But already she could hear sirens, see people pulling over to the side of the road. Where was Diana? If she'd made it out, she should be trailing after them, she should be crossing the road right now. But she wasn't. Maybe she hadn't made it. Maybe she was lying broken in the ruins of the temple. Maybe she'd been captured.

"Alia, we have to move. *Now.*" Jason seized her wrist and pulled her after them.

Alia cast a last look over her shoulder, and then they were charging through the trees, crashing toward the baseball diamonds. Jason was yelling into his cell phone as the Great Lawn came into view.

Alia heard a teeth-rattling shriek, and Jason threw his arms out. "Stop!"

"Holy crap," said Nim as a jet roared overhead, impossibly close, wheels brushing the tops of the trees.

They put up their hands as the wind battered them with a hail of dust and tiny pebbles. The jet touched down on the wide, empty expanse of the Great Lawn, sending up a fountain of dirt in its wake as the wheels tore into the earth and the plane bobbled wildly.

"Is there enough room?" Theo asked.

"The Great Lawn is fifty-five acres," Nim said.

"More trivia?" he yelled. "I just want to know if he has enough runway."

"This isn't my kind of runway," retorted Nim, but her voice was wobbly.

The little plane slowed, nearing the tree line.

"He's not going to make it," Jason said.

Alia clapped her hands over her mouth.

But the plane skidded to a halt mere feet from the trees.

Theo whooped as the jet turned in a slow, tight circle.

"Come on," said Jason.

As they bolted across the lawn, Alia cast another look back toward the trees, but the park was silent and dark.

The jet was painted blue and gold, the Keralis Labs logo—a golden *K* bracketed by laurel leaves—emblazoned on the side. Alia had been on it a few times before. As they drew closer, she could see the deep furrows the jet had left in the lawn.

The door on the side of the jet opened, and the stairs descended. A burly man with coppery hair leaned out and raised a hand in greeting.

"I guess the lines are better here than at JFK?" he said. Ben Barrows. He'd been flying with the family a long time. Alia remembered he was former military.

Jason herded them up the stairs and inside. "How did you do it, Ben?"

"Talent, grit, and a shit ton of luck," he said. "Sorry, kids."

"We were just shot at," said Theo, slumping onto one of the banquettes in the lounge area at the front of the plane. "I think our tender ears will survive."

"I'm gonna need you to get into a proper seat and buckle up for takeoff. All of you."

"Can you get us off the ground?" asked Jason.

"Yeah, but getting back on it is going to be trickier. We sustained some damage to the landing gear."

"How much trickier?"

"I can handle it. But we need to get out of here or we're going to have NORAD up our asses. I told Teterboro I needed to make an emergency landing, but they're going to notice I didn't reach LaGuardia. We don't get airborne pronto, we're not going to make it off the coast."

"Everyone, buckle up," Jason ordered. "Ben, get us in the air."

The others obeyed, strapping themselves into the row of seats facing the lounge.

Ben reached for the handle beside the door, but Alia grabbed his arm.

"Don't," she said. "We can't just leave her, Jason."

Ben hesitated, eyes moving from Alia to her brother.

Jason pointed at one of the empty seats. "Alia, get your ass in a seat. You saw that explosion—"

"We're not leaving without her."

"Ben," said Jason. "Do it."

Alia moved to block Ben, but Jason took her by the shoulders, forcing her away from the door and into a seat. Ben yanked the handle down, and the door began to close.

Jason's grip was like steel. *"Alia,"* he said angrily. "Diana was trying to protect you. We're all trying to protect you. We need to get out of here now or none of us is making it to the other side of this night."

The plane lurched forward, and Alia realized Ben was back in the cockpit.

A burst of gunfire sounded from outside.

"Um, guys?" said Nim.

Alia shoved against Jason, and when he didn't budge she turned and bit his hand. Hard.

He yelped, and she pushed away from him, scrambling past Theo and Nim to look through Nim's window, nearly falling against it as the plane rumbled over the uneven terrain, picking up speed.

Diana was racing across the Great Lawn, blue dress in shreds, dark hair streaming behind her. A group of soldiers exploded from the woods, close on her heels.

"Jason, she's coming!" Alia shouted.

Jason grabbed her arm again, trying to pull her back as the plane picked up speed and Theo and Nim braced themselves against their seats. "Those men are coming after *you*, Alia. To kill you."

Your cause is mine.

A voice crackled over the radio. "Learjet N-535T, we have emergency vehicles en route to crash site. Please report your status."

"Ben, if you take off, you're fired!" Alia yelled.

"She can't fire you!" Jason retorted.

"He signs the checks," Ben called over his shoulder.

"Alia, we have to go!" said Jason.

"Diana!" Alia shouted pointlessly, face pressed to the window.

As if she had heard her, Diana put on a burst of speed.

"Damn," said Theo. "That girl can run."

She almost seemed to be flying, her strides long. Alia could see that the fabric of her gown was singed, and there were welts on her skin, but she seemed whole and unharmed.

Alia braced her hand against the side of the jet and faced Jason. "Open the door," she demanded.

"We can't stop, Alia. There's not enough runway."

The jet jounced along, faster and faster.

"We need her help to get to the spring!" she insisted.

And she saw it then. The doubt that flickered over his face. Jason had agreed to go to the spring because he'd wanted to give her hope, but he'd never really believed.

"Jason, if you don't open that door, I will find a way to end my life before the new moon. I swear it on our parents' lives."

The words struck him like a slap. Alia almost regretted them, but if that was what it took to make him listen . . .

"Damn it," Jason swore. He strode to the door and yanked down on the handle. Immediately, an alarm began to sound.

Ben's voice crackled over the radio. "Don't know what you're doing back there, but this is your captain speaking, and he'd like you to cut it the hell out."

"Diana!" Alia screamed again. The door opened wider, spreading like a clamshell, the night air rushing through. Alia could see the brightly lit baseball diamonds and Diana hurtling toward the jet.

She shouted something, but Alia wasn't sure what. She was waving her arms frantically.

"Something's wrong," Alia cried, then realized it was a ridiculous understatement.

"No, you idiot," said Theo. "She's saying get out of the way."

Theo shoved up from his seat and yanked her away from the door just as Diana took two huge strides and *leapt*, launching herself through the air like a missile. She dove through the door of the plane, tucking into a somersault and slamming hard against the banquette. Gunfire pelted the side of the jet.

Jason jammed the handle up, and the door started sliding back into place as Alia's stomach lurched and the jet lifted off. She stumbled backward into Theo, nearly falling into his lap.

Jason threw her into a seat, hurling himself down beside her, and then they were in the air, climbing.

Alia heard a horrible crunching sound as the plane jolted and shook. *The wheels*, she realized. They'd scraped the tops of the trees. She dared to look down through the window as the plane arced over the park. Craning her neck, she could just make out the baseball diamonds, the men standing on the ruin that had been the Great Lawn.

She blinked, trying to clear her vision. For just a moment she'd thought— But that was impossible. Had she hit her head again? Were the fear and adrenaline playing tricks on her? She thought she'd seen what looked like a chariot drawn by four massive black horses cutting across the field toward the soldiers, floodlights glinting off the driver's plumed helmet. Alia gave herself a shake. She needed a good night's sleep. She needed a *month* of good night's sleep.

"Learjet N-535T, you are not cleared for takeoff," said the voice over the radio. "Report your status."

The crackle of static died as Ben switched off the radio. "My status is most likely looking at a career change," he said. "Everyone okay back there?"

"You tell me, Ben," said Jason.

"We're in a wait-and-see situation. If we triggered a scramble out of Barnes, we're going to know pretty quick when they shoot us down."

Alia swallowed hard. She peered through the window as the city lights gave way to the vast, unending black of the Atlantic. Would she see death coming? She tried to breathe, to leash her heart rate. Silence enveloped the cabin, the only sound the thrum of the jet's engines as they all waited, wondering what might be headed toward them in the dark.

Beside her, she saw that Jason had somehow managed to split his lip during the fight, and the sleeve of his jacket had become almost completely detached. Across the aisle, Theo had his head tipped back and his eyes shut. Alia didn't know if he was praying or if he'd actually fallen asleep. Past him, Alia could see Nim staring straight ahead. Her eyes were ringed with mascara, and there was blood on her jumpsuit; her chest rose and fell in rapid, panicked hitches. Alia wished she could put her arm around her, tell her it would be all right. But that was a lie. Nothing was all right. Maybe nothing would ever be right again.

Diana had pulled herself onto the cream-colored banquette and sat rigidly in place, fingers digging into the cushions. Alia realized she'd probably never been on a plane before. Her dress had been reduced to what looked like a bedraggled ice-skating costume. The fabric was charred black near its edges—all but the lasso in a tangle at her waist, still as pristine as it had been when they left for the party. Her skin was pink in places.

Where the bullets struck, Alia realized. The wounds had already healed.

Alia had known Diana was strong, that there was some kind of magic at work on her island, but this was different. She'd thrown tables like Frisbees. She'd leapt into a moving plane. She'd survived an explosion and a gunfight with little more than a few bumps and scratches.

Theo shook his head and laughed, the sound strange in the quiet cabin. "Damn, Jason. You really know how to throw a party."

Nim buried her face in her hands. Jason was watching Diana.

"What is she?" he muttered beneath his breath, low enough that only Alia could hear.

Amazon. Born of war, destined to be ruled by no one but herself. But that wasn't Alia's secret to tell.

"I don't really know," Alia said. "I'm just glad she's on our side."

CHAPTER 16

They sat in silence until Ben's voice came over the speaker. "You are now free to move about the cabin, fellow lawbreakers. We are clear."

Alia released a shuddering sigh of relief, and Jason gave her hand a squeeze.

Theo unbuckled his seat belt and stumbled over to the jet's bar by the banquettes. There was no turbulence, but Alia couldn't blame him for being unsteady on his feet.

"You're going to start drinking already?" said Nim, her tear-stained face bleak.

"No," said Theo. "I'm going to *continue* drinking."

"Theo," Jason said warningly.

"Would everyone relax?" he said. "I just want some ginger ale. My tummy gets upset when I fly, and almost dying doesn't help, either."

Alia wanted to laugh, but she was afraid she might just start crying. She felt shaken and exhausted now that the adrenaline was leaving her body, but she also felt grateful. Theo was alive. Nim was alive. Once again, Alia had evaded death. They'd all made it out. Maybe Diana was right and they *were* destined to survive and reach the spring.

Alia knew they needed to talk, but she wanted a chance to gather her thoughts and get cleaned up. The jet was equipped with a shower, so she retrieved her small travel case from where it had been stashed beside Diana's pack in the rear of the plane and headed into the bathroom to shed her golden scales.

The water was hot enough, but she didn't linger beneath it. She stepped out of the shower and stared at herself in the mirror. Her body was covered in new cuts and scrapes, and she knew she was going to have more bruises from all the tumbling and falling she'd done during the fight. She had blisters on her toes from those ridiculous shoes Nim had picked out.

She looked at the heap of finery and again felt the events of the night, of the last few days, threatening to overwhelm her, but she pushed that panic away. In a day, this would all be over.

Alia pulled on the jeans she'd packed and a ratty old T-shirt with a double helix on it that she'd gotten at science camp years ago. She frowned at her reflection as a memory came back to her: a brawl that had erupted at the closing picnic that year. She and the other kids had thought it was hilarious. They'd called it the Great Nerd Battle. But when the fight had been broken up and some semblance of calm had returned, Alia had heard two of the counselors talking. A boy had almost been choked to death by one of the staff, and a fire had been set in the dining hall. They were just lucky it hadn't spread. The camp had closed permanently after that.

At the time, it had just been something shocking for the campers to talk about, a story Alia brought home to her parents and Jason. But now she remembered her parents' expressions when she'd told them about the fight, the look they'd exchanged. From then on, they spent their summers traveling or at one of the family's houses. There were no more trips to camp.

Alia wasn't sure what to do with the wreck she'd made of her beautiful dress, so she crushed it into a ball and shoved it to the bottom of her bag. No doubt Nim would be appalled, but she couldn't bear to look at it. Thinking of how happy and hopeful she'd felt when she'd put that dress on, of how she'd imagined Theo looking at her in it, made her skin prickle with embarrassment. It seemed silly now, and dangerous, too. Diana had been right: The people pursuing her were relentless. They clearly had resources they were willing to use—on innocent people on a boat in the Aegean, and now in full view of some of the wealthiest members of New York society.

Alia untangled the pretty gold chain from her braids, pulled on her sneakers, and took a last look in the mirror. Warbringer. Had Helen's legacy passed through her father's bloodline? Through the Keralis name to Alia? It didn't matter. She was her mother's daughter, too. She'd thought it had taken all of her courage to leave New York and sign up for the trip aboard the *Thetis* without Jason's permission, but she'd been so wrong. That had been just a scrap of her courage. Since then she'd faced shipwreck, a near drowning, and a gunfight, and she was still here, still standing. She was going to make sure no girl ever had to live with this curse again. And Alia knew it was because of the way her mom had raised her. For all her mother's caution, she'd never wanted Alia to be meek. *Look them in the eye*, she'd always told her. *Let them know who you are.* When someone asked where you were *from*. When a new kid at Bennett wanted to know if she was on an athletic scholarship. *Look them in the eye.*

Another memory came to Alia—sitting in the office of the penthouse, her mother sliding a needle into her arm, the syringe filling with Alia's blood. "Just for tests," her mother had said, covering the injection site with a cotton ball and a Band-Aid, and planting a kiss on her cheek. Alia had never given it a second thought.

Her parents had believed something good could come from Alia's heritage, that the terrible power inside her might be turned to better purpose. They hadn't lived to make that a possibility, but

Alia could at least make sure the world didn't pay for their choice to keep her alive.

"I'm Alia Mayeux Keralis," she said, surprised by how steady her voice sounded. "And I'm going to stop a war."

She pulled her braids into a knot atop her head and returned to the front of the plane. Theo was sprawled out on one of the padded banquettes. Nim was still slumped forward with her head in her hands. Alia sat down next to her and gently bumped her shoulder against Nim's. "Are you okay?"

"No," Nim said into her palms.

"Gemma—"

"I watched her die," said Nim, still not looking at her. "No, that's not right. It happened too fast to watch. We were just talking. I was looking at the butterflies on her dress. I was thinking about the color, the bead count. I was thinking Gemma was pretty but"—Nim hiccuped a sob—"pretty but boring. And then people were screaming. We heard the gunshots. We tried to get down. Why did they shoot her?"

"I don't think they meant to," said Alia. *I don't think they cared.* She barely knew Gemma Rutledge, but she'd seemed nice enough. All of those people she'd been complaining about having to talk to had seemed nice enough. How many had been hurt? Killed? She held tight to Diana's promise that there was a purpose to this mission, that all of it would mean something if they could just get to the spring.

"There's a shower," Alia said. "And some Keralis Labs gear if you want to change."

Nim sat up, wiping the back of her hand across her eyes like a child woken from a deep sleep. "I don't want to change. I want to know what's going on. What just happened?" Her voice was pleading. "Why did Jason have a gun? Who are we running from?" She turned to Diana. "And how did you do those things?"

Diana sat cross-legged on the banquette, methodically untying the knots in her lasso. She said nothing, only shifted her gaze to Alia, waiting.

"Well?" said Theo, resting his glass of ginger ale on his stomach. "I think it's fair to ask what the hell is going on. Even if Nim is the one asking."

"Just shut up," said Nim. "What are you even doing here? What if your father didn't make it out of the party?"

"My father wasn't there."

"What?" said Jason. He'd disappeared into the back of the plane and emerged in jeans and a T-shirt. He set a pile of sweats on one of the seats and began to dig through the jet's medical kit.

"My father took off," said Theo. "He said he had to be on a call to Singapore or something. Good timing, right?"

"When was this?"

"I don't know," Theo said. "He wanted me to come with him. 'You're going to embarrass yourself, Theo, blah, blah, blah.' The usual stuff. It was right around Alia running off and us being shot at."

Alia felt something cold uncoil in her stomach. Could it be a coincidence? She met Jason's gaze and knew he was thinking the same thing. Could Michael be involved? What if he knew what she was? He'd been like a father to them both, but "like a father" wasn't a father. Maybe he'd been willing to make the sacrifice Alia's parents hadn't.

"Don't look so worried, guys," Theo said. "I'll call him when we're on the ground."

"No!" they said in unison.

Theo's brows shot up. "Why not?"

Jason pinched the bridge of his nose between his forefingers. "It's just really important that no one know where we are or where we're headed."

"Okay," said Nim. "Fine. How about you tell us why?"

Jason and Alia did their best. They answered question after question from Theo and Nim. At first the queries came fast and loud, one piling on top of another: Who had attacked them? Why? Were the gunmen terrorists? What did they want? Was it because of the Foundation? But as Jason calmly explained that these people had a different agenda in mind and Alia was at the center of it, Nim and Theo grew quiet.

Jason set the medical kit aside and handed around some of the files he'd printed, a copy of the scroll, and a laptop with the documents from the flash drive. Big chunks of text had been redacted from some of the files, and others seemed to be incomplete, but there were more than enough to make the point.

Alia felt a little like she was standing naked in the middle of Times Square. The story sounded so much less far-fetched with Jason telling it—especially with all of those documents to back him up. But that only made it worse. She'd pretty much accepted the fact that Theo was never going to see her as more than an annoying kid, but what if he looked at her now and saw a monster? And Nim had been her friend through everything, but "everything" had never included bringing about the end of the world.

When Theo finally looked up from Jason's files, he focused his attention on Diana. "What about you? What's your deal? Right now, my best guess is government super soldier."

"Government what?" said Diana.

"You know . . . like, genetically altered killing machine."

Diana clenched the pile of gleaming rope in her lap. "I'm not a killer." She said it with such conviction, her chin tilted at an almost regal angle. But the words of the vow they'd spoken still resonated through Alia. Diana would honor it.

"Okay, okay," said Theo. "Member of a bionic-ninja fight squad."

"I'm not trained as a ninja, either." Diana looked down at the lasso and said, "Where I come from, we train for war."

"Why?"

"Because men are incapable of living without fighting, and we know that one day the fight will come to us."

"But the things you did—" said Nim.

"I'm stronger, faster than . . . well, than ordinary people. All of my sisters are."

"And you can shrug off bullets like mosquito bites, knock over temples, and survive fiery explosions?" said Nim.

Diana opened her mouth, then closed it, as if uncertain what to say. In that moment, she looked less like the brave, self-assured girl who casually wrecked the egos of subway-going bros in business suits. She looked dazed, a little lost. Like a girl who'd stayed too late at a party and missed her ride home.

"Honestly, I'm not totally sure what I can do," Diana said. "I've never done it before."

"Well, you're one hell of a quick study," grumbled Jason as he extracted a roll of gauze and packets of what looked like aspirin from the medical kit. Alia wanted to reach across the aisle and slap him. She knew he was hungry for concrete answers, but Diana had saved their lives. She deserved to keep whatever secrets she wanted to.

"Let's say I choose to believe all this," said Nim. "What happens next?"

"We get to the spring," said Diana.

"In Sparta," said Theo, "where dudes run around yelling in leather undies."

"I've never heard that particular story," Diana said. "But Sparta is where Helen was born and raised, and where she was worshipped after her death."

That didn't sound right to Alia. "People worshipped Helen? I thought everyone hated her."

"There were those who did. But Helen wasn't just the cause of the Trojan War. She was a mother and a wife, and a girl once, too. There are stories that she used to run races along the banks of the Eurotas." Diana smiled slightly. "And she won."

It was strange to think of Helen before she was *Helen*. "Her tomb is in Therapne?" Alia asked.

"That's right," said Diana. "It's called the Menelaion, but before that it was known as Helen's Tomb. '*Where Helen rests, the Warbringer may be purified.*'"

Nim tapped her fingers against the frayed knees of her jump-suit. "Okay, so we just have to get to the spring before the bad guys get to Alia."

Alia wanted to say a long prayer of thanks that Nim seemed to be taking all of this in stride and hadn't tried to throw herself out of the airplane. But if they were going to tell the truth, they should tell all of it.

"Actually," said Alia, "I'm not sure they *are* the bad guys."

"They blew up the Sackler Wing of the Met," said Nim. "They're *monsters*."

Theo took a sip of his ginger ale. "Or maybe just not art lovers."

"They're people willing to do anything to see Alia dead," said Jason grimly. "And a lot of people lost their lives because of it."

"Right," said Theo softly. "Sorry."

Jason wasn't wrong, but Alia also knew that they were all deal-ing with their fear and horror as best they could.

She gestured to the laptop propped on the banquette. "From what I can see, plenty of people are looking to identify and eradi-cate Warbringers—"

"In other words, *you*," said Theo.

"Yes, me. And they have pretty good reasons."

Nim tossed her sheaf of black hair from her eye. "How good can their reasons be if they're trying to kill you?"

Alia sighed. "They don't know about the spring. They're just trying to stop a world war. So, according to everyone but present company, they're pretty good."

"That's perfect," said Theo, sitting up.

Jason crossed his arms. "How's that exactly?"

"We're the villains! It's always cooler to be the villain. You get to wear black and have a lair and brood. Besides, girls can't resist a bad boy."

"You are such an idiot," said Nim.

He tapped his temple. "It's not my fault you lack the vision."

Nim opened her mouth to reply and Alia cut in with a sharp,

"Hey! Have you guys ever noticed that you get along fine except when I'm around?"

"That's not true," said Theo. "We have never gotten along."

"Think about it. Do you go home and rant about how much you hate Nim?"

"I—" Theo hesitated. Even his locs looked like they were thinking. "Well, no. It's just when—"

"Just when you're around me. So next time you guys feel like killing each other, maybe take a break and go to your corners. Literally, just get away from me or each other."

Theo and Nim shared a skeptical glance.

"See?" said Alia. "You both think I'm nuts so you have something to agree on already."

"What will your people make of the attack on the museum?" Diana asked.

"I'm not sure," said Jason, his voice weary. "There's a lot of bad stuff happening around the world right now. They'll probably chalk it up to terrorism, an attack on the Foundation because of its international policies. We've had threats before, problems at some of our facilities abroad."

"But nothing on this scale," said Theo.

"No," said Jason. "Nothing with a body count."

"And do we have any idea who those particular good guys were?" Nim asked.

"They were speaking German," said Theo. "*Ich bin ein* blow the museum up."

Jason shuffled through a stack of files. "There are a number of international organizations who make it their business to try to track the Warbringer's bloodline. There used to be more, but either they've gone to ground or just died out. There's the Order of Saint Dumas, and a splinter group called Das Erdbeben that once operated out of Hamburg, but it's hard to tell which are real and which are fiction."

"Those bullets seemed awfully real," said Nim.

"But why now?" asked Alia. "Why wait until so close to the new moon to try to . . . get rid of me?"

Jason shifted uneasily in his seat and looked down at his hands. "I think that may be my fault."

"As long as it's not *my* fault," said Theo.

Alia waited, and Jason smoothed his thumb over the knee of his jeans. "Mom and Dad hadn't transferred a bunch of the old files to digital. I thought I should back everything up, make a record. So I scanned it all in—"

"On a Keralis Labs computer?" Theo said, sounding genuinely horrified for the first time since they'd started talking. "Were you even running encryption?"

"Yes," said Jason. "And we have all kinds of confidential information on those servers. Research. Proprietary data. It should have been safe."

"But someone in the company could have recognized something," said Diana. "All it would take was one word, one mention."

"I'm sorry, Al," Jason said. He looked physically ill. "I never really believed in all of it. Not the way they did. I should have been more careful."

Alia sighed. How could she be angry with him for something he couldn't possibly have understood? "I don't know whether to smack you for being so stupid or do a victory dance to celebrate the fact that this time you're the one who screwed up."

"You could incorporate a smack into your victory dance," suggested Nim.

"Efficiency," said Alia. "I like it."

"Efficiency," Diana repeated thoughtfully. "It's possible these organizations are exchanging information now. It would be the strategic thing to do. As near as I can tell from the scroll, tracking and identifying Warbringers was no easy task. The first recorded assassination of a Warbringer happened in the modern world. That can't be a coincidence."

"One more thing to blame on the Internet," said Theo.

Alia held up one of the folders. "What about all the text that's been blacked out? Are there complete versions of the files anywhere?"

Jason shook his head. "Not that I've found. I think Mom and Dad may have been pursuing separate lines of research at some point. I'm not sure."

Theo refilled his glass. "Okay, we get to Greece, we find the spring, we're all good."

So they weren't going to run screaming. Alia could have hugged Theo. But that was pretty much always true.

"Theo, this isn't your fight," said Jason. "Or yours, Nim. I'm going to have Ben put us down at an abandoned landing strip near the airport in Araxos instead of the airport in Kalamata. From there, I can arrange for a flight back to—"

"Stop," said Nim, holding her hands up. "If people are willing to blow a hole in the side of the Met to get to you, then they know who we are, and as soon as we pop back up on the grid they'll be coming after us, trying to find out where you went."

"She makes a good point," said Diana. "We can't afford to underestimate these people again."

"All right," Jason said, considering. "We'll find a safe house. Someplace secure—"

"You're going to find some olive grove to stash us in?" said Theo indignantly.

"I was thinking a hotel," said Jason.

"Forget it. If our roles were reversed, would you just sit around sipping ouzo while I was in danger?"

"No," conceded Jason.

"Then I'm coming with you."

"Me too," said Nim.

Alia shook her head. "No way. You saw what we're up against. You could get hurt. Maybe killed. I couldn't bear that."

"I know," said Nim. "It would be a terrible loss for you *and* the world. But you're my best friend. And honestly, I'd rather be shot at than spend a week in a hotel room with Theo."

Alia knew she should argue harder. Tell them to hide out, do what Jason had suggested, make a real effort to ensure their safety. But despite the danger and their constant sniping, she wanted them with her. She and Jason had lost so much, and Theo and Nim had become their family—loving, supportive, and, occasionally, completely insufferable.

Alia met Diana's eyes. "Can we keep them safe?"

"I don't know," Diana said honestly, and Alia felt grateful for that truth. "But I'm not sure leaving them behind somewhere would be much better. If they were caught . . ."

Diana didn't have to finish the thought. If Theo and Nim were caught, maybe it would be by one of the *good* good guys. Or maybe it would be by one of the groups who wouldn't think twice about torture.

Alia didn't like it, but they were out of real choices. "All right. You can come. But let's try not to do anything too stupid."

Nim reached out and gave Alia's hand a sharp squeeze. "Don't ask Theo to make promises he can't keep."

Maybe Alia's warning had gotten to him, or maybe Theo was just in a good mood, because all he did was grin and lift his ginger ale.

"A toast," he said. "To the villains."

CHAPTER 17

Diana longed to wash the battle from her skin. The smell of smoke was in her hair, caught in the remnants of her gown. With every breath she was pulled back to the chaos of the attack, the terrifying sight of bodies on the ground, the echoes of the war cry that continued to reverberate in her blood.

Even though she still wasn't used to the feeling of being airborne, she forced herself to leave the reassuring solidity of the cushioned banquette and make her way back to the showers. She washed and changed into the leathers she'd stowed in her pack, looping the lasso at her hip. Diana would be conspicuous on the ground in Greece, but they'd be traveling quickly, and she felt more herself in Amazon clothing. If they faced another attack, she wanted any advantage she could get.

For a while she read through the files Jason had brought, keeping her back to the jet's window. She didn't like looking out into the dark and seeing her own face reflected back at her. She didn't want to think about the fact that she was hurtling through the air in a machine that mortals had constructed from metal and plastic and what seemed to be an unwarranted optimism in their own innovation. If she'd been the one at the controls it might have been different, but she did not like being in someone else's hands, no matter how reassuring Ben's manner and military experience might be.

Eventually her eyes grew heavy. Tucked into the plush seat, lulled by the sound of the engines, she managed to sleep. She dreamed that she was back on the battlefield that she'd seen in the Oracle's waters. She heard what she now knew was gunfire, saw the blackened ruins of an unknown city around her, the piles of bodies. But this time it was Tek who looked on as the jackal-headed beast tore out Diana's throat.

Diana woke gasping, hand clutched to her neck, still feeling the monster's long teeth lodged in her flesh.

The jet's cabin was silent. How much time had passed while she slept? Light gleamed from beneath the drawn window shades, and Diana realized they'd caught up to the sun.

Alia was curled next to Nim on the banquette, Theo across from them. Jason was in the back of the plane. When the girls had fallen asleep, Diana had seen Theo pour himself a drink that wasn't ginger ale. She said nothing, but she wondered if his behavior was out of habit or fatigue or something darker. Did he suspect his father's involvement in the attack? Could he be responsible himself? She didn't want to believe the worst of someone Jason and Alia cared about, and Theo's surprise and confusion about Alia's identity as the Warbringer had seemed genuine. But Diana didn't trust her instincts when it came to mortals and their deceptions. She felt like she was wandering in the dark through this world, catching only flashes of understanding, grasping one thing, then stumbling on to the next.

Alia's eyes moved beneath her lids, and Diana wondered if she should wake her. The dream she was having did not look pleasant. Her brow was furrowed, and she clutched one of the file folders in her arms.

Project Second Born. That had been the name Alia's parents had given to their research using Alia's blood. The majority of their information came from documents and artifacts passed down through the Keralis line, family legends, and the work of private investigators they'd hired to pursue leads on Helen's other descendants. There were photographs of archaeological sites, of private digs they'd funded at the locations of ancient battlegrounds, diving expeditions that ranged off the coast of Egypt to the depths of the Black Sea. They'd set up what seemed to be a secret division of Keralis Labs devoted to archaeogenetics, and though they'd begun their research looking for an answer to the problem of the Warbringer line, it was clear their minds had been engaged by the possibilities of what might be gleaned not only from Alia's biology but from the DNA—or aDNA—of the heroes and monsters they had come to accept might be more than legend.

Diana had flipped through page after page on the laptop's screen. It had taken some getting used to, and her fingers still hungered for the feel of paper, but her mind was greedy for the information that flowed before her. One after another, the images slid by, covered in annotations—Achilles with his famous shield in hand, Hector gifting his sword to Ajax. Aeneas. Odysseus. Helen's brothers, the legendary Dioskouroi. But there were other images, illustrations and models that had sent a chill skittering up her spine: the Minotaur with his great bull's horns in the labyrinth at Knossos; the sea monster Lamia, queen and child-eater; six-headed Scylla, with her triple rows of shark's teeth; the cannibal giants of Lamos; the fire-breathing chimera. What had the Keralises been tampering with? The files were troubling enough, but the gaps and missing pages worried her, too.

Now she looked at the screen filled with an image of Echidna, mother of all monsters, part woman, part snake. There were extensive notes on possible uses for gene therapy and the extraction of DNA, as well as a list of possible sites for Echidna's cave, where she was thought to have died. Diana shuddered. *No wonder I had nightmares.*

Jason emerged from the back of the plane. Somehow he managed to look as formal in jeans and a T-shirt as he had in a suit. He retrieved two bottles of water from the bar and offered her one, then took the seat across the aisle from her and leaned forward, resting his elbows on his knees.

He didn't look at her when he said, "I owe you an apology." He turned the bottle of water in his hands. "You put your life at risk to save Alia. All of us. We never would have made it out of the museum without you there." He paused, took a breath. "And I guess I should say that I'm sorry she was at the party in the first place. I'm trying to protect Alia. I'm trying to protect the Keralis name. I don't seem to be doing a good job of either."

"You're doing your best."

To her surprise a slight smile tugged at his lips. "High praise."

Diana couldn't help but smile herself. "I'm sorry. I forget the way people coddle one another here."

Jason barked a laugh, then stifled it as Alia stirred in her sleep. "I'd hardly call it coddling."

"You made a mistake. You acknowledged it. I respect that. Mitigating the repercussions of those choices or their outcome would be a lie that served no one."

He leaned back in his seat and cast her a sidelong glance. "You're right. I'm just not used to . . . people being that straightforward."

Diana remembered Nim's description of Jason. "Because you're rich and handsome?"

Now he grinned that startling, deep-dimpled smile. "Exactly." He gestured to the open laptop on the seat beside Diana. "My parents raised me on those stories. I thought that's all they were. Tales of gods and monsters and heroes."

"Heroes?"

"Theseus—"

"A kidnapper."

"Hercules—"

"A thief."

Jason's brows rose. "Well, you know what I mean. In the books they're heroes."

"I think we were raised on different tales."

"Maybe," he said. "When I got older, I forgot those stories, and it was all about the comic books. Put on a cape, rescue the girl."

"Which girl?"

"The girl. There's always a girl."

Diana snorted. "We definitely grew up on different stories."

That grin again. "Did you have a favorite?" he asked.

"Probably the story of Azimech, the double star."

"I don't know that one."

"It's not very exciting." That wasn't true, but it also wasn't something she wanted to share. "There's another story I liked, one about an island," she said cautiously. "A gift from the gods, given to their favored warriors, a place that could never be touched by bloodshed. I liked that story."

"Now that's definitely fiction."

And there was that smug tone again. It made her bristle. "Why?"

"Because no one can stop war entirely. It's inevitable."

"In your world, maybe."

"In any world. The problem isn't war; it's what humanity has made of it."

Diana folded her arms. "I imagine all wars look the same to those who die in them."

"But it's so much easier now, isn't it?" Again, he gestured toward the laptop. "In the old stories, war was a hero striding onto the battlefield with a sword in his hand. It was a monster to be vanquished. But now? It isn't even a general commanding armies. It's drones, nuclear stockpiles, air strikes. Some guy can push a button and wipe an entire village off a map."

Diana knew those words and the horrors associated with them. She'd been schooled in all the ways mortals had found to destroy each other.

"You sound a little like my mother," Diana conceded. "She says people find ways to make life cheap."

"And death."

"Are you afraid to die?" Diana asked curiously.

"No," said Jason. "Not if I die well. Not if it's for something I believe in. My parents . . ." He hesitated. "Keralis Labs isn't just their legacy. As long as it thrives, their names live on and they do, too."

Jason really had taken the old stories and legends to heart. It was the way the ancient Greeks had viewed the afterlife. "Being remembered is a kind of immortality."

Jason looked at her sharply, surprised. "Exactly," he said. "That's what I want for them."

"And maybe for yourself?"

"Is that stupid?" he asked. It was the first time she'd seen him look anything less than sure of himself. "To want a chance at greatness?"

Diana didn't think it was stupid at all.

But before she could say so, Ben's voice came over the speaker. "We've entered Greek airspace and are beginning our descent. We should be on the ground in Araxos in about twenty minutes. I'm expecting a bumpy landing, so please do buckle up and keep your prayer beads handy."

Whatever spell had been woven in the sleepy cocoon of the jet had been broken.

Jason shifted, his expression shuttering. "Not long now."

Alia and the others stretched and yawned. Nim hardly looked like herself in her Keralis Labs sweatsuit, her face scrubbed free of makeup. Theo smacked his lips and ran a hand over his crest of dark hair. He still wore his shiny suit trousers, but he'd abandoned the jacket and tie for a Keralis T-shirt.

"Are we there?" Alia asked, voice muzzy with sleep.

"Almost," said Jason.

"What happens when we land?" asked Theo, abandoning the banquette to plunk himself down in a seat and strap a seat belt across his lap.

"Ben will put us down near Araxos. We'll have to find someone to drive us south, but from there it's only about four hours by car to Therapne. It would have been faster to set down in Kalamata, but I was worried about landing at such a busy airport."

"Still," said Alia, "we'll be at the spring in a matter of hours." Her gaze met Diana's, and Diana felt a spark of excitement pass between them.

She stretched and wiggled her jaw, trying to ease the uncomfortable pressure in her ears.

"Never been on a plane before?" asked Jason.

"No. I—"

Suddenly, an alarm blared through the cabin.

Nim clutched Alia's arm. "What is that?"

"Get in your seats, both of you. *Now*," Jason ordered.

"What's happening?" said Nim as they threw themselves into the row behind Theo.

"We have a problem," Ben said over the speaker, an edge to his measured voice.

"The jet is equipped with an early-warning system," said Jason.

"Someone's firing on us?" Theo said incredulously.

"I don't suppose we can fire back?" asked Alia.

Jason gripped the armrests. "We don't have that particular upgrade."

"Deploying flares," Ben said.

Diana shoved up the window shade. She heard a *thunk*, and in the glare of the afternoon sky she saw two bright bursts of light followed by trails of white smoke. She glimpsed something shooting toward the flare on the left, and then *boom*.

The little jet shook and tilted wildly.

Theo swore. Alia shouted. The jet righted itself. The flare had drawn off the missile, but the alarm was still sounding.

Jason tore his seat belt from his lap and lunged toward the back of the plane, emerging seconds later with what Diana realized were parachute packs. She'd seen them on the bodies of downed pilots.

"You can't be serious," said Alia, eyes bright with panic.

"Put it on," commanded Jason, shoving a pack at her. "You've jumped out of a plane before."

"For your stupid eighteenth birthday!" Alia said, but she was already reaching for the straps.

"Listen to me," he said as he hurled packs at Nim and Theo and shoved another at Diana. "Get your goggles on. We're at about ten thousand feet. As soon as we get below seven thousand, we're going to jump. We go five seconds apart. Count it out so you don't crash into each other."

"*Ai meu Deus,*" said Theo.

"What about you?" said Alia.

"Ben has a pack in the cockpit. We'll go in tandem. As soon as you jump, I want you to get stable and belly down, then deploy the main canopy. Try to face upwind and be prepared to duck and roll when you hit the ground."

"This isn't happening," said Nim, wriggling into the parachute harness.

"It is," Alia said, and Diana was struck by the steadiness in her voice. "But we're going to be okay."

"Liar," moaned Nim.

"Optimist," countered Alia. There was fear in her eyes, but somehow she forced a smile.

"Stay where you are once we're on the ground," said Jason. "The packs have trackers in them." He touched Diana's shoulder briefly. "I'll find you."

A loud *clang* sounded, and the jet shuddered slightly.

"What the hell was that?" said Theo, pulling his legs through the straps of the harness.

Diana looked up at the roof. "There's something on the jet."

They heard a metallic clatter above them.

"Are those foot—" Alia said, and then her words were lost as the jet's door was torn open. A thunderous roar filled the cabin. The rest of them were strapped into their seats. All but Jason.

In the space of a breath, Diana felt the pack torn from her hands. She saw Jason's eyes widen.

"No!" she cried. She reached for him, but it was too late. The force of the vacuum lifted him like a doll and sucked him into the waiting sky.

Alia was screaming. Theo and Nim were shouting. Diana

looked at where Jason had stood a bare moment before. *There and then gone.*

Two men in black battle armor swung through the hole they'd torn in the plane's side, cables attached to their backs, and stalked toward them.

Diana wrenched free of her seat belt and hurled herself at the armored men. They tumbled backward, perilously close to the open door. She felt a pistol pressed tight to her side and one of the soldiers unloaded his clip.

She screamed as her organs ruptured, the bullets tearing through her, and for a moment the world went black. The soldier on top of her pushed the barrel of his gun against her skull. Diana wasn't sure what she could survive, and she didn't intend to find out.

She unleashed a howl of rage and broke his hold, shoving at him with all her strength. He shot upward and struck the roof of the jet, then crumpled in a heap.

Diana pulled herself to her feet, clutching her side, and her blood turned to ice. The other soldier had Alia in his arms. He leapt from the plane as the wind caught Alia's cry.

"Oh no you don't," snarled Diana.

She grabbed the lasso from her hip, wedged herself against the ragged metal side of the door, and cast the rope after the soldier with all the force she could muster. It shot downward in a gleaming arc, a lash of golden fire against the blue sky.

The loop closed over Alia and the soldier, snapping tight as Diana yanked back hard. The soldier's head connected with the lip of the door as he was pulled back into the plane. He and Alia toppled inside, but his body was limp. Nim and Theo fell on them, drawing Alia close as she clawed at the lasso, trying to get away from the soldier.

Diana gave a shake of the knot, and it slithered loose. She leaned against the wall of the jet, panting. She could feel her body healing—a cool, crawling sensation that rippled over her flesh. The wound at her side had closed, but she was still reeling from the pain, from the wet feel of her own blood on her fingers. At least the bullets had gone clean through.

At that moment, the wail of the alarm picked up speed.

"Incoming," Ben's surprisingly calm voice noted over the speaker. The plane banked hard left. They tumbled against the seats.

A sound like a thunder crack split the air, and the jet quaked with a cacophonous *boom*. A strange quiet descended as the alarm and the engines went silent. For a moment, they were in free fall. Then one of the jet's engines roared to life, and Ben pulled them out of the dive.

"Kids, it is time to exit the aircraft in an orderly fashion," he said over the radio. "I will not be setting this bird down."

Diana dragged herself to her knees, pulling Alia up with her. "Go."

"You don't have a parachute—" Alia began.

Ben appeared in the cockpit doorway, a pack strapped to his shoulders. "We can go together," said Ben. "I'll take her."

Another *clang* sounded above them. Footsteps racing toward the door. Who were these men? How were they doing this? All Diana knew was they were determined to see Alia dead.

"We only have one chance," said Diana. "I'll block them; you all get out. No arguments. Ben, get behind me with the others."

Ben cocked a pistol. "With all due respect, ma'am, a SEAL doesn't hide behind a lady's skirts."

A flood of soldiers dressed in black poured through the door.

"Now!" Diana shouted. She and Ben rushed the soldiers. She heard gunfire, felt the sear of a bullet grazing her thigh, and then she was grappling with one man, two.

These soldiers were strong, better equipped and better trained than those she had faced at the museum. Maybe Alia's foes had realized what they were up against.

The pain in Diana's side was slowing her movements, but all

that mattered was getting Alia and the others clear. She allowed herself a swift glance at the door and saw Nim leap with a shriek and vanish from view. Theo must already be gone. Alia met Diana's eyes, touched her fist to her heart. *Sister in battle.* Then she squeezed her eyes shut and jumped.

Diana grunted and seized a wide wrist, felt bones splinter, kicked hard. The soldier screamed and collapsed, but another soldier was already at her back, grabbing her arms.

In horror, Diana saw Ben slumped against the banquette, eyes blank and staring, his chest riddled with holes. Apparently, courage couldn't stop bullets, even for a SEAL.

Two soldiers had hold of her now, yanking her wrists behind her. One of them drove a fist into the still tender wound at her side, and she screamed as pain exploded through her, stealing her breath.

"Heard about you," said one of the soldiers from behind his black helmet, advancing on her with a notched knife in his hands. "Heard you can take a bullet. Let's see how you do when I carve the heart out of your chest."

From the corner of her eye, Diana glimpsed movement, but her mind refused to believe what she was seeing. Someone was clinging to the wing of the plane.

Jason was clinging to the wing of the plane.

Impossible. No mortal had that kind of strength. But as she watched, he pulled himself over the side and launched himself back into the jet.

He slammed into the helmeted soldier, knocking his knife free, and with one swift gesture snapped his neck.

It can't be.

The soldiers reached for their guns and took aim at Jason. Diana seized them and threw them hard against the walls of the jet. They slumped to the floor.

For a moment, she and Jason stared at each other, the jet shaking as it plummeted toward the earth.

"You lied to me!" she shouted over the roar of the wind.

Jason bent and pulled the parachute from Ben's back, looping it over his own shoulders. "No more than you lied to me." He
offered his hand. "Is it worth dying over?"

Diana took his hand. He yanked her close.

"Hold tight," he said, and then the sky had them.

CHAPTER 18

The terror of the fall came at Alia like a wave. The world rushing up to meet her, her brain trying to remember everything about skydiving at Jason's birthday party and instead spitting out a list of the bones in the human body—every bone she was about to break.

The details of the earth grew clearer—in green, gray, brown, ridges and shadow, clusters of trees. Her fingers fumbled over the latches and bits of metal at her shoulders.

Her body felt heavy, impossibly awkward as she tried to hold the position Jason had described. Jason. She saw the wind grab him, hurl him from the jet. It had happened so fast. A hard fist of despair pressed at her chest, fear and sorrow and disbelief tangling together inside her.

The wind and the pounding of her heart filled her ears. All of that tough talk about Diana killing her for the sake of peace and the only thought in her head: *I do not want to die.* She grabbed hold of the toggle at her hip and yanked hard. A whirring sound. She'd pulled the wrong cord—for a moment she was sure of it, certain she'd made some horrible blunder. Then her body was yanked upward with a hard jolt. A choked sound between a sob and a bleat escaped her lips as the harness dug into her thighs and her momentum slowed. She was pretty sure she'd left her shoulders and pelvis somewhere above.

She forced herself to scan the terrain. She knew she needed to try to find somewhere flat and treeless and steer into the wind. She pulled gently at the toggles, testing them. The world looked alien and mysterious beneath her. Her mind registered barns, houses, cultivated land. She needed a field, someplace flat. She tugged gently at the toggles, turning left, then right, trying to slow her descent.

One moment she was gliding over the shine of a river, and in the next, the earth was too close, speeding by beneath her. She lifted her feet and hit the ground with a painful thud, then tumbled forward, unable to control her momentum. She felt her ankle twist, felt rock scrape along her back and sides. She tucked her knees and rolled. The canopy caught the wind, dragging her along, then finally collapsed. She skidded to a halt.

Alia lay on her side, trying to catch her breath, trying to make her rational mind catch up to the adrenaline coursing through her body. She batted at the latches and straps of her harness and wriggled free. Her left ankle throbbed. She could only hope it wasn't broken. She forced herself to sit up, but every part of her felt like a Jell-O mold that hadn't quite set. She was at the base of a terraced hillside covered in tarps and netting to prevent erosion.

She heard a shrill whir and peered up into the sky, saw a trail of smoke—the jet spiraling downward. It disappeared behind a rise of hills, and Alia heard a loud *boom* that shook the earth beneath her. A scream rose in her throat as a plume of black smoke blossomed from the horizon.

She glimpsed a shape moving through the sky, the translucent bowl of a parachute trailing behind it. Could it be Diana? Ben? One of their attackers?

Alia struggled to her feet. Jason had said there were trackers in the packs. *Jason.*

"Alia!" Nim's voice. Alia had never heard a more beautiful

sound. She turned, saw Nim stumbling toward her, and forced herself to stand. They staggered the rest of the distance to each other, and Alia threw her arms around Nim, wishing she could hold her close and keep her safe forever.

"Did you see where Theo came down?" Alia asked.

"No," said Nim. "It all happened so fast."

Alia felt panic swelling up to choke her breath. "Let's get to the top of the hill," she said. "Maybe we can see more."

Alia leaned on Nim, and they scrambled past the tarps and netting as fast as their wobbly legs would carry them. When Alia looked west she could make out a sapphire strip of sea. To the east she saw only farmland.

"There!" she said, pointing to where the parachute was sailing toward the earth near what might be a grain field. It had to be Ben and Diana. *It had to be.* They stumbled down the other side of the hill, Alia limping slightly, trying to walk the pain out of her ankle as Nim rolled the sleeves of her Keralis T-shirt up over her shoulders. It was late afternoon, but the sun above was strong.

Alia wanted to slump down right there, cover her head with her hands, and just scream. She couldn't stop seeing Jason's face as he vanished through the jet door. *Keep going,* she told herself. *Just keep moving. If you stop, you'll have to think.*

They rounded an overgrown hedge, and she thought she heard voices.

Nim's head snapped up. "That sounds like—"

"It can't be," said Alia, but she would have known her brother's voice anywhere. Especially when he sounded angry.

"I don't owe you an explanation," Jason spat. "You've been lying and dodging my questions since the moment we met."

"No ordinary man could do what you did," came Diana's reply.

Alia stepped around the hedge and saw Diana pacing back and forth in a field spotted with poppies, as Jason lay on the ground, trying to untangle himself from a mess of parachute cords. He was alive. He was okay. She didn't care how or why, just that it was so.

"Help me out of this thing," he said to Diana.

"Help yourself," Diana shot back.

Alia exchanged a glance with Nim. "We interrupting?" she asked.

Jason and Diana turned and saw her at the same time. "Alia!" they shouted.

Diana loped toward her and swept Alia up in her arms, swinging her around like a little kid. "You made it!" She threw an arm around Nim's shoulders and pulled them both into a hug. "You made it."

Jason gave a frustrated growl and said, "Would someone please help me out of this thing so I can hug my damn sister?"

Alia limped over to him, tears in her eyes, and said, "Yes, I'll help, you big grump."

He dragged her down and hugged her tight. "I thought I'd lost you."

"Same here."

"Are you getting snot all over my shirt?"

"Probably," she said, but she didn't let go. "How the hell did you get down here?"

Jason sighed. "It's a long story. I'll tell you all of it, but we need to go. Whoever shot us down will have people on the ground, searching."

"Did Ben get out before the plane went down?" Nim asked.

Jason shook his head. "No."

"He died bravely," said Diana.

"But he died just the same," Alia replied. Another death on her conscience, and all the more reason to make it to the spring.

After a few minutes of fiddling, they managed to get Jason free, though Diana kept her distance, arms crossed, jaw set. He pulled a Velcro patch free from one of the straps of the parachute pack, revealing some kind of screen. His fingers moved over it, entering a code, and a cluster of green dots appeared beside an electronic compass rose.

"That's us," said Jason, using his fingertips to zoom out. Another green dot appeared to the southeast.

"And that's Theo," said Alia.

"Or his parachute at least."

She punched Jason hard in the arm. "Don't say that."

They followed the signal through the poppy field into an olive grove, through row after row of gnarled trees. In the late-afternoon light, their gray-green leaves took on a silvery cast, like boughs clustered with clouds of sea foam.

Nim stopped short. "Oh God," she said, and when Alia followed her horrified gaze, she saw Theo's limp body hanging from the twisted branches of an olive tree, like a puppet gone slack on its strings.

"No," said Alia. "No." She had done this. She might as well have snapped his neck herself.

Then one of Theo's pointy shoes wiggled, his knee, his thigh, up to his wrist. Alia grabbed Nim's arm, relief gusting through her. "He's alive!" she said on a happy gasp.

"I should have known I couldn't get rid of him that easily," said Nim, but she was smiling.

Diana peered at Theo's wiggling form. "What exactly is he doing?"

Jason sighed. "I'm pretty sure he's doing the wave."

Alia cocked her head to one side. "Maybe the robot?"

Diana frowned. "Is this the way your people celebrate cheating death?"

"What exactly are you doing, Theo?" Alia called.

He tried to twist against the strings, to no avail. "Alia?" he shouted. "Guys?" His feet bicycled futilely through the air. He was only a few feet off the ground, but it was a crucial few feet.

"He looks like a manic Christmas ornament," said Nim. "And God, who told him those pants were a good idea?"

Personally, Alia thought the pants were great. Was it wrong

to notice how good someone's butt looked when a second earlier you'd thought he was dead?

It only took a few moments for Diana to scale the tree and cut Theo loose. He fell to the ground in a heap and gazed up at them from the dirt. "Can we never, ever do that again?"

"Sold," Jason said, offering him a hand. He pulled Theo up and drew him into a quick hug, clapping him on the back. Alia wanted to plant kisses all over Theo's ridiculous face, but she was going to have to fall out of a few more planes before she had the guts to do it.

"How did they find us?" said Nim. "How did they know we were headed to Greece?"

"I don't know," said Jason. "It's possible they found the jet via satellite. Maybe they were just waiting to see where we intended to land, and once we were in range—"

"They took a shot," said Theo.

"They'll have seen where the jet went down," said Diana. "We need to move. If they don't already know we escaped the crash, they will soon."

"But where are we?" said Nim. "And where do we go?"

Theo pulled out his phone.

"Don't!" said Alia, swatting it out of his hands onto the ground. "Hey!"

"Maybe that's the answer to how they found us," said Nim.

Theo looked almost insulted. "You seriously think I let anyone track me through this thing? If anybody goes looking for Theo Santos, they're going to think I'm sunning myself on Praia do Toque. Which, honestly, I wish I was."

"I wish you were, too," said Nim.

"Does anyone else have a phone?" said Jason.

Nim shook her head. "It was in my clutch at the party."

"I never got a new one," said Alia. "And Diana doesn't have a phone."

Theo clutched his chest. "No—no phone? How do you function?"

Diana cast Theo a haughty glance that looked like it had been pulled straight from Nim's playbook. "I wear practical shoes and avoid the branches of olive trees."

"So cold," said Nim with a grin. "So accurate."

"*Shhhh,*" Theo said to his pointy-toed shoes. "She didn't mean it."

"Just keep the phone off for now," Jason said.

"Fine," Theo retorted. "But for a guy who knows so much biology, you don't know shit about tech. This thing is literally untraceable."

In the end, Diana led them southeast, the setting sun to their backs. They made their way through olive groves and farmland for hours, lurching along, lost in their own thoughts. They kept away from the roads and left a wide perimeter as they skirted farms and houses, keeping Theo at the front of the line and Nim at the back, since they didn't seem to be able to stop insulting each other, regardless of the danger. Alia still caught them throwing angry glares each other's way.

Occasionally, Diana or Jason would jog ahead to scout their route, and it was nearly dusk when Diana returned to say they were on the outskirts of an area called Thines.

"Do you think we've gone far enough?" asked Alia. She refused to complain, but her feet ached and her whole body felt weary with fatigue. Though her ankle was obeying, she was desperate to take her weight off it for a while.

"Even if we aren't, it's getting too dark to see," said Jason. "We need to find shelter for the night."

"I don't think we should risk seeking lodging," said Diana. "I saw what looks like an abandoned building not far ahead."

"How are you not tired?" said Nim grumpily.

Alia smiled. She'd almost gotten used to Diana's limitless reserve of energy. "Annoying, isn't it?"

They followed Diana through another mile of orchards and across a dry creek bed, where the stones glowed nearly white in the gathering dusk, then back into another olive grove. Through the trees, Alia occasionally caught sight of lit windows or the shape of a building. Once they passed close enough to a house that she glimpsed a television through the window, flickering blue in the living room. She felt like she'd looked through a portal to another planet. How could something so ordinary be happening when they were running for their lives? She was glad when they left the cultivated groves and began picking their way up a low rise, through a tangle of dense trees and scrub that provided plenty of cover.

Eventually, they came to a building that looked like it had once been a chapel but had long since been abandoned. They'd almost missed it, tucked into a copse of cypress and deadfall. Hopefully, the men looking for them would head straight for the neighboring farms and never think to seek them out here.

Alia felt along the wall near the door and found a small lantern hanging from a rusted hook. "It still has oil in it," she said. A few more minutes of fumbling and they'd found safety matches in a tin box tucked into a niche in the wall.

"Keep the flame low," Jason said.

Alia lit the wick and turned the little bronze key as low as it would go. By the dim light, they could see whitewashed walls reaching up to a blue enamel dome and a packed-earth floor beneath them. Rusted hulks of farm equipment and piles of rotting pews had been stacked haphazardly in the apse, but there was still plenty of room.

"We can spend the night here," said Jason.

"We're far enough from the farmhouses?" said Diana.

"I think so."

"And we're stopping for the day?"

"Yes."

"Good," she said. In a single movement, she freed the lasso from her hip and slung it over Jason's shoulders. "Then what exactly are you, Jason Keralis?"

CHAPTER 19

Diana snapped the lasso tight, and for a moment, its fibers seemed to glow in the dim light of the church. Jason stumbled but kept his footing, thrashing at the end of the rope like a fish on a line. Despite what she'd seen on the jet, the reality of his strength still came as a shock.

"Diana!" Alia yelped.

"Oh dang," said Theo.

"What is that thing *made* of?" said Nim.

Diana ignored them. "Who are you?" she demanded. "What are you?"

"I'm exactly who I said I am," Jason said through gritted teeth.

"How did you catch hold of the jet's wing at those speeds? How did you hang on? What are you, Jason Keralis? Speak."

Jason gave an angry growl, his muscles flexing, the tendons in his neck drawn taut. But he was no match for the lasso's power.

"What's happening to him?" Theo asked, a frantic edge to his voice. "What are you doing?"

"He's fine," said Diana, though she wasn't entirely sure that was so. "The lasso compels the truth."

Jason grimaced. "I am a descendant of Helen and Menelaus, just as Alia is."

Of course he was—he was Alia's brother—but that didn't account for his abilities. "Another Warbringer?"

"Something . . . else." He spoke the words as if they were being torn from him. "I carry hero's blood. The blood of Menelaus and the Spartan kings before him. My mother and father helped me keep my strength secret."

"Why didn't you tell us?" Alia said. Diana could sense the worry she had for her brother, but the hurt in her voice was clear, too.

"Mom and Dad didn't want anyone to know," said Jason. "It was dangerous for all of us."

"You held back when we fought at the hotel," Diana said as realization dawned.

"I've been holding back my whole life," Jason snarled. "Now get this thing off me."

"Let him go," Alia said. "This is wrong."

Diana narrowed her eyes but let the rope slacken.

Jason pulled it over his head, casting the lasso away from him like a snake. "What the hell is that thing?"

Diana yanked the lasso back. "A necessity in the World of Man. You've been lying this whole time. To all of us."

"And you've been so forthcoming?" He pointed an accusing finger at her. "You come out of nowhere. You shrug off bullet wounds like they're paper cuts. You can outfight my best security guards."

"I've made no attempt to hide my gifts," Diana replied. "The secrets I protect do not just belong to me."

"You think that lets you off the hook?" Jason made a sound of disgust and stalked through the chapel door. He looked back once over his shoulder. "If you want the truth so damn much, maybe you should think about offering it in return." He vanished into the dusk.

Alia moved to follow, but Theo laid a hand on her shoulder. "Maybe give him a minute. If there's one thing Jason hates, it's feeling out of control."

"You shouldn't have done that," Alia said to Diana. "You shouldn't have used that thing on him."

Diana coiled the rope at her hip, using the time to quell some of her anger. Alia was right. Maybe Jason was right, too. But he was also a hypocrite. The whole time he'd been badgering her for information, he'd been keeping his strength a secret.

"Well," said Theo into the silence. "I guess now I know why he always wrecked me at basketball."

Alia cast him a skeptical glance. "I've seen you play basketball, Theo. He beat you because you're terrible."

With great dignity, Theo stated, "I'm good on the fundamentals."

Nim hooted. "And I'm the queen of the Netherlands." She glanced in the direction Jason had gone. "It kind of makes sense, though. Alia, has Jason ever been sick a day in his life?"

Alia shook her head slowly. "No. Never missed a day of school. Never took a day off work. I thought he was just . . . I don't know, Jason being Jason. Like a cold wouldn't dare be caught by him."

"Also, his sweat smells like pinecones," said Nim.

Alia's gaze snapped to her. *"What?"*

Nim blushed and shrugged. "Why do you think I liked his dirty T-shirts so much? He smells like a sexy forest."

Jason *did* have a pleasing scent. Almost better than new car. But Diana didn't intend to discuss it.

Alia gagged. "You're disgusting."

"I'm honest," Nim said with a sniff.

"Well, there's no way I'm going to stop giving him crap about his cologne," said Theo.

It was almost fully dark now. Diana sighed. "It would be best if Jason didn't stray far."

"I'll go," Theo said.

"Great idea," said Nim. "Maybe you can find a ditch to fall into."

Alia pulled the parachute-tracking screen from her pocket. "Here," she said, handing it to Theo. "The screen is pretty bright. You can use it as a flashlight."

"I wish I could use it as a sandwich. Next time we throw ourselves out of a plane, remind me to grab a bag of pretzels."

Alia pointed toward the grove. "We have olives and also olives."

"Maybe we can cook and eat Nim," he grumbled as he headed out the door.

Nim ran a hand through her black hair. "I would be delicious."

Diana considered offering to go after Jason instead of Theo, but she knew she wasn't quite ready to apologize, and she doubted he was ready to hear it. Besides, someone needed to remain with Alia.

At least there was one apology she could make and mean. "I'm sorry I lost my temper," she said quietly.

Alia blew out a long breath. "I'm mad at him, too," she said. "I'm just so glad he's alive, I'm having trouble staying mad."

Maybe that was part of what Diana resented, that horrible moment of watching Jason vanish, of believing he'd been lost for good. She thought of the soldiers they'd left behind on the jet, of Gemma Rutledge, someone she'd never met, a blond girl in a party dress lying dead beside Nim. She thought of Ben's chest pocked by bullet holes. She'd never known someone who had died. She'd barely known Ben, and yet she felt the weight of loss pressing down on her, all that courage and easy humor gone forever. Jason was right. Death was too easy here.

They bedded down against the cold, packed earth. Eventually, Theo returned with word that Jason would take the first watch.

"Let him sulk," he said with a shrug, curling onto his side a short distance from Nim and Alia.

Diana wasn't quite ready to trust Theo. Once the others were breathing deeply, she slipped out of the chapel and crept silently through the trees and underbrush until she spotted Jason's shape in the dark. His back was to her, his head tilted up at the stars. He looked like a figure carved in stone, a statue of a hero, still standing as everything around him fell to ruin. Or maybe just a lonely boy keeping watch with the stars. What had it been like for him to hide the truth of himself even from his best friend, his sister?

Diana didn't ask. Without a sound, she turned and made her way back to the chapel. She lay down beside Alia and let herself fall into a deep, dreamless sleep.

Jason woke her sometime after midnight. He said nothing, and wordlessly, Diana left to take up the watch as he bedded down on the chapel floor.

The hours passed slowly with nothing but her thoughts and the ceaseless buzz of the cicadas to keep her company, but at last the sky began to brighten, and gray dawn light spilled across the grove below. Diana made her way back to the chapel, eager to begin the day's journey. She pushed open the decaying door and saw Alia sleeping peacefully on her side, Jason on his back, brow creased as if expressing disapproval even in his dreams.

And Nim crouched on top of Theo, her hands locked around his throat. Theo was clawing at her arms, his face red with suffused blood.

"Nim!" she shouted.

The girl turned her head, but the thing looking back at her was not Nim. Her eyes were hollows, her hair a mane of star-strewn night, and from her back sprang the filthy black wings of a vulture. The image flickered and was gone.

Diana launched herself at Nim, knocking her off Theo and rolling with her over the chapel floor.

"What's going on?" Jason said blearily as he and Alia came awake.

But Theo was already shoving to his feet, coughing and gasping. He roared and rushed at Diana and Nim.

In a heartbeat, Jason leapt up and seized Theo's arms, holding him back. "Stop!" he commanded. "Stop it."

Theo thrashed in his grip. "I'll kill that little bitch—"

"You should have died in the crash!" shouted Nim, hissing and spitting as Diana attempted to restrain her without hurting her. "You shouldn't even be here! You're as worthless as your father says!"

Theo snarled. "Fat, ugly, stupid co—"

Jason snagged Theo's jaw in his hands and clamped it shut, silencing him forcibly. "Shut your damned mouth, Theo."

Diana hauled Nim off her feet and slung her over her shoulder, hearing the breath go out of the tiny girl in a disgruntled *whuff*. At least she couldn't keep shouting insults. But Nim did not cease her snarling and struggling until they were several hundred yards away in a stand of cypress trees.

Diana dumped her onto the scraggly grass.

"Nim," said Alia, coming up behind them. "What the hell?"

"I . . ." Nim panted. "I . . ." She unballed her fists, a look of horror dawning on her face. Her shoulders slumped, and she burst into tears. "I wanted to kill him. I *tried* to kill him."

Alia met Diana's gaze. "It's getting worse, isn't it?"

Diana nodded. Maybe the terror of the past few days had made Theo and Nim more susceptible to Alia's power, or maybe it was simply the coming of the new moon. Only one thing was certain: They were running out of time.

"We have to find some way to keep them separated," said Alia.

"You're not leaving me here," Nim said, wiping the tears from her eyes.

Alia offered her a hand. "That wasn't what I was suggesting, you nerd. But we have to do something before you guys murder each other."

"We'll just have to try to keep them apart as much as possible," said Diana.

"Being near you helps," Nim said.

Alia's brows rose. "Are you saying that because you enjoy being carried like a sack of flour by a cute girl?"

Nim planted her hands on her hips. "I'm serious. As soon as she separated me from Theo, I could feel my mind start to clear. It just took a little while for the rest of me to catch up."

"It's possible," said Diana. "Remember how you were healthier when you were near me on the island?"

"Okay," said Alia. "But we have to watch them. I'm not going to be responsible for my friends killing—"

Diana caught a flicker of movement from the olive grove below. "Silence," she whispered.

There were dark shapes moving through the trees. They were still far enough away that Diana could just make them out, but they were drawing closer, and Diana could only whisper a prayer of thanks that they hadn't overheard her conversation with Alia and Nim. She needed to be more cautious. They all did.

Diana gestured for Alia and Nim to follow, and as quietly as they could, they traced their steps back to the chapel.

"Maybe they're not looking for us?" Nim murmured.

"Yeah," whispered Alia. "They're probably going to use those guns to shoot the olives off the trees."

Theo and Jason were seated near the entry. Theo's eyes narrowed as they drew closer, but Diana laid a hand on his shoulder and some of the tension in his body seemed to ease.

"There are armed men approaching the chapel," she said.

Jason was on his feet instantly. "Damn it," he said. "We need to get out of here."

"We need a car," said Alia.

Jason shook his head. "What if they're watching the roads?"

"He's right," said Diana. "They may even have set up roadblocks. We'd be better off continuing on foot until we can get farther from the crash site."

They did their best to hide the evidence of the night they'd spent in the chapel and hurried down the south slope of the hill, keeping away from the main highway, scurrying over fields that offered little cover, through orchards where they plucked their breakfast from the trees, and past a scrubby pasture where a scrawny goat bleated furiously at them as they passed. In a small backyard, they found a clothesline strung with damp laundry, and Nim and Theo exchanged their Keralis Labs shirts for a linen undershirt and a bright-blue button-down.

The previous night, they'd tacked east, but now they moved back toward the coast, where campers and beachgoers might provide some camouflage for their oddly dressed crew. At one point, they crested a series of low ridges and Diana caught a view of the bright waters of the Ionian Sea. The blue was more like her home waters than the sullen slate of the Atlantic, but it was still nothing compared to the coast of Themyscira. She was closer to home than she'd been since she'd crossed into the World of Man, and yet she'd never felt farther away.

As they looked out at the water, Diana was startled to hear Nim say, "Sorry about this morning, Theo."

Theo kept his eyes trained on the sea. "I'm sorry I called you names. You're not fat or ugly."

Nim cut him a glance. "I am fat, Theo, and far too hot for your sorry ass."

A smile flashed over Theo's face. "I think you mean my worthless ass."

Diana couldn't help but respect their willingness to set their anger aside. She knew those insults must have stung.

They continued on, keeping as much distance as they could between Theo and Nim without losing sight of each other, just in case the reconciliation didn't take. The situation suited Diana just fine, since it meant she and Jason had to stay away from each other, too. They hadn't spoken a word since the previous night, and Diana wavered between feeling that was best for everyone and crafting an apology in her head.

She matched her pace to Theo's. He'd removed his new shirt and tied it around his head, revealing dark freckles on his narrow brown shoulders.

"Theo?" she began.

"Yes, Big Mama?"

She raised a brow at the nickname. "This morning, when Nim was—"

"Trying to kill me?"

"Yes. Did you see . . . anything odd?"

"You mean like a hideous winged hellbeast?"

Diana didn't know whether to feel relieved or distressed. "Exactly."

"Yeah, I saw it," said Theo. He shivered despite the heat of the sun. "When I looked into her eyes, they were . . . ancient, and I could feel . . ."

"What?" Diana prodded.

"She was happy. No, *gleeful*." He shuddered and shook his arms as if trying to rid himself of the memory.

"She had wings, black eyes, what else?"

"Wild hair—not really hair at all, like you were looking into the dark—and gold smeared all over her lips."

Diana hadn't noticed the gold on her mouth. Her stomach clenched. "Gold from the apple of discord. That was Eris, the goddess of strife."

"A *goddess*?"

Diana nodded, her stomach churning at the possibility. She had been raised to worship the goddesses of the island, to make the proper sacrifices, speak the appropriate prayers. She knew they could be generous in their gifts and terrible in their judgment. But she had never *seen* a god, and she knew they didn't make a habit of revealing themselves to mortals, either. "She's a battlefield god. She incites discord and thrives on the misery it creates."

Again, Theo shuddered. "It was like there was a chorus in my head, egging me on. I hated Nim. I would have killed her if I had the chance. I didn't just feel mad—I felt *righteous*." He blinked. "And I'm a lover, not a fighter!"

"There are others," said Diana. "The Algea, full of weeping," she recited. "Até, who brings ruin; Limos, the bone soldier of famine. The brother gods, Phobos and Deimos."

"Panic and Dread," said Jason, catching up to them.

"And the Keres."

"What do they do, exactly?" asked Theo.

"They eat the corpses of warriors as they die."

He winced. "Maybe we don't need to stop for lunch."

"Is it possible Alia's power is drawing them?" asked Jason.

"I don't know what's possible anymore," Diana admitted. It was a frightening thought.

She loped ahead to scout the territory before them. She needed to think, and she wanted to be away from mortals for a moment, from their squabbles and hungers and wants.

The landscape here reminded her of parts of Themyscira, but there was no mistaking this place for anything but the World of Man. She could hear the rumble of cars in the distance, smell burning fuel in the air, hear the buzz and crackle of telephone lines. Through all of it, in the pulse and flow of her blood, she could still feel the pain and worry of her sisters on the island. She hated that they suffered, that she'd been the one to cause it, but she couldn't deny that she was grateful for the connection, for the reminder of who and what she was.

Had she and Theo truly seen Eris? The gods of battle had been the creatures of her earliest nightmares. They were the enemies of peace, more terrifying than ordinary monsters because their power didn't lie in jagged teeth or terrible strength but in their ability to drive soldiers to the worst atrocities, to drown the empathy and mercy of warriors in terror and rage so they were capable of things they'd never imagined. What if Jason was right and they were coming to the mortal world, drawn by the prospect of war?

As the day wore on, the heat rose, and the group's pace slowed. By late morning, Diana could see that Alia's steps were weaving and Nim was bleary-eyed from exhaustion. She dropped back to talk to Jason.

"We can't keep on this way. We're going to have to get a car and risk the roadblocks."

"Seconded," said Nim over her shoulder. "Or you're going to have to leave me by the side of the road."

"Well—" began Theo. Alia hurled an olive at him.

"We can't stay away from the roads forever," said Diana. "They're just going to keep widening the perimeter of their search.

Besides, there's no way we can make it over the Taygetus Mountains on foot, not before the new moon."

"Is there another way around?" asked Theo.

Alia shook her head. "Not without backtracking north. Therapne is backed by mountains to the east and west. It's part of what made Sparta so easy to defend."

Diana grinned, surprised, and Jason cast Alia a speculative look. "How do you know so much about it?"

"I did a lot of reading on the plane. I wanted to know about Helen. Where she came from." She wiped the sweat from her brow and glanced at Diana. "You realize you're suggesting stealing a car?"

"I'm suggesting *borrowing* a car," Diana corrected. "Surely there's a way to compensate the owner."

Theo reached into his back pocket and pulled out his wallet. "I have twenty-six bucks and my Better Latte Than Never card. Only one more stamp for a free cappuccino."

"Wait a minute," said Jason. "Can any of us even drive?"

"I drove," said Theo. "Once."

"That was a golf cart," said Alia.

"So? It had four wheels and went *vroom*."

"You crashed it into a tree."

"I'll have you know that tree had been drinking."

"Everybody, relax," said Nim. "I can drive."

"Where did you learn to drive?" Alia asked incredulously.

"With the rest of the peasants on Long Island."

"We have a driver," Diana said, new hope surging through her. "Now we just need to find a car."

"You know this means I get to choose the radio station," said Nim as they set out across the field.

Theo whimpered. "How about I just let you run me over?"

It took far longer to locate a car than they'd hoped. Many of the farms they passed didn't seem to have much in the way of vehicles beyond donkey carts and bicycles, and in one case, a truck set up on cement blocks, its wheels long vanished.

As they were approaching a promising-looking farmhouse with Jason in the lead, he snapped, "Get down."

They sank to their bellies in the grass just as two men emerged from the front door of the house.

"Police?" whispered Alia.

"Those guns don't look like standard police issue."

The men wore nondescript blue uniforms, but the long, ugly guns they carried looked like those Diana had seen their attackers use.

"That's some serious firepower," said Theo.

"Are you surprised?" asked Jason.

"That they're willing to just walk around the Greek country-side brandishing semiautomatics? Kind of."

"They weren't afraid to attack us in a New York City museum," said Jason. "Why would they hesitate here? They know the stakes."

"And it's possible Alia's power is at work here, too," said Diana, "eroding the barriers to violent action."

"Ironic," said Nim.

"That's not technically irony," said Theo.

"Do I need to remind you that I tried to strangle you this morning, loser?"

"Let's get moving," Alia said hurriedly.

They made sure the men were leaving, then circled around the back of the farmhouse to a dilapidated stable. A horse nickered from a stall on the intact side of the structure. The roof on the other side had almost completely caved in and was covered by a tarp, but there were two vehicles parked beneath it: a truck with its hood open that seemed to be missing part of its engine, and a funny bubble-shaped car the color of a tangerine.

Theo shook his head. "We're going over a mountain range in a Fiat?"

Diana eyed the car doubtfully. "It doesn't seem very . . .

sturdy." In fact, it looked less like a real vehicle than one of the pretty handbags Nim had shown them.

"We don't have a lot of other options," said Alia. "Unless you want to try the horse."

"I'm not really the noble-steed type," said Theo.

Diana sighed and glanced over at the horse watching them with dark, steady eyes. She would have preferred riding, but she knew they needed the little car's speed.

"So . . . ," said Alia. "Does anyone actually know how to steal a car?"

"We could break into the house," said Nim. "Take the keys."

"There are people in there," said Alia. "What if they catch us?"

Nim tossed her hair back from her eyes. "Well, you guys are the science geniuses. Can't you just hotwire it or something?"

"We're biologists," said Jason. "Not electrical engineers."

"All I'm hearing are excuses, people."

But for once Theo wasn't weighing in. He was silently contemplating the car. "I can do it," he said slowly. "But I'm going to need to use my phone."

"Out of the question," said Jason.

"I told you it's untraceable," said Theo.

"Even so—"

"You know, I can actually be helpful if you'll let me." Theo's tone was light, but Diana heard the edge in his voice and felt a surge of sympathy for the skinny boy. She knew what it was to be underestimated. But was he trustworthy? If he'd wanted to harm them or alert their captors to their whereabouts, he'd certainly had plenty of opportunities.

She met Jason's gaze and gave a short nod. "Let him try."

Jason blew out a long breath. "Okay."

"Okay?" said Theo.

"Yeah," said Jason more firmly. "Do it."

Theo's smile was small and pleased, far shyer than Diana would have expected.

"All right, then." He pulled the phone from his pocket, his thumbs moving rapidly over the screen, and said, "If this were an older car, we'd be screwed. No Bluetooth. No wireless. But everything's digital now, right? Cars are basically just tricked-out computers on wheels."

Jason folded his arms, unconvinced. "And you have a magic phone?"

"This *phone* can't be sold in some countries because the computer inside it is powerful enough to operate a missile-guidance system, and I can use it to access my desktop through a spoof IP I set up on the dark net."

"Okay, okay," said Jason. "All hail the mighty phone."

"Thank you," said Theo. "The phone accepts cash gifts by way of apology. Now, all we have to do is mimic the signals the key sends to tell the car to unlock the door. It's not like the car cares if the key is there."

"Same with the human brain," said Alia. "We see something, we react based on the stimulus, real or artificial. It's all just a collection of electrical impulses."

"Divine lightning," said Diana.

Alia frowned. "Huh?"

"I second that huh," Theo said, not looking up from the little screen, thumbs moving so fast they blurred.

Diana shrugged. "It's just what you were saying reminded me of Zeus. He's the god of thunder and lightning, but what you're describing in our minds, those electrical impulses . . . It's another way of thinking about that power."

"Divine lightning," repeated Alia. "You know, it's kind of fundamental to the way we think about thinking. Like a big idea at the right time is catching lightning in a bottle."

"Or when you're dumbfounded, you say you're thunderstruck," said Nim.

The corner of Jason's lips tugged upward in a small smile. "And when you connect with someone, you call it a spark."

Despite the morning's long silences and her lingering anger, Diana was glad to see that smile again. She couldn't help returning it. "Exactly."

Theo held up his phone. "Who's ready for a little divine lightning?"

"Just do the thing," said Nim impatiently.

He jabbed his finger down on the screen. *"Shapow!"*

Nothing happened.

"Oh, wait a second." His thumbs flew over the screen again. He cleared his throat. "What I meant to say was, *shablammy*!" He gave the screen a firm poke. The car doors released a satisfying *clunk*. "I'll ask you to hold your applause. And now the engine—"

"Wait," said Jason. "Let's roll it out to the road before we start it."

Diana raised a brow. He was so dedicated to this falsehood. "Do we really need to roll it? Wouldn't it be faster and quieter just to . . ."

A moment later, they had hefted the car above their heads, Diana gripping the front bumper, Jason at the rear.

"Maybe Nim doesn't need to drive," Theo said, panting as the others hurried to keep up. "Jason and Diana can just carry us."

"Don't make me strap you to the roof," grunted Jason.

They jogged the car across the field and down the road from the farmhouse, then deposited it on the dirt road.

They waited beside the little vehicle as Nim slid behind the wheel. She wedged the seat up as far as it could go to accommodate her short legs. "Okay, let's do this."

"When was the last time you actually drove?" asked Alia.

Nim flexed her fingers. "It's not the kind of thing you forget."

"Ready?" said Theo.

"Wait," said Diana. She placed her hand on his shoulder. She didn't know what he could accomplish with that little computer, but just in case he was feeling hostile toward Nim, she wanted him as calm as possible. From the sheepish look he cast her, the gesture was warranted.

His thumbs sped over the screen, and a moment later the car roared to life.

Theo broke out in a dance that looked like it might cause lasting damage to his spine and did a victory lap around the car. "Who's the king?"

Nim cast Alia a meaningful glance and whispered, "You have terrible taste."

"Whatever," said Alia. "Shotgun!"

Diana seized Alia and slammed her to the ground, shoving her body beneath the car for cover. She rose with bracelets raised, ready for the onslaught, but the others were just standing there staring.

"Um, Diana," said Alia, peeking out from beneath the Fiat. "It's just a saying."

Diana felt her face heat.

"Of course," she said, helping Alia up and dusting her off. Jason's expression was bemused, and Theo's whole body was shaking with laughter. "Naturally. And it means?"

"When you call shotgun, you get the seat next to the driver."

"Why?"

"It's just a rule," said Alia.

"It's from the Old West," said Nim. "On a stagecoach, there was the driver, and the guy who rode next to him carried a shotgun in case they were attacked."

"Or in case someone started spouting useless trivia and had to be murdered," said Theo.

"Go stand in front of the car."

It did take some time to negotiate where everyone would sit. Eventually, Jason took the passenger seat, and Diana squashed in between Alia and Theo in the back, her knees nearly up to her chin—that way she was ready to protect Alia if need be, and Nim and Theo were separated as much as possible.

To preserve the battery life of Theo's phone for controlling the car, they used the old-fashioned map folded up in the glove compartment and picked out a route that took them south via side roads and narrow byways. It also occasionally trapped them behind a slow-moving cart drawn by mules, or required that they stop to let a herd of bandy-legged goats cross the road.

Despite the need for haste, Diana almost welcomed the pauses from Nim's reckless pace.

"She has a much different style than Dez," she murmured to Alia, thinking longingly of the smooth way the black town car had passed through traffic.

Theo moaned as they jolted against a divot, the Fiat's tires momentarily losing touch with the road.

"Maybe she's just trying to kill me slowly," he speculated, looking a bit green.

They turned on the radio, flipping through the channels, until they found something that sounded like the news. Jason and Alia's Greek wasn't good enough to follow the rapid-fire conversation, but Diana understood it all. There were reports of more conflicts across the globe, another bloody coup attempt, world leaders issuing angry threats, but eventually the speaker mentioned the crash.

"The wreckage of the plane hasn't been identified yet," she translated. "There are reports of several casualties, but the bodies haven't been identified, either." *Bodies.* Again she thought of Ben. She remembered what Jason had said about living on in memory. At least she could do that for the pilot who had stood by her so bravely.

"It's just a matter of time before they identify the aircraft," said Jason, his eyes trained on the passing scenery.

"Everyone's going to think we're dead," said Theo.

"Oh God," said Nim. "My parents must be worried sick. They knew I was at that party with you guys."

For the first time, Diana wondered what her mother would think when she found her daughter missing from the island. Grief? Anger? Diana might never have a chance to explain what she'd done.

She reached forward and gave Nim's shoulder a squeeze. "You'll be back with them soon."

"Yeah," said Nim, her voice a little shaky.

"My dad's going to be so disappointed to find out I'm alive," said Theo.

"That isn't true," Jason said.

"And it's a crap thing to say," added Alia, the echo of old grief in her words.

Theo ran a thumb over the shiny knee of his pants. "You're right."

"Did anyone even know we were on that jet?" asked Nim, taking another corner so fast she veered into the opposing lane and had to jerk the wheel back.

"I'm not sure," said Jason, only gradually releasing his death grip on the door handle. "We didn't exactly file the appropriate papers when we left New York."

"But they'll know it's a Keralis jet," Alia said.

"So be it," said Jason.

"But the board—"

"The board will do what it's going to do," said Jason, shoulders stiff. "The company will survive. Our parents built Keralis Labs on innovation. If they lock us out, we'll just keep innovating." Diana wasn't sure if Jason believed his own words, but she did. She could hear the iron in his voice.

They saw no police and there were no indications that they were being followed, but Diana remained watchful as they steadily tacked southward. They stopped once to fill the Fiat's tank with gasoline, the rest of them watching through the window as Jason approached the attendant, whose gestures and angry exclamations made it clear he wouldn't accept American money. Jason turned away from the attendant, scrunching his fist, frustration radiating in every line of his body, and for a moment Diana thought he might strike the man. Instead, he unslung his watch from his wrist and handed it over.

"That belonged to our dad," Alia said quietly.

The attendant's demeanor changed instantly. He disappeared into the little store while Jason filled the tank, then emerged with his arms full of potato chips and bottled soda, and a big plastic jug of water that he shoved through the open window at them. Diana wasn't sure if the water was for them or the little car's radiator as they crossed the mountains. A few minutes later they were back on the road.

Jason stared straight ahead, and Diana saw him touch his fingers briefly to his now-bare wrist.

"Jason," Alia said tentatively.

He gave a short, sharp shake of his head. "Don't."

They drove on in silence, but after only a few miles had sped by Nim pulled to a halt by the side of the road where several cars were parked, their drivers somewhere down on the beaches below.

"Why are we stopping?" asked Diana. They still had until sunset the next day to get to the spring, but the farther they could get from their pursuers, the happier she'd be.

"We should switch the plates," said Nim. "The license plates. That guy at the gas station is going to remember us. We don't want this car matching up with a missing Fiat."

"Or we could *borrow* another car," Theo suggested.

"No," said Nim. "We steal a car, it gets reported, we're back on the grid, and they know which way we're headed. But no one pays attention to license plates. They won't notice the change until we're long gone, if they notice at all."

Alia leaned forward and gave Nim a tight hug over the back of the seat. "You're brilliant."

Nim beamed. "How much do you love me?"

"So much."

"How much?" hissed Nim.

Diana saw her fingers dig deeply into the flesh of Alia's arms. They were black talons, her arms corded with muscle. A stench filled the car, the dusty smell of decay. "If you loved me, you would let me kill him. You would let me kill them all."

"Nim!" Alia cried out, trying to pull away.

"Let go of her!" Jason grabbed Nim's wrist, then recoiled, his hand seared an angry red.

"I see you, Daughter of Earth," said Eris. Hollow black eyes deep as wells met Diana's in the rearview mirror. "You and your sisters have evaded our grasp far too long."

Diana shifted to launch herself forward, but Theo grabbed her arm.

"Our time draws near," he said, and Diana saw that he was not Theo. His face was pale as wax, his teeth yellowed points wet with blood. He wore a battered black helm, crowned by the face of a Gorgon.

Diana growled and shoved him from the car, tumbling with him to the ground.

"Get out of here, Alia!" Jason bellowed.

Diana heard the car door open and Alia's footsteps as she ran.

"Phobos," Diana said, looking down into the face beneath her. God of panic. A *god* beneath her.

He was beautiful until he smiled, the points of his teeth like spikes of sharpened bone. "We see you, Amazon. You will never reach the spring. War is coming. *We* are coming for you all."

She could feel his power coursing through her, flooding her mind with terror. Her heart pounded a frantic rhythm; cold sweat bloomed on her brow. She had failed. Failed her mother, her sisters, herself. She had doomed them all. A wild, gibbering panic slashed at her chest. She couldn't breathe. *Run*, her mind commanded. *Hide*. All she wanted was to obey, to let her legs carry her as fast and as far as they could, to find somewhere she could bow her head and weep. She wanted to cry out for her mother. Her mother. Through the horror, she held to the image of Hippolyta, warrior and queen, subject to no one.

"We are stronger," Diana gasped. "Peace is stronger."

"If only you believed that." His grin widened. "Can you imagine the pleasures that await? I can already taste your suffering on my tongue. . . . And it is sweet." He drew the last word out, his tongue waggling obscenely from his mouth.

It isn't real, she told herself. *Nothing terrible has happened. There's still time to reach the spring. This fear is an illusion.*

She needed something real, something indestructible and true, the opposite of the false fear Phobos created. Diana seized the lasso at her hip and pressed its golden coils against Phobos's throat. He screamed, a sound that seemed to pierce her skull, high and rattling.

"Get out," she snarled.

"Out of what?" Theo said desperately, batting at her arms. "Just tell me and I'm gone."

Diana rocked back on her heels. He sat up, looking dazed, his face as sweet and ordinary as it had ever been. She shook her head, eyes blinking furiously, body still trembling from the terror that had washed through her.

She shoved to her feet and rounded the other side of the Fiat. Nim was sobbing, but she was Nim again. The skin of Jason's hands and forearms looked badly blistered, though she could see they were already starting to heal. Apparently, the blood of kings was powerful stuff. Alia stood a few feet away, arms tight around herself, chest heaving.

Diana could feel the fragility of these mortals, and for the first time, something inside her felt breakable, too.

"We need to go," said Alia. She kept her arms wrapped around herself, as if trying to keep from flying apart, but her voice was steady, resolute. "Nim, can you drive?" Nim nodded, shakily. "Diana, can you and Theo switch the license plates?"

"Alia—" Jason began.

"We're getting to that spring. If they didn't think we were going to make it, they wouldn't be trying to frighten us."

Gods don't work that way, Diana thought but didn't say. Amazons were immortal. They didn't think in minutes or hours or even in years, but in centuries. And the gods? They were eternal. Alia's power had called to them, and like hibernating beasts they'd come awake with empty bellies. She could still hear Phobos crooning, *Can you imagine the pleasures that await?* The mirth in Eris's teasing voice when she'd said, *You and your sisters have evaded our grasp far too long.*

Diana retrieved Theo from where he was lying on his back, panting in the dirt, and set about making herself useful, afraid that if she faced Alia now, Alia would see the truth in her face. Because Diana knew that Phobos and Eris weren't worried. They'd been sure of themselves, smug. And they'd been hungry. What Alia had sensed in them was not anxiety but anticipation.

Now Diana understood what this war would really mean, and the terrible truth of the vow she'd made settled over her. If they did not reach the spring, she would have to face the horror of killing Alia, or live with the knowledge that she had helped set the gods' terrible appetite loose upon the world—and offered her own people up for the feast.

CHAPTER 20

They drove on, all of them weary and shaken. They'd faced bullets, missiles, a plane crash. Still, thought Alia, it was different to know that the forces allied against you weren't just humans who happened to be better trained and armed, but that actual gods were trying to take you down.

For a while, Diana and Jason passed the map back and forth, debating the best route to take to Therapne. They could save hours by cutting east across one of the major highways, but those roads would also probably be the most closely watched. Instead, they agreed to keep heading south to a twisting mountain road that would take them directly through the Taygetus. It was steep, empty of people, and rarely used by anyone but tourists eager for scenery. The sharp cliffs and rock overhangs also meant they'd be hard to get eyes on from the air.

The sun sank low over the horizon, and Nim's pace slowed. They used their brights when they could, but sometimes they had to double back when they missed road signs, and they were all getting sleepy. Nim's yawns grew more frequent. They rolled down the windows, turned the radio up loud. Jason kept offering her swigs of sugary soda from their supplies. But it was no good.

"I'm sorry," she said. "If I don't stop, I'm going to fall asleep at the wheel."

"It's okay," Alia said gently. She could sense Diana's frustration with their progress, but she also knew Nim had pushed as hard as she could. They all had. If the gods had meant to scare them off, they'd failed.

They'd been wending their way down the eastern side of a steep series of hills, and when they reached a flat-enough area, Nim steered the car carefully off the road behind a stand of lush poplars and brush that would hide the car from anyone on the road.

"We'll camp tonight," said Jason. "If we get an early start tomorrow, we'll be in Therapne long before sunset."

"We have to be," said Diana. "At dawn, the new moon rises and Hekatombaion begins."

Nim punched a button and the car's engine went silent. She turned off the headlights.

"We have the blankets Diana took from the farmhouse," said Jason. "Two people can sleep in the car."

"Or we could all sleep in the car," said Theo. "Not that I'm afraid of the dark. Which I am not."

Nim's hands gripped the steering wheel. "I'm not sure that's a great idea. Not if our . . . friends come back."

They opened the Fiat's doors and stepped outside into the balmy air. The stars glimmered brightly, gilding the trees around them in silver. Diana dropped into a lunge, stretching her long legs, and Alia felt a pang of sympathy. If she felt this stiff after being crammed in that car, Diana must really have been hurting.

"Do you hear that?" said Theo. "It sounds like running water."

They picked their way through the trees and brush toward the sound and emerged at the top of a wide outcropping of rock. Alia took a deep breath, something in her heart eased by the beauty of what she saw.

A waterfall. Two waterfalls, really. One that fed the small pool beside them, and another that cascaded over the rocks in a misty white veil, emptying into a wide, dark pond below.

Theo picked up a rock and tossed it over the cliff. It hit the surface with a resonant *plunk*, sending silver ripples marching toward shore. "Seems pretty deep."

"Look," said Nim. "A bell."

She was right. An old iron bell hung from a metal bar that had been driven between the rocks. "I think there's a cave back there," said Alia. "But why a bell?"

"It might be a hermit cave," said Diana. "Mystics—"

But her voice was cut off by the sound of Theo's whoop as he ran past them stark naked and leapt off the rock. A tremendous splash sounded, and they raced to the edge to see him emerge in the frothing water and shake his head like a dog.

Did I really just see Theo Santos naked? Alia thought. *Do not giggle,* she warned herself, but it was really hard when her mind kept conjuring up the image of Theo's starlit backside.

"Good news!" he called from below. "It's deep enough!"

"He is *unhinged,*" said Nim.

Diana frowned. "How did he even get his clothes off that fast?"

"We don't have time for this," Jason grumbled.

"I don't know," said Alia. "We have to stop for the night, and that water looks pretty good." Just for a minute, she wanted to forget all the horror they'd seen. She wanted to pretend she was an ordinary girl on a road trip, even if she knew the illusion wouldn't last.

"Alia—"

"Jason, I am tired, sweaty, and grumpy."

"That's like three of the Seven Dwarfs," said Nim. "I don't want to know what happens when she gets to four."

"I am part man!" Theo shouted from far below. "But also part fish!"

"Besides," said Alia, nudging Jason with her shoulder, "we need something good right about now."

"She's right," said Diana. "We can't keep driving, so it's not as if we're losing time." She unbuckled the straps of her top and pulled it over her head.

"What are you doing?" squeaked Alia, trying not to stare. "Why is everyone suddenly allergic to their clothes?"

"I thought you wanted to swim," said Diana, untying her sandals and yanking her leather trousers down.

"You're . . . you're . . . ," said Jason. He looked at the sky, the rocks, and then somewhere just over Diana's shoulder. "You don't have anything on."

A furrow appeared between Diana's brows. "Did Theo?"

"I don't . . . I mean—"

"Is something wrong?" Diana asked, planting her hands on her hips as if she were about to start a cheerleading routine.

"Absolutely not," said Nim. "Jason, Alia, you shut your mouths. I fell out of a plane. I got possessed by a war goddess. I deserve some happiness."

"A thing I thought," babbled Jason. "I had a thinking—"

"You should swim, too," said Diana. "You may be suffering heatstroke."

She turned her back and strode to the end of the rock, raising her arms overhead, her muscles flexing, her hair a gleaming tide over her shoulders. "Come on!" Diana called happily, and then she leapt, her body forming a perfect arc, her skin shining as if lit by some secret source of moonlight. A splash sounded from below.

"I should exfoliate more," said Alia.

"This is the best moment of my life," said Nim.

Jason had apparently given up on speech.

They swam for well over an hour. Alia had been sure Jason wouldn't join, but eventually he'd cannonballed over the top of the falls and made a very un-Jason-like splash.

Despite the laughter and Theo's continued crooning of "Don't go chasing waterfalls," she was aware of how cautious everyone was being, the distance Nim and Theo kept from each other, the alert way that Diana and Jason watched them. And yet she was right: They'd needed something good, and this—lying on her back in the water, the stillness of the pond filling her ears, the spangle of stars so dense above her it felt like she was looking into time itself—was very good.

Tomorrow they would reach the spring. Would its waters feel different on her skin? Would she know something inside her had changed forever?

When they were all thoroughly waterlogged and pruny, Diana jogged back up the hill to retrieve her leathers and brought their clothes and a blanket down from the car. Since they were away from the road, it seemed safe to make a fire and, after they gathered enough kindling, Diana set the little pile ablaze with ease.

"If all the Girl Scouts looked like her, I would have joined," Nim murmured.

"And worn that green uniform?"

Nim retched. "Never mind."

Diana claimed there were rabbits in the woods and offered to hunt them, but Nim was a vegetarian and no one was quite hungry enough to go that rustic. They ate most of what was left of the snacks from the gas station, and warmed themselves by the crackling of the flames.

"I'm exhausted," said Alia at last. "But I don't know if I can sleep."

"Theo and I will crash outside tonight," said Jason. "You guys can take the car."

"I know you're not going to like this," said Diana. "But we should probably restrain both Theo and Nim."

"I don't mind," said Nim. "I really don't want that thing in my head again."

Theo shuddered and nodded.

"We can rig something up with the blanket for Theo," said Jason. He paused. "Can you use the lasso on Nim?"

Diana's fingers brushed the golden loops of rope at her hip. "It's not really meant to be used that way. I've heard of people being driven mad when bound too long in its coils."

"Why?" asked Alia.

"No one wants to live with the truth that long. It's too much."

"I'll say," said Nim. "Jason looked like his head was going to explode."

"Nim!" said Alia. Did she really have to go kicking that particular beehive?

But Diana just looked Jason in the eye and said, "That was wrong of me. To use the lasso on a compatriot without his consent. I swear it won't happen again."

Jason held her gaze, and Alia felt a little like she was witnessing something private. "I should have told you. You gave me the chance, but I was too cowardly to take it." Then he seemed to remember they were sitting around a campfire. "I should have told all of you. Mom and Dad had their theories about where my strength came from, that it was tied to the bloodline and had just somehow skipped Dad, but . . . I never really believed it all."

"So that thing," said Nim, pointing at the lasso. "It really compels the truth?"

"Yes," Diana said.

"Had you used it before?" said Jason.

"No," she admitted.

He raised a brow. "What if it hadn't worked?"

The faintest smile tugged at her lips. "I wanted the truth. I was going to get it."

"But where did it come from?" said Nim. "How did you make it?"

"I didn't. It was woven by Athena on a spindle forged in Hestia's fire, of fiber harvested from Gaia's first tree."

A few days ago, Alia would have laughed, but after tangling with a pair of spiteful battle gods, she wasn't inclined to scoff.

"Big deal," said Theo. "You can probably get one on eBay."

"Off what coast is that located?" Diana asked.

Theo opened his mouth. Shut it. "Good question."

"So it's basically organic, locally sourced super string," said Nim. "Athena is the goddess of war, isn't she?"

"She's the goddess of war, but also of knowledge, and the pursuit of knowledge is basically—"

"The pursuit of truth," said Jason.

Diana nodded. "And like the truth, the lasso can't be altered or broken. I think that's why I was able to use it against Phobos. It's true in a way that the terror he inspires isn't."

"Nothing's indestructible," said Nim.

Diana looped a coil around her hand and flung the rope into the fire, sending up a shower of sparks.

Alia gasped, but the lasso didn't catch. It lay in the flames, unaltered, visible through the fire like a stone through clear water.

Diana drew it back and passed it to Nim. "See?" she said.

Nim squealed. "It's not even warm!"

"We should try it," Theo said.

"Jumping into the fire?" said Nim. "Definitely go for it."

"The lasso, *Nim.*"

"It isn't a toy," Diana said.

"Come on," said Theo. "One question each. Like truth or dare."

"I don't know . . . ," said Alia.

"Please?" Nim begged.

"You're actually agreeing with Theo?"

"I'm curious! And Jason survived."

Jason shook his head. "You don't want to mess with this. I've felt the lasso's power, and you're not going to like it."

"Meaning you're tough enough to handle it, but we aren't?" said Theo. His tone was light, but Alia could sense the tension in his words.

"That isn't what I meant."

"Come on, Diana," Theo said. "Let's do this."

Diana hesitated, and Alia wondered if she knew just how much of Theo's pride was wrapped up in this moment. She breathed a small sigh of gratitude when Diana said, "Okay, but only for a second."

"Me first!" shouted Nim.

"But I—" protested Theo.

"I called it, and by Holy Right of Dibs, it is mine."

Theo rolled his eyes. "Go on," he said. "I hope it melts your tiny brain."

Diana bit her lip and formed a loop with the lasso. "You're sure?"

Nim bobbed her head. "Hit me."

Diana slipped the rope over Nim's head and down to her shoulders.

Suddenly, Nim's eyes went blank. She sat up straight, slack-jawed.

"Nim?" said Alia.

"What do you wish to know?" Nim replied. Her voice was oddly formal.

"Umm . . . what should we ask her?" said Alia. "Quick!"

Diana frowned. "I'm not sure. I've never seen anyone react that way."

"Did you cheat on our U.S. History final?" said Alia.

"The system is corrupt. It was my duty to subvert it."

"Are you kidding?" said Alia.

"I must tell the *troooooth*," said Nim. "You should own more than one color of lip *glossssss*."

Alia punched Nim in the arm. "You are the worst."

"I am the best. See? Truth. And I can't believe you would ask me something that boring. Of course I cheated on the history final. Mr. Blankenship is a terrible teacher. If he wants to bore me to death, he should expect me to cheat on his crappy test."

"What was I supposed to ask you about? Were you the one who put shaving cream in Alicia Allen's locker?"

"Yes, but only because she kissed me at the harvest party and then pretended it never happened and then called me a lezzie to all her friends." Nim clapped her hands over her mouth.

Alia stared at her. "Are you serious?"

"I—I didn't mean to say that." Nim's eyes looked slightly

panicked. "I . . ." Sweat broke out on her brow, and her breath came in shallow pants.

Diana pulled the rope free. "I'm sorry! I warned you."

A tremor passed through Nim's body. "That was so weird."

"Alicia Allen?" said Alia. "Really? You're always saying how awful she is. You said she had a face like a weasel."

Nim scowled. "She's actually kind of human when she isn't with her crappy friends. I don't know. Not a lot of girls at our school show an interest, okay? I don't get to pick the lesbians."

"My turn!" said Theo.

Jason picked up a stick and jabbed it into the fire. "This is a bad idea. We should stop."

Theo shuffled over on his knees and crouched in front of Diana, his back to the flames. "Ready."

Alia saw the look that passed between Jason and Diana. Jason gave the barest shake of his head. Did he really think Theo would get hurt? Or was he afraid of what Theo might say?

Diana considered for a moment, then looped the lasso over Theo's body.

Alia searched her mind for something silly to ask him. She knew what she wanted to say, but even if they'd been alone, she still wouldn't have had the guts. *Have you ever seen me as anything more than Jason's annoying little sister? Could you?* Just thinking the words made her cheeks flame.

But before she could order her thoughts, Nim said, "Did you or your dad tip off those Germans so they could attack the museum?"

"Nim!" Jason said sharply, but Diana made no move to draw back the rope.

"Of course not," said Theo, his face shocked. "I didn't know anything about it."

"What about your father?" Nim said harshly.

"No!" shouted Theo.

Alia felt a tiny knot of tension beneath her ribs unspool.

Theo yanked the rope free and cast it aside. "How could you even think something like that?"

"We were all thinking it," said Nim. "Your dad disappeared at a pretty convenient time."

Theo rocked back on his heels, staring at them with wide, hurt eyes. "You really thought I could be involved in something like this?" He turned his wounded gaze on Alia. "You thought I'd help people hurt you?"

Alia shook her head furiously. "No! I . . ." What had she believed? That she was destruction walking. That Theo or his father would be entirely justified if they wanted her gone.

"There are spies on Jason's security team," Diana said gently. "Informers within Keralis Labs. No one knew what to think."

"What about you, Jason?" Theo asked.

Jason scrubbed a hand over his face. "You could have tipped someone off without even realizing it."

"So I'm not evil, I'm just incompetent?"

"Theo—" Jason began. But Alia had the feeling whatever he said next was just going to make things worse.

"My turn!" she blurted. They all stared at her. "For the lasso," she continued. "Put it on me, Diana."

"Seriously?" said Jason.

Diana hesitated, but the pleading in Alia's eyes must have done the trick because she gave a disbelieving shake of her head and said, "All right."

"Great!" Alia said with false enthusiasm. "But only one question." Under her breath, she whispered, "Nim, help me out here."

"Got you," murmured Nim.

"You're sure about this?" said Diana.

Absolutely not. Why hadn't she thought of some other way to change the subject? *An interpretive dance. How 'bout those Mets?* Really, the options were endless.

She tried to look calm as she let Diana loop the lasso gently over her shoulders. Its fibers were cool against her skin, and Alia felt a curious lightness overtake her. She saw that she feared the lasso because she feared everything. That she was afraid of the world in a way that Theo didn't seem to be, or Nim or Jason. That she loved Nim but resented her ease with people. That she feared Nim would tire of her, stop wanting to be her friend, go off to have adventures with someone more fun. That Nim would never forgive her for the trauma of the last few days. That Alia simply was not worth the trouble. All these truths passed through Alia's mind in the barest second, horrible in their clarity. Every small lie she'd ever told herself torn away to reveal something ugly but unburdened beneath.

She saw Nim open her mouth to ask a question, but Theo said, "What's the most embarrassing thing you've ever done?"

"Oh, I know the answer to this," said Nim with relief. "She fainted in gym class."

Alia parted her lips to agree, but instead she said, "I wrote Theo a love letter."

"What?" Nim shrieked.

"What?" Jason barked.

"Oh," said Theo, looking a little stunned. Or was he totally horrified? She couldn't tell.

Diana was already leaning forward to remove the lasso.

Alia wanted to blurt a denial. Her mouth formed the words to say "Just kidding," but instead she heard her own voice saying, "When I was thirteen. On pink princess stationery, and I sprayed it with lemon Pledge because I didn't have any perfume. I put it in one of his books."

This was easily the worst moment of her life, and that included every recent near-death experience. Diana yanked the rope over Alia's head, but Alia couldn't get free fast enough. She wriggled it past her braids and stood up, heat flooding her cheeks.

I'm going to die right here, she thought, eyes jumping from Nim's grimace to Jason's wince to Diana's worried blue gaze. She refused to look at Theo. Because the earth wasn't going to do her the courtesy of opening to swallow her. She'd live with this humiliation burning through her every time she looked at him, the same way it had been for months after she'd given him that note.

He'd been fifteen and string-bean skinny and perfect, and she'd been completely mad for him in a way that had seemed totally inevitable at the time. He would mutter to himself in Portuguese while he was scribbling away at his homework, and Alia thought it was the most adorable thing she'd ever seen.

The night Alia had signed the note with a flourish and placed it between the pages of Theo's math book, her sense of elation had lasted all the way to her bedroom. Then she'd panicked. She'd raced back to the living room, but Theo had already returned to the table, and there was no way to retrieve it. Eventually, he'd picked up his books, tucked them into his bag, and headed out, all while Alia sat there, pretending to conjugate French verbs, certain she was going to be sick. She'd tried to retrieve it after school the next day, but when she'd opened the math book, the letter was gone.

Alia would never forget the horrible, sickening cringe she'd felt in that moment—especially now that she was feeling it all over again.

Theo had never said anything, but she'd noticed he made sure never to be in a room alone with her again. Or maybe he hadn't and she'd imagined it. Alia could never be sure. But the sheer strain of trying to act casual over the next few months had been completely exhausting. Then Theo had gone away for the summer, back to São Paulo with his dad, while Alia and Jason had stayed in Martha's Vineyard, and Alia had been almost relieved. Except when Theo came back, he was nearly half a foot taller, that smattering of acne gone. He didn't even seem human anymore. And she looked exactly the same.

Now Alia smoothed down her damp T-shirt. "Well," she said. "That was the worst thing ever."

"Alia," said Theo, on his feet now. "It's no big deal. Honestly, it's awesome."

Theo had ignored her, he'd teased her . . . but Theo pitying her?

"Good night, everyone!" she chirped with forced cheer, and stumbled toward the path, ignoring Diana's call of "Alia!"

She marched up the hill, tears choking her throat. It wasn't the embarrassment. It wasn't the memory. It was everything that had come with it, every hateful thought she'd ever had about herself like a chorus in her head. The lasso was like looking into a mirror that stripped away each illusion you used to get yourself through the day, every bit of scaffolding you'd built to prop yourself up. And then there was just *you*. Boobs too small. Butt too big. Skin too ashy. She was too nerdy, too weird, too quiet around people. In the grips of the lasso, she'd known that she was glad that Theo and Nim didn't get along because Nim was funnier and braver and more interesting than Alia would ever be. She was like a gorgeous little fireball, while Alia was an ember, banked fire, easily overlooked in the face of all those flames. The idea that Theo might look at Nim one day and want her, choose her, had made Alia hate them both a little, and made her hate herself even more.

Alia crawled into the backseat of the Fiat and curled up against the car door. She could still see the stars through the window, but now all she felt was small.

A while later, she heard Nim open the door and climb into the driver's seat. "You awake?" she whispered.

"Yeah," Alia replied. She didn't feel like pretending.

"What did it show you?"

Alia glanced briefly at Nim. She sat face forward, gaze focused on the windshield. Maybe it was easier to talk this way, in the dark, without having to look each other in the eye.

Alia leaned her head back against the glass. "Basically that I'm a petty, jealous jerk. You?"

"That I'm a coward."

"That's ridiculous. You're the bravest person I know. You wore shorts with suspenders to a dance."

"That look worked."

"Like I said."

Alia heard Nim shift in her seat. "For all my big talk, I've never brought a girl home. I've never even hinted at that stuff to my parents. I'm afraid if I do, it will all fall apart."

Alia blinked, surprised. She'd figured Nim would come out to her parents when she was ready. They were one of the most loving families she knew. "I don't think that's true."

"It doesn't matter if it's true. It *feels* true."

Alia hesitated. She dug her fingernails into her palm. "Don't give up on me, okay?"

Nim twisted around in her seat and shoved her sheaf of hair back from her face. "What?"

Alia made herself meet Nim's eyes. "Once I go to the spring, it'll change. I won't have to be as scared to go out. I'll do better. Go to more parties. Whatever you want."

"Alia, it doesn't matter if you start hanging out at warehouse parties till dawn or if you stay in your room looking at balls of cells the way I know you want to. It's always going to be you and me against the world."

"Why?"

"Because everyone else sucks, and you don't need a magic lasso to know that's the truth."

Alia grinned, some of the shame and hurt sliding away. She closed her eyes, suddenly feeling like she might actually be able to sleep.

"Alia," she heard Nim murmur.

"Hmm?"

"No offense, but this is the worst vacation ever."

"I told you we should go to the Grand Canyon," Alia managed before fatigue overcame her, and she let herself drift into a deep sea of sleep.

CHAPTER 21

Diana packed dirt over the remnants of the campfire to make sure they wouldn't catch again, and wondered if she should apologize to Alia. After Alia had scurried up the hill, they'd all stared at each other for a long moment in tense silence, Theo standing awkwardly at the edge of the fire.

"Should I—" he'd hazarded.

"No," Nim had said. "Just let her shake it off, and then pretend it never happened."

"But—"

"She's right," Diana had said, though she'd wanted to follow Alia herself. She'd dealt with her fair share of humiliations, trailing after her mother and her Amazon sisters, always the slowest, always the last, excluded from their understanding of the world. When her pride was smarting, she didn't want to be reminded of her failures. She wanted the solitude of the cliffs. She wanted to be alone until the hurt dwindled, until it was small enough to pack away. "Just let her be."

Jason peered up at Theo and raised a brow. "She sent you a *love* letter?"

"It wasn't a big deal."

"How come you never mentioned it?"

Theo had jammed his hands in his pockets. "She was just a kid. I didn't want to embarrass her."

"Why did you even ask that stupid question?" Nim said grumpily.

His shoulders shot up to his ears. "I thought she would say something dumb, like she drank too much fruit punch and vomited on her bunk at sleepaway camp."

"That seems awfully specific," said Diana.

"Yeah, well, it could happen to anyone. Don't we need to get some rest? Big day tomorrow? Mystical cleansing?"

"I'm going back to the car," said Nim. "I know Alia needs her space, but if I stay down here much longer, I'm going to try to drown Theo in the pond."

Nim had headed up the hill, but as they'd gathered their empty chip bags and soda bottles and extinguished the fire, Diana's mind was still on Alia. Though the stories of the lasso and what it might accomplish were so varied she hadn't known what to expect, she still felt guilty.

Mortals weren't meant to trifle with these things—and her mother would have been furious if she'd known Diana was playing party games with a sacred weapon. Although she supposed it would be the least of the things her mother would be furious about right now. She ran her thumb over the golden fibers, the lasso glowing faintly at her touch. It felt oddly friendly, like another companion who traveled with them. It wasn't meant to sit behind glass in a cold room. She'd read once that there were jewels that required wearing to keep their luster. She couldn't help but feel that the bracelets, the lasso, even the heartstone still tucked into her pocket, were gifts that weren't meant to be locked away.

She looked up to realize that Jason was studying her.

"What are you thinking about?" he asked.

"Why?" She rose and dusted her hands off on her leathers as they started up the trail.

"He's hoping you're thinking about him," said Theo with a laugh.

Jason gave Theo a light shove that nearly sent him careening into a tree.

"Hey!" said Theo. "Use your words!"

Diana cast Jason a swift glance. His jaw was set, his shoulders stiff as always. *Was* that what he'd been wondering? Or, as Alia would say, was Theo just being Theo?

She cleared her throat. "I'm wondering what tomorrow might bring," she said. "I can't imagine it will be as simple as just finding the spring. We don't know what might be waiting for us."

"Sure we do," said Theo, swatting at a branch. "We get to the spring, Alia gets cured. We argue over the best choice for our We Saved the World victory dance."

"I do enjoy your optimism," said Diana.

"And I admire your ability to lift a car over your head without breaking a sweat and look fine as hell doing it," said Theo with a bow.

"Why do I have the feeling it's not going to be as easy as you think?" Jason said.

"Because you're a glass-half-empty kind of guy."

"Whereas you're an it-will-all-work-out-or-someone-else-will-take-care-of-it kind of guy?"

"Unfair."

"I'm serious, Theo. If this all goes to hell, you can't just reboot or re-up or whatever."

"You mean one-up. And good to know you're concerned, even if you did think I was some kind of traitor."

"Theo—" Jason attempted.

Theo clapped Jason on the back. "I get it, okay? Just maybe give me a little more credit. You guys are my family. More than my dad has ever been. Besides, without me you'd currently be riding a mule over a mountaintop."

"The mule would talk less," Jason noted.

"Probably smell better, too," said Theo.

Was it really that simple? A shared joke, a pat on the back, forgiveness given when no apology had been offered? She'd seen Jason's frustration with Theo's glib ways, Theo's irritation at how easily Jason dismissed him. But they seemed perfectly happy to avoid talking about any of it. Boys were peculiar creatures.

Diana left Jason and Theo to set up their makeshift camp across the clearing from the car. Through the windows of the Fiat, she could see Alia and Nim already dozing. She hated to wake them.

"Sorry," she whispered as she slipped inside and used two knotted socks to bind Nim's hands together.

"It's okay," said Nim sleepily. "My mom duct-taped oven mitts on my hands when I had the chicken pox."

Diana wasn't sure what cooking and infectious diseases had to do with anything, but she made a polite humming noise.

She shifted in the passenger seat, trying to find a comfortable position, listening to the quiet of the night. She wanted to sleep, but the car was miserably cramped, and her mind didn't want to shut down. A run might help.

She slipped outside as silently as she could. Someone was snoring loudly from the other side of the clearing, and based on the timbre, she suspected it was Theo. Diana stretched, then walked back to the outcropping to listen to the rush of the waterfall and see if she could find another trail.

She was surprised to see Jason standing there, gazing out at the water. He'd shed his shirt again, possibly to bind Theo's hands, and the mist from the falls had beaded on his skin.

As if sensing her presence, he turned sharply.

"Sorry," she said. "I wasn't spying. I couldn't sleep." Well, maybe she'd been spying a little. She liked looking at him. But hadn't Nim said that most girls did?

"Me neither," he said. "Theo snores."

"So I heard."

Jason looked back out at the falls. "What if it doesn't work?" he said quietly.

Diana didn't ask what he meant. "The Oracle didn't lie."

"Then maybe she made a mistake. Oracles have been wrong before."

"Not this one."

He leaned against the rock by the bell and crossed his arms. "Would you have played the game if we'd kept going?"

"With the lasso? I don't know. Would you have?"

He expelled a short breath. "Absolutely not."

Diana perched beside him on the rock. "I meant what I said. I'm sorry for using the lasso on you."

Jason shrugged, the muscles shifting smoothly beneath his skin. "What I am, what I can do, I've kept it secret a long time. Keeping people out gets to be a habit."

"I shouldn't have forced my way in. Truth means something different when it's given freely."

He tilted his head back, watching the stars. "Early on, my parents saw that I was stronger than the other kids, faster. And I liked to fight. I was on the way to becoming a bully. They taught me to hold back, to be careful not to hurt anyone. But sometimes I feel it in my blood, the desire to use this strength, to prove myself."

Diana tried not to show her surprise. This was exactly the behavior she'd been told to expect in the World of Man. And yet, Jason recognized the urge to violence that had been passed down to him through the Keralis line. He'd struggled to temper it.

"Is that why you value control so highly?"

"It's that. But it's also the way I was raised. My mom taught Alia and me that our money could only protect us so much. People would be waiting for us to fail, to prove we didn't deserve what we had."

"I know that feeling," she admitted.

He cast her a skeptical glance. "Do you? It's a trap for us. Alia and I always have to be better. We always have to be a step ahead.

But the stronger you get, the more you achieve, the more people want to make sure you know your place." He bumped the back of his head gently against the rock. "It's exhausting. And all that caution doesn't leave much room for greatness."

Maybe she understood less than she thought. On the island, Diana had always known her failures meant more, but she'd also known her achievements would be her own, that if she ran quickly enough, fought hard enough, thought fast enough, her sisters would treat her victories with respect.

She nudged her arm against his. "It wasn't stupid. What you said on the plane. We all want a taste of greatness."

Jason turned his head to look at her. "What if you want more than a taste?"

Something in those words made her pulse quicken. "How much more?"

"I don't know." His gaze shifted back to the sky. "You take a bite. You take another. How are you supposed to know when you'll be full?"

I see you, Daughter of Earth. I see your dreams of glory.

"Then your desire to run Keralis Labs, your parents' legacy—"

"Their legacy," he repeated, and released a bitter laugh. "Do you know some part of me wants to believe Alia's power caused the car accident that killed our parents?"

Diana drew in a sharp breath, and he glanced at her, dark eyes glinting.

"How's that for truth?" he said. "It's why I pushed Michael so hard on the investigation. I wanted there to be a conspiracy, an explanation, a reason for all of it. If wanting to do great deeds isn't stupid, that is. It's the way little kids think."

What would it do to someone to lose so much in a single night? Who wouldn't search for order, for some measure of control?

"You wanted to find meaning in their deaths," she said. "There's nothing wrong with that."

Jason pushed off the rock and prowled to the edge of the cliff.

"I wanted to remake the world. Make it into something I under-stood." He crossed his arms, profile turned to the sky, and she remembered seeing him alone in the orchard, a stone sentinel, keeping the watch. "I still do."

"That's why you want to retain control of the company."

He cocked his head to one side and slowly made his way back to the rock. "Why do I feel like I'm always the one who ends up talking instead of you?"

"I'm an excellent listener?" she ventured.

He snorted. "I'll make you a deal. We'll play twenty questions. You answer, and I'll forgive you for the lasso."

She cut a hand through the air. "Twenty is way too many."

"Ten."

"Three."

"Three?" he said incredulously. "That's nothing!"

She thought she knew what he would ask, and she felt ready to tell him the truth about who and what she was—maybe not all of it, but some. She'd taken that much from him by force. She could give it back.

Diana shrugged. "In the stories it's always three. Three wishes. Three questions."

He sighed and settled next to her on the rock again. "Fine. But you have to tell the truth."

"As much as I can."

He rubbed his hands together in anticipation. "Okay, Diana Prince, do you have a boyfriend back home?"

She laughed. That wasn't what she'd expected at all.

"No."

"A girlfriend?"

"No. You realize you're terrible at this, right? That was two questions."

"But—"

"Rules are rules. One more question, Jason Keralis."

She waited. She knew what he would ask next.

"Fine," he said. "What's the story of the double star?"

She sat up straighter, surprised. No questions about her home? Her people? "You remember that?"

"Yes, and I knew you didn't want to tell me about it."

She scowled. "Am I that easy to read?"

"Maybe I'm just an excellent listener. Go on. Story."

Diana leaned back against the rock, listening to the wind in the pines. This was a different kind of secret to share. She'd already admitted the story was her favorite. She didn't want to look foolish.

She studied the night sky. "Do you know how to find Ursa Major?"

"The Big Dipper?" said Jason. "Sure."

She pointed, tracing a path. "If you follow the handle, you'll see Arcturus there beside it. And if you keep going, you'll see the star known as the Horn, or Azimech. It's one of the brightest in the sky."

"Can't miss it."

"But it has a secret."

He clucked his tongue. "Never a good idea."

"Never," she agreed. "It's really two stars, orbiting the same center of gravity, so close they're indistinguishable. The story is that there was a great warrior, Zoraida, who swore she would never give herself to anyone but her equal. But none could best her in battle."

"I'm guessing this is where the hero enters."

"Zoraida is the hero. But another champion did come to try to win her, a man just as prideful and just as strong. He swore he would defeat her or die in the endeavor, and so, on a rosy dawn, they met and clashed, Zoraida with her trusted axe in hand, and Agathon with a sword that gleamed bright as morning." Diana closed her eyes, remembering the words of the story. "From the start, it was clear they were evenly matched, and the valley echoed with the sounds of the blows they rained down on each other. On and on they fought, for hours and then days. And when Zoraida's axe shattered on Agathon's gauntlet, and Agathon's sword broke against Zoraida's shield, still they battled, neither willing to cede victory."

"Who won?" said Jason.

Diana opened her eyes. "Neither. Or both. Depending on how you look at it. As they fought, their respect for each other grew. They fell in love, but as they were matched in strength, so were they matched in stubbornness. They died in each other's arms and, with their last breaths, spoke their vows. The gods placed them in the sky, where they might remain forever, neither diminished by the other's brightness, ruling their corner of the night in haughty isolation."

"*That's* your favorite story?" Jason's brows were raised in the bemused expression she was coming to expect from him.

"Yes," she said defensively.

"That is some grim stuff. You a Romeo and Juliet fan, too?"

Diana scoffed. "Hardly. I prefer Benedick and Beatrice."

"But they weren't doomed!"

"Doomed isn't a necessity."

"Just a nice perk?"

Diana threw up her hands. "It's a tragic love story."

"I mean, it's definitely *tragic*."

"It's romantic. They found their equals." From the first time Diana had heard Zoraida's story, she'd been fascinated by it. It had seemed filled with all of the danger and enticement of the World of Man. What would it mean to want someone so much but hold to your beliefs in spite of it? If she'd lost her heart to Agathon, would she have given in or kept to her vow? Maybe the story was a *little* melodramatic, but that didn't mean she had to stop loving it. She turned to find Jason watching her again. "Why didn't you ask me about the island?" she said. "Where I'm from?"

He smiled, and his dimple made a shadow in his cheek. "Truth means something different when it's given freely." He bobbed his head toward the valley. "How far away do you think that mountain peak is?"

Diana grinned. "Let's find out."

With a laugh, they were plunging down the hill, past the pond, through the silver wood.

Diana shot past him, leaping over a fallen log, under a low branch, her heart pounding a happy rhythm as the forest unfolded before her. She burst from its trees onto a gravelly hillside, sliding more than running as the powdery soil gave way beneath her feet in a shower of pebbles. She heard Jason whoop somewhere behind her, struggling to keep up but apparently enjoying every minute of it.

They were on open ground now, low rolling hills pocked with boulders and scrub clinging to rough planes of granite. She heard Jason's steady footsteps, and then he was running beside her, matching her step for step. *He's not hiding anymore*, she realized. She laughed, and his smile flashed white in the darkness.

Diana let go and ran. *You do not enter a race to lose.*

She felt the slap of her sandals against the earth, the stars whirling above her. She didn't bother to pace herself or to worry about how far or how high the mountain might be. She simply ran, Jason's steps pushing her faster, the hound at the heels of the stag—but she felt no fear, only exhilaration. She didn't need to worry about what it might mean to lose or how she should comport herself as a princess. There was only the race, the desire to win, the thrill of her wild heartbeat matched to his as they leapt the rocky gully of a stream and began to climb the peak's steep slope, pushing through thorny scrub and fragrant pine until . . . there, an old cart track, barely visible, overgrown with weeds and broken by tree roots.

Diana hooted in triumph as her feet met the path, sprinting higher to where the trees were sparse, their trunks bent and twisted by the wind. They looked like women, frozen in a mad dance, the tangle of their hair tossed forward in abandon, their backs arched in ecstasy or bent in supplication, a processional of dancers that led Diana up the mountainside.

Run, they whispered, *for this is what happens if you let your feet take root*. But wasn't that the life Diana's sisters had chosen?

Bound to one spot, safe but locked out of time, preparing for a war that might never come?

She rounded a bend and saw the crest of the peak before her, a small shrine near its apex, a Madonna surrounded by withered flowers and packages of sweets, small offerings. Diana somehow knew that there had always been shrines here, holy places where the gods' names were spoken, where prayers were offered beneath the black and limitless sky.

She put on a spurt of speed, lengthened her stride, and gave a shout as she passed the shrine and reached the mountain's highest peak, raising her arms in victory.

Jason padded up behind her, jogging the last few yards. His laugh was breathless as he bent double, hands on his knees. "Not nice to gloat," he panted.

Diana grinned. "We should have made a wager."

She gazed out over the valley to the peaks of the Taygetus far in the distance, a world painted in black and silver, the sky a dark vault of stars. It seemed to go on and on, unbounded by seas or barriers, a world that might take a hundred human lifetimes to explore. But when they reached the spring, she would have to leave all of these horizons behind.

"Well, I guess I'm no Agathon," Jason said. "I barely kept up with you."

She gave him a grudging nod. "You kept up fine."

"Did I?" he asked, and somehow she knew that was not really the question he was asking. Starlight gilded the lines of his profile as he turned to her.

"Yes," she said, the sound caught on a breath.

Jason leaned forward, and she felt her own weight shift as if snared by his gravity, by the shape of his lips, by the shift of muscle beneath his skin. His mouth met hers, warm and smooth, the first summer plum, ripe with promise, and hunger bloomed in her like an eager vine, its tendrils uncurling low in her stomach. He slid his hand into her hair, drawing her closer. But beneath his strength and speed, she could feel how very mortal he was, his life as fleeting as a kiss, a captured spark. He would not last. And so she let herself feel the fierce beat of his heart, the heat of his skin, the ferocity of a life that would shine for the barest moment, there and then gone.

CHAPTER 22

Alia woke at dawn to birdsong—and a crescent moon visible on the horizon, a slender, perfect scythe. The reaping moon. Hekatombaion had begun. *We're almost there,* she reminded herself. *We just have to reach the spring before sunset.*

Either binding Theo and Nim during the night had done the trick or the gods of battle had found some other group of people to harass because no one seemed to be screaming or trying to commit murder. Diana and Jason were already awake, the last of their food stores set out on a rock as they debated the merits of which route to take to Therapne and how they hoped to find the spring once they were there. They sat close together, their shoulders almost touching, the animosity that had hummed between them since that first meeting at the Good Night seemingly gone. *Maybe it wasn't animosity,* she considered as she rolled her head, trying to work the crick out of her neck. *Ugh.* If Jason was making moves on her friends, she didn't want to know about it. *Though he could definitely do worse.*

Alia left Nim still snoozing in the reclined driver's seat and went to wash her face and hands in the upper pool of the falls.

She heard Theo before she saw him, the happy whistle of some song she didn't recognize floating around the bend in the path. Before she could turn and run, he was rounding the corner in his shiny, battered trousers and the stolen blue button-down that now seemed to be missing its sleeves. He was carrying the full water jug in front of him with both skinny arms and stopped dead when he saw her. His crop of locs looked more awake than he did.

"Hey," he said.

Well, this isn't going to be awkward at all. "Hi," said Alia, making her best effort to sound normal. "How'd you sleep?"

"Good, good. You?"

"Great," she said, continuing past him toward the falls. *Easy. Now you just have to spend a few hours crammed in a car with him. No problem.*

She heard a *thunk* and his footsteps and realized he'd set the water jug down and was jogging to catch up with her. Maybe she could just stick her head underwater and hold her breath until he went away.

"Listen . . . ," he began.

"Theo, whatever you're going to say is only going to make it worse. It's not a big deal. I was thirteen. I had a crush."

"Because my eyes are golden as a sunset sea?"

For a second Alia was just confused, and then the memory came back to her with gut-clenching clarity. *Your eyes are golden as a sunset sea. I could drown in them a thousand times.* That horrible letter.

"Oh God," Alia groaned. "I was hoping you never read it."

Theo grinned. "I read it."

"Well, it was a long time ago," she said with an awkward laugh. "I wrote like ten of those. One was to Zac Efron."

"Oh." He actually looked a little disappointed. "That's too bad. It was pretty much the nicest thing anyone's ever said to me."

Alia thought of the string of girls she'd seen with Theo the last few years. "Sure."

He ran his hand back and forth over his locs. "Do you even remember what you wrote?"

"Not exactly. Every time my brain tries to go back there, I cringe so hard I have to stop or risk an aneurysm."

Theo looked down at his pointy-toed dress shoes. They were scuffed beyond repair, the houndstooth pattern on their sides nearly hidden by dust. "You said I was smart and that if people didn't always get my jokes, maybe it was because they couldn't keep up."

"I did?" Well, she'd been right about that. Alia remembered how much she'd hated the way Michael picked on Theo, how kids at school had called him weird and goofy. As they'd gotten older, everyone had seemed to realize that Theo's taste in music and clothes and everything else wasn't so much weird as interesting. She'd watched girls start to fawn over him and had felt like a disgruntled hipster. *I knew he was cool before you did.*

"You compared me to a pistol shrimp," he said.

Alia closed her eyes. "Are you trying to get me to drown myself?"

"No, it was amazing. You said the pistol shrimp was tiny, but it has this claw that can produce a bang—"

"Louder than a jet engine," said Alia. "Yeah, I remember. I was really into marine biology that year."

"Right," said Theo eagerly. "So it makes this bang that can shock big fish or whatever, but you said it survives by being noisy, not by trying to blend in."

"How do you even remember all that?"

Theo's grin went lopsided. He jammed his hands into his pockets and bounced once on his heels. "I kept it."

"Really?"

He shrugged. "It was a good reminder. When things weren't going great."

Alia folded her arms. "If it meant so much to you, why didn't you say anything?"

Theo rolled his eyes. "Because there was a lot of ridiculous kissy stuff, too, and you were *thirteen* and my best friend's sister. I thought you might pounce on me in the TV room and ask me to marry you. I mean, there's half a page dedicated to all the signs that we were soul mates. One of them was we both like ketchup."

Alia covered her head with her hands. "Stop."

"Lotta loopy stalker talk, some seriously convoluted metaphors."

"Okay, that's enough. Go away and leave me to enjoy my humiliation in peace."

"But that's what I'm saying—I'm sorry that note embarrasses you." She lifted a brow. "Okay, I'm not that sorry, because you're kind of cute when you're embarrassed, but that letter meant everything to me. You told me you liked the way I wasn't like anyone else, and that was really what I needed to hear right then."

"Then . . . I guess, you're welcome?" said Alia, unsure of what else to say. She supposed she could live with a little embarrassment. "But you still have to leave."

"Why?"

"Because I really need to go."

"Right, to the spring!"

"No," she said, cheeks heating. "To *go*."

Theo gave her the thumbs-up. "And I'm out."

He headed back down the path, but when he picked up the water jug, Alia said, "Hey, Theo?"

"Yeah?"

"The night of the party at the Met, how come you complimented everyone but me?"

He grinned. "Because you in that gold dress turned my brain to mush."

She rolled her eyes. "Right."

He took a couple of steps, then paused. "Alia?" he called back.

"What, Theo?"

"That night, at the party? You looked like buried treasure."

*   *   *

Alia took her time getting back to the car, mostly because she couldn't shake the goofy grin from her face, and when she finally returned to the clearing, Diana was pacing and Jason looked suitably grouchy. He opened the Fiat's door to usher them inside, and Alia was pretty sure that if he'd still had a watch he would have tapped it impatiently.

They squeezed into the same formation they had the previous day: Nim behind the wheel, Jason in the passenger seat, and the rest of them wedged into the back, Diana sandwiched between Alia and Theo like the really gorgeous filling in a pressed panini. Alia felt almost guilty for the room she had behind Nim and silently blessed her friend's short legs.

They decided to keep to their plan to take the Langadha Pass, and a few hours later they skirted the town of Kalamata, pausing only to get gas—after a negotiation that went considerably more smoothly with Diana doing the talking—before they joined up with the road heading east through the hills.

It didn't take long to realize why locals didn't use this particular route. It clung to the cliff in a narrow ribbon, bracketed on one side by unforgiving gray rock and on the other by a steep plunge into a tree-choked ravine.

Alia tried to control her nausea as they snaked around another hairpin turn. The road shrank to a single lane in some sections, with no way to see who might be coming the opposite direction or how fast. Even when there were two lanes, they were so cramped that whenever another car sped by, the Fiat shuddered. Alia told herself it was just because of the change in pressure between the two vehicles, but attaching Bernoulli's principle to the shaking didn't make her feel any less like they were one careless driver away from a crash that would smash them into the side of the mountain or send them sailing into nothingness.

"This is an ancient road," said Diana, looking past Alia out the window. "Telemachus traveled it by chariot when he rode from Nestor's palace to meet Menelaus in Sparta."

"Menelaus? As in Helen's husband?" asked Alia.

"I bet Telemachus didn't get stuck behind a tour bus," growled Nim, laying on the horn.

"Hey," said Jason. "We're trying not to attract attention, remember?"

"Don't worry," said Nim, punctuating every word with a horn blast. "No. One. Is. Paying. Attention. To. Me."

Eventually, the bus found a place to pull to the side and Nim zoomed by as Alia clenched Diana's arm and squeezed her eyes shut.

"Nim," she gasped, "I realize we're fleeing for our lives, but that's not going to matter if we don't actually survive this drive."

"It's fine!" said Nim, taking another turn with such enthusiasm everyone in the car slid hard to the left.

They'd had to sacrifice the car's air conditioning to the climb up the hill, and now that they were free of the bus's exhaust fumes, Alia tilted her head out the open window and breathed deeply.

The part of her brain that wasn't preoccupied with trying not to vomit could appreciate the beauty of this place, the dense clouds of pine, the jagged peaks and twisting spires of the pass. There were places where the rock hung low over the road like a wave frozen just before it broke, others where the road narrowed and the car passed through a slender, rough-hewn furrow in the stone. Whoever had cut through the rock had left little room on either side. Alia felt like the Fiat was caught in some monster's gullet, and that at any minute the beast might clear its throat.

They flew past a sign and Jason said, "That was the Kaiadas pit."

"The what now?" said Alia.

"It's where the Spartans dropped their enemies so no one would find them. It's supposed to be bottomless."

"Yeah, and their kids, too," said Theo. "If the babies weren't up to snuff."

"That's awful," said Alia.

"It was a martial culture," Jason said. "They had different priorities."

Theo flicked Jason's ear. "So you're saying it was okay for them to dump anyone who wasn't a perfect physical specimen like yourself?"

"I'm just saying it was a different time."

Nim shuddered. "A barbaric time."

"Is the world we live in so much better?" said Jason.

"Flush toilets," offered Nim.

"Antibiotics," said Alia.

"Smartphones," said Theo.

"But that's what I mean," said Jason. "Antibiotics have created new strains of super bacteria. People are so dependent on their phones that they don't bother learning anything for themselves anymore."

Alia leaned forward and swatted Jason's arm. "I cannot believe you're talking smack about science."

Jason held up his hands defensively. "I'm not! I'm just saying all those things that make our lives so convenient have a price. Think about the way technology has changed modern warfare. How much courage do you need to launch an air strike from behind a computer screen?"

"It's true," said Diana. "You're efficient killers."

"Sure," said Alia, thinking of all the advances her parents had made at Keralis Labs, even the things they'd been working toward with Project Second Born. "But we're also efficient healers."

"And that has a cost, too," said Jason. "Every generation is weaker than the last. Unable to adapt and thrive without being propped up by vaccines, gene therapy."

Theo kicked the back of Jason's seat. "Jesus, Jason, you're sounding more Spartan by the second."

"It's just biology," Jason said. "I'm not saying it's good or bad."

Theo slumped back in his seat. "Yeah, well, all I know is I would have been the first one over the cliff. The Spartans probably weren't big on scrawny nerd babies in a *martial culture*."

"It's a myth," said Diana.

Alia wasn't sure what that meant anymore. "You mean like Warbringers and battle gods?"

"No, I mean, one of the most famous Spartan poets was blind from birth. They had a king with a clubfoot. They knew there was more to being a warrior than strength. All that stuff about leaving babies to die was Athenian propaganda."

"Hey," said Nim. "Do you know what the Spartans said when the Persians demanded they lay down their arms and surrender?"

"No," said Theo. "But I bet it was followed by a lot of yelling and a slow-motion fight scene."

"Molon labe," said Jason.

" 'Come and get them,' " murmured Diana.

"Ha!" said Theo. "Someone knows more than the know-it-all."

Nim hurtled them past the next turn. "Theo, I'm pretty sure we have time to detour to that bottomless pit."

Come and get them. Alia wondered if Diana thought they might be facing a battle today. Was she afraid? Or was she like a concert violinist looking forward to a chance to play?

"Alia," said Theo, ignoring Nim, "what's the first thing you want to do once you're purged of all your Warbringer-ness?"

Alia opened her mouth, then hesitated. In all the terror and desperation to get to the spring, she hadn't really thought about what might come after. "Do you think I'll feel different?" she asked Diana.

"I don't know," Diana said, "but I think the world will."

Theo laughed. "You mean we're all going to join hands and sing folk songs?"

"That sounds unpleasant," said Diana.

"Come on!" said Theo. "Peace, love, the Age of Asparagus."

"Aquarius," corrected Nim.

"Is this really what you think peace is?" Diana said, clearly amused. "It sounds like a bad one-act play."

"No, no, no," said Theo. "It's definitely a musical."

"Oh God," groaned Nim.

"When the *moooon* is in the something something," crooned Theo.

Nim gripped the steering wheel. "Theo, shut up."

"And *Jooopiter* is wearing *paaaants*—"

"Theo!" snarled Nim. "*Shut up*. There's something behind us."

Alia craned her neck to see out the back window. There was a truck there, flashing its brights. "Maybe he just wants to get by."

But at that moment the truck accelerated, its bumper kissing the back of the Fiat, sending the little car lurching forward as they all screamed.

Alia looked back again, and through the window she saw the driver's hollow black eyes, his lips pulled back in a rictus grin, his monstrous face framed by a lion's helm. The truck flickered, and Alia saw the shape of a chariot drawn by four massive horses, their eyes red as blood, their huge hooves sparking against the asphalt. Fear flooded through her. She needed to get out of this car.

Diana grabbed her hand, keeping it from the door handle.

"Don't give in to the fear. It's Deimos," she said, keeping her voice low, steady, though Alia could see her pupils had dilated and a sheen of sweat had broken out on her brow. "God of terror. Phobos's twin. Nim, you have to slow down."

The driver laid on his horn, the sound too loud, filling Alia's ears. In it she heard the trumpets of war, the screams of the dying.

The truck roared forward and banged against their bumper again. The car jolted, swung far into the left lane, nearly colliding with a car coming the other direction.

Nim clutched the steering wheel, pulling them back into their lane, and hit the gas, trying to outpace the truck. "What do I do?" she gasped, voice trembling. In the rearview mirror, Alia could see the terror on her face, her knuckles white on the steering wheel.

"Slow down," commanded Diana.

"He's right on my butt!" Nim yelled.

"Listen to Diana. He won't try to kill us," Jason said, his fists clenched, knuckles like white stars. "Slow down. They don't want the Warbringer dead."

"Do it, Nim," said Alia, though everything in her screamed to run as far and as fast from the monster behind them as they could. She made herself squeeze Nim's shoulder. "Do it."

Nim huffed a low sob, flexed her fingers, and took her foot off the gas. The car slowed.

Again the truck's horn blared, and Alia covered her ears. Over it all, she heard the roar of the engine, the thunder of hooves. The truck had moved into the opposite lane and was pulling alongside them.

"He's going to run us into the cliff!" cried Theo.

"We need to stop," said Jason.

"I can't!" sobbed Nim. "There are cars behind us."

Innocent drivers. What did they see? A little Fiat packed with tourists, slowing and speeding up, driving erratically? A truck trying to pass? Or something worse? If Nim stopped the car, the other drivers might have time to slow and stop safely, or those people might go careening off the cliff into the gorge.

The sound of the chariot seemed to shake the little car, the pounding of hooves was the detonation of mortars, the clatter of its wheels the earsplitting percussion of gunfire.

Theo laughed, and Alia saw Phobos beside Diana. He kicked at Jason's seat in ferocious glee as Diana put her arm out to restrain him. The Fiat shot forward.

"Nim, *slow down!*" Alia cried.

But Nim's only answer was a ragged cackle, her star-strewn hair a glittering tangle, as Eris shoved her foot down on the gas, racing the chariot.

Deimos grinned and cracked his whip, a long black coil that gleamed like a slick-skinned adder in his hand. The chariot roared ahead—one car length, two—and cut into their lane. It screeched to a halt, and Alia saw the truck's trailer slide around so it was blocking the road. They were going to crash.

She opened her mouth to scream. Jason grabbed the steering wheel and yanked it hard right. The Fiat jounced off the highway and onto a side road, its back wheels squealing against the blacktop as it skidded into a spin and careened off the pavement into the brush, branches crackling against the windshield. Alia realized Diana had braced her body around hers, then heard a loud *bang.*

One of their tires had blown. The car slowed and finally rattled to a halt.

The air went still, the silence strangely loud in Alia's ears, until one by one the sounds of the ordinary world seemed to return: insects, the chirp of birds, the rhythm of her own frantic breathing.

Jason had his arms straight out, hands flat against the dashboard, nostrils flaring as he inhaled, exhaled, eyes closed. Theo leaned his head against the back of Jason's seat, muttering, "Shit, shit, shit."

Diana's face was pale, her blue eyes wide. She pushed the braids back from Alia's face. "Are you all right?"

Alia managed to nod.

Nim shoved open the driver's-side door, stumbled two weaving steps, crumpled to her knees, and threw up.

Alia batted at the door handle. She couldn't quite make her fingers work. Diana leaned forward and released the lock. Alia slid out after Nim, her legs rubbery. For a moment the world tilted and she thought she might faint. Then she was next to Nim, holding her tight as they both shook.

She heard the car doors open and made herself take a proper look around. They were in a shallow gully pocked with olive trees. It had been sheer luck that they hadn't slammed into one of them and wrecked the car completely.

"So they weren't trying to kill us, huh?" said Theo, leaning against the side of the Fiat.

"They stopped the truck there for a reason," Diana said. She dug into the car's trunk and brought the water jug over to Nim, crouching down to offer it to her. "Drink," she said gently.

Jason paced in tight circles. His eyes were a little wild. "They wanted to slow us down. They knew the side road was here. They drove us off the highway on purpose."

"The chariot," Alia said, voice dazed. "I saw a chariot when we took off from the Great Lawn. I think it was one of them. I think he was helping us get away, driving the soldiers back, keeping me alive."

Nim took a sip of water, rinsed her mouth, spat in the dirt, then took another gulp and wiped the moisture from her lips. "Is there a spare?"

"Nim—" said Alia. There was no way Nim was ready to get back on the road.

"*Is there a spare?*" Nim repeated, her gaze fierce.

"Yeah," said Theo, looking in the trunk. "There is."

"Then get to it," she said, waving at Diana and Jason. "One of you human jacks should be able to get the tire changed fast enough."

Diana rested her hand on Nim's shoulder. "Nim, are you sure you can do this? You've already proven your strength."

Nim shook her head. "Alia and I have spent half our lives being bullied. If those asshats think they can scare us into not fighting back, they're in for an education."

Nim held up her right pinky and Alia locked her own finger into it. Alia raised her left hand, and after a moment of confusion, Diana hooked her pinky with Alia's, then offered her other pinky to Nim.

"Are you guys forming a coven?" called Theo, the spare slung over his bony shoulder.

"Bubble, bubble," said Nim with a determined grin.

Alia squeezed her pinkies and felt Nim and Diana squeeze back.

They answered together, "Make some trouble."

CHAPTER 23

Instead of returning to the pass, they took the back roads. Whether it was the scare with Deimos and his kin or the fact that they had only three proper tires, Diana wasn't sorry Nim had tempered her exuberant driving style, and they progressed at a more reasonable pace. The Fiat had been badly banged up, its back bumper dented and its cheerful tangerine paint scratched along both sides, but its engine still hummed and it soldiered on. It seemed as if the Fiat and Nim were kindred spirits, tiny and indefatigable.

Human courage was different from Amazon bravery. She saw that now. For all the suspicion and derision she'd heard from her mother and her sisters about the mortal world, Diana couldn't help but admire the people with whom she traveled. Their lives were violent, precarious, fragile, but they fought for them anyway, and held to the hope that their brief stay on this earth might count for something. That faith was worth preserving.

The road they took away from the gorge was gentler, leading down into the vast green valley watered by the Eurotas River and bordered by the peaks of the Parnon Mountains beyond. It felt like a modern road, its wide lanes and mild curves leading them back to signs of civilization. The passing scenery made a strange dissonance, boxy houses with television aerials on their roofs and shiny cars in their driveways nudged right up against tumbling stone ruins or the crenellated walls of some ancient monastery.

It was neither city nor country, but eventually they passed through a small town, the patios of the little hotels on its main square pocked with fat palms. Clouds of orange trees hung over whitewashed walls, and the air was sweet with the smell of their fruit.

Then they were moving on, speeding through flat groves of olive trees bordered by metal fences, past a church capped in terracotta tiles and built of stone that glowed gold like the terraces of Themyscira, until the road was dappled by the shade of plane trees and quivering fronds of fern. The countryside became suburbs, and those gave way to a modern town, wide boulevards bracketed by apartment buildings, offices, open-air cafés set with plastic umbrellas, metal streetlamps marching steadily toward the town center.

"God, it feels so ordinary here," said Nim.

It was all still too new to Diana to feel ordinary, but they were surrounded by traffic, people. It felt safe somehow, as if the modern world might beat back the terror of the old gods. Too soon they were jogging north and crossing the Eurotas.

As they passed over the river, Alia murmured, "We're close, aren't we?"

"Only a few miles left," said Jason. He tapped a nervous rhythm on his thigh, every muscle in his body taut with worry. It was hard for Diana to believe he was the same boy who had run with her, laughing beneath the stars, who had kissed her on a mountain peak. She shook the thought from her head.

"Does it feel different to you here?" she asked Alia. The landscape had changed subtly once again, grown more lush. They passed gated quarries, and here the olive trees' twisting gray trunks emerged from soft green grass. Even the color of the rock had changed from gray to a rich red.

Alia let her hand float outside of the window, riding the currents. "It feels familiar."

Clouds scudded across the sky, and the air blew cool against Diana's skin as the road began to climb through the low hills.

"No cars," said Theo. "No tour buses. I guess we'll have the tomb to ourselves."

"They forgot her," said Alia. "Everyone remembers Helen of Troy. But she was from Sparta; this was her home. The queen who lived and died here, they forgot."

Nim's pace had slowed to a crawl as she wended around the road's wide, lazy curves. "Does it seem . . . I don't know, too quiet to anyone?"

Alia shivered and rubbed her arms. "You mean like something's going to go horribly wrong?"

"You know what they say," said Theo. "Don't shoot a gift horse in the mouth."

"I'm pretty sure that's not what they say," said Nim.

Alia took a deep breath. "Everybody just . . . stay relaxed."

Jason shifted uneasily in the passenger seat, a muscle ticking in his jaw. Diana knew they were all thinking the same thing. After the horrors of the pass, there should have been something worse waiting for them as they neared the spring, and yet there was no sign of trouble.

The road climbed steadily, surrounded on all sides by rocky pasture, more olive trees, the stark trunks of telephone poles. They passed through a small town that seemed to appear up against the hills for no reason and a large cemetery blooming around a church like a crop of white crosses.

As it turned out, the sign for the tomb was so small they had to double back twice before they found it—a dented metal rectangle tilting woozily on its metal pole, nearly hidden by yellow wildflowers. The words were written in Greek and English: *Menelaion, Sanctuary of Menelaus and Helen.*

"At least she made it onto the sign," muttered Alia.

There was nowhere to hide the Fiat, so they had to park it up against the dirt shoulder of the road.

"It feels weird to just leave her out here in the open," said Alia.

"It's a girl?" said Theo.

"Sure. Isn't it obvious?"

"This feels too easy," Diana murmured to Jason, as they fell in step behind the others.

"It's possible we lost whoever attacked us on the jet," he replied, eyes scanning the surroundings. "They had no way of knowing we were headed to some obscure tomb."

"Even so, where's Eris? Where are the twins? They don't need satellites to track us."

"They could still make a showing," he said.

They might. But another voice spoke inside Diana—what if it had all been a ruse? The Oracle had said the spring at Therapne, but what if Diana had somehow misunderstood. Maybe there was some other place sacred to Helen. Maybe Eris and her horrible nephews had just been a distraction, driving them on, making sure they were focused on the wrong target as the hours until Hekatombaion winnowed away.

"Diana," said Jason, startling her from her thoughts. His hand brushed the back of hers, and she remembered how it had felt to kiss him beneath the night sky. "When this is over, will you go home?"

"Yes," she said without thinking.

"Ah." He trained his eyes on the ground. "For good?"

How could she explain the rules of the island? She supposed that, after all of this, even if they succeeded, she might be exiled. But time passed differently on Themyscira. While Diana was tried and sentenced, years would pass in the mortal world. And even if she could somehow find her way back to her friends, could that ever temper the pain of losing her home? Of never seeing her mother or her sisters again?

"I don't know," she said. "I don't belong here, Jason."

"But you could," he said, still not looking at her. "In time."

"Is this it?" said Theo from up ahead, standing near the top of the hill, hands on hips.

The ruins were less dramatic than Diana had expected. She knew there had once been a vast settlement here, shrines and temples dedicated to Helen and her husband. But now all that remained were a few overgrown foundations surrounding an unimpressive pile of earth that looked like a cross between a burial mound and what might have once been a temple, its stone walls slowly being swallowed by wildflowers. Beyond it, the green bowl of the valley glowed golden, as if the sun had pooled between the mountain ranges, glinting off the banks of the Eurotas far below.

"It doesn't look like much," said Nim. "And where's the spring?"

"Maybe it's a metaphorical spring," said Theo. "Like the spring is inside all of us?"

"Why didn't I run you over when I had the chance?"

"Diana?" said Alia.

The sick sensation in Diana's gut worsened. "The Oracle just said the spring at Therapne."

"Could she have meant somewhere else?"

"Where?" said Diana. "There are no other monuments to Helen in Therapne. *'Where Helen rests, the Warbringer may be purified.'*" She could feel her frustration rising. "This is where Helen was laid to rest. It was *her* shrine first, before it belonged to Menelaus."

"There's nothing here," said Jason.

Theo turned in a slow circle. "We came all this way for nothing?"

Jason shook his head. "Alia, we have to get you out of here. You could still be in danger."

"I'm not going anywhere." Her eyes met Diana's. "I held up my end of the bargain. The sun will set soon."

No. They'd barely looked for the spring. They hadn't thought this through.

"We still have time," said Diana. "We'll find some other solution."

"How much time do we have left? An hour? An hour and a half? There is no other solution. I won't live knowing I could have stopped this."

"Alia," Jason said sharply. "I am not letting you kill yourself."

"It isn't up to you," she said. Her voice was clear and strong and rang with conviction, the sound of steel against steel. "This is between me and Diana."

Sister in battle. It wasn't supposed to come to this. Diana had *known* in her heart they were meant to reach the spring together. What other lies had she told herself?

"You can't be serious," said Nim desperately. "What if this is all some kind of big mistake? For all we know this Warbringer thing is just—"

"Nim, after everything you've seen, everything we've been through, you know this is real."

"We're not going to kill you off as a precautionary measure," said Theo. He gripped her shoulder, more serious and more frightened than Diana had ever seen him. "There has to be a way to fix this."

But Alia shrugged him off. She took a step closer to Diana, and Diana had to will herself not to move away from her.

Your cause is mine.

She'd sworn to become a murderer, stain her hands with innocent blood. She'd given her oath, but Diana had never truly believed she'd be forced to fulfill it. She could not; she *would* not, and yet how was she to turn away from the conviction in Alia's eyes? Alia had fought with everything she had to reach the spring, to reach the future Diana had promised might be hers.

"Sister in battle," Diana said, ashamed of the tears that roughened her voice. "I have failed you."

"You haven't," said Alia, taking another step toward her. "Not yet."

Jason moved to block her path. "Enough. We never should have come here. You would be safe right now if—"

"No," Alia said, and Diana heard the anger in her voice. "Your solution was to hide. Ours was to fight. Don't you dare blame us for trying. Diana, you gave me your word."

Diana could feel the oath that bound her, as powerful as the lasso, as indestructible. She could not live with herself if she violated the vow she'd given. But how could she live knowing she'd taken Alia's life? She was immortal, and that would give her an eternity to endure this terrible shame.

"Make your choice, Daughter of Earth."

Eris. So she had come after all. To gloat. Diana looked to Nim, expecting a monster's face, but saw Nim's wide brown eyes, her mouth agape as she stared at a figure perched at the apex of the rocky ruins, black wings spread wide, the tips of her filthy feathers nearly touching the ground. Her hair flowed around her face in curling tendrils of darkness, and the gold smeared across her lips glinted in the sun. "Foolish girl, with your noble quest and your heart that yearns for glory. Can you do it? Cut her throat to keep us at bay?"

"Is that what I looked like?" Nim asked in disgust.

A wind rose, billowing up from the earth around them, and the sound of hoofbeats filled the air. The dust collected in the shape of two chariots, cutting a path around them, the hooves of their horses seeming to fly over the ground.

"I don't know," said Theo, backing up so they stood clumped together at the base of the tomb. "I look pretty cool." Phobos smiled from his chariot, his hideous pointed teeth emerging. "Or not."

Had the battle gods grown stronger this close to sunset? Was that why they didn't need to possess Nim and Theo any longer? Or had that just been a game to them?

"You have laid a feast before us!" shouted Phobos, his voice rising shrill above the clatter of wheels and hooves.

"And, O young warrior," cried Deimos in exultation, the crack of his whip like a bomb blast, "we will eat our fill!"

Eris rose in the sky, beating her shield with her sword, the clamor unbearable. Diana covered her ears with her hands, but she couldn't block out the sound of her regret. She'd gotten it wrong, all of it.

"The reaping moon has come. In an hour the sun sets and darkness rises, yet here you languish," Eris cackled. She rose higher, her vast wings blotting out the sun, casting them in shadow. "What will you tell your sisters? Your mother?"

"And you, Warbringer," Deimos mocked as his chariot raced faster. "What will you tell your mother in the afterlife?"

Phobos bellowed laughter. "She will wear a veil in the underworld and hide her face for the shame you've brought her, *haptandra*, the cursed."

Diana and the others clustered in a frightened circle, back to back, shoulder to shoulder, as the chariots circled, their steeds sending up clumps of earth, the horses' lips pulled back as they snapped at their golden bits, their muzzles trailing blood-flecked foam.

The shields, the hooves, the whip, the rumble of the wheels, the sound was overwhelming, filling Diana's skull, shaking her teeth.

"I can't think!" Theo shouted. "They're too loud."

"But why?" yelled Alia. "This is different from last time! Why are they making so much noise?"

Jason shook his head, hands clamped to his ears. "They've won, and they know it!"

He was right. Alia and the others were grasping at false hope. It was the way of mortals. And yet, if Diana had been wrong all along, why interfere at all? For the fun of it? On Themyscira, she'd grown used to the extraordinary, to the knowledge that the gods made demands, that their will dictated the rules of the island. But nothing in the mortal world was as it had been on Themyscira, and the gods of the battlefield were not the goddesses of her home. They hungered for blood and sorrow. They required it and needed mortals to provide it. So why exactly were they here? Had they simply come to enjoy her suffering in this last hour?

Her suffering—but not her terror. She was scared, frustrated, furious with herself—yet that gibbering, mindless horror wasn't flooding through her. Why wouldn't the battle gods want them terrified? Unless they didn't want the group to run. What if they simply wanted them to stay here, stay still—paralyzed and deafened. What if Alia was right? What if they'd come with a purpose? What if all this din was to drown something out?

She remembered the way Phobos had hissed at the touch of her lasso. Could its touch kill a god? It didn't have to. She just needed to drive them back. She just needed to buy some respite from that clamor.

Diana gritted her teeth and removed her hands from her ears, the noise rising to a jaw-shaking roar.

She unhooked the lasso and swung it over her head, a steady rhythm, matching it to the beat of her heart. It felt comforting in her hands, and yet so slight. Was this a weapon with which to face the gods? She let it swing farther and farther in a widening loop, then unleashed it with a snap. It glowed golden in her hands, lashing out like a tongue of yellow flame at the wheels of Phobos's chariot and sending him veering off course. *Snap.* It snatched at Deimos's helmet like a hungry serpent, forcing him to shake his reins and break his horses' stride. The sounds of their shields and chariots faded. Maybe it was *just* the weapon she needed.

Diana swung the rope wider and wider, the lasso seeming to lengthen impossibly in her hands, the gust of its momentum forcing Eris back, her wings flapping grotesquely as she let fly a hideous shriek, and sunlight burst over them once more.

"Diana!" shouted Alia. Her face was alight; her braids made a halo around her head as if borne aloft by invisible current. She was bracketed by two figures of light. They were Nim and Theo, but Diana knew then they were also the Dioskouroi, Helen's twin brothers and guardians, legendary warriors.

"Diana," said Alia, "I hear it!"

"Hear what?" shouted Jason, his face grim and disbelieving. "I don't hear anything."

"Listen," urged Alia.

He tugged on her arm. "Enough, Alia! We have to get out of here *now.*"

Alia shook her head. She smiled, and the air around her seemed to shimmer. "They're singing."

CHAPTER 24

The song was faint, so quiet that at first Alia felt sure she was imagining it. She dismissed it, her mind still reeling from the sight of Eris wheeling in the sky above them, of Diana keeping Phobos and Deimos at bay, the lasso a bolt of lightning in her hands. Then there it was—a ringing in her ears, the wind in the trees—no, something more, a melody. One voice became two, ten, twenty. She didn't understand the words, but she knew they were guiding her.

"What did the Oracle say, Diana?"

Diana glanced at her, confused, the lasso still whirling in her hands. "I told you—"

"No, what were her exact words?"

"*'Where Helen rests, the Warbringer may be purified.'*"

Where Helen rests. "The spring isn't here," she said. "It's one of the springs that feeds the river." The Eurotas, the wide, slow river that had paralleled the road as they approached the Menelaion, that lay only a hundred yards below.

"*This* is her tomb," said Jason. Every bit of his patience had vanished, replaced by an angry urgency. "Stop grasping at straws, Alia."

Why couldn't he hear them?

"*No,*" she said. She needed to make him understand. The girls were singing, and their song was one of mourning, a farewell to a friend. "Don't you see? By the time Helen died, it was too late. She wasn't Helen anymore, not really. She was Helen of Troy. She was Menelaus's wife. Her tomb didn't even keep her name."

"The race," said Diana, new hope kindling in her blue eyes. Alia had hated to see that light go out, even for a minute. "That was the last moment, when she was still allowed to compete side by side with her companions."

The battle gods shrieked and howled, and Alia knew she was right.

"It was her last moment of peace," she said. "Before she became a bride, before she stopped running. We have to get down to the river."

"Well, we'd better move quick," said Theo, pointing to the road.

Far in the distance, a parade of armored vehicles crawled along the winding road like gleaming beetles, dust rising in a cloud behind them.

"If we could just explain," said Nim.

"They may not give us the chance," said Diana. "To the river. *Now.*"

Down the hill they plunged, Eris circling above them, beyond the reach of Diana's lasso, trying to disrupt the chorus with her screams and the banging of her shield, Deimos and Phobos alongside, their chariots making a furious clatter.

But the girls ran with them, too, Helen's companions, hair streaming behind them, laughing and unafraid. And now that she'd heard the song, Alia could hold it, keep the thread of its melody in her mind. It was the song they sang when one of their own was chosen to be married. A chorus of celebration, but also one of mourning for the girl who had been lost, for the freedom that had vanished with a vow, for the future races she would never run.

Helen had won a race, before anyone knew what sorrow she would bring to the world, before she was Menelaus's bride or

Helen of anything but herself. She'd run side by side with the boys who would someday don armor and fight to their deaths in her name. She'd run barefoot with the wind at her back, and when the gods had granted her victory, she'd gone to the banks of the river Eurotas and laid a lotus wreath on the great tree that grew there; she'd poured a libation of oil upon its roots. *Libation.* An offering. These were old words, old ideas, but Alia knew them in her very bones. For years, girls had come to that site to worship Helen and to sing for their friends.

Alia tried to catch her breath as they reached the bottom of the footpath and sprinted across the paved road, then stumbled down a gentle slope, dense with brush and whispering plane trees. Their trunks were gray as stone, the thick, twisting arms of their branches bowed low over the water as if trying to drink, and the blaze of the late-afternoon sun made their leaves look curiously weightless, as if clouds of green butterflies had alighted in their boughs but might vanish at any moment, leaving the trees bare.

Somewhere far in the distance, she heard the rumble of engines. The voices of the girls grew louder, drawing her onward. They were fifty now, one hundred, the sound so lovely it brought tears to Alia's eyes. When had she stopped being a child? The first time a guy had whistled at her out of a car window when she was walking to school? The moment she started wondering how she looked when she ran, what jiggled or bounced, instead of the pace she was setting? The first time she'd kept from raising her hand because she didn't want to seem too smart or too eager? No one had sung. No one had told her how much she would lose until the time for grieving was long over.

But now they'd reached the sandy banks of the river and there was no more time or breath for sadness. She followed the girls, running beside them, caught up in their joy. They would always be young and unafraid. They would forever run this race.

"They're coming!" Theo shouted, but he didn't mean the runners. On the road above, armored vehicles screeched to a halt, men in gray camouflage emerging and crashing down the slope toward the water. A Humvee was charging down the riverbed, a wide, menacing military jeep with tires that seemed to eat up the ground.

"There!" Alia cried. A tree on the banks, its massive trunk giving way to heavy branches. The water at its base was flat and smooth like no other part of the river, reflecting the image of the tree so brightly it might have been a mirror. Alia blinked and saw girls dancing on the riverbank, the tree's trunk laden with wreaths of lotus blossoms, its roots crowded with tiny offerings.

"The water by the tree!" said Diana, taking her hand, pulling her forward. "Alia, you just have to reach it."

But the soldiers were in the river now, surrounding them, blocking their path to the spring, their boots splashing through the water and kicking up plumes of silt. A hard breeze shook the leaves of the plane tree as a helicopter descended, hovering over them. Alia could swear she heard Eris's wings in the steady whir of its propeller blades.

"Please!" Diana shouted, throwing her arms out to shield Alia. "Listen to me! This girl is no danger to you. The river is sacred. It can purge the Warbringer line and end this madness forever!"

"I'm sorry," said Jason from behind them. "I can't allow that."

He seized Alia's arm and yanked her tight to his side, backing away up the banks.

"Jason," said Diana. "We just need to make them understand."

"They understand just fine."

Alia tried to break free of his grip, stumbling in the soft sand. "What are you doing?" she said, the voices of the girls' song lost, fading on the wind.

"It's okay," her brother said gently—his voice as steady, as familiar, as controlled as ever. "You are just as you were meant to be. This is all as it was meant to be, and no one will hurt you." His eyes were bright. His dimple creased his cheek. She realized he looked happier than she'd ever seen him. "You must live, Alia. And war must come."

CHAPTER 25

Diana stared at Jason, at his fingers digging into Alia's arm, at the soldiers fanned out around them. Their eyes were alert, scanning the area, but they kept returning to him—not as if assessing a target, but as if awaiting a command. They looked a bit like the boys Jason had spoken to at the gala—paler, sterner, but with that same smug ease. The Humvee rumbled to a stop half in and half out of the river, and only then did Diana realize that aside from the rhythmic whir of the helicopter blades, the air was still. Eris and the twins had gone. Had they retreated in defeat or because their victory was secure?

"What is this?" said Diana. "What are you doing?"

"I'm sorry," Jason repeated. He sounded sincere. "I didn't really believe we'd get this close. I hoped I wouldn't have to intervene, that we could just let the clock run out and the sun set."

"Jason, man, what are you talking about?" said Theo. "You got us on the jet that brought us here."

"I know. It wasn't what I wanted. But you have to understand how hard it's been to keep Alia safe." He turned to his sister, his grip still secure on her upper arm. "First you run off to Istanbul and board a boat before I can send anyone to intercept you. When the *Thetis* went missing . . . I nearly lost my mind." He expelled a long breath, and his brows rose in that bemused look that had become so familiar. "But then you show up in New York, safe and sound, with an *Amazon* in tow."

Diana flinched. "You knew?"

"From the first moment we tangled in that hotel hallway. Did you really think you could pretend to be an ordinary mortal, Diana? There's nothing ordinary about you."

Anger unfurled inside her. That was why he hadn't asked about where she came from or what she was. Not out of respect, but because he already knew.

"What better bodyguard could I dream of for my sister?" Jason said. "An immortal warrior willing to stop at nothing to keep Alia alive."

"So we could reach the spring," Alia said, her dark eyes dazed and lost, as if she was waiting to be told this was all a joke.

"The *spring*." Jason said the word as if he wanted to rinse its sound from his mouth. "You two were set on trying to reach it, so why fight you? We'd go to Greece. I'd let you chase your tails, and all the while Diana would be using her strength and skill to protect the Warbringer."

Diana's hand inched toward her lasso, and Jason held up a scolding finger. "Easy now. There are snipers on the ridge. You might survive a bullet to the brain, but I doubt Nim or Theo will."

Alia winced. "Jason, have you lost your damn mind?"

"I'm just being cautious," he said softly. "The way I always have."

Nim planted her hands on her hips. "But you helped us! You could have flown us anywhere on that jet and—"

"My team was waiting for us on the ground in Araxos, but our enemies had other plans. After the crash, there were too many hostiles in the area. If I'd called in my forces, they might have led Alia's pursuers straight to us. So I had them track us and follow at a safe distance."

"The tracker for the parachute packs," said Theo suddenly. "It wasn't just receiving signals. It was transmitting, too."

Jason lifted a brow. "I'm surprised you didn't figure it out before now."

Nim pointed her finger at Jason. "That's why you didn't want Theo to use his phone to start the car. You weren't afraid of us being found. You were trying to slow us down." Her eyes widened. "Oh God . . . That first day driving, you were handing me soda."

Diana remembered Jason digging through the medical kit on the jet, pocketing pills. "You drugged her?" she asked incredulously. Could he have done such a thing to a girl he'd known his whole life? Who was this boy standing before her? This boy she'd whispered secrets to in the dark?

"I'm not proud of it," he said, and he *sounded* ashamed. "But I had to do something. You were all so determined."

"To stop a war!" shouted Alia, her voice fraying.

"Humans aren't made for peace," said Jason. "We've proven it again and again. Give us the chance and we'll find something to fight over. Territory. Religion. Love. It's our natural state. Ask Diana why her people turned their backs on us. They know what humans are."

"Diana?" Alia asked.

Diana wasn't sure what to say. She had been taught her whole life that mortals hungered for war, that they couldn't resist the urge to destroy one another, that there was no point in trying to stem the tide of bloodshed.

As if he could read her mind, Jason said, "Don't look to her for answers. Her people don't care about us. And why should they? Look what we've become. Cowards and weaklings playing with weapons like they're toys."

"Weaklings," Alia repeated. "Every generation weaker than the last. . . ." She reared back as realization struck. "Our parents' work. You didn't continue it."

"I did. Our father's work."

"What does Dad have to do with any of this?" Alia asked desperately.

"The files," said Diana, remembering the missing pages, the blacked-out passages. "You redacted the text."

"Dad saw the potential for what our blood could do, what it might mean for the world, before Mom interfered."

"You mean before she talked sense into him?" Alia shot back.

Jason gave her arm a slight shake. "Vaccines. Gene therapy. Supercures. *That's* what they ended up using our bloodline for. The blood of heroes like Ajax and Achilles. To prolong the lives of those who had no right to their strength."

What had Jason said on that winding road through the cliffs? *It's just biology. I'm not saying it's good or bad.*

Alia tried to pull away from him, and Diana stepped forward. A bullet struck the water by Theo's feet.

"Shit!" shouted Theo, backing up and nearly falling. Nim shrieked.

"Jason," pleaded Alia, "call them off!"

"Behind me," commanded Diana, spreading her arms wide, eyes scanning the road above and the ridge of the ruins beyond it for snipers.

They stood in strange formation: Jason and Alia on the sandy riverbank, Diana with Nim and Theo crowded against her in the shallows—as if she could protect them when they were surrounded by men on all sides.

Theo held his hands up. "Jason," he said, voice reasonable. "Think about what you're saying. Who are you to decide who's weak and who's strong?"

Jason blew out a breath. "I don't expect you to understand, Theo. You'd rather hide from the world behind a screen than face it."

Theo's head snapped back as if Jason had struck him. "Is that really what you think of me?" He lowered his hands slowly, his face bewildered. All of Jason's jibes and judgments—they hadn't been the teasing of someone who wanted more for his friend, but actual contempt. "I thought—"

"That we were friends? Because we collected comic books together when we were twelve? Because we liked the same cartoons? What do you think I've been doing while you've been wasting your life on games and make-believe?"

"If you say 'growing up,' I'm going to punch that smug expression right off your face."

Jason's smile flashed again. "Do you even know how to make a fist?"

Theo's lip curled. "If I'm such a loser, why waste your time on me?"

"It was an easy way to keep tabs on your father."

"My father?"

"He was always trying to track expenditures at the labs, monitoring the projects I wanted to approve. He thought it was about money. It's never been about money. It's about the future."

The future. Jason's words by the waterfall came back to her. *I wanted to remake the world.* The ferocity in his eyes when he'd said, *I still do.* A boy who'd lost his parents in a single terrible moment. A boy who longed to be remembered, who longed to see his gifts recognized. Diana could see him standing at the party at the museum, like a soldier surrounded by enemies. She'd thought she'd understood, but she hadn't come close to grasping the scope of his vision. The tension she'd sensed in him as they'd drawn closer to Helen's tomb hadn't been fear for their safety. He'd just been afraid he would have to reveal his true goals before he was ready.

"You were never with us," said Diana. The betrayal was worse for the shame it brought, the feeling that she should have known, anticipated the wound, stanched the bleeding. "You never wanted to stop this war."

"We *can't* stop war," said Jason. "But we can change the way wars are waged."

"War is war," said Alia. "People will die."

Jason rubbed a hand over the back of his neck and took a deep breath. He released Alia's arm and put up his palms as if in surrender. "I know how this looks," he said, gesturing to the artillery and the stone-faced men gathered around him. He gave a short laugh. "I know how I sound. But think for a minute. What if we weren't fighting one another? What if the monsters from the stories were real and we had to band together to face them? What if war could bring us together instead of tearing us apart?"

"Monsters?" said Alia.

"*Real* enemies. Scylla, Charybdis, the Nemean Lion, Echidna, the mother of all grotesques."

From inside the Humvee, Diana heard a slithering thump, as if something massive had shifted its weight.

And then Diana knew. The thing Tek had faced in the Oracle's vision, the monster with the jackal's head—it was one of Jason's creations. She remembered the images on the laptop. How many of those creatures had he found? How many would he bring back?

"You don't understand what you'll unleash upon the world," said Diana. "This won't be like one of the stories you loved. It won't be a heroic quest. I've seen the future you speak of, and it is not glorious. It's a nightmare of loss."

Jason waved her words away. "Whatever vision the Oracle showed you was only one version of the future, one possible outcome."

"It's not a risk worth taking!"

"An immortal has no right to make that choice for humanity," he said, a bitter edge to his voice, as if he resented his own mortality, as if he resented *her* for being something more. "You say we deserve a chance at peace, but why not a chance at *greatness*? The biological material my parents found at those ancient battle sites, the work they did on gene therapies. They didn't know it, but it was all for this." Jason threw his arms wide, encompassing his troops. "These are soldiers like no others, warriors to rival Odysseus and Achilles. They will do battle with creatures born of myth and nightmare, and the world will rally behind them."

"You guys are gonna die," said Theo, glancing at the grim-faced soldiers. "You get that, right?"

"Yes, we'll die," said Jason. "But we'll live on as legends."

"Like a hero in a story?" Diana asked.

"They aren't just stories. You and I both know that."

We'll live on as legends. Jason wanted an opportunity to be the hero he was born to be. He wanted to live in a world that made sense. He wanted the death his parents had been denied, a death with meaning, a chance to be remembered. Immortality.

"And what about me?" asked Alia, anger seeping through her disbelief.

Jason touched her arm, and she batted his hand away.

"Alia," he said, "I'm the one who wants you to *live*."

"With thousands of deaths on my conscience?" Her voice cracked on the words. "Knowing that I was the reason so many innocent people had to die?"

"So a new age of heroes can begin." Jason turned his gaze on Diana. "I lied to you. You lied to me. But there's only truth between us now." He stepped forward, and for a moment, the world dropped away. They were standing once again on that rocky hill, the stars wheeling above them. "The Amazons are warriors. They're not meant to live out of time, isolated on that island. You know it's true. You left Themyscira for the chance to be a hero, to give meaning to your life. Don't you think humanity deserves that, too?"

The late-afternoon sun glittered off the water and made a mantle of gold that shimmered over Jason's features. Diana saw in him the blood of kings, of heroes, the daring and the ambition.

"Stand with me," he pleaded, "as we were meant to—side by side, seeking glory as equals."

She'd thought her path would lead one of two ways: to the stifling familiarity of home or the terror of exile. Jason was offering her another future: a life lived without caution or fear of reprisal. One drenched in blood and glory, and she could feel her warrior's heart fill with hunger at the call.

"Humans can't hold to peace, Diana," Jason said. His gaze was steady, certain, and in his words she heard the echo of her mother's voice. "We're brutes and have been since our beginning. If we can't have peace, then at least give us a chance at a beautiful death."

"*Diana,*" Alia said desperately. And in that moment, Diana knew that Alia was pleading for her own death; that frightened as she might be, Alia would rather die than see the world fall to Jason's vision. That was courage. That was its own kind of greatness. Diana had not been raised to be just any warrior. She was an Amazon, and she knew true strength when she saw it. If Jason wanted this glorious future, she would not simply hand it to him; he would have to fight for it.

She met his gaze, and when she spoke, she heard her mother's voice, Tek's voice, Maeve's. "You may well be my equal in strength," she said. "But you are no match for Nim's ingenuity, for Theo's resilience, for Alia's bravery. Might does not make a hero. You can build a thousand soldiers, and not one will have a hero's heart."

Jason didn't turn angry. His face didn't regain the cold control he'd shown so often. His voice was gentle when he said, "You were a story to me, too, you know. An Amazon. A legend come to life." His smile was small, sweet, and something in her chest twisted at the words. "I sought you for so long, Diana. I dreamed of finding Themyscira, some remnant of a lost civilization that might yield a vital scrap of Amazon DNA. Instead, I found you."

The ache in her chest became the cold press of something hard and unforgiving. So that was the truth of his desire, not for her, but for the power that might be gleaned from her.

"I can't wait to meet the soldiers your blood will raise," he said. "The secrets your genes will give up to me."

She shifted into fighting stance. "*Molon labe,*" she said in the language of Jason's ancestors. *Come and take them.*

"Oh, I will," he said calmly. "I began building a serum from your DNA the first day we met. You left traces of your extraordinary bloodline all over my house. Hair. Skin cells. Who knows what treasures a supply of your blood will yield?"

"Never."

"You're as weak as your sisters, turning your back on greatness as they turned their backs on the mortal world."

"Come closer and speak again of my sisters."

"No, Diana. I have other plans for you." He turned to the soldiers standing at attention beside the Humvee parked on the sand. From inside the vehicle, Diana heard harsh chittering, like a beetle clicking its wings, and then a wet, hungry sound like . . . like something smacking its lips. Jason's eyes glittered as he gave the order. "Open the cage."

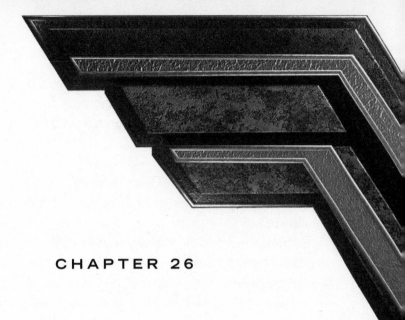

CHAPTER 26

"Stay behind me," Diana commanded Nim and Theo, trying to keep her eyes on Alia and on the Humvee. There was a loud clatter as the vehicle seemed to rock on its mighty wheels, and the soldiers stepped forward, one with his gun raised to offer cover, the other with a long metal stick attached to some kind of collar. He threw open the rear doors. For a moment they were caught in shadow, and then they were backing into the sun, calling orders to the other soldiers as they dragged a huge shape from the depths of the Humvee.

"I call her Pinon," said Jason. "The Drinker." She had the head and torso of a woman, her breasts bare, her arms muscled, her red hair a ropy tangle. But her lower half was the segmented body of a glossy black scorpion, and a massive tail curled grotesquely behind her. "Part warrior, part arachnid, part parasite. She can drain an opponent's blood in a matter of minutes, but she won't digest it. Not until she needs it. Or in this case, I do."

One of the soldiers used a hook to throw something at Pinon—a T-shirt emblazoned with "I ♥ NY." *Enjoy the best, prepare for the worst.* He'd been planning this from the start. Pinon caught the shirt in one fist, breathed deeply of the scent, and cast it aside. Her vibrant green gaze fastened on Diana.

Jason signaled to a soldier, who tossed a sword at Theo's feet in the shallows.

"Seems like a fair fight," said Nim bitterly.

"Jason," Alia pleaded. "Don't do this."

"You'll grow stronger without these crutches to lean on, Al."

"Jason—"

"Drain the Amazon," he ordered. "Kill the others."

His guards fell into formation, dragging Alia up the hill as she began to scream.

"Alia!" Diana cried, but Pinon skittered forward to block her path. The creature's movements made her skin crawl. There was something unnatural in the creeping of her legs, the slither of that segmented body, but worse were her intelligent eyes.

"Find cover!" she yelled at Theo and Nim as she took her lasso in hand. But the remaining soldiers had fanned out in a half circle, cutting off their retreat and forming a kind of arena in the shallow waters of the river. They carried no guns, only swords and shields at the ready. Apparently, this was the kind of clean fight Jason thought the world needed.

Nim knelt to pick up the sword, but it looked almost as heavy as she was, and Theo took it from her, holding it awkwardly out before him, his narrow shoulders bunching with effort.

They crowded together, back to back, and edged deeper into the water, the river cold around Diana's sandaled feet as she herded them toward a cluster of boulders that might provide cover. Pinon followed, her tail curling and uncurling behind her.

"On a scale of one to 'we're definitely going to die,' where would you put this?"

"Shut up, Theo," murmured Nim, her voice breathless with fear.

But they did not cower, did not weep. These people Jason discarded with such contempt, whom he could sentence to death with a few brief words, stood at her back, stubborn and courageous as they had always been.

Neutralize Pinon. Deal with the soldiers. *Find a way*, she told herself. *Find a way to keep them safe.*

Diana feinted left, and her hand shot out, hurtling the lasso at Pinon's tail in a bright lash. Too slow. The creature dodged in a blur of speed, far faster than her leisurely approach had indicated. Pinon reared up, forelegs waving hideously. She ducked her chin, her smile small and close-lipped, almost coy. She launched herself forward.

"Get down!" Diana shouted, hoping Theo and Nim would comply. She swept the lasso out, hooked it over a boulder, snapped it tight, and swung the rock. Pinon tried to dart away, but the boulder caught the edge of her shoulder, knocking her backward with bone-shattering force.

The monster gave a high, mewling shriek, her tail lashing the air as she turned back to Diana. There was that intelligence again, a gaze that promised punishment.

"Get ready to run," Diana instructed.

"Born ready," said Theo.

Diana yanked the boulder back to her, swung it once to build momentum, then sent it barreling into two of the soldiers. She hooked it back, attacked with it again, the rock shooting forward like a missile, knocking two more of the men to the ground.

"Go!" she shouted. Nim and Theo scrambled to their feet, but the soldiers closed ranks quickly, blocking their escape and drawing the circle tighter.

Pinon was creeping forward, flexing her injured shoulder, tail twitching. Diana whipped the boulder toward her, and the creature slithered back onto the sand.

Diana tightened her grip on the rope and swung the boulder wide, launching it at the soldiers again, trying to make a way out. Two fell easily, but the next soldier braced himself and blocked the impact with his forearms. A chunk of the boulder flew free.

Heroes' blood. No ordinary man could withstand a blow like that.

"Diana!" Theo cried.

Pinon had skittered closer. She was in striking distance.

Diana shook the boulder free, swinging the lasso in her hand.

Pinon lunged at Diana, but she had anticipated the movement. She cast the lasso over the creature's head, yanking her forward and driving her foot into Pinon's abdomen.

The monster squealed in pain, seizing the rope with her long white fingers, her tail snapping forward. It had a pincer at its tip, not a stinger, and Diana had the briefest second to wonder why before she dodged away, barely keeping hold of her end of the lasso, snapping it snugly around Pinon's neck.

The creature thrashed, her eyes rolling backward. Diana did not want to know what truths the lasso had revealed to make the monster scream that way. Had Jason made her from nothing, a nightmare spawned in a lab? Or had she been an ordinary girl once, before she was transformed? Diana lowered her shoulders, trying to keep her grip on the lasso.

"Give me the sword, Theo!" she commanded.

"They're coming!" he shouted. Diana glanced over her shoulder and saw the soldiers advancing.

Nim gripped a rock in each hand. "You want some of this?" she yelled.

"You look like a bunch of jocks at a costume party!" taunted Theo.

Were they out of their minds? *No, just mortal.*

Two soldiers shot forward with what should have been impossible speed.

"Run!" she cried. But Theo didn't run. He held up his sword.

Diana heard a *clang* as the soldier struck, and Theo stumbled beneath the force of his opponent's blade. They were too unevenly matched.

She released the lasso and leapt toward the attacking soldier, slamming him backward. She turned in time to see the other soldier bring his sword down in a sweeping arc. Two more men were running at Nim.

"No!" she cried, but it was too late. The blade cut deeply into Theo's side.

He fell to his knees, then slumped sideways into the water, the blood flowing from his body into the Eurotas in a billowing flood of red. *No.* Diana whirled frantically.

A soldier had lifted Nim off her feet and raised his sword to skewer her. But Nim swung one of her fists, the rock tucked into her hand, and cracked it hard against the side of his head. The soldier bobbled on his feet, and she struck his left temple with the second rock. He let go, and she fell on her backside in the river.

Diana seized Theo's sword from the riverbed and sprinted toward Nim.

She heard a splash behind her and knew Pinon had freed herself of the lasso. Diana whirled, slashing out in rage. Her blade struck the creature's side, slid along the plating of its exoskeleton. She swung again. From the corner of her eye, she caught a blur of movement, and suddenly she was on her back in the water. She gasped for air, felt something fasten around her ankle and yank her upward.

Diana dangled upside down in the air before Pinon. Now she knew what the pincer on the creature's tail was for.

She heard a stream of high-pitched swearing. *Nim.* Diana twisted in Pinon's grip and saw that one of the soldiers had grabbed Nim from behind. He was laughing, shaking his head in amusement as she struggled.

"Bubble, bubble, you asshole," Nim said, and brought her head back. The soldier flinched as her skull connected with his face.

"Little bitch," he growled.

His grip shifted, and Diana saw what he meant to do.

The sound was like a branch snapping. Nim's body went limp. Diana screamed. The soldier tossed Nim aside and wiped his hands on his pants, as if he'd handled something unclean. Her small body floated faceup in the shallows, her head resting at an unnatural angle on her broken neck, her blank eyes open to the sky.

No, no, no.

Pinon gave Diana a shake, as if demanding her attention. The pincer dug into the flesh of her lower leg, but all Diana could think was *They're gone. I was supposed to protect them, and they're gone.* She should have taken the sword from Theo at the start. She should have kept Nim closer. She should have made them stay behind, somewhere safe, no matter the risk to her quest. A howl tore free from Diana's chest, grief and rage quaking through her.

Pinon smiled that sweet, coy smile, as if the sound of Diana's misery gave her pleasure. Her lips parted, and two hooklike barbs emerged. Before Diana could react, Pinon yanked her higher and latched her wet mouth to Diana's throat, the barbs sinking deep into her flesh. *She was made for this,* Diana realized as Pinon's lips sealed tightly over her skin and she felt her blood drawn in a rush from her body. *She was engineered to bleed her victims, upside down, like pigs brought to slaughter.*

Then there was only pain, the agony coming in waves as Pinon drank in great, pulling gulps. Diana could hear the click of every satisfied swallow, timed to the waning beat of her heart. She could feel her body trying to heal, her strength attempting to return, but Pinon was too fast and too efficient.

Diana thrashed weakly. In the distance, she could hear Alia's screams, the whir of helicopter blades. She'd sworn to keep Alia from this very fate, but she had failed more terribly than she ever could have imagined. The Oracle had been right. Her mother. Tek. They'd all been right. She should never have ventured off Themyscira. She had never been a true Amazon, and now the world would pay for her pride.

"Protect them, Athena," she gasped as the life drained from her body and her vision blurred. *Mortal and immortal, weak and strong, deserving and undeserving. Protect them all. Protect Alia from the burden of her fate. Protect my mother and my sisters in the war to come.*

She thought of Maeve's freckles that seemed to float above her skin, of Rani's gentle nature, of Thyra's giddy laugh. Would they know when she was gone? Could they sense her pain now? She thought of her mother seated at the table in the palace beside Tek, turning to greet Diana as she raced up the stairs, opening her arms to welcome her home. *What did you learn today, Pyxis?* said Tek with a smile, and Diana felt no bitterness now, only the ache of knowing there would be nothing more. She heard the wet release of Pinon's mouth.

Protect them, she prayed, and then she thought no more.

CHAPTER 27

Alia thrashed in the arms of the soldiers dragging her along the road, past a line of armored trucks and Humvees.

"Jason, stop this," she pleaded. "You can't let them die. Not Nim, not Theo. They're no threat to you. You can let Diana go home. Please. Jason—" She didn't even know what she was saying anymore; it was just a series of entreaties, one more desperate than the last. She knew she was crying. Her voice was raw. Her arms ached where Jason's soldiers had hold of her. Their fingers felt unnaturally strong, like steel prongs.

When they reached the back of one of the trucks, a soldier passed Jason a canteen full of water. He drank deeply, but when he offered it to her, she slapped it from his hands. The soldiers yanked her arms back tighter, and she snarled at them, kicking out with her legs as they lifted her off the ground. Jason sighed.

"Alia!" he barked. He set his hands on her shoulders. "Alia," he said more gently. "*Stop*. You're going to hurt yourself."

A sound that was half sob, half laugh ripped free of her throat. She stared at him. Her brother. Her protector. Her friend. His face so like hers that it was almost like looking into a mirror. "Jason," she said quietly. "Please. I am begging you. Help them."

He shook his head, and she saw true sorrow in his eyes. "I can't, Al. A war is coming. People like Nim and Theo won't survive it. This is a kindness."

"Stop talking that way."

"I'm sorry. This is how it has to be."

The emotion that rose in her felt like something rupturing down her center, cracking her in two. Jason, who had read to her, who had let her cry herself to sleep curled into his side, who had walked to school with her every day for months because she'd been afraid to ride in a car after the accident. He couldn't be doing this thing, this horrible thing.

"No, it doesn't," she said. Jason was the reasonable one, the steady one. She had to make him understand. "It doesn't. We can undo this. We can make it right."

"Alia, I know you don't see it, but I know what's right for both of us." He glanced over his shoulder. "And I'm afraid it's too late."

Alia followed his gaze and retched, her mind rejecting the horror before her. Pinon, Jason had called her, the Drinker. She was emerging from the trees, being herded toward the open back of a Humvee. But she didn't look as she had when his men had unleashed her by the river. Her body was bloated, the skin gray and distended; her swollen tail dragged on the ground behind her. *Kill the others. Drain the Amazon.*

Diana was dead. She was dead, and this thing was full of her blood.

"Have her disgorge and bring me the ampoules," Jason commanded. "I want to start processing the data on the way to base."

Two of the soldiers dragged Pinon into the back of the Humvee. Through its doors, she could see part of it had been converted to cages.

Another of Jason's men said, "Will you be taking the helicopter to base, sir?"

Sir.

"No, I want the Seahawk keeping an eye on the surrounding territory and making sure we didn't draw any unwanted attention. We're safer on the ground, and we don't have much time until the sun goes down. Set a fire once we're a few miles out and make sure the bodies burn."

How could he say these things? "You're talking about burning our friends."

"I'm doing what has to be done."

"I will never forgive you, Jason. Never."

Jason's gaze was sad, but it didn't falter. "You will, Alia. Because you'll have no one else. You are the Warbringer, and when the sun sets, you will fulfill your destiny and pave the way for me to fulfill mine. One day, you'll learn to forgive me. But if you don't, I'll find a way to live with that. It's the price I'm willing to pay for a world transformed. That's what heroes do."

Now she did laugh, an ugly sound of serrated edges. "You *were* my hero. The wise one. The responsible one. But you're the kind of guy Mom and Dad would have hated."

"Dad would have understood."

"This is really about him, isn't it?" Alia said as the pieces shifted into place. "All that talk about generals and warfare, but this is about Dad. This is because you're so desperate to be a Keralis instead of a Mayeux."

"*Be careful. Be cautious,*" he sneered, mocking their mother's warnings. "Is that how you want to live? Playing by their rules instead of making our own?"

"You *are* playing by their rules—choosing the strong over the weak, turning against the people who always had your back."

"*These* are my people," he said, spreading his hands wide. "Heroes. Winners."

Alia shook her head. "You think you're going to save the world and everyone's going to finally thank you for it? You think all your new gun-toting friends are going to take your side when the battle is over? This isn't going to change anything."

"You don't see it, Alia, but eventually you will."

"Tell yourself what you want. You're not a hero. You're a little boy playing war."

"That's enough."

"I'll let you know when it's enough," she snapped.

His eyes narrowed. "You are a child, Alia. You've had the luxury of being a child because I kept the watch, because I made the hard choices. I can't protect you forever."

The pain inside her was a living thing, a wounded animal that strained at its leash.

"What's going to happen to me, Jason? Is someone going to betray everything I believe in and murder my friends? Is that what you're going to protect me from?"

"Stop being a brat."

She spat in his face.

Jason recoiled. He wiped his face clean with the hem of his shirt. For a moment he was just a boy, her brother, in a dirty T-shirt and jeans. Then he spoke, and the illusion shattered.

"Get her in the car," he said to two soldiers standing at attention nearby. "But be cautious. You aren't immune to her power the way I am. I don't want you fighting among yourselves. We'll change drivers as we travel."

The soldiers hauled her toward the backseat of one of the Humvees, but they paused when Jason said, "Alia, the world's about to become a very ugly place. Everyone will need allies. You may want to think about how alone you are."

He was scolding her, like a kid being sent to bed without supper. She loved her brother, maybe she even understood the hurt that drove him, but she would never forgive what he had done.

When she spoke again, she didn't recognize her own voice. It was a low, thrumming thing, the rage within her burning like a crucible, making it something new.

"I'm a daughter of Nemesis," she said, "the goddess of divine retribution. You may want to think about how well I can hold a grudge."

"Cuff her," said Jason as the soldiers dragged her away. "I don't want her trying to hurt herself in some misguided attempt to save the world."

Sister in battle, I am shield and blade to you, she repeated to herself as the soldiers tossed her into the back of the Humvee, as they used plastic zip ties to fasten her wrists to the metal console that divided the backseat. *As I breathe, your enemies will know no sanctuary.*

I'll find a way, Diana, she swore. *For you, for Theo, for Nim. While I live, your cause is mine.*

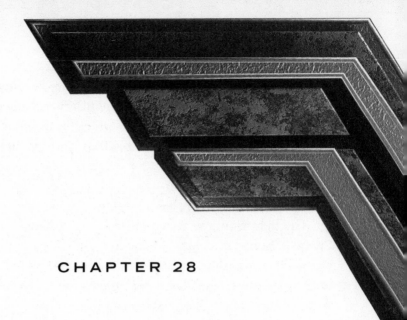

CHAPTER 28

Diana could see the silver waters of the Eurotas, her own body, face-down in the river, limbs sprawled at graceless angles, drained of blood and white as bone. She made the shape of a shattered star. Nim lay a few yards away, and there was Theo, his arm hooked around a rock, as if he'd been trying to hold on to it, fingers fluttering in the current.

She watched Pinon make her slow progress to the road, her movements sluggish, her blood-bloated tail dragging through the brush as she returned to her master. As if from a great distance, she could hear the whir of helicopter blades, and Alia shouting. She was sorry she could not go to her friend, but the emotion was a faraway thing, a thought that came and went like a memory of sorrow. Diana felt nothing. Without her body, there was nothing to hold to, nothing to keep her tied to the earth.

So this was how it ended. This was death.

Yes, Daughter of Earth, this is death. And rebirth.

Diana saw her then: the Oracle, crouched by the great gray trunk of the plane tree, leaning over the waters of the spring and stirring them with one long finger, as if it were her scrying pool back on Themyscira. Was she real or just a dying vision?

I am as real as anything, said the Oracle. Her hood slid back, revealing piercing gray eyes, a full mouth, her features framed by a golden helm. Diana had seen the Oracle in this guise when she'd first visited her, but she hadn't realized she was looking into the face of a god.

Athena.

See me now as I truly am, Daughter. See us.

The light from the water shifted, and Athena's face was gone. She was Aphrodite with her gleaming curls; Hera in her jeweled glory; Artemis, glowing bright as the moon; veiled Hestia, who burned like an ember; Demeter in her crown of wheat; and then Athena once more. She was too beautiful. Diana wished she had eyes so she could look away.

We made Themyscira for the Amazons that they would have sanctuary, and in the guise of the Oracle, we watch over our daughters still.

It is time to return home, Diana, and take your true place among your sisters. You fought bravely for the innocent. You died with honor. And in your final moments, you cried out to me.

The Oracle rose, and Diana saw her shape shift—a warrior, a wife, a woman seated at a loom, an archer with arrow drawn.

Come, Daughter of Earth, and be reborn as your sisters once were, with all the strength that is your due. A war is coming, and you must help your people to prepare. You have earned your place among the battle-born at last.

Battle-born. Diana had dreamed of those words, longed for them. *I am an Amazon.*

Could she truly return to Themyscira? Fight side by side with her sisters in the war to come? The Council would never allow it. She'd violated the island's most fundamental laws.

They will never know, said the Oracle. *It will be as if you never left. Come, Diana. Come home.*

Home. The images were bright in her mind. The trumpet flowers climbing the window outside of her bedroom. The palace kitchens bustling with life. The woods with their vast trees, where she and Maeve had spent long hours exploring. The northern shore with its cliffs and secret coves. The cliffs she knew better than anyone, where she'd first heard Alia's cry for help.

Alia. To whom she'd sworn an oath. *As I breathe, your enemies will know no sanctuary. While I live, your cause is mine.* That vow was unbreakable, as binding as the golden lasso.

Diana thought of Ben, who had piloted the jet with such calm assurance, facing down assailants he knew were better armed; of Alia's parents, who had tried to make a better world. She thought of her pinky twined with Nim's; of Theo picking up a sword, though he had no idea how to wield it. The Amazons were her people, but these had become her people, too. She had to find a way to protect them.

These people, these mortals—fragile, foolish, brave beyond all common sense—deserved a chance at peace. It was not too late. The sun had not yet set.

Daughter, said Athena, *we see your good heart. But this cannot be.*

Please, Diana begged. *Let me remain.*

No, said the goddess, and her voice was stern.

But from the first moment she'd met Alia, Diana had refused to do as she was told. Why start now?

Give me another chance, she pleaded. What was she asking? What price would the gods demand? *Give Theo and Nim another chance.*

This is not possible. Their moment is past.

You are goddesses, Diana said, taking her courage in hand. *You decide what's possible.*

You bargain for the lives of mortals? A different voice this time, clear as a horn calling the hunt. *Why?*

They are my soldiers, said Diana. *I can't win this battle alone.*

And these are the warriors you choose? that clear, cold voice asked, her amusement rippling like moonlight.

Another voice spoke, sweet as a lyre. *If the girl wishes to make a foolish choice, she would not be the first.*

Then if we are to bargain, said another, *let us name our terms. What do you have to offer, Daughter of Earth?*

Nothing. She had nothing with which to barter for her friends' lives. No trinkets or vows to offer, no worthy sacrifice. But that wasn't quite true, was it? She had the gift she'd just been given. She could risk her own life, her own future.

Think, Daughter, said the Oracle, once more the golden-helmed general. *Think what you will be giving up for the sake of these mortals, these brief, impossible creatures.*

But Diana didn't need to think anymore.

I offer my life as an Amazon. If I fail to stop this war, if I die at Jason's hand, I relinquish my right to return to the island.

You would go to your true death? said the Oracle.

Yes.

A chorus rose: a thousand languages, the voices of a thousand goddesses, all the deities who had entrusted their daughters to the sanctuary of Themyscira, all who knew what war would bring.

Then, abruptly, the Oracle went silent. The goddesses waged their arguments in private, and all Diana could do was wait. An age passed. A bare second.

Athena spoke, and Diana heard both pride and caution in her voice. *We will answer your entreaties. Your compatriots will have their chance and so will you. Seek victory, and should you find it, return to your sisters as a true Amazon. But heed us, Daughter of Earth—you have bartered the last of your chances.*

Diana felt a tremor of fear at these words. The gods did not deal in favors. There was always a price.

Here are the terms of our bargain: Should you die in the World of Man a second time, you will pass on to the Underworld as mortals do. You will never see Themyscira's shores, or your mother or your sisters again. Athena paused. *Do you understand, Diana? Your life will end. There can be no backward step. We will not intercede on your behalf. Speak not our names to plead for mercy.*

Diana thought of exiled Nessa standing on the shore, stripped of her armor, as the earth shook and the winds howled. She remembered the poet's words: *What can we say of her suffering, except that it was brief?*

Diana had made her choice with that first leap from a high cliff, with that first plunge into the sea. Her mother and her sisters had chosen to turn their backs on the World of Man, to build a new world with peace at its heart. *Their work is done*, thought Diana. *But mine is just beginning.*

This is my fight, she told the Oracle. *Let me claim it.*

A sound like thunder rent the air with a *crack.*

Diana gasped for breath—the roar of the storm was the pounding of her heart, echoing in her ears as her body filled with blood, her lungs with air. Her eyes flew open. She saw gray water, reeds. She inhaled, and water flooded her nostrils. She remembered her arms, her legs, forced herself to turn over and sit up, coughing.

The air around her seemed to snap with electricity.

Demeter lifted her hand, and the reeds along the riverbank grew taller, sheltering them from view.

Hera knelt beside Nim. The goddess cradled her head in her lap, straightening the angle of Nim's neck as Aphrodite dipped a shell into the river and sprinkled its contents over Nim's limp form. Nim's chest began to rise. She blinked once, twice, sat up in shock, water streaming from her hair, looking around frantically, but the goddesses were gone.

Over Theo's wound, Hestia's fingers dripped fire, and as the flames touched the cleft the sword had made in his side, the flesh knit together, smooth and unscarred. Artemis drew an arrow from her quiver, ghostly and glowing as if forged of moonlight. She drove it into Theo's chest, and he twitched, gasping as his heart began to beat once more. His eyes flew open, and he scrambled backward on his hands, reaching for a weapon, seeking his attackers.

"Diana? What the hell just happened?" said Nim. "Where's Alia? Where's that—that thing?"

There was no sign of the goddesses or the Oracle, but Diana heard Athena's words ringing in her ears: *Speak not our names to plead for mercy.*

There were men headed down the hillside; they had cans of gasoline in their hands.

Theo touched the place where his wound had been. "Did I die? Oh shit, am I a zombie?"

"There's no time to explain," said Diana. "Jason has Alia."

Theo's face went grim. "Then let's go get her."

Diana glanced at the horizon. "And we have less than thirty minutes until the sun sets."

Nim nodded. "Then let's get her *quickly*."

She'd chosen her soldiers. It was time to go to war.

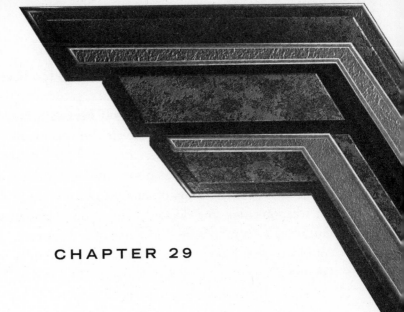

CHAPTER 29

They crept into the bushes, skirting the men with the gasoline cans who had made it down to the banks of the river and were discovering there were no bodies to be found.

"What the hell?" one of them said. "I saw Pinon finish the Amazon, and Rutkoski took care of the skinny guy."

"I broke that Indian kid's neck myself," said another.

"Asshole," muttered Nim.

"So where are they?"

"Maybe the river carried them downstream?"

They set off, boots splashing through the shallows.

"Come on," said Diana. "We won't have long until they report back to Jason."

At the edge of the blacktop, they paused. Jason's vehicles had blocked off the road, and she wondered if his forces had set up a perimeter to stop ordinary traffic. She could see men milling around two Humvees at the head of the caravan. Three armored trucks clustered closer to their hiding place, along with a third Humvee. This was the one that carried Pinon. Diana could tell from the heavy bolts that had been added to the rear doors, but she was relieved to see no sign of the creature. Hopefully, she was securely locked up and sleeping off her feast inside the vehicle. The helicopter had taken to the air and was making a wide circle over the valley.

A group of soldiers was piling into one of the armored trucks. Through the open doors of another, she could see a mini armory of weapons and what looked like a mobile laboratory. Jason was speaking to a man seated in front of a computer, test tubes full of blood—her blood—parceled out for him to play with. The sick shame of betrayal pooled in her gut. He'd lied to her, taken her trust, and stolen the very life from her body.

"How can he look so damn calm?" Theo said. Beneath his anger, Diana heard all the hurt and bewilderment of the moment Jason had turned on them.

"It's worse than that," said Nim, nothing but disgust in her voice. "He looks *satisfied.*"

She was right. The rigid tension had gone from Jason. He'd changed into a clean shirt and a combat jacket, and he wore them like cloth of gold. He looked like a king at the moment of his ascension.

Diana curled her hand into a fist. He wasn't a king; he was a thief. And he'd taken enough from all of them.

"Theo," she said, "if you had access to one of those computers, could you find a way to, I don't know—"

"Infiltrate Jason's network and decimate his data stores, corrupting every bit of information he's gathered and rendering his research worthless?"

"Um, yes, that."

"Sure."

"That easy?" said Nim.

Theo shrugged. "I helped build Jason's networks and firewalls."

Nim whistled. "No wonder he wanted you dead."

Jason jumped down from the truck and headed for the front of the caravan, pausing beside the second Humvee.

"Alia will be in there," Diana said. "They'll take second position on the drive in case of ambush. I can get to her."

"You sure?" said Theo. "Those are a lot of soldiers all juiced up on hero blood."

"I can get to her," Diana repeated, hoping that was true. She would have only one chance at this. "But we need to get you to the lab truck. Jason said he had snipers in place, and I doubt he'll have them stand down until the caravan is in motion."

Nim pointed to a spot near the crest of the Menelaion, then left and right at the lower ridges. "They'll be there," she said.

"What do you know about snipers?" asked Theo.

"Nothing, but I know plenty about sight lines. Those are the three spots that will give them direct views of the caravan and anyone approaching from either side of the road."

"That's remarkable," said Diana. "Can you pick out a path to follow that will get us to the lab truck without drawing their fire?"

Nim cocked her head. "I can get us there, but not without the guys in Pinon's Humvee seeing us."

"Then that's our first stop," said Diana. "Nim, take the lead. Let's move."

They dropped into a crouch and crept along the side of the road, following Nim's directions, using the brush and trees as cover. Nim's zigs and zags as they approached the vehicles seemed counterintuitive to Diana, but she could admit she didn't have Nim's particular gift for the visual. They emerged from the brush, wriggled directly under one of the armored trucks, and then crawled along its opposite flank. From there, they slid into a wide pocket of shadow by the driver's side of the Humvee.

"Stay close," she said, and yanked open the driver's door.

Before the stunned soldier could say a word, she'd pulled him from the vehicle and slammed him against the Humvee's side. He dropped to the pavement.

"Hey!" said the soldier in the passenger's seat, his hand on his radio. She slid into the car, seized the scruff of his shirt, and cracked his head against the dashboard. He slumped forward.

Diana looked behind her. The rear of the Humvee held two large cages. Pinon lay in one, curled on her side and snoring.

She picked up the handheld radio and slipped back out of the Humvee. Nim and Theo were rolling the driver's unconscious body beneath the vehicle.

"Nim," said Diana. "Get us to the lab truck."

In a few quick steps, they were there. Diana threw the back doors open and leapt inside.

The man at the computer station scrambled away, fumbling for the gun at his hip.

Diana yanked it from its holster and held it easily out of his reach.

He raised his hands. "Please. I'm a scientist."

"I'm not going to hurt you." She saw his hand creeping toward a yellow panic switch and brought the butt of the pistol down on his head. "Much."

She waved Theo and Nim inside and shut the doors behind them.

"Keep an eye on him," she said. "If anyone realizes you're here—"

Nim snatched a semiautomatic rifle from the wall. "We'll be ready."

Theo was already bent over the computer, his fingers flying over the keyboard.

A machine was whirring at the workstation, row after row of glass test tubes filling with dark red blood, then shifting left so another row could be filled.

"Oh hell," said Nim. "Is that your blood?"

Diana narrowed her eyes. She scanned the mini armory in the truck and pointed to a row of incendiary grenades. "When Theo is done, I want you to get clear, then blow this truck and the vehicle with Pinon in it. Can you do that?"

"Yes," said Nim.

Her answer was a little too quick and a little too confident for Diana's liking. "Without blowing yourselves up?"

"Possibly," said Theo.

The radio crackled. "We are ready to move out. Collins, remain in position until the site has been cleared, over." They stared at the black box. The voice sounded again. "Collins, do you copy?"

Theo snatched up the radio, fumbling it clumsily, then pressed a button and said, "Copy that . . . pal."

"See you back at base, over."

Theo put the radio aside and returned to his work. Diana grabbed a short sword and a shield from the racks.

"I don't understand," said Nim. "All the swords and stuff. Are Jason's soldiers really tough enough to go up against bullets and bombs?"

"He's going to deploy EMPs," said Theo. He pointed to the screen, where a long string of text scrolled by. Diana's confusion must have shown, because he continued. "An electromagnetic pulse. It's not much different from lightning, just a lot bigger. It will disable all major weapons systems. No nukes, no missiles, no access to weapons stockpiles."

"A fair fight," murmured Diana. *I wanted to remake the world.*

"Sure," said Theo. "If you've been taking your hero-blood vitamins. The Keralis Foundation has footholds all over the world. He's going to throw us back to the Stone Age."

"The Bronze Age," corrected Nim.

"Was dying once today not enough for you?" said Theo.

Diana touched each of them on the shoulder, hoping they could get along well enough to manage this task.

"Stay quiet and stay safe," she whispered, heading for the doors. "And lock up behind me."

"Diana," said Nim. "Kick Jason's ass."

She frowned, confused. "Specifically his ass?"

"Yeah."

"Why?"

Without looking up from the keys, Theo said, "New York tradition."

Diana nodded and cracked the doors. She edged outside. The

last of the day's sunlight cast long shadows across the road. She'd hoped to be able to sneak up on Jason's vehicle, but there was no time for stealth. The caravan was already moving.

Diana broke into a run. Instantly, she heard gunfire. She kept her shield up, hearing bullets ping against the metal. She sprinted ahead, slipping alongside the last truck in the caravan, keeping pace with it and using it for cover. She heard voices shouting and saw the lead cars put on speed as the truck beside her screeched to a halt.

She couldn't afford to wait to see what emerged from it. She raced ahead and dove for the back of the Humvee, seizing the base of its metal bumper, using one hand to keep her shield above her, and the other to lift the vehicle's back end off the ground.

The Humvee's front wheels spun as it tried to surge forward. Diana gave a grunt of effort and planted her feet. A bullet struck her left thigh; another struck her calf, the pain coming in bright shocks that jolted through her body. She glanced behind her and saw soldiers pouring out of the other truck, racing toward her with guns drawn. They were far enough away that their weapons weren't doing much damage, but she couldn't maintain this position.

Diana sucked in a breath and flung her shield at them in a sweeping arc. She let go of the Humvee. It roared forward on a burst of speed. With a running leap, she sprang onto its back, charging up and over the roof. Gunfire exploded around her, the bullets striking her body in a painful hail. She ignored them and launched herself off the Humvee's hood, directly into its path.

She rolled into a somersault, came up standing, and barely had time to plant her feet and turn, hands held out before her. The Humvee barreled into her, driving her backward, her sandals sliding over the pavement. The force of the impact quaked up her palms, and she gritted her teeth, bracing her shoulders, as the Humvee's engine roared.

She heard footfalls, soldiers running toward her. How many?

Ten? Twenty? More? How fast were they? How strong? Could she fight them all?

Diana looked to the west. The sun had turned a fiery red as it drew closer to the hills. How long did she have until it set completely? How long until darkness fell and their last chance vanished?

CHAPTER 30

When a voice came over the radio declaring, "Sir, we have an incoming hostile," Jason didn't seem remotely concerned.

"Local law or big guns?"

"Uh, neither, sir. It's that girl."

Alia sat up straighter, the plastic zip ties around her wrists digging into her flesh.

"Girl?" Jason said, craning his neck as gunfire exploded behind them.

Alia was afraid to look, afraid to hope, but she made herself turn.

Diana, sprinting through a torrent of bullets, her shield raised above her head. She leapt forward and seized the rear bumper of the Humvee.

"That isn't *possible*," Jason said, his brow lowered as if he was trying to solve a particularly difficult equation. "Pinon drained her. No one can survive that."

Men were descending on Diana, drawing closer, the gunfire growing louder. She hurled her shield at them and released the Humvee, but a moment later, Alia heard footsteps on the roof, and in the next second, Diana was standing in the Humvee's path.

"Take her down," said Jason.

The driver gunned the engine, and Alia screamed.

They struck Diana head-on, the impact throwing Alia forward against her seat belt. But Diana hadn't moved. She was planted in the road, her lips drawn back over her teeth, her hands braced against the Humvee's crossbar.

"My God," Jason said, peering through the windshield, admiration in his voice. "Look at her."

He didn't sound scared. Alia wanted him to sound scared.

"Sir?" said the driver, unsure of himself.

"I want the prota guard. Swords and shields, no guns. Oh, and tell them to try and keep her alive if they can."

How could he talk this way? As if this was a game—no, an experiment—and he couldn't wait to record the outcome.

The soldier communicated the order over the radio, and in seconds Alia saw a wave of men flanking Diana as the Humvee's wheels whirred.

"These are my finest soldiers," Jason said. "They've been blessed with the strength of the greatest heroes to ever walk this earth, but they've never faced a challenge like Diana."

Alia glared at him. "They're no match for her."

"Maybe not," Jason acknowledged. "But they'll make quite a mess of her while we wait for the sun to set."

Fresh fury spiked through her. She pulled futilely at her cuffed hands. Diana was here, back from the dead, and Alia could do nothing to help her. She wanted to scream. All of this power inside her, an apocalypse waiting to be born, and what use was it to her?

"I wish we could stay to watch her fight," Jason said as his prota guard advanced with swords and spears and . . . nets.

"Why do they have nets, Jason?" she asked, though she wasn't sure she wanted to know.

"I was shortsighted before. Okay," he admitted with a small, painfully Jason shrug, "I was overeager. I shouldn't have had Pinon drain her dry. Alive, she'll provide me with a permanent supply of genetic material to work from."

Something dark tore lose in Alia. Jason might not be right about their parents, but he wasn't totally wrong, either. Her whole life, she'd been told to be careful, to keep her voice low, to make sure she only drew the right kind of attention. Stay calm. Don't give them a reason. Don't ever give them a reason. But she'd had a right to her anger then, and she had a right to it now. And what had being careful gotten her, anyway? There had to be justice for Theo, for Nim, for all the pain Jason had caused. *Careful* wasn't going to get it. *Nemesis. Goddess of retribution.*

She heard the beat of wings and recoiled, thinking of Eris, but this sound came from within her, the rustle of something that had slept for too long. *Haptandra. The hand of war.* What if she were the one to reach for this power?

I am done being careful. I am done being quiet. Let them see me angry. Let them hear me wail at the top of my lungs. The sleeping thing stretched its wings, black and glossy, lit by dark fire. It rose, a dagger in its hand.

Nemesis. What if this power wasn't only a curse but a gift, something unwieldy and dangerous, passed from a goddess to her daughter, and on and on, something that longed to be used? What if it could be a weapon in Alia's hand?

She closed her eyes and reached toward that dark, winged thing. She grabbed hold, fastening it to her, so that she was only anger now. Alia could almost feel the shift of wings between her own shoulder blades—and there was no fear, only a vibrant surety. *This is mine. This is my right.* She nudged at the power inside her and felt it take flight.

The soldier in the passenger seat lifted his radio and smashed it into the driver's head. Jason flinched back as the driver turned on his attacker and they began to grapple in the front seat.

"Scholes!" Jason shouted as the driver took his foot off the pedal and the Humvee decelerated. "Chihara! What the hell are you doing?"

Alia opened her eyes, saw the ring of soldiers. She reached toward her power, and this time she *shoved*.

Suddenly, the soldiers outside were screaming, shouting, their swords clanging as they turned on one another.

"Damn it," said Jason. "This must be because we're so close to sunset."

"Yeah," said Alia. "That must be it."

"Do—" Jason began, then shouted as the Humvee tilted forward and the front of the vehicle hit the road with a loud metallic clang. "What the—"

"I think she took the front tires off." The Humvee's rear sank with a sudden *thunk*. "And those would be the back tires."

"Where is she?" he said, turning in his seat.

"She's coming for you." Alia looked through the windows and smiled at the havoc she had made. It was only the beginning. "*We're* coming for you."

"Don't look so pleased, Alia," Jason said, and she could see only frustration in him, no terror, no worry. If anything, he looked almost eager as he drew a long sword from the Humvee's main compartment. "This fight is just starting."

He threw the door open, blade gleaming in his hand.

CHAPTER 31

Diana cast the last of the tires away in time to see Jason crawl from the box that had been the Humvee and launch himself to his feet. He was armed with a sword and paused only to snatch a shield from the inert arm of one of his fallen men.

There was no time to survey the chaos around her, to worry if, back in the lab truck, Theo and Nim would succumb to this battle madness, too.

The soldier closest to Diana had knocked his compatriot to the ground and was slamming his shield against his opponent's face. Diana seized it on the upswing and cracked it once across the soldier's head. He dropped forward, cheek to cheek with his comrade.

She faced Jason now. They were ringed by fighting men. The other truck had driven off the road.

Diana tested the weight of the sword in her hand. It was fairly short, but its shape would make it good for both cutting and thrusting. Though the steel was of average quality, the blade seemed sharp enough.

"Your men aren't coming to your rescue," she said.

Jason rolled his shoulders. "I don't need a rescue."

"You already lost to me once on the way up the mountain."

"Let's say I let you believe what you wanted to believe."

Diana shook her head, realizing he'd feigned his fatigue on that starlit peak. "You lie as easily as you breathe. Always you held back. Well then," she said, "let's see what your best looks like against an Amazon."

They circled each other slowly. But Jason had no reason to wait to assess her strengths. He'd been doing that for days. He lunged.

Their swords met, clashed, the sound of steel against steel ringing off the hillside. Diana felt the force of the blow all the way up her arm. He was strong and knew how to use his weight.

They drew apart, blades sparking. He attacked, and Diana parried, spinning left, keeping her shield up as he made a fresh jab at her ribs. *Strong*, she noted, *but also used to being the strongest player on the field*. He slammed his shield into hers, expecting her to fall back. Instead, she shoved, sending him flying.

He crashed into the side of one of the trucks but was on his feet in the blink of an eye. He shook off the pain of the impact and smiled. "The soldiers I am going to build from your blood."

Not if Theo can help it, she thought as Jason rushed at her, his sword glinting like a flash of lightning in a bank of clouds. He moved in a flurry, swiping and thrusting, driving her backward. She shifted her weight, returning each blow. It was startling, strange. How many hours had she spent preparing for such a moment? And yet this was nothing like the drills or sparring matches in the training rooms of the Armory. Because now her opponent was prepared to deal a killing blow.

"You're fast," she noted.

Jason smiled, and the dimple that had charmed her so easily appeared. "You're not just fighting me," he said, his breathing even. "You're fighting the warriors who defeated the Amazons. Achilles, who bested Penthesilea. Telamon, who brought low Melanippe. Hercules, who defeated Hippolyta."

She hated hearing her sisters' names, her mother's name on his lips.

Diana raised a brow. "A wise warrior learns from her mistakes." She adjusted her stance. "And you're forgetting who taught me to fight."

She brought her sword down in a furious arc. Jason raised his shield to block the blow but stumbled. Diana kicked out with her right foot, driving her heel into his solar plexus and knocking the wind from his lungs.

This time he did not rise so quickly. She descended on him with every bit of skill she'd learned, the echo of her sisters' teachings reverberating through her movements, the lessons they'd learned and passed down to her.

Jason returned the blows, but his movements had slowed. He was still feeling the force of her kick, struggling to catch his breath. She slashed and he pivoted right, avoiding the strike, but she'd never intended to make contact. She checked her attack, changing direction, and brought her blade down in a swipe against his shield arm. He hissed as blood bloomed along his skin. She took the opening and brought the hilt of her sword down swiftly on his shield, knocking it free of his hand. It hit the ground with a dull clang.

Diana changed her grip and swept her blade hard right, batting his sword away.

He scrambled backward, his left arm dripping blood. He looked less frightened than confused, as if he couldn't quite fathom where his weapons had gone. "No," he said. "This is all wrong. Achilles, Hercules, they won. In all the stories, they best the Amazons. They are the victors."

"Those are the stories your poets tell, not mine. Surrender, Jason Keralis."

Jason growled his frustration, circling left. "Did Menelaus surrender when Paris stole his bride? I know you aren't willing to deal a killing strike."

"You can't win. Only my sisters can match me in fair combat."

A fevered look came into his eyes. "Then put aside your weapons. Fight me hand to hand. Best me and take your victory."

Would that end this? Give him the defeat in honest combat he sought? She doubted it. Diana shrugged, tossed her sword and shield far out of reach.

Jason sighed and shook his head. "So honest, so righteous." His lips curved, the beginnings of a smile, sharp as a knife blade. "So easy to dupe. Only your sisters can match you?" He drew a syringe from his pocket. "Then you will fall to the might of the Amazons."

She remembered what he'd said on the banks of the Eurotas. *I began building a serum from your DNA the first day we met.* Her cells, her strength.

"No!" Diana cried.

He jammed the needle into his thigh and depressed the plunger, then tossed the empty syringe aside. Jason straightened, cracked his neck. His grin widened. Diana took a step back.

"The sun sets," said Jason, flexing his fingers as if testing the feel of his new strength. "An age of heroes begins. And I believe I promised you a beautiful death."

He advanced and Diana retreated, eyeing him warily. "There's nowhere to run now. I wonder," he said, his hands forming fists, "how it will feel to be brought low by strength born of your own blood."

He swung left. Diana dodged the blow. He came up hard right—a hook to her gut with tremendous force. Diana grunted as his fist landed. Jason released a *whoof* of air and drew back, startled.

He shook it off and lunged at her. She pivoted, intending to wrap her ankle around his and use his own momentum to bring him down. But he was faster now. He halted his motion, seized her shoulders, and twisted, hurling her to the ground.

He grunted as if he were the one who'd been thrown on his back, whirled as if expecting to find someone behind him.

Diana rocked backward and sprang to her feet.

Jason threw himself at her, unleashing a flurry of punches and driving elbows; she bobbed left, right, landed a punch to his gut. He drove the palm of his hand upward in a strike to her chin.

Diana's neck snapped back; the metallic tang of blood filled her mouth.

Jason reeled away, holding his hand to his jaw as if he'd been struck. He touched his fingers to his mouth, but there was no blood there. His eyes were wide and wild. "What is this?"

Diana licked the blood from her lip. Now she was the one to smile. "This is what it means to be an Amazon. My pain is theirs, and theirs is mine. Each wound you deal will be one you suffer yourself."

"But it's not just the—" Jason shook his head as if trying to clear it. He took a step toward her, stopped. "What is that *sound*?"

"Come, Jason, strike me. Grant me the beautiful death you promised. But with each blow, you will feel the agony of every Amazon fallen in battle. In each attack, you will hear the chorus of their screams."

Jason clapped his hands to his ears. "Make it stop."

"I can't."

He lurched forward, dropped to his knees. "Make it stop!" he screamed. "Don't you hear it? Don't you feel it?"

"Of course," said Diana. "Every Amazon bears the suffering of her sisters, lives with it, and learns to endure it. It's why we value mercy so highly." It was what helped them remember that despite their greater strength, their speed, their skill, the promise of glory was nothing in the face of another's anguish. Diana crouched down and took Jason's chin in her fingers, forcing him to meet her gaze. "If you cannot bear our pain, you are not fit to carry our strength."

"You meant to do this," he hissed. "You tricked me."

It was true. Jason knew she would not kill him, and she had known he would never surrender without the hero's death he so longed for. "Let's say I let you believe what you wanted to believe."

"Kill me!" Jason yelled. "You can't leave me like this!"

"You haven't earned an honorable death—neither a beautiful one nor a quiet one. Live in shame instead, Jason Keralis, unmourned and unremembered."

"You'll remember me," he panted, his face sheened with sweat.

"I was your first kiss. I could have been your first everything. You'll always know that."

She looked deep into his eyes. "You were my first nothing, Jason. I am immortal, and you are a footnote. I will erase you from my history, and you will vanish, unremembered by this world."

Jason gave a high, keening shriek, his entire body shuddering. He slumped over on his side, curling into himself like a child, and wrapped his arms over his head, rocking back and forth, his howls of rage becoming sobs.

She heard a loud *boom* and saw a spurt of flame rise from where she'd left Theo and Nim at the lab truck. A second later, another explosion sounded. Pinon's cage.

Diana gave Jason one swift kick in the ass, as was tradition, then yanked the door from an armored truck and wrapped it tightly around him. That would hold him for a short while at least.

She glanced over her shoulder. The sun was about to set. They had only a few minutes left, and the spring was almost a quarter mile away.

She raced to the Humvee and threw open the passenger door.

"What did you do to him?" Alia asked when she heard her brother crying inside his metal cocoon.

Diana snapped the plastic bands binding her wrists.

"Nothing," she said. "He did it to himself." She turned her back to Alia. "Now get on."

This time there was no argument. Alia leapt onto her back, and they were running toward the spring.

CHAPTER 32

Alia held tight to Diana's neck, taking in the chaos she'd unleashed, trying to forget the sounds of Jason's whimpers as they sprinted toward the spring. Had Theo and Nim survived, too? How much time did they have left?

Branches struck her cheeks as they clambered down the slope to the river, racing along its sandy banks.

"What if we're too late?" Alia panted, unsure why *she* was out of breath.

"We won't be."

"But what if we are?"

"I don't know," Diana said, unslinging her as they neared the plane tree. "I guess we just keep fighting. Together."

They splashed into the shallows of the riverbed, the water growing deeper as they plunged toward the spring. Around her, Alia heard the chorus building once more, girls' voices multiplying as she sank waist deep in the water, stumbling over slick stones, soaked sneakers searching for purchase on the river's sandy bottom. She saw Eris high above them, heard her horrid screeching, saw the twins in their chariots racing along the riverbanks, both of them laughing, shrill and victorious.

Too late. Too late.

As the sun sank below the horizon, Alia hurled herself into the shining waters of the spring. She plunged beneath the surface, and the world went dark and silent. The water was far deeper than she'd expected, the cold like a hand sliding closed around her. Her feet kicked, but she could feel nothing beneath her. She was no longer sure which way she was facing or where the surface might be. There was only darkness all around.

She could feel that winged thing inside her, thrashing, but she couldn't tell if it was fighting to keep hold or to break free.

Don't go. The thought came unbidden to her mind. She didn't mean it. She'd fought too hard to release the world from the horror this curse would bring. But some part of her wished she could keep a scrap of this power for herself. She'd done good with it, saved Diana with it. For a brief moment, that righteous anger had burned bright in her heart, and it had belonged to no one but her.

Her lungs tightened, hungry for air. Had the spring done its work? She didn't know, but she didn't want to drown finding out. She expelled her remaining breath, watched the bubbles rise, and knew which way to go. She shot upward and broke free of the river's grasp, hauling herself back to shallower water, sucking in great gulps of air.

"Well?" shouted Nim from the shore, Theo beside her in the blue light of dusk. A bolt of joy—they'd made it. But . . .

"What happened?" asked Diana, offering Alia her hand and helping her rise.

"Nothing."

Alia looked up at the sliver of moon that had appeared in the twilight sky, helplessness weighting her heart.

A rumble filled the air. Alia looked to the road, wondering what fresh disaster was headed their way, but the sound didn't seem to be coming from there.

"What is that noise?" said Theo.

It was coming from everywhere. She began to pick out different pieces in the roar: the punishing din of artillery fire, the thunder of tanks, the shriek of fighter jets. And screams. The screams of the dying.

"Oh God," she said. "It's starting."

Diana blinked, her eyes deep blue in the fading light. Her shoulders sagged, and it was as if an invisible crown had slid from her head. "We failed. We were too late."

Was it my fault? Alia wondered. Had she doomed them in that last moment? In her selfish desire to keep some of that mysterious power for her own?

They stood hip deep in the river as the sound grew, shaking the earth and the branches of the plane trees. It rose like a wave, towering over them, the coming of a future thick with human misery.

And then, like a wave, it broke.

The sound receded in a rush, the tide retreating—and then gone.

Diana's breath caught. "Alia," she said. "Look."

Three figures stood by the plane tree, their bodies glowing golden in the gathering dark. Their features were indistinct, but Alia could see that one of them was a girl.

Helen. The girl stepped forward, her feet light on the ground, older than when she'd been allowed to race near the banks of the Eurotas. She placed a glowing wreath of lotus flowers against the plane tree, touched her fingers once, lightly, to its gray trunk.

In the golden sheen cast upon the waters of the spring, Alia saw armies retreating, soldiers laying down their weapons, crowds of angry people breaking their stride. The light faded, and Alia watched as Helen and her brothers drifted away from the river, until she could no longer find their shapes in the shadows. Wherever they were going, she hoped they found peace.

She met Diana's gaze, almost afraid to speak. "Is it over?"

Diana took a shaky breath. "I think so," she said tentatively, as if she couldn't quite believe it. "We changed the future. We stopped a war."

From the road, Alia heard the cry of sirens and saw the flashing lights of police cars and fire trucks approaching.

She and Diana made their way to the riverbank, and Nim seized Alia in a tight hug.

"I thought you were dead," Alia said, the ache of tears pressing at her throat.

Nim's laugh was part sob. "I kind of was."

"Hey, so was I," said Theo. "I did some really good dying."

"He also put a wrecking ball through Jason's firewall," said Nim.

"Yeah," Theo said, shoving his hands into the pockets of his ridiculous trousers. "I can't guarantee that there won't be some fallout at Keralis Labs, though."

Alia winced. "I'm betting after all of this, the board isn't going to want me or Jason anywhere near the company."

Theo's shoulders lifted. "Sorry?"

"I'm not," Alia said. "I'll be fine. I'll build something of my own."

Angry voices drifted down from the road, shouting in Greek.

"Should we go up there?" said Diana.

"No," said Alia. "I don't think we should. Let Jason explain why he has a heavily armed militia in the middle of a country road."

"What's going to happen to him?" said Nim.

They sat down beneath the drooping branches of a willow. In the dark, no one looking down from above would see them, though if anyone came investigating, they'd be easy enough to spot. But why would they? The battle had been waged on the road. There were no signs that it had spread to the river's banks, that beneath the branches of a plane tree an age of bloodshed had been prevented.

"I don't know," said Alia. "I hope there's some way to reach him, to help him. I still can't quite believe that my brother did this."

"And my best friend," said Theo.

"No offense," Nim said, "but that douchebag tried to kill me—I hope he rots."

Theo nodded. "Fair point."

Diana clutched Alia's arm. "Alia, they're agreeing."

"Hey," said Nim, "that's true. And I haven't wanted to stab you for a solid fifteen minutes, Theo."

"How about now?" he asked.

"Nope."

"How about now?"

"Theo—"

"How about now?"

Nim grimaced.

"Don't worry," said Alia. "Even I want to stab him."

The shining scythe of the reaping moon hung low over the valley, visible once more, and they sat together, side by side, watching the stars appear and the lights of the city multiply in the distance. After a while, they heard more cars arrive, and then others depart.

"I guess someone is making decisions," said Alia.

"How do you feel?" Diana asked.

"Tired," Alia said. "Sad. Sore."

"But do you feel different?"

"No," she said cautiously. "I feel bruised all over and more than a little freaked out about what the hell I'm going to do with the brother you turned into a gibbering bowl of jelly, but I just feel like me."

"Just you is pretty good," said Theo, and Alia felt her cheeks go warm.

"Just me is pretty hungry," she said lightly.

Nim flopped backward. "We don't have any money."

"We'll live off the land!" said Theo.

Nim groaned. "Unless the land is made of pizza, you can forget it."

Alia nudged Diana's shoulder with her own. "I'm thinking we find a nicer place to stay than the Good Night, but I'm not totally sure how we're going to pay for it." When Diana didn't say anything, she amended, "I promise we won't steal. Or borrow."

"It's not that," said Diana. She pulled her knees up to her chin. "I'm not sure I'm ready to go."

"Seriously?" said Nim. "I've had about enough of southern Greece to last a lifetime."

"No, I mean home. To Themyscira."

Alia froze. "But . . . you don't have to go, do you? Not right away."

"I have to get back. I need to know if the island is okay, if my friend Maeve is all right. I . . ." She drew in a long breath as if fortifying herself. "I need to face my mom."

"Is your mom anything like you?" asked Theo.

Diana grinned. "Tougher, faster, and really good at the lyre."

But Alia didn't want to joke, not now. She'd already lost too much tonight.

"Will you be able to come back?" she said.

"I don't know. I may still face exile, punishment."

"Then don't go!" said Nim. "Stay with us. You can be my date to the Bennett prom. Alicia Allen will lose her damn mind."

"Or you could be my bodyguard," said Theo. "I've been told I'm not a very intimidating specimen."

"You held your own with a sword for a solid ten seconds," said Diana with a smile.

"Fifteen, at least!" he said. "I was counting."

Why is everyone acting like this is okay? As much as Alia loved Nim and Theo, she just wanted them to shut up.

"Don't go," she said to Diana. "Not yet. I know you liked New York. I could tell. Even the grubby parts. So what if they decide to take you back on Cult Island? Is that really what you want? To spend forever there?"

Slowly, Diana shook her head. "No," she said, and for a moment, Alia's heart filled with hope. "But my family is there. My people. I can't take the coward's way."

Alia sighed. Of course she couldn't. She was Diana. Alia rested her head lightly on Diana's shoulder. "Promise me you'll come back someday."

"I promise to try."

"Make me the oath." There was magic in those words. She'd felt it.

"Sister in battle," murmured Diana, "I am shield and blade to you."

"And friend."

"And always your friend." Her eyes were bright with unshed tears.

Maybe the oath didn't matter if that much was true.

"I will never forget you," said Diana. She looked at Nim, at Theo. "Any of you, or the way you face the world with courage and humor—"

"And impeccable style?" said Nim.

"That, too."

They linked pinkies then, Diana and Alia and Nim and Theo, like little kids at the start of an adventure, even though they knew it was the end.

Diana rose.

"Now?" asked Alia, getting to her feet.

"Before I lose my courage."

Alia had to laugh at that. When had she ever seen Diana be anything but brave?

She watched her friend wade out into the waters of the spring and slip the heartstone from her pocket, clutching it in her palm. The river began to churn, the waters turning white with foam. Starlight collected around her, bright on the black waves of her hair. Alia wanted to call her back, beg her to stay, but the words caught in her throat. Diana had a path to follow, and it was time for Alia to stand on her own. Jason had been her hero, her protector for so long, and Diana had been her hero, too. A different kind of knight, one who'd chosen to protect the girl the world wanted to destroy; one born to slay dragons, but maybe to befriend them, too.

Diana raised her hand, her shape little more than a silhouette in the dark.

Alia lifted her own hand to wave, but before she could, Diana had plunged into the whirling waters of the spring.

A moment later, the river calmed and she was gone, leaving not even a ripple in her wake.

Alia wiped the tears from her cheeks, as Nim and Theo placed their arms around her shoulders.

"You should bring friends home more often," Nim said softly.

"Guys," said Theo after a minute, "how are we getting back to town?"

Nim shrugged. "I'm pretty sure the Fiat's where we parked it."

They began to make their way to the now-deserted road, Alia trailing slightly behind them.

She hadn't been entirely honest with Diana. She *did* feel changed by the spring. Alia reached out to that dark, winged thing inside her—its shape was different now; it felt more wholly hers, and the dagger in its hand was sheathed. She gave it the tiniest nudge.

Nim's fist shot out and punched Theo in the arm.

"Ow!" Theo yelped, and gave her a not-too-gentle shove.

Alia yanked her power back hurriedly. She was a Warbringer no longer. The spring had altered the legacy inside her, but it hadn't taken everything. That strength was still there, hers if she wanted it, more gift than curse now, something she could choose to use or ignore. *Make some trouble.* She just might. For all the right people. She'd done good with this power before. Maybe she could find a way to do good with it again.

Alia glanced back once at the river, at the silver waters of the spring, but whatever ghosts once dwelled there had gone.

"Sister in battle," she whispered once more, less a vow than a prayer, that wherever Diana was she would remember those words and keep her promise. That someday Alia might see her friend once more.

CHAPTER 33

Diana couldn't breathe; the water had her, the current driving her forward with impossible speed. She kept her arms straight before her, her body taut as she arrowed through the dark, the rush of the water like thunder in her ears. Some part of her ached for the friends she'd left behind, trembled with fear at what might lie ahead, but she refused to be distracted. There could be no mistakes this time.

She shoved all of her will into the heartstone, her only thought: *Home*. The bright shores of Themyscira, the little cove that cut into the northern coast, the cliffs that rose above it, the landscape of her heart.

Behind her closed lids, she sensed light, but she could not open her eyes against the force of the water, and then, with a tremendous burst of speed, she was hurled ashore. She slammed against the sand with enough force to rattle her bones and send her head spinning. No—not sand, stone. She was lying in the blue-lit hollow of the Oracle's temple, sprawled wet and bedraggled in the moat that ran along the bramble walls.

The Oracle sat beside the bronze tripod, a slender curl of smoke rising from the brazier into the night sky.

Slowly, Diana pushed the heavy tangle of her hair back from her face and rose. She didn't know what to say. It had been hard enough facing the Oracle before, but now she knew she was in the presence of the very goddesses who had founded Themyscira, who had given her a second chance to save herself, to save Alia. What did you say to a goddess when you had no tribute to offer? Maybe a simple "thank you."

But in the next moment, she heard voices. They were coming from the tunnel she'd braved to visit the Oracle only days ago.

"This was inevitable." Tek's voice. "We've been living on borrowed time since—"

"Do not say my daughter's name again," said Hippolyta, and Diana's heart squeezed at the sound of her mother's voice. "Not in this place."

"Let us hope the Oracle accepts our sacrifices," said another voice, familiar but less well known.

Diana froze, unsure of what to do. Hide? Face them here in the Oracle's sanctuary? The Oracle extended her arm, one long finger pointing, and Diana heard a whispering behind her. The brambles parted. She hesitated for a moment, then hooked her hands into the twisting gray vines and climbed into the wall.

The brambles closed around her, but Diana felt only the briefest panic. There was something gentle in the movement of the branches now, in the way they shifted so she could turn and peer through the spaces between them into the Oracle's chamber.

Diana could see her mother and Tek emerging from the tunnel with Biette, Sela, Arawelo, Marguerite, and Hongyu—all members of the Amazon Council. It was Hongyu's voice she'd heard.

The Amazons waited in respectful silence on the other side of the moat.

The Oracle rose. Her hood slipped back, revealing the face of an ancient crone. "Sisters of the Bow and Spear, have you come to make your offering?"

"We have," said Hippolyta. "We bring you gifts and pray you find them wor—"

"I will accept no offering this day."

The members of the Council exchanged stricken looks.

Hippolyta shut her eyes briefly. "Then we've come too late. The island's sickness, the earthquakes—"

With a start, Diana realized her mother wore the same purple silks and amethysts she'd been wearing when Diana had left. The Council had been meeting to decide whether to consult the Oracle, and this must be the delegation they'd sent. That meant only hours had passed on Themyscira. If that was the case—Diana tried to temper her hope and failed. She'd been sure she would return to exile and punishment, but what if they didn't know she'd gone? She could slip back into the city and be at Maeve's bedside in under an hour.

"Why did you wait so long to visit my temple?" asked the Oracle.

A crease appeared between Hippolyta's brows. "The Council meeting was unusually contentious. At one point, I feared we'd come to blows."

Could that have been Alia's power? Diana wondered.

"Is there no way to save Themyscira?" asked Tek impulsively. "Can we not—"

Lightning flashed and thunder rumbled through the temple. "I have accepted no offering, and yet you dare to speak these questions?"

Tek bowed her head, her hands clenching into fists. She wasn't particularly good at meek. "I beg your forgiveness. I seek only to protect our people."

The thunder faded, and the Oracle's voice calmed. "You need not fear for your people, Tekmessa." Tek's face snapped up. "Nor for the island. This time of trouble has passed."

Though they held their tongues, the Council exchanged worried looks, and Diana sensed their confusion.

The Oracle made a disgruntled humming noise. "And still you wait for explanations." She waved a gnarled hand. "The island was thrown into imbalance by a disturbance in the World of Man, but the unrest is at an end."

A slow smile spread over Hongyu's face, and a sigh of relief seemed to pass through the Council members. Hippolyta blew out a surprisingly un-queenlike breath, and Tek grinned, slinging an arm around her shoulders. Hippolyta reached for Tek's hand and let their fingers entwine.

"I was so sure it was something worse," she murmured. "Nothing like this has ever happened before."

"Just be glad it's over," said Tek. "Can you do that?" Hippolyta returned her smile.

But the Oracle spoke again. "Do not think to rest, Daughters of Themyscira. I have looked into the waters and seen a battle waged in the World of Man. One of your own will wade into the mortal fray to face this turmoil, a trial that will test her and decide the fate of this island and us all."

Tek squared her shoulders. Hongyu lifted her chin. Even in her mother's eyes, Diana saw the light of battle burning. Diana wondered which of the Council's great warriors would face the challenge the Oracle described.

"Go now," said the Oracle. "Rebuild your walls, set your cities to rights, and trouble me no more."

The Amazons made their bows and departed silently through the tunnel of brambles. Diana was afraid to watch her mother go. She wanted to run after them, offer some foolish explanation, hold her mother close. She even wanted to hug Tek. Instead, she forced herself to wait.

When their footsteps had faded, the Oracle turned to Diana and the vines parted, allowing her to pass from the wall.

"So you see, Daughter of Earth, I have kept your secret."

Diana longed to ask why, but she knew any question to the Oracle would come at a price.

"You are one of them now," said the Oracle. "Battle-tested. Even if they do not know it, you do."

Battle-born at last. They would never know what she'd done, the quest she'd completed. There would be no songs sung about it, no stories of glory shared. It didn't matter. She knew who she was and the ordeal she'd faced. She was an Amazon. The knowledge burned like a secret flame inside her, a light no one could extinguish, no matter what names they called her. Diana knew that she deserved her place here—and she knew there was more than just this life on this island.

"Thank you," Diana whispered.

"You took the chance as we hoped you would," said the Oracle. "We did nothing."

But that wasn't quite true. "When I came to ask about Alia, you told me I wasn't a true Amazon."

"Did we?"

Well, not exactly, but the meaning had been clear. "You told me I would fail."

"We couldn't know you would succeed."

Realization struck Diana with the force of an unexpected wave. "You wanted me to go. That's why you said those things."

"Better to choose a quest feeling you have something to prove than take it on as a burden. We needed a champion, and you needed a chance to learn what you are capable of."

"But I almost failed!" Diana said, her mind reeling. "The world was almost plunged into an age of warfare! What if I'd lost?"

"But you didn't."

"What if I'd chosen to come back to Themyscira when you offered me the chance, instead of facing Jason?"

"Then we would have known you aren't the hero we hoped for."

"But—"

The air rumbled with distant thunder. Diana ground her teeth in frustration. Maybe the Oracle was right. Maybe she'd needed to choose the path for herself. Maybe she'd fought harder because she'd known she had no one else to believe in her. Then she remembered Nim at the gala, saying, *Oh man, do you have one of those tough-love families? I just don't buy into that.*

"Nim had it right," she muttered.

"Oh, very well," said the Oracle. "Draw closer, Daughter, and never say we are not generous in our gifts."

The waters of the moat shimmered, and in them, Diana saw a great swath of green set like an emerald into the gray spires of a city. *The park*, Diana realized. The one she'd seen from the windows of Alia's bedroom. The image shifted, and she saw a stone terrace marked by arches, a circular fountain with a winged woman at its center. Two figures sat at the edge, their faces turned to the sun.

"Alia," she whispered. Alia was holding Theo's hand. They looked older somehow, and Diana wondered what time she was peering into, how long it had been since the fight at the spring, if all those memories had faded for them.

Another figure appeared—Nim zooming by on roller skates, a pink bandage on one of her dimpled knees. She turned in circles before them, her flowered skirt flaring. She was saying something, but Diana couldn't make out the words.

Another girl whizzed by on skates. She was tall and blond with a pretty—if somewhat weaselly—face. She snagged Nim's hand, and they spun away, laughing.

Theo and Alia rose, ready for whatever adventure Nim had suggested, and as Theo lifted Alia's hand to plant a kiss on her knuckles, Diana saw something on her wrist—a red tattoo in the shape of a star. The heartstone. *Promise me you'll come back someday.*

Diana reached toward the water, and the image faded.

Was it a promise she could keep? It seemed impossible, but she'd thought so much was impossible, and again and again she'd proven herself wrong.

"I miss them," she said. Her voice sounded small beneath the stars of the Oracle's sky. "They're worth fighting for."

"Princess," said the Oracle. For a moment, she took a new shape, one Diana had never seen before—a soldier standing with sword and shield in hand. She wore an armored breastplate, a lasso at her hip. Her blue eyes flashed, her black hair lifted by a distant wind. There was something familiar in her features. "You will have the chance to fight for them again."

The soldier vanished, replaced once more by the crone. "Go home, Diana," said the Oracle. "Maeve will be waiting for you." Grateful tears pricked Diana's eyes—her friend was well. The Oracle nodded at Diana's bracelets. "Just make sure to stop at the Armory first."

Diana smiled. She thanked the Oracle and hurried through the tunnel, her steps hastening, her heart full of joy. She did not know what the future held, only that the world—full of danger, and challenge, and wonder—was waiting to be discovered.

She ran to meet it.

AUTHOR'S NOTE

Don't try to land a Learjet on the Great Lawn. That's actually a crash, not a landing, and you won't be able to take off again. The waterfall that Diana and her friends visit does not exist but is inspired by the Polylimnio and Platania falls, where you can find a hermit's cave and a small church built into the rock. The Nemeseia was usually celebrated on 19 Hekatombaion. Also, while there has been some debate over the site of Platanistas (the shrine dedicated to Helen of the Plane Trees), it was originally believed to be located not far from the Menealaion, near the Eurotas, as described in these pages. More recent theories locate it north of the site of ancient Sparta, closer to the Magoula River. In our skies, the Dog Star shines blue, not red. The star known as the Horn or Azimech is more commonly known as Spica. As for the location of Themyscira, I recommend consulting a trusted Amazon.

ACKNOWLEDGMENTS

It has been an honor and a joy to write a chapter in Diana's story, but I couldn't have done it alone. Luckily, I know a lot of heroes; I owe them all a huge debt of thanks.

Chelsea Eberly shepherded me through this project with patience and smarts. Thank you for being a brilliant editor and champion diplomat. Many thanks also to the entire team at RHCB, especially Michelle Nagler, Nicole de las Heras, Dominique Cimina, Aisha Cloud, Kerri Benvenuto, John Adamo, Adrienne Waintraub, Lauren Adams, Joseph Scalora, Kate Keating, Hanna Lee, and Jocelyn Lange. Thanks also to Ben Harper, Melanie Swartz, and Thomas Zellers.

All the love to Joanna Volpe, Jackie Lindert, Hilary Pechone, and the rest of my family at New Leaf Literary, aka the League of Badasses, for their constant support on this project. (And a special shout to Pouya and Mel Shahbazian for the last-minute language assist.)

Angela DePace, Kelly Biette, and Clarissa Scholes helped sort the science of this story and lent their gigantic brains to Keralis Labs and Alia's interests. I'm glad they use their powers for good. Dr. Katherine Rask generously guided me through ancient religions and archaeogenetics and introduced me to Helen of the Plane Trees. She is a stalwart champion of YA lit, and her expertise and creativity were indispensable to the writing of this novel. Andrew Becker and Dan Leon were kind enough to help me sort my choices on ancient Greek. David Peterson brought his conlang genius to the construction of the Warbringer's many names and found me a kind soul to correct my Bulgarian. Thomas Cucchi talked me through flight protocols and private jets. Poornima Paidipaty gave excellent goddess guidance, and Sarah Jae Jones advised on skydiving, which I can say is something I never, ever want to do. I also want to say a special thank-you to Aman Chaudhary, who let me hash through the starting point of this story with him on the way to San Diego Comic-Con.

Kelly Link, Holly Black, Sarah Rees Brennan, and Robin Wasserman read the earliest pages of this book when I still thought Diana should have a pet leopard. Daniel José Older (who fielded long phone calls), Robyn Kali Bacon (who put up with late-night texts), Rachael Martin (who did both), Gamynne Guillote (*prota adelfis*), and Morgan Fahey (trusted reader #1) helped me find my footing with Alia and Jason, and helped me navigate the story as a whole.

Thanks also to Marie "Gotham Needs Me" Lu, Amie Kaufman, Kayte Ghaffar, Susan Dennard, Gwenda Bond, the superhumanly adorable Flash Martin, and, of course, my mom, who has put up with my Wonder Woman obsession lo these many years. Speaking of which, I'm grateful to the Superfriends for introducing me to Diana over soggy Saturday-morning cereal, and to Lynda Carter for cementing my love for Wondy forever.

Many books, articles, and essays influenced the Warbringer world, including *The Amazons: Lives and Legends of Warrior Women Across the Ancient World* by Adrienne Mayor; *Choruses of Young Women in Ancient Greece: Their Morphology, Religious Role and Social Functions* by Claude Calame; *On the Origins of War: And the Preservation of Peace* by Donald Kagan; "Platanistas, the Course and Carneus: Their Places in the Topography of Sparta" by G. D. R. Sanders; *The Secret History of Wonder Woman* by Jill Lepore; *A Golden Thread: An Unofficial Critical History of Wonder Woman* by Philip Sandifer; *Wonder Woman Unbound: The Curious History of the World's Most Famous Heroine* by Tim Hanley; and, of course, the work of the inimitable Gail Simone.

And finally, to the Amazons of the world, to every woman or girl who fights for peace and on behalf of one another, thank you for inspiring me.

ABOUT THE AUTHOR

LEIGH BARDUGO is the #1 *New York Times* bestselling and *USA Today* bestselling author of *Six of Crows*, *Crooked Kingdom*, and the Shadow and Bone Trilogy. She was born in Jerusalem, grew up in Los Angeles, and graduated from Yale University. She fell under Wonder Woman's spell early and spent a good chunk of her childhood making construction-paper bracelets and spinning herself dizzy in her driveway. These days, she lives and writes in Hollywood, where she can occasionally be heard singing with her band.

leighbardugo.com

@LBardugo

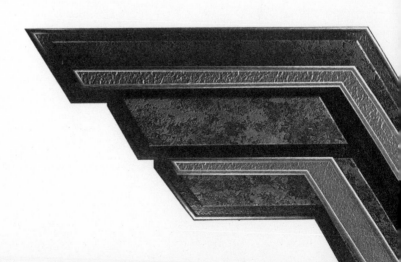

THE NIGHTWALKERS
ARE HUNTING GOTHAM CITY'S ELITE.

BRUCE WAYNE IS NEXT ON THEIR LIST.

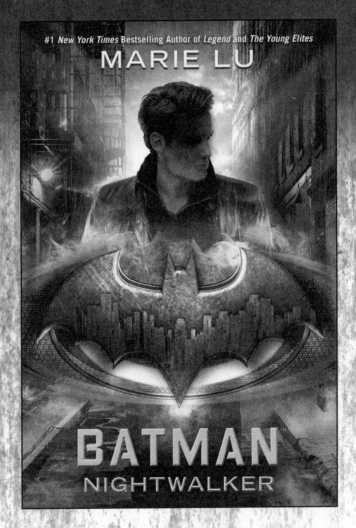

TURN THE PAGE TO SEE HOW
BRUCE'S ADVENTURE BEGINS,
IN THE NEXT DC ICONS STORY!

As Bruce rounded another bend, the police sirens suddenly turned deafening, and a mass of red and blue lights flashed against the buildings near the end of the street. Cement barricades and yellow police tape completely blocked the intersection. Fire engines and black SWAT trucks clustered together, with the silhouettes of officers running back and forth in front of the headlights.

Inside his car, the electronic voice came on again, followed by a transparent map overlaid against his windshield. *"Heavy police activity ahead. Alternate route suggested."*

A sense of dread filled his chest.

Bruce flicked away the map and pulled to an abrupt halt in front of the barricade—right as the unmistakable *pop-pop-pop* of gunfire rang out in the night air.

He remembered the sound all too well. The memory of his parents' deaths sent a wave of dizziness through him. *Another robbery. A murder. That's what all this is.*

Then he shook his head. *No, that can't be right.* There were far too many cops here for a simple robbery.

"Step *out* of your vehicle, and put your hands in the air!" a police officer shouted through a megaphone, her voice echoing along the block. Bruce's head jerked toward her. For an instant, he thought her command was directed at him, but then he saw that her back was turned, her attention fixed on the corner of a building. "We have you surrounded, Nightwalker! This is your final warning!"

Another officer came running over to Bruce's car. He whirled an arm exaggeratedly for Bruce to turn his car around. His voice harsh with panic, he warned, "Turn back *now*. It's not safe!"

Before Bruce could reply, a blinding fireball exploded behind the officer. The street rocked.

Even from inside his car, Bruce felt the heat of the blast. Every window in the building burst simultaneously, a million shards of glass raining down on the pavement below. The police ducked in unison, their arms shielding their heads. Fragments of glass flew toward Bruce's car, dinging like hail against his windshield.

From inside the blockade, a white car veered around the corner at top speed. Bruce saw immediately what the car was aiming for—a slim gap between the police barricades, where a SWAT team truck had just pulled through.

"I said, *get out of here*!" the officer shouted at Bruce. A thin ribbon of blood trickled down the man's face. "That's an *order*!"

Bruce heard the scream of the getaway car's tires against the asphalt as it raced toward the gap. He'd been in his father's garage a thousand times, helping him tinker with an endless number of engines from the best cars in the world. At WayneTech, Bruce had watched in fascination as tests were conducted on custom engines, conceptual jets, stealth tech, new vehicles of every kind.

And so he knew: whatever was installed under that hood was faster than anything the GCPD could hope to have.

They'll never catch him.

But I can.

His Aston Martin was probably the only vehicle here that could overtake the criminal's, the only one powerful enough to chase it down. Bruce's eyes followed the path the car would likely take, his gaze settling on a sign at the end of the street that pointed toward the freeway.

I can get him.

The white getaway vehicle shot straight through the gap in the barricade, clipping two police cars as it went.

No, not this time. Bruce slammed his gas pedal.

The Aston Martin's engine let out a deafening roar and sped forward. The officer who'd shouted at him stumbled back. In the rearview mirror, Bruce saw him scramble to his feet and wave the other officers' cars forward, both his arms held up high.

"Hold your fire!" Bruce could hear him yelling. "Civilian in proximity—*hold your fire*!"

Bruce narrowed his eyes and tightened his hands on the steering wheel. Few things in his life seemed within his control right now—but this? This moment was his.

The getaway car made a sharp turn at the first intersection, and Bruce sped behind it a few seconds later. The street zigzagged, then turned in a wide arc as it led toward the freeway—and the Nightwalker took the on-ramp, leaving a trail of exhaust and two black skid marks on the road.

Bruce raced forward in close pursuit; his car mapped the ground instantly, swerving in a perfect curve to follow the ramp onto the freeway. He tapped twice on the windshield right over where the Nightwalker's white vehicle was.

"Follow him," Bruce commanded.